The Art of Rebellion

Published by Rebelight Publishing Inc.
Editor: Deborah Froese
Cover and interior design: Melanie Matheson
Map design: S. Osterdal

Rebelight Publishing Inc.
23-845 Dakota St., Suite 314
Winnipeg, Manitoba, Canada R2M 5M3

www.rebelight.com

Library and Archives Canada Cataloguing in Publication

Leahy, Brenda Joyce, author
        The art of rebellion / Brenda Joyce Leahy.

Issued in print and electronic formats.
ISBN 978-0-9948399-8-5 (paperback).--ISBN 978-0-9948399-9-2 (ebook)

        I. Title.

PS8623E255A89 2016   jC813'.6   C2016-903169-1
                                              C2016-903170-5

This book is a work of fiction. Names, characters, places and incidents are products of the author's imagination or are used fictitiously. Any resemblance to actual events or locales or persons, living or dead, is entirely coincidental.

Printed and bound in Canada
10 9 8 7 6 5 4 3 2 1

The Art of Rebellion

BRENDA JOYCE LEAHY

2016 rebel!ght PUBLISHING INC.

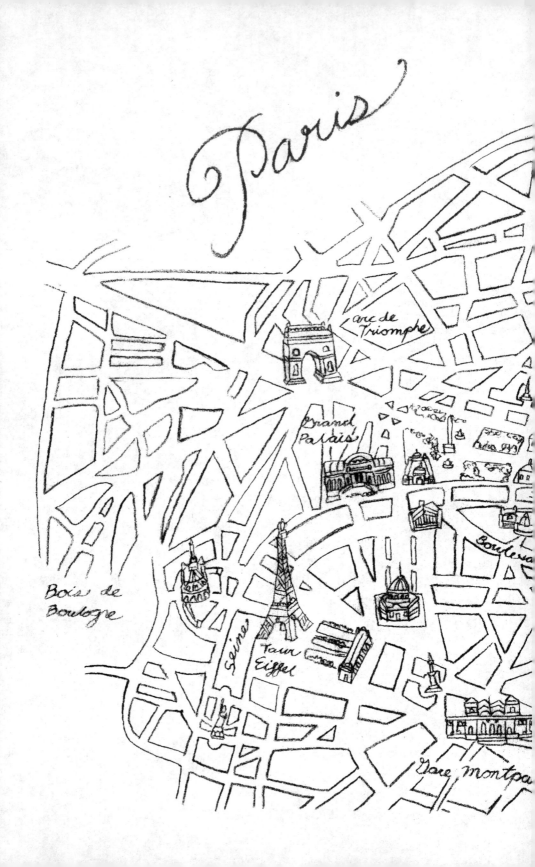

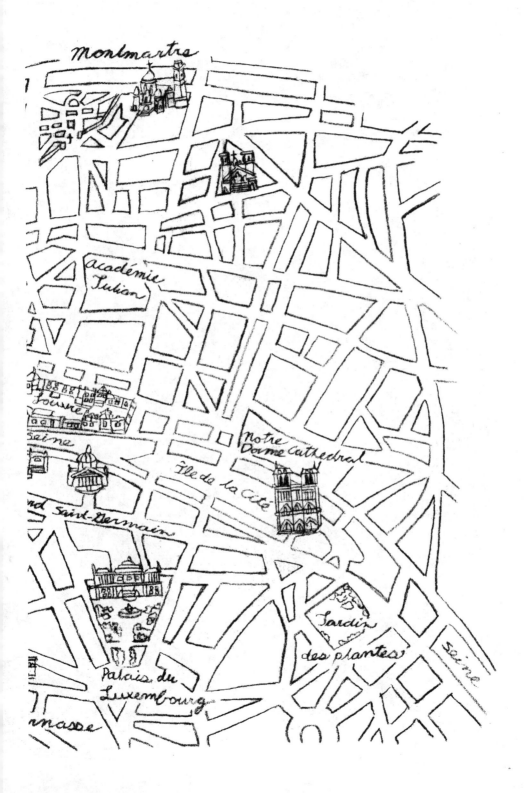

1. rue Cortot
2. rue Gabrielle
3. Place du Tertre
4. Sacre Cœur
5. Église Saint-Pierre
6. Moulin de la Galette
7. Lapin agile
8. Funiculaire
9. Place Pigalle
10. Cimetière de Montmartre
11. Moulin Rouge

rue Caulaincourt

rue Lepic

rue Lepic

Blvd. de Clichy

Blvd. de Rochechouart

Montmartre

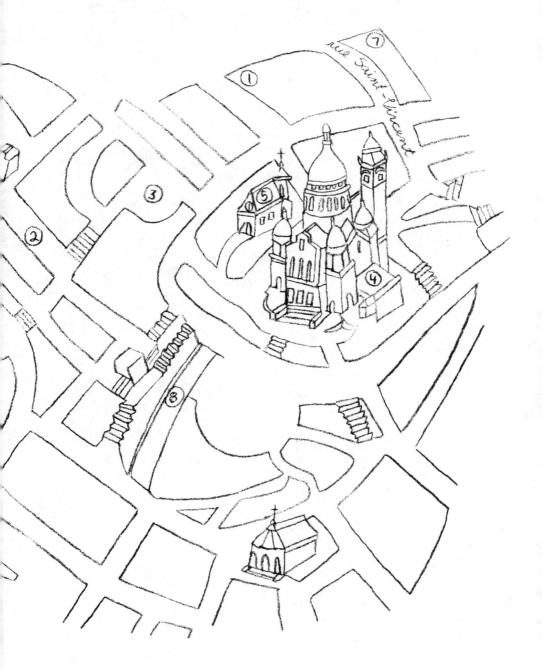

This book is dedicated to my mother, Frances Gabrielle Carmen.

"Be like the bird that, pausing in her flight awhile on boughs too slight, feels them give way beneath her, and yet sings, knowing that she hath wings."

~Victor Hugo

June, 1900
Laval, France

Chapter One

A SHRILL BLAST OF THE TRAIN'S WHISTLE jolted me. I ran through a veil of steam and scrambled up the rail car steps, my heart thudding in a prayer of thanks for slipping away unnoticed.

I ducked inside, quickly found my seat, and settled my art box and bags beneath it, my parasol on the seat beside me. My eyes were drawn to the window. The early morning light revealed a handful of people on the platform waving farewell. I turned away. No one would be out there to wish me a safe journey. I'd made sure of that.

A loud thump on the panel behind my head informed me the adjoining compartment was occupied. Children argued loudly over where to sit and a thin, tired woman's voice begged for quiet.

I smoothed my blue kid gloves, a secret parting gift from my older sister Nacia. She alone was privy to my plans. My blue felt hat, speared into submission by Grand-mère's hat pin—six inches of sterling silver topped with a crimson *cloisonné* bead—hopefully created the impression of a young woman much older than sixteen years. I tucked my undesirably large feet, pinched into fashionable heeled slippers, under a froth of petticoats and skirts and waited nervously for the train to depart.

Despite the early hour, a slick line of sweat snaked a path between my shoulder blades and dampened my corset laces. Was sneaking away like a thief in the night a mistake? I glanced out the window once more, for it might be the last I saw of Laval.

The clouds of steam thinned, and I locked eyes with a tall, imposing woman wearing an outrageous hat of stuffed birds.

I gasped. Madame Dupont, the worst gossip among Maman's society friends.

Her eyes widened. She took a few steps forward but an attendant blocked her path as he stopped to assist a woman overloaded with baggage. Madame Dupont tilted one way then another, craning her neck as she searched me out.

I flinched and turned away. When I dared look again, she was gone. No doubt she would rush to spread the scandalous news: Sebastian and Désirée's youngest daughter rode the express train bound for Paris—without a chaperone.

With a deep breath, I shoved Madame DuPont to the back of my mind. I could not stop her. There was no going back.

I pulled a creased envelope out of my purse and stroked it for courage. It held Grand-mère's photograph and an address acquired only recently. An address in the capital. Paris. The very word promised the fulfillment of every wish.

One more whistle, and the sharp grinding of iron wheels on the rails signalled our departure. Just as the train shuddered and began to leave the station, a man boarded the car. He stuck his head into my compartment and gestured to the empty bench across from me. "I believe this is my seat, mademoiselle."

I nodded sharply, trying to disguise my dismay. I'd paid extra to have the compartment to myself. That cheat of a ticket seller!

The stranger stowed his bags on the rack above, setting his top hat beside them with care. He sat down and snapped open a newspaper. Every now and then, he let the paper drop and peered at me over his wire-rimmed spectacles. I averted my gaze each time, but not before sneaking my own look at him.

He appeared to be in his mid-twenties, about the same age as my older brother, Charles. His suit wasn't custom tailored, yet he held himself with the same dignity as any high-born gentleman. Even behind spectacles, his cobalt blue eyes exuded a notably intense hue. Clean-shaven with a slim build and broad shoulders, he looked strong and athletic. As a caricature, he would make a fine thoroughbred horse, albeit one with a jagged scar spoiling his facial features.

The train shuddered and creaked as the tracks curved deeply around a gorge. The art box slid forward from its spot under my seat and stopped at the feet of the stranger across from me.

He leaned forward and picked it up. "I believe this is yours, mademoiselle. Perhaps I can stow it in the rack above for you?"

"*Non, merci.*" I retrieved the case and stroked the mother-of-pearl design on its top before sliding it back under the seat.

"It looks very valuable."

"It is to me." Not in the sense he was probably thinking, but yes, valuable. It had opened the world of art to me. The art box was a gift from

Papa after my grandmother's mysterious departure from our home four years ago. A sturdy mahogany case with brass fittings, it bore scars and scuffs from a multitude of outdoor painting excursions. Filled with watercolour paints, brushes, pastels, paper and a clever folding easel, it contained my life. A life that Maman had very nearly destroyed.

And yet as the train shimmied and shook around another bend, I still worried about how angry she would be when she found the note I had pinned to my pillow.

Dearest Maman and Papa,
By the time you read this, I will be in Paris with Grand-mère. Please try to understand and do not send anyone after me. I am an artist and not meant for marriage. Forgive me for any embarrassment I have caused. One day you will be proud of me.
Your loving daughter, Gabrielle

A heavily whiskered man in a bowler hat lurched into the compartment, his arms extended for balance as the train's rocking motion jostled him back and forth. As the man's eyes roamed about the car and then rested on me, any regrets for the mess I'd left behind in Laval were momentarily forgotten.

"Terribly warm morning, mademoiselle." He drew out a handkerchief and wiped his brow, beaded with perspiration. Some of it dripped down his deeply veined nose. His gaze lingered on me far too long.

I looked away, hoping he'd quickly move on.

"Would you care for some company, mademoiselle?"

Out of habitual politeness, I looked up. He tipped his bowler hat and bowed slightly. The train jolted, and so did he. A silver flask flashed from his jacket pocket, and he very nearly landed on top of me.

Madame Dijon, my etiquette teacher, would have been highly incensed at the man's rude behaviour. I sat up straighter and mimicked her most disapproving expression. "This seat is taken, monsieur." I said in a decidedly unfriendly voice. "My husband is away for but a moment." I glanced pointedly at the exit.

The man's face turned an unpleasant hue of vermilion, nicely matching his nose. Clearly he was unaccustomed to being addressed so by a woman. And certainly never by someone as young as me. He nodded curtly and left.

The spectacled man with the newspaper stared openly across the compartment. I squared my shoulders. If he took offence at the way I'd spoken to the bowler-hatted man, it was simply too bad. I had to take matters into my own hands.

As the stranger continued to stare, I hoped I wouldn't have to fend off any other unwanted advances. He looked harmless, not at all like the villains I read about in novels. His newspaper, *L'Ouest-Éclair*, was the same conservative one Papa preferred. And of course, those intriguing blue eyes couldn't belong to a criminal, could they?

He leaned forward, his brow furrowed. "Are you all right, mademoiselle?"

I nodded, my throat too tight to speak.

The man folded his glasses and tucked them in a pocket. "Excuse me if I am being too bold, but are you not travelling alone?"

I pulled my handbag closer. "Oh, non, monsieur."

"Non?"

"My . . . my brother Charles is with me. He's attending business meetings in a private car." I gestured vaguely. "No more than a shout away." The ease with which I lied bothered me only slightly. I would have enjoyed my brother's company if he'd been free to escort me, however, his gambling and reckless lifestyle had caught up with him. He had dishonoured Papa and would soon ship off to the wilds of Canada to live with Maman's brother, Uncle Luc.

The stranger had the nerve to look amused. "And your husband?"

"Ah, well . . ." I tried not to squirm under his gaze. "That was a necessary fiction."

Chapter Two

FICTIONAL HUSBANDS are preferable to the flesh and blood kind.

I know this to be true. Only a few weeks before leaving home, I endured one of Maman's *soirées* on an evening that could have been spent painting *en plein air*.

Our only guest, the Baron d'Argente, was strategically seated between my two older sisters, Nacia and Genevieve. Maman had great plans for one of them to snare a betrothal by evening's end.

Maman's smug expression made me think of a field marshal surveying her troops. Aside from a few streaks of grey hair, she didn't look like a woman who'd been through seven pregnancies. She was still encased in black *crepe de chine* for mourning, though the last of my three baby brothers had been buried over four years ago.

Dear Papa sat quite properly at the head of the table, but it was Maman at the opposite end who presided over the parade of nauseatingly rich food, clever conversation and insincere flattery. My only consolation was the presence of Bernadette, my best friend. Charles, my older and only brother, sat between us.

Bernadette leaned across Charles and spoke, *sotto voce*. "I adore Nacia's new *coiffure*." Her own white blonde hair was styled fashionably, short bangs above her heart-shaped face, tight curls pinned in place with jeweled combs. Despite her obvious beauty, she never failed to complement others. "Your sisters are really shining tonight."

"It took them all day to prepare. Nacia and Genevieve are dressed for a quick sale." My words sounded heartless, but attending endless match-making parties wearied me. My sisters were, after all, willing participants and didn't need my support or encouragement.

"You don't fool me," Bernie whispered. "You'll miss them terribly once they are wed and have households of their own.”

It was true. I loved my sisters. Until recently, we had been as close as the three rows of pearls on the choker circling my throat. “I hardly know them any more, Bernie. They’re too busy with endless fittings for gowns or dancing with suitors at the *bals blancs*.”

Charles cleared his throat. “Are you two going to talk fashion all evening? Papa and monsieur le baron already bored me with their yammering about business and politics before dinner.”

“I thought you enjoy discussing fashion, *mon frère*, since you are obsessive about your own attire.”

As usual, he was dressed impeccably. He wore a hand-tailored dove grey suit with a pin-striped vest, his white shirt crisply pressed and grey silk cravat expertly knotted. Pomade fashionably slicked down his thick dark hair.

“*Touché, petite.*” He tipped his head at me. “But let’s discuss something much more interesting.” He rubbed his hands together. “A wager, perhaps. Who will be the first to start name-dropping? Maman, our sisters, or our honourable guest? My money is on the baron.”

I smothered a giggle and glanced across the table at Genevieve, whose slender hands fluttered gracefully in an animated conversation with monsieur le baron. With every practiced gesture, her gown of emerald silk shimmered under soft lamps and candle light. “I’ll take your money, mon frère, for I am certain it will be Genevieve.”

“Shush. You shouldn’t make jokes about it.” Bernadette’s face flushed. “Your sisters are anxious enough.”

“Especially Nash,” I agreed. “She looks ready to bolt.”

Nacia appeared lovely and fragile, just as a prospective bride should. Her auburn hair was backcombed over a hair rat and swept into a full Pompadour with mother-of-pearl combs keeping stray wisps in place. The deep gussets of her new sapphire satin gown enhanced her slender figure and fair complexion. Alas, her round green eyes remained fixed on her plate. She was extremely shy, most particularly around men.

“Come on, Bernadette. Have some fun,” Charles teased. “I’m going to put you down for five francs on Maman.”

Bernie’s dimples flashed. “If I must.” She had a secret crush on my brother. She’d sworn me to secrecy, a promise I intended to honour. Although I loved him best of all my siblings, he was far too worldly for Bernie.

“What are you three scheming about?” Genevieve’s perfectly modulated voice cut through the air. “Let us all in on the conspiracy.” She sounded playful, but her hazel eyes flashed a warning that I’d ignored previously at my peril. I had to admire her poise, for as she lowered her gaze, the candlelight glinted off her jewelled hairpiece. She and I were similar in looks, much darker versions of Nash, yet I'd never mastered such grace—nor did I bother to learn.

I bit my lower lip to hide a smile. "Only a small wager, *chérie*. Nothing—"

"Thank you, Gerard." Maman spoke firmly.

Our butler entered the dining room, carrying a large tray of Matelote d'Anguille—eels stewed in red wine. The kitchen maids followed, armed with dishes of roast pork, asparagus smothered in hollandaise, Grenouilles a la Provençal—frogs' legs—and baskets of Cook's fresh breads and garlic butter.

"Do be more careful, Claudine," Maman scolded the nearest maid. "You very nearly burned the Prince last week!"

The baron's eyes lit up. "The Prince of Wales? Apparently Laval is not the backwater some might think."

My father bit his lip while Charles and I exchanged an amused look. No Prince had graced our home last week—or ever.

"Indeed, we are much more than linen mills and dairy cows," Maman said.

Her canny ability to neither deny or confirm what prince she referred to made me smile.

As I studied the baron to gauge his reaction, my fingers itched to sketch a caricature of him. With little exaggeration, he reminded me of a preening crow. Classically handsome except for his fleshy jowls, he was nearly as old as my father. He repeatedly licked his fleshy, oddly feminine lips. But his resemblance to a crow surfaced when he strutted around our home during aperitifs as if he already owned the house and all its contents. And how he constantly groomed himself, picking at his lapels for lint or smoothing down his moustache and goatee. Glossy coat tails hung behind him like shiny black plumage.

Especially crow-like, though, were his heavy-lidded, glinting eyes. As they swept around the room, I imagined him assessing the monetary value of our fine furniture and décor and carting off the gold and glitter to his nest.

Crows are common enough birds, as are noblemen with grand estates and insufficient wealth to sustain the lifestyle they desire. That's where well-to-do, cultured families with eligible daughters fit in.

When the dish of eels came my way, I declined and selected only delicate portions of the other dishes, afraid not for my figure but my digestion after such rich food. Not so, apparently, for Genevieve. Despite her air of confidence, she had much riding on the evening and seemed to steady herself by elegantly nibbling morsels of every heavily-sauced dish served.

Bernadette helped herself to the frogs' legs and addressed Genevieve. "I adore your gown, Genevieve." Bernadette fancied herself an expert on fashion and studied all the magazines from Paris and London. "I believe I saw a similar style in *La Mode Illustrée*."

My eldest sister's face shone. "Merci, Bernadette." She glanced at the baron, no doubt to ensure he'd heard the compliment.

The baron cleared his throat. "Your gown is indeed lovely and complements you beautifully. Tell me, is it from the House of Worth?"

"Non, Monsieur le Baron. Madame Charlotte, our *couturière,* created it for me." Genevieve's hand carefully flitted to the modest lace-trimmed neckline of her silk gown. The baron's eyes followed the gesture. She wore Maman's best emerald necklace, a strategic choice. The oversized jewels glinted in the gas lighting and emphasized my sister's delicate collarbone.

"We never travel to the capital, Monsieur le Baron," Maman added. "I insist on supporting Laval's businesses. Besides, Madame Charlotte was trained in Paris, at the Maison Paquin. "

"I am surprised to hear that you never travel to Paris, Madame." The baron's dark eyes narrowed as he regarded her for a moment. "I understand your mother lives there."

I sucked in my breath. Grand-mère in Paris? That was news to me, for after she left us so suddenly, Maman forbade any mention of her name. I searched my siblings' faces. They looked as surprised as I was. My father emptied his wine glass and fiddled with his cutlery, his gaze on the table

Maman's expression turned stony. Did the baron know about the scandal surrounding my beloved grandmother?

Several awkward moments of silence were punctuated only by the baron's knife and fork scraping his plate. The rest of us waited, all movement suspended.

Maman's lips slowly stretched across her teeth in a form of smile. "You are mistaken, Monsieur." Her tone left no opening for further discussion. Apparently, even the hope of snaring a noble title was not reason enough for Maman to unbend and speak of her mother.

Murmured conversation resumed around me, but I could not focus. Grand-mère was living in the very city where I was determined to study art. Surely fate had delivered this news to me. I could live with Grand-mère! She would support my studies. And oh, what sights we'd see. What adventures we could—

"Gabrielle!" My mother's sharp voice invaded my daydreams.

"*Oui,* Maman?"

"Monsieur le Baron asked you a question."

I dabbed my lips with my *serviette de table*. "I apologize, your Excellency. My mind was elsewhere."

He inclined his head to accept my apology. "I was curious, Mademoiselle Gabrielle, whether you will be performing tonight, along with your talented sisters." His dark eyes glinted, but he smiled, his nearly perfect teeth gleaming.

"You will be spared from any performance by me, Your Excellency. I am learning to play the mandolin, but have as little musical ability as Genevieve has artistic sensibility."

Genevieve choked on a mouthful of eel. Maman reached over to pat her on the back and shot me a murderous look. Apparently, I'd committed another *faux pas*. No matter. Plans were hatching in my head, plans that had nothing to do with the womanly art of conversation and entirely to do with true art.

After dinner, Bernadette excused herself to attend a family birthday party. Charles gallantly offered to escort her home, leaving me without an ally for the remainder of the evening.

The rest of us retired to the parlour for "musical entertainment" from my sisters. Nacia clutched her violin and hovered near the back of the room, while Maman showed the baron to the gilt-edged Bergère chair set up directly in front of the piano where Genevieve was poised.

"May this be mercifully short," I murmured to Papa as I joined him on the settee behind our guest, fanning myself.

His eyes crinkled and a slight smile lifted his lips. "This is your sisters' evening, chérie. I'm happy it isn't what you desire, for I'd hate to lose your charming company so soon." He squeezed my hand. "But this is what they want. Let us indulge them."

"And I only want the best for them. But is this man truly what's best?"

Maman shushed me as Genevieve fluffed her skirts and sat, gracefully smoothing each sleeve before placing one delicate slipper on the foot pedal. A sheen of sweat beaded her brow. She raised her hands above the keys as if to begin but then stood abruptly, knocking over the chair. Her hand flew to her mouth, and her eyebrows rose to her fringe of bangs.

What on earth was wrong?

I rushed toward her, but the baron arrived first, standing between Genevieve and the door. "May I help you, Mademoiselle?"

Genevieve stared at him in alarm for several heartbeats and then convulsed. Vomit spewed across the carpet and onto the baron's shiny buckled shoes.

His face paled and twisted in dismay, and he backed away.

Genevieve bolted from the room, tears streaming down her cheeks.

"I am so sorry." Maman clutched her throat, her face as pale as the baron's. I feared she would vomit as well. "Gabrielle, Nacia, please see to the baron." She scurried to follow my sister.

Nacia stared wide-eyed at me, clutching the arm of the settee.

"Get Claudine," I ordered her as I swiped at the baron's shoes with my lace handkerchief. "Not to worry, Your Excellency. Your shoes will recover."

He pressed a monogrammed handkerchief to his nose.

Claudine flew into the room with damp rags and wiped at the mess on the floor, while Papa stood nearby, apparently struck dumb by the incident.

I excused myself to wash up. By the time I returned to the parlour, Maman was back, supported on Papa's arm as she apologized profusely to the baron. Nacia still sat alone on the settee, pale. I shook my head and joined her. "It's up to us to salvage tonight, Nash."

"I . . . I'm not feeling well, either." She dabbed her forehead with a handkerchief and stood.

The baron headed toward us, smouldering cigar in hand.

Nacia bolted for Maman.

"Nash!" I muttered and grabbed at her elbow but missed, biting down a curse.

Undeterred, the baron joined me on the settee, sitting closer than propriety would dictate. "I hope you aren't feeling sick also, Mademoiselle Gabrielle." He chuckled.

I slid as far from him as I could. "I am a trifle nauseous."

"My, you are a shy one, not at all like your older sister." He sidled closer. "I enjoy a challenge."

"I'm certain that Genevieve will be anxious to apologize. It is most unlike her to be ill." The stink of cigar and a sharp male odour rose from him and pinched my nose. I leaned away until I was pressed up against the arm of the settee.

Genevieve re-entered the parlour and stood beside Maman, looking nauseated still. She caught my eye and glared as if I'd deliberately enticed the baron.

As usual, her ill humour ignited my desire to tease her. I turned to the baron, eyelashes so a-flutter that even Madame Dijon would have approved. I felt Genevieve's eyes boring into my back. "Genevieve tells me you have many examples of fine art at your estate, Monsieur le Baron."

But she had done no such thing. Although she'd been to his grand country chateau once for a ball, she could speak afterward of nothing but the "noble proportions" of the great hall and ballroom, and she couldn't recall a single statue or painting in the entire estate. I'd had to rely upon my own sources for this one bit of interesting gossip about the baron.

He scowled. "My grandparents and parents nearly bankrupted our family through their lavish patronage of artists." A snort escaped him. "One good thing came of it—I've been selling it off."

I gasped. A mansion full of masterpieces by Corot, Delacroix, David and more, and yet he cared not? *"C'est vrai?"*

He nodded, oblivious to my shocked tone. "Of course, I am forced to keep a few of the more famous ones for when my royal cousins stay with me. It's a pity, for those pieces would bring in the highest prices."

"Yes, a pity," I forced myself to agree. What on earth does Genevieve see in him? Someone ought to step on his toes for such an ignorant view of priceless art. "I am studying art and plan to make a career of it," I said smugly.

His reaction was as expected: eyebrows raised, nose pinched in disapproval. "I would advise you to reconsider, Mademoiselle. Your gender is emotionally unstable with a delicate disposition. Be content with what you do best. Marry and bear children." He took my hand in his and pressed his lips against it.

My throat tightened with anger. I snatched my hand from his and struggled to reply.

"Gabrielle!" Maman's sharp voice carried across the room.

I jumped up. "Excuse me, Your Excellency." I felt his eyes bore into me as I crossed the room to Maman and Genevieve, who pressed one hand to her stomach. She still had a sickly sheen on her face.

I felt badly for flirting with her potential suitor and put my arm around her. "Shouldn't you be resting in bed instead of here?"

She shook my hand away and lifted her pretty chin. "Don't be ridiculous, Gabbi. I'm perfectly well."

"But you spewed your dinner—"

"Gabrielle," Maman interrupted in a hushed but scolding tone. "Ladies never speak of such things."

"*Mon Dieu,* Maman! What shall we speak of then?"

Her face darkened. "If you cannot conduct yourself as a lady, then you are excused for the evening." She nodded at Genevieve, who scurried to the baron's side.

I took my leave before she could change her mind.

Chapter Three

WHO KNEW THAT GENEVIEVE'S sour stomach would lead to an even greater disaster? I gazed out the train window. The panorama of passing villages and the gentle rocking of the car reassured me I was safely on my way to Paris.

Enfin. Nothing and no one could stop me.

The other passenger in the compartment folded his newspaper, laying it on his seat before he extended his hand. "May I introduce myself? Philippe Lucien."

"*Bonjour,* Monsieur Lucien. I'm Gabrielle Carmen Désirée Jean d'Arc de Villiers. Mademoiselle, that is." I gave him my gloved hand, and he shook it firmly. I liked that. So much firmer than the baron's limpid lips, leaving their damp mark on my glove.

Stop it, Gabrielle! Enjoy your freedom.

"May I assume you are travelling to Paris, Mademoiselle?"

"Oui, I'm going to see my grandmother." Saying it aloud made my dream seem within reach. At that moment, I felt as if I could conquer the world. "And are you also headed for Paris, Monsieur?"

"Yes."

Maman would not have approved of such direct questions, yet I continued. "Do you know Paris well? It will be my first time."

"*Mais oui,* I've been there many times."

I glanced at the envelope in my handbag. "Do you know the 18e *arrondissement*? That's where my grandmother lives."

He frowned. "I know of it. It's the old village of Montmartre, in the north end of the city, where the quarries and mills are." He paused and his nose wrinkled. "It's mostly rural, filled with pig pens, cabarets and carnivals. Popular with anarchists, artists and the like. Are you sure you have the correct address?"

"Yes, I'm sure." He lumped artists in with anarchists! "Grand-mère's not an ordinary grandmother." Certainly not ordinary.

"I daresay."

"She practically raised me when my mother became ill." I didn't add that Grand-mère was proud to be a feminist. Or that she'd once been arrested and spent a night in prison after a women's march turned unpleasant. She moved away from Laval the day after she was released from prison. "I haven't seen her for over four years."

"It sounds as if you've missed her, *n'est-ce pas?*" He leaned forward and gazed at me sympathetically.

I pulled back against the seat, surprised and not a little uncomfortable. Perhaps I'd been too trusting, too open with him.

He cleared his throat. "I have been meddlesome. Please excuse me, Mademoiselle."

"No, no. It's fine." I did miss Mémère. And I was anxious to locate her, slightly troubled she'd not responded to my hasty telegram: "Urgent I come and live with you in Paris Stop Forced to marry unless you accept me Stop Love Gabbi."

We spent the next part of the journey in silence. Philippe returned his attention to his newspaper, and I gazed out the window. Farms and small villages flew past. I got out my sketchpad and tried to capture impressions before they were out of sight. A church steeple, an old stone barn tilting dangerously, and a ghostly herd of white Charolais cattle took shape in quick strokes.

"Can I see?" A timid voice at my elbow startled me. It must have been one of the children from the compartment behind mine. She had a sweet smile beneath a smattering of freckles across her nose and cheeks.

"Oui." I slid over so she could sit beside me and tilted my sketchpad so she could see the page better.

"Those are cows," she said solemnly. She wiped her nose with her sleeve and then ran out.

"I want to see too." A boy, slightly older but with the same pattern of freckles, leaned over my shoulder, peering down at my picture.

I smiled up at him. "Do you like it?"

Instead of answering, he grabbed the sketchbook out of my hands and darted into the aisle as quickly as a street urchin.

"Hey!" I grabbed at his shirt but missed.

Philippe stood swiftly. "Allow me, please." With a few long strides, he caught up to the rascal and snagged him by the collar before he reached the car's vestibule. "Not so fast, young man."

Philippe brought the lad back to me, maintaining a tight grip on his collar. When the boy stared at his boots in silence, Philippe put a hand on his shoulder, squeezed lightly and said, "Come on, then. What do you have to say to the lady?"

The boy couldn't meet my eyes, but he held out my sketchbook and muttered, "I'm sorry."

"I accept your apology." I took my sketchbook back and flipped through the pages to ensure none were torn.

Philippe released the boy, who stomped back into the aisle and disappeared from sight. The compartment door next to ours slammed shut.

Through the walls, a thin tired voice admonished the boy, no doubt his mother. His muttered reply was too quiet to catch, but I wasn't at all sure he was contrite.

I hugged my sketchbook close. "I am in your debt, Monsieur. I might have lost all of my work."

He waved off my thanks. "Think nothing of it. The little ruffian simply needs a firm hand." His voice was loud enough for the boy and his mother to hear. "Although I can't say I blame him for being curious."

I laughed at his blatant hint. "Would you care to see my sketches?"

He dipped his head. "I'd be honoured. Thank you."

I passed him my sketchbook, my pulse racing as a terrible thought struck me. Perhaps the praises of my art teacher, Madame Magne, had been given out of kindness or even worse, pity. I gripped my hands together and brought to mind a quote by Victor Hugo that never failed to hearten me: "Be like the bird that, pausing in her flight awhile on boughs too slight, feels them give way beneath her, and yet sings, knowing that she hath wings."

I'd taken that advice to heart and decided to sing. But I had to develop a thick skin about my work. Surely one man's opinion shouldn't cause me to be so nervous. If only I could control my flushed cheeks.

Early sketches were studies of paintings Madame Magne shared from her art journals. Philippe paused at my interpretation of seaside scene by Gaston Lachance, a contemporary artist whom Madame admired greatly. I wondered what Philippe thought of my many portraits of Bernadette as he gave them his full attention. He couldn't fail to see her beauty. Petite, blonde and curvy, with porcelain skin, she was everything my mother had hoped I'd be. Alas, I'd grown tall and rail-thin, with mud-puddle brown eyes instead of Bernie's china blue ones.

I longed for Bernie's loyal presence as Philippe continued to examine my sketches. He pointed at my caricatures of the baron and smirked. "Who is this unfortunate man?"

"He was courting . . . my sisters," I told him, amending the truth while suppressing a shudder. For that was not the entire story.

After Maman had summarily dismissed me from the soirée, I escaped to my room. A few hours of painting never failed to restore my spirits. I donned my smock and set out my supplies to begin a self-portrait.

It took shape quickly. After a few short hours, I stood back to consider its progress. Dark Medusa-like snakes of hair escaped their combs against a vermilion background. An elongated triangle of yellow ochre represented my face, with slashes of black for eyebrows. Another smear of venetian red slashed my cheekbone.

My best work seemed to follow an argument with my mother. I didn't want to consider what that said about my artistic future.

Claudine knocked on my door. "Excuse me, Mam'selle." She curtsied slightly. "The baron has left, and Madame has requested that you see her downstairs."

I found Maman in the foyer, fussing with a mass of white roses displayed in an antique vase on the round table.

She looked up briefly before resuming her task. "Must you always be on the run, Gabrielle? It's time for you to behave like a young woman, not a wild colt."

"Sorry, Maman." I kept my gaze on the black-and-white tiles, determined not to rise to her bait.

She sighed. "Really, you could try to be more like your sisters and learn some grace. You're old enough to receive your own suitors."

My head snapped up. "If I'm old enough to receive suitors, surely I am old enough to travel to Paris and study art."

"We've been over this. Your age is not the issue." She stopped shuffling the rose stems and faced me, her gaze intense. "It's a question of who you are. You are meant for better things than working like a tradesman."

"There's nothing wrong with creating art, Maman! And I'm not like Nacia or Genevieve. They'll happily marry the baron or any other nobleman you throw at them. Although I don't know how you can seriously consider that horrid man. He's ancient!"

"The baron is only forty-five," she said, her voice ominously mild. "Besides, what matters is that he can open doors for us. He can introduce us to *le gratin,* the best of society."

"He's a boor."

Maman's dark eyebrows drew together, a warning I too often ignored. "I will not have you insulting the men we entertain, especially not the baron."

My scalp prickled. "Why especially not him?"

"For some inexplicable reason, he has expressed a preference for you. If only Genevieve hadn't . . . ." She shook her head. "He's asked for permission to court you."

I stared at her. "Court me? But that means . . . ." No, no, no, my heart pounded. I took a step back. "Maman . . . I don't want to . . . not him, please!"

"I've already agreed." She set her jaw. "You will marry the man I choose."

I felt faint and it wasn't my corset. "Papa would never—"

"Don't even think of running to your father. In these matters, he agrees I know what's best. And what's best for you is a husband, someone who will put a stop to your childish fantasies about art. Once and for all."

My tongue thickened, threatening to choke off my breath. Courtship inevitably led to marriage, at least in our circles. I hadn't seen this coming. My older sisters should have married before Maman set her matchmaking sights on me. My plan was to have established a successful art career before then, a sure deterrent for any man foolish enough to propose marriage. I had to stop this madness. "I'll never marry the baron or any other man. I won't do it!"

Maman's face flushed, and her nostrils flared like bellows fanning embers into a flame. Then she slapped me.

I gasped and touched my cheek. She'd never struck me before. I turned and fled to my room.

No amount of pleading with my parents had deterred them. The courtship progressed alarmingly fast and plans to announce our engagement were made without my agreement. They left me with no alternative.

A sigh of relief escaped me as the distance between the baron and I increased with every clackety-clack of the iron wheels.

Philippe remained bent over my sketchbook for several more minutes, taking time on each page, nodding at times, murmuring at others. Finally he passed it back. "Thank you for showing me your work. I'm particularly impressed by your pastel portraits. Your use of colour and your ability to capture emotions in your subjects' expressions is remarkable."

My cheeks warmed with his praise. "You know something about art?"

"One of my older sisters dabbles in watercolours."

My face flushed. "It's not just a hobby for me," I snapped. What did he know of art, after all? He thought artists and anarchists were of the same ilk. I took a deep breath but my corset stays only rankled me more.

He held up his hands as if in self-defence. "I didn't mean to cause offence, Mademoiselle. Please forgive me. It's just that—well, you must realize it's highly irregular for a woman to study art seriously. None of my acquaintance, certainly."

"It's 1900, *la belle époque*! You may choose to remain rooted in the past, but I intend to be a part of the new way of doing things." My voice was sharp, but I didn't regret it. I had to speak plainly. I shifted my gaze out the window to cut off any further discussion.

With the possible exception of my brother Charles, the men I knew believed women were unsuited for anything but child-bearing and housewifery. We were expected to be attractive and charming, knowledgeable about running a house, all with the ultimate goal of making a man's life easier. Nonsense, of course, but most of the girls I went to school with viewed it as the gospel truth.

Even Bernadette accepted this silly view. Until recently, she dreamed of designing *haute couture* for Worth or Paquin. By the end of term, she began to fantasize about the man she'd marry, the house she'd manage, and she even chose names for the children she'd bear. It was exceedingly difficult to listen to such drivel, and I was almost glad when school ended, and she left with her family for a month of holiday in Brittany.

Almost.

I glanced at Philippe. His head was buried in his newspaper, a clear signal he didn't care for conversation either. Why did it bother me what this stranger thought? He was no more enlightened than Papa when I'd begged him to free me of the baron and to support my plans to study in Paris.

Chapter Four

THE MORNING AFTER THAT DISASTROUS night when Maman had informed me of the baron's intentions, I rose early and marched to Papa's study. As I raised my hand to knock, muffled, angry voices pierced the air. The door jerked open, and Charles stormed out with Papa on his heels, almost knocking me over

"You've run out of chances," Papa shouted. "Do this or I wash my hands of you!"

Charles's crimson face bore a mixture of hurt and rage. He glanced at me before disappearing down the hallway.

"Clearly, this is a bad time," I said to my father. "I can come back later."

"No, no, come in, petite." Looking much older than his fifty years, he eased into the chair behind his desk, an open ledger in front of him. He pushed the papers aside and ran a hand through his thinning hair.

The air in the study was thick with remnants of their quarrel. "Is anything wrong with Charles?" I asked.

"There's always something wrong with him."

I smiled. At least Papa's sense of humour was still intact. "I meant something new."

"You'll find out soon enough, I suppose," he said with a deep sigh. "I'm sending Charles to Canada to live and work with your uncle Luc."

"Canada! Why?"

Papa's lips thinned into an unrelenting line. "Gambling debts. Allegations of a dalliance with a married woman. And last night, he was accused of cheating at cards and challenged to a duel."

"A duel?" I gasped. "Oh, Papa, surely not."

He put up his hands. "I've smoothed that over. But I'm at the end of my wits with him. He must learn he can't continue his reckless lifestyle without consequences."

I stood to leave. "I'd better come back another time."

"I assume you're here about the baron?"

A bitter taste arose in my throat. I swallowed it with difficulty. "Maman says you have agreed to that . . . that man courting me. Papa, is it true?"

"The baron has a long and noble ancestry. More importantly, your mother believes you need the steadying influence an older husband can give you." He sounded as if he were dutifully repeating my mother's words rather than speaking out of his own conviction.

"I don't need any husband at all, Papa." I struggled to keep a reasonable tone. "You know I'm meant to be an artist, not a wife."

"Sit down, petite."

I strode to his desk and planted my hands on it. "I'm begging you. Get rid of the baron. Better yet, insist he marry Genevieve! It's what she wants. Please, Papa. Let me go to Paris."

He looked at me with what I thought was pity. "I'm sorry, *ma chérie*. Ask me anything but that." He held his hands out, palms open and empty. "We couldn't refuse him and cause a scandal, not once we'd invited him into our home for this very purpose. Yes, he chose you when it should have been one of your sisters, but to renege on our word would destroy your sisters' chances for their own futures."

I stared at him in disbelief. How could my beloved Papa condemn me to such a life? "All Maman wants is a noble title, and she'll do anything— including sacrificing me—to get it!"

"That is quite enough, young lady. I won't allow you to speak about your mother like that."

Words spewed out of my mouth without thought. "First she sent Grand-mère away, and now she's selling me to the highest bidder. I hate her!"

He stood, hands knuckled on top of his desk. "You must never say that."

"Why not? She hates me!"

He shook his head. "She loves you. We both do. Which is why we accepted the baron's request to court you. It's why we can't let you go to Paris."

"Can't or won't?"

He came around his desk and grabbed my hands. "Don't do anything foolish. Promise me."

I pulled away and fled to my room. My self-portrait mocked me from its easel. I dipped my thick sable brush in cadmium yellow and raw sienna and slashed the canvas with golden bars—so many bars that I exhausted the tube of colour and myself as well. But no amount of painting could ease the pain of my father's complicity and betrayal.

I leaned my head against the train window.

"Mademoiselle? Are you all right?" Philippe's voice broke into my thoughts.

I shook Papa and the baron from my head as if emerging from a bad dream. "I am fine. Thank you."

"I believe there is a bar on this train. May I bring you some refreshment?" His brow was creased in concern.

"Merci. I would enjoy a glass of lemonade."

"I'll be most happy to oblige."

Philippe soon returned with a refreshing lemonade for each of us. The sight of it reminded me how thirsty I was, and that it would be hours still before we reached Paris.

"À *votre santé,*" he said, raising his glass.

"Santé." I sipped my drink, stealing glances at him. Those carved lips of his cried out to be sketched, as did that intriguing scar. "May I draw your portrait?"

"A portrait or a cartoon?" He chuckled.

I liked the sound—deep, genuine. "You'll have to trust me."

"On one condition." He held up an index finger, his mouth stern but his eyes crinkled.

"Oui?"

"That you allow me to take a photograph of you."

Uneasiness crept into my belly. For what possible reason could a stranger—a man, no less—want a photograph of me? "Perhaps I've given you the wrong impression, Monsieur."

"I am sorry. Was my request too forward? If so, I apologize once again. I'm afraid I'm not well versed in the art of conversation with modern women."

I gave him a hard look, uncertain as to whether he was teasing or not, but he returned my gaze steadily, his expression sincere. What harm would a single photograph do? Our entire family made annual trips to the photographer's studio in Laval. Was a photograph any different than a portrait, really? Yet a small voice inside me still resisted, warning me that this request was of a different nature altogether.

I looked at my hands, cupped together on my lap. My mother and etiquette teacher would certainly have refused Philippe, but I was now on my own. I had exactly what I longed for, the freedom from tiresome rules and conventions. Freedom to choose, "oui" or "non." I glanced at my sketchpad. Other than Papa and Charles, I'd never had an opportunity to sketch a man. It would be challenging but a real addition to my work. And there were hours yet to fill before Paris.

"One photograph in exchange for a portrait." I stuck out my hand once again, and we shook firmly on the deal.

Philippe grinned broadly. "*Bien.* Now, how do you want me to pose?"

"Perhaps you could gaze out the window with your hand under your chin, like this." I showed him what I wanted.

He took off his glasses and slipped them into his jacket pocket, then sat in the position I'd demonstrated.

My hand hovered over the sketchpad before beginning. I fantasized Berthe Morisot whispering in my ear, tutoring me in the art of portraiture. "Sketch in the outline lightly, paying close attention to the underlying facial structure . . . ."

I flipped to a fresh page and roughed in Philippe's profile, then his neck and shoulders. I studied his features between each stroke on the page: a sharply defined jaw with faint darkish stubble, prominent cheekbones and curly, dark hair that flopped over his forehead. Combined with his full, carved lips, he could have been the model for Michelangelo's David, if not for the pale scar from his temple to his jaw.

He straightened his shoulders slightly and rolled his neck. "Can we talk while you work?"

I sketched in his dark eyelashes, straight nose and wide brow. "Certainly, except when I'm drawing your mouth."

He grinned.

"Can you hold that smile?"

He spoke through gritted teeth. "How's this?"

I laughed. "Terrible. Go back to your serious look." I tried to correct his mouth, softening the line of his lower lip. "Tell me, are you a photographer by profession?"

He shook his head. "Photography is my hobby." He shifted again, forcing me to re-adjust his shoulders in the sketch.

I shaded in the faint indentations left by his spectacles on the bridge of his nose. "Then what is it that you do for a living?"

"All I can say is that discretion and secrecy are at the heart of what I do." He smiled slightly, as if it were a private joke.

"So, police or government work, perhaps?"

He grimaced. "Surely you don't think I'm as boring as that? No, something much more exciting."

I softened the line of his scar with my gum eraser. Discretion, secrecy and excitement? "You're not a master criminal, are you?" A nervous laugh shook my hand and created an uneven line along his shoulders. I would have to cross-hatch the background to cover it up.

He glanced at his top hat before resuming his pose. "No, I assure you my work is all above board."

A criminal would have given the same answer—and nefarious activity would explain the nasty scar. I took a deep breath and ordered myself to concentrate on the portrait, tossing suspicion to the rubbish heap in the back of my mind.

"Can I take a break?" he asked finally.

"Oh. I'm sorry. Yes, of course."

He rubbed the back of his neck with one hand. "I had no idea modelling was such hard work."

"You are an excellent model." I blushed. It sounded as though I were flirting, which I was most definitely not. "I believe I'm finished, in any event."

"May I see?"

I handed him his portrait and he held it at arm's length, studying it for several heartbeats. "I like it much more than a photograph. You've made me better looking than I really am."

Better than a photograph? "Merci, Monsieur." A blush bloomed on my cheeks again, this time from such praise. "You may have it, if you'd like."

His broad smile was enough reward. "I'd be honoured. Would you sign it, *s'il vous plaît?*"

I scribbled my signature on the lower right. Another first. It wasn't exactly a sale, but very nearly.

Philippe cleared his throat. "And now, for your side of the bargain."

I nodded. "How is this for a pose?" I tipped my hat at a fashionable angle, smoothed down my bodice, and then turned slightly away from him.

He smiled. "Absolutely perfect." He retrieved his top hat from the luggage rack and donned it before taking his seat again.

"You are taking my picture, not your own, aren't you?" I asked, slightly amused.

His eyes sparkled with mischief, and he put a finger to his lips. "You of all people should know how important it is for the subject to hold her pose."

"True enough, but you haven't got your camera ready."

"Oh, but I do." A bright grin flashed across his face. "All right, I'm done."

"What? Where on earth is the camera?" I scanned the entire compartment. My face flushed. Was I the target of a joke? "What's the meaning of this? Explain yourself, Monsieur."

He removed his top hat carefully and handed it to me. "Look closely."

The hat was much heavier than it looked. A small hole pierced the front piece of the crown. The shiny grey satin lining appeared normal, but the interior of the hat was shallower than it should have been. I guessed it hid a mechanism of some sort high in the crown. A long narrow cord dangled from the back of the hat.

"It's a portable camera," he explained. He pointed at the small hole. "This is the lens. There's a magazine of several photographic plates inside the crown to capture the images."

"Rather clever," I said. "I suppose you hide that cord in your suit pocket?"

"Yes." His voice rose with enthusiasm. "This is only one of many miniaturized cameras. Subjects never even know they have been photographed. Quite the invention, wouldn't you say?"

"Hmmm."

"My favourite is one I saw last month in Paris. The Soda and Brandy Glass camera." He leaned toward me with boyish eagerness. "It's a large tumbler with a double bottom hiding the lens, the plate and so on. You fill your glass and begin to drink. You can keep the bottom of your glass at any angle you wish and take a photograph while in the very act of drinking. Most clever, isn't it?"

"Clever? I suppose." I bit my lip, knowing I might be considered rude but I simply had to speak my mind. "It is also very invasive of another's privacy."

The smug look on his face disappeared. He drew himself up as if a rod were suddenly jammed into his spine. "Have you never sketched a subject without their permission?"

"Well, yes, every artist does. It's entirely different."

"Really? How so?"

"Well . . . it just is." I had to gather my thoughts. Why was it acceptable to sketch people without their permission, yet offensive to do so with a camera? I thought back to the caricatures I'd made of the baron, along with many other impromptu sketches I'd done of people unaware of what I was doing.

Philippe crossed his arms and wore an expression of amusement.

A flash of annoyance ran through me. "For one thing, your photograph takes only an instant, whereas my sketches take several minutes, or hours even. It's very difficult to draw someone without them knowing."

"Perhaps we shall agree to disagree." He snapped open his newspaper and hid behind it.

"Fine." Annoyed, I stared out the window once again.

A crumbling castle ruin atop a hill in the distance caught my attention. It reminded me of the medieval castle in Laval where I used to play make-believe with Bernadette. I wondered if she'd received the letter revealing my bold plans. At the bottom, I had made a small sketch of myself boarding a train with an easel under my arm, waving gaily.

She'd be shocked at first, certainly, but would support me even if she didn't understand my need to escape.

Eventually the houses along the tracks became more numerous. No doubt we had reached the outer fringe of Paris. Imagine Grand-mère's surprise when I arrived at her apartment! Four years was a long time. I slipped her photograph out of its envelope and rubbed the image with my thumb. She looked the same as I remembered her—a heart-shaped face framed by a cloud of white curls, a determined look in her eyes as she smiled straight at the camera, her arm linked through another woman's. A name was scrawled on the back: Séverine.

The train's wheels squealed as it slowed, and the conductor popped his head into our car. "Final stop. *Gare* Montparnasse."

Paris! I put away the photograph, clutched my art box and luggage tightly, and rose just as the train lurched to a halt. I was thrown onto Philippe, very nearly spearing him with my parasol.

He caught my elbow to steady me. "Whoa, Mademoiselle Gabrielle, what's your hurry?"

A pleasant shock ran up my sleeve, but I pulled my arm away. "I need to catch up to my brother, Monsieur. *Adieu.*"

"The pleasure was all mine," he said. "*Au revoir.*"

I felt his eyes on my back as I rushed to the exit.

Chapter Five

GARE MONTPARNASSE, A CAVERNOUS train station of stone and high glass windows, burst with people of all shapes and sizes. The noise level nearly deafened me. Men shouted, women greeted arrivals with shrieks, and children wailed their displeasure. Odours of the hot food hawked in stalls underlay the sharp choking stink of coal and something else, something unfamiliar that I fancied was unique to Paris—the reek of two million souls living together.

A hard object thumped me from behind.

"*Pardon,* mademoiselle."

I turned in time to avoid further attack from a grey-whiskered man encased in a light linen suit and straw boater hat who clutched a heavy leather case. When I sidestepped him, more travelers buffeted me from all sides, flowing past as if I were nothing more than a pebble in a stream. Some people carried their own baggage, like me, while others strode ahead of porters with barrows heavily burdened with cases, crates, and trunks.

I stopped in front of a newsstand which displayed a bewildering variety of newspapers and journals. Headlines in bold type topped copies of *Le Petit Parisien, Le Figaro, Le Monde, La Fronde.* I passed over them, choosing a map of the city instead. I then found a bench to spread it out upon.

It was easy to pinpoint Gare Montparnasse, but *rue* Cortot wasn't marked anywhere. From what Philippe had told me of Montmartre, that wasn't terribly surprising. Trusting I could get directions along the way, I pushed aside a niggling worry that the street might not even exist.

I joined the queue for the ticket agent. When it was my turn, I shoved my map at him. "*Excusez-moi.* Can I take the omnibus or tramway to get to Montmartre?"

The agent, surely no older than I, looked up with a bored expression. "You can't get there from here by public transport, even if the Metro was open, which it isn't until next month."

"Then I suppose I'll have to walk. Could you help me with directions?"

He stared at my shoes. "Walk? Not in those heels. You'd best take a carriage for hire, mademoiselle. There's a cab stand outside." He gestured vaguely and motioned for the next customer to move ahead.

It was already late afternoon when I exited the station. Despite ominous clouds promising thundershowers, I hugged myself and whirled around. I was in Paris—at last! My outburst quite probably revealed me to be a country bumpkin, but I didn't care. I wanted to savour the moment. I, Gabrielle de Villiers, threw caution to the wind and ran away from home. Paris, here I am!

I laughed aloud at my pretensions of grandeur. But with Grand-mère's backing, I could take on any challenges life threw at me, even pressure from Maman to marry the baron. Indeed, I would master painting and surprise them all—my family, the Madame DuPonts of the world, and most of all, the art critics.

But first, I had to locate Grand-mère.

The chaos I'd experienced inside the station was multiplied outdoors. Omnibuses, carriages, and even bicycles jammed the streets. Coachmen cracked their whips, horses clopped along the pavement, harnesses jingled, and newsboys wailed the day's headlines.

The smell of gasoline caught my attention. I whirled around, half-expecting to see Charles zoom past on his new gas-powered bicycle. Instead, a strange horseless carriage the shape of a cigar flew by. An automobile. The goggled driver of the exhaust-spewing machine honked his horn as he slewed around a double-decker omnibus and cut back in front.

Top-hatted men in the upper level of the omnibus cursed while the coach-man fought to keep his team of horses from bolting. "Get a horse!" he yelled, but the automobile's driver seemed oblivious of the havoc he'd created. His white silk scarf flew out behind him as he sped away.

I laughed as I pictured Charles behind the wheel of such a machine, equally heedless.

Or perhaps, one day, that would be me.

All of the cabs were engaged by the time I located the stand. With my bags at my feet, I raised one arm to hail one of the carriages rattling past. None stopped. An unpleasant stench of manure and garbage swirled about me as I waited.

A woman balanced on a bicycle passed by, reminding me of Bernadette. Upon our graduation the previous week, my parents had given me a thick choker of pearls while Bernie had received her wonderful "freedom machine"—a bicycle.

I last saw her less than a week before, on our final day of school. Our year-end art projects lay on our desks, ready for critique by Madame Magne. I was especially anxious, for I'd chosen a dead finch for my subject instead of a safer composition such as a landscape or portrait.

As we waited for class to begin, I studied my picture with growing dismay. It was crucial that Madame approve of my picture, for I intended to ask her for a reference letter to the Académie Julian. Yet something was missing— that indefinable spark of uniqueness. Dare I work on it? One misstep and it would be ruined. I checked the gold watch pinned to my shirtwaist—three minutes. Madame was always punctual.

My hand hovered over the rainbow of pastels on my desk. I had to risk it. A few strokes of vermillion in the background, a touch more crimson on the bird's torn wing, a spot of white to suggest a reflection of light in its pupil.

I sat back and studied my work. Yes! A warm glow spread through my veins from belly to fingertips. This was why I devoted myself to art.

The piece wasn't conventional or even pretty. In the foreground, the bird was splayed out in death, exposing a portion of fine bones in one wing, its delicate tendons shredded where our cat Fantine caught the poor creature in her jaws. In the background, a light sepia rendering caught the finch mid-air, wings spread with the joy of flight.

Angeline, a classmate fond of stirring up trouble, pointed an accusing finger at my picture, drawing a crowd of girls around us. "Mon Dieu! What a hideous subject!"

"Oh, for heaven's sake, Angeline." Bernadette pushed through the other students to stand by my side. "What a fuss over nothing. Have you never seen a dead bird before?"

Angeline shuddered, and her pretty mouth twisted into a grimace. "It's positively disgusting."

Someone else gagged loudly. "How could you draw something so grotesque?"

"I think Gabbi's drawing is powerful," Bernadette declared, her hand on my shoulder. "And poetic."

Mediocre at art, she excelled at friendship.

I would miss her company while in Paris, but by August she will have returned to Laval from her family holiday in St. Malo. By then, I'd be settled in with Grand-mère and could invite Bernie to Paris. Perhaps she'd come to her senses and pursue her dream of joining the world of *haute couture*. What fun we would have together, carving out a niche for ourselves as modern women.

First things first. I had to find my grandmother's apartment. With no bicycle at the ready and no coachman prepared to stop, I had no choice but
to walk. After consulting the woman who sold me the map, I headed in a
generally northern direction toward the Seine River. From her garbled directions involving unfamiliar avenues and landmarks, I gathered I could take an
omnibus to the foot of Montmartre, once I crossed the river.

My bags gained weight with every step. I managed for a few blocks but had
to stop at the next intersection to rest my arms. Bright posters plastered on
lamp posts advertised cabarets, scientific lectures, art gallery openings, cafés,
and even a circus at L'Hippodrome. I hugged myself again, certain I'd made
the right decision. No doubt Grand-mère and I would see it all.

I couldn't wait.

I hefted my bags and crossed the street, narrowly missing an encounter
with a highly polished black and gold *fiacre*, the coachman's whip cracking
over his blinkered horse. Traffic dust settled on my pinched shoes, wafted up
my nose, and made me sneeze. Despite gathering storm clouds, the day was
hot and perspiration dripped under my corset. It wasn't quite the glorious
beginning I'd envisioned. At least I wasn't sitting demurely at home as my
engagement was announced, waiting to receive endless streams of gossiping
women. I was walking toward my future, even if I wore the wrong shoes.

My head high and filled with lofty thoughts, I stepped into a steaming pile
of horse droppings. *Merde!* I swiped at my shoe with my handkerchief, ruin-
ing them both in the process. After discarding my handkerchief, I carried on,
ignoring the slight stench dogging me with each step. A nasty blister devel-
oped on my right heel, and I began to limp.

The sky began to spit thick, wet drops. I struggled with my parasol, but by
the time it finally unfolded, the rain pelted down and the hem of my skirt was
sodden. Could things get any worse?

"Bonjour, Mademoiselle Gabrielle Carmen Désirée Jean d'Arc de Villiers."

I recognized that teasing male voice at once. But then, who else could it
have been, for no one knew me here. I looked up to see Philippe waving out
the window of a closed fiacre, his fine sleeve quickly drenched. The coachman, hunched on his perch in front of the cab, was exposed to the weather.
The reins looped from his slack hands to a sway-backed nag. They would
make a striking composition, so I tried to memorize the details for later: the
finely matched pair, rain dripping off their long noses and rain-slick backs.

"Bonjour, Monsieur Lucien." I wondered at the coincidence of seeing
him again.

He leaned out his window, his intensely blue eyes gazing at me with sympathy. "Please, take my carriage, Mademoiselle."

"I couldn't." It would be most improper to share his ride, although I wanted to. My feet hurt, I wasn't sure where I was going, and soon I'd be soaked through to the skin. And, despite his irritating views on women, women artists in particular, I had enjoyed his company on the train.

"You don't want to stay out there in the muck and the rain, do you?"

Then again, he wasn't a stranger—not really. Still, I hesitated.

"You are headed to Montmartre? Please, take my coach." He stepped out of the carriage and into the now pelting rain, holding open the door.

His meaning suddenly became clear. He was offering the coach for my sole use. He would stay and get soaked.

"I can't possibly take your carriage. There are no others to be had."

"Please, get inside before you catch your death of a cold." He hefted my now-damp bags into the carriage. The door remained ajar. Rain pelted inside, wetting the leather bench.

A bold proposal occurred to me. I imagined myself, unchaperoned in a closed fiacre with him. The gusting wind drove sheets of rain beneath my parasol, wetting my skirts, and yet I never felt better. I was a thoroughly modern woman. "I cannot leave you here in the rain. I will accept your offer, but only on the condition that we share the carriage."

Chapter Six

IT WAS PHILIPPE'S TURN TO HESITATE. He frowned, shifting his weight from one foot to the other as if trying to find his balance. He nodded sharply at last and bowed slightly. "As you wish, Mademoiselle." He held out his hand.

I accepted his help, lifting my skirts only high enough to climb up without tripping. The snug cab was a tight fit for the two of us. I pressed my shoulder against the far window to keep a proper distance. "My grandmother's address is 16 rue Cortot."

He called out, "To rue Cortot, in Montmartre."

The coachman shouted back, "You realize that's across the whole city? It'll cost you much more."

Philippe waved his objections away. "Don't worry, you'll get paid."

As the carriage lurched forward, Philippe turned to me and asked, "Did you miss your brother at the station?"

I suppressed a twinge of guilt. "No doubt he'll meet me at our grandmother's."

He raised his eyebrows but changed the subject. "Were you planning to walk all the way to Montmartre?" He sounded annoyed or even angry. "It's nearly five kilometres from here to the Seine, never mind climbing the butte."

Five kilometres? A startling distance. I tucked my shoes under my skirt and wiggled my toes to ease the growing blisters. "I tried to hail a cab but none would stop for me."

"Ah, yes. We Frenchmen are not yet ready to accept independent women, are we? I apologize on behalf of all the men in France, Mademoiselle."

Was he making fun? "I accept your apology," I said rather sharply.

"Coachmen aren't allowed to pick up fares outside of the cab stands," he said, sounding amused. "So, it had nothing to do with your gender."

Chastened, I looked at my hands clutched in my lap. "I suppose there is much I have to learn about the city." Then, albeit reluctantly, I added, "I must thank you for your chivalrous offer of your carriage, Monsieur Lucien."

"You are most welcome, Mademoiselle." He cleared his throat. "Would you consider dropping the formalities and calling me 'Philippe' instead of 'Monsieur?'"

Maman, never mind Madame Dijon, would be horrified by such informality. "Thank you, Philippe. You may call me Gabrielle."

"Excellent, Gabrielle."

I couldn't tear my gaze from Philippe's remarkable eyes. In the dark interior of the carriage, they became a deep cobalt blue, the very colour of our kitchen at home, my favourite room. The room where Grand-mère would ply me with Cook's fresh croissants after school and tell me wild stories about her youth, or romantic stories about my grandfather, who died before I was even born.

The kitchen was also the last place I'd seen her in our home.

She had called me into the kitchen during breakfast. With a hushed voice, she told me she was taking me to a parade in the town square.

"Does Maman know?"

She put a finger over her lips. "It's our little secret."

I glanced back at the door to the dining room. "But what about Nacia and Genevieve?"

"It's just you and me." She winked as she tied her bonnet. "Come now, let's not be late."

"Will I miss school?"

"Do you mind?" She peered at me, a worried look on her normally cheerful face.

"Not one bit." I linked my arm through hers, my pulse racing. Adventures always happened for my grandmother and this time, she was taking me along. "What kind of parade is it, Mémère?" I asked once we reached the sidewalk and headed for the main square.

She grinned. "It's a parade of women."

That didn't sound like much fun. "What will they be doing, embroidering pillow cushions as they walk?"

She chuckled. "Hardly, chérie. We have signs demanding that men recognize our rights, like voting and managing our own money. We're going to show men how serious we are."

I dropped her hand. Maman would be furious with her. And with me. She and Grand-mère often argued about what Maman called my grand-mother's "political nonsense." It meant nothing to me. "Why should I care about any of that?"

She caressed my cheek. "You don't much like spending hours with embroidery, do you? Or those ridiculous etiquette classes your Maman sends you to?"

I shook my head.

"My dear child, what do you think your mother is preparing you for?"

I stared at her as it dawned on me. "Marriage?"

She nodded. "Exactly. That's fine, if it's what you want, like Genevieve and Nacia. But I think we both know you want more out of your life. What if you want to attend university? Don't you want the right to choose an occupation? What about the right to manage your own money, to make decisions about your own future? Don't you want the same opportunities Charles has?"

I nodded vigorously as my mind whirled through the implications of what she had said. I hadn't imagined my life as an adult until then. "Let's hurry, we don't want to be late," I said.

Grand-mère laughed and I skipped beside her. I'd have a great story to tell Bernadette at school the next day.

But I never got that story.

As we neared the square, my grandmother's hand tightened on mine.

"What is wrong, Mémère?"

She pointed to Papa, standing on the sidewalk. "I'd forgotten that your father's shop is on the square."

Papa was peering up at the new sign he'd recently installed—*Les Caves de Villiers et Fils*. Villiers and Son. Charles, recently home after completing his studies at the Sorbonne and a tour of Europe, was joining Papa in the family business.

Papa spotted us and waved.

Grand-mère halted and took a deep breath. Her steps slowed as we joined Papa, and mine matched her pace. "Bonjour, Madame Lucille." He tipped his hat to her. "Why aren't you in school, Gabbi?"

I looked to Grand-mère. She glanced at the square. Women of all ages, dressed in everything from humble homespun cotton to tailored suits began to fill the grassy expanse. Many of them hoisted hand-lettered signs over their heads. "She's getting a different kind of education this morning, Sebastian."

Papa's normally cheerful expression clouded over. "Lucille, you know Désirée wouldn't approve. It's one thing for you and your feminist friends to take part in a demonstration, but you can't involve Gabbi. It could be dangerous."

"I will look after her," she promised.

He shook his head and held out his hand to me. "Come, petite. I'll take you."

I tightened my grip on Grand-mère's arm. "Papa, please? I want to be here."

"I'm sorry," he said.

Grand-mère sighed. "Your father is right, Gabbi. Perhaps I shouldn't have brought you."

I looked over my shoulder at the women beginning to form lines, as if they were soldiers readying for war. "*S'il vous plait,* Papa?"

My father seldom refused me, but I could tell from the set of his jaw that he wouldn't change his mind. Reluctantly, I let go of Grand-mère and followed my father to school.

I have regretted leaving her ever since. I couldn't shake the belief that I might have somehow prevented what came next. We heard later that the *gendarmes* tried to stop the marching women, that some of them resisted, striking out at the gendarmes. Many were arrested, Grand-mère amongst them. She spent the night in prison, and by the time I returned from school the following day, she'd packed and left our house. Maman forbid any of us to even speak her name, but I never forgot her.

Now, after four long years, I was finally going to see her. I sighed deeply, smiling to myself. No doubt great adventures were ahead.

Chapter Seven

THE HIRED FIACRE LURCHED through heavy traffic as rain streaked the windows. I rubbed the fog off the inside of the glass with my glove. "What's that large building and park, there?" The scene looked familiar, as if it had popped out of the pages of an art journal.

Philippe leaned forward to peer out my window and the warmth of his body invaded my space. His scent—a clean smell of soap, pomade and something spicy—sent my pulse racing.

"That's the Luxembourg Palace and Gardens. Such a shame you arrived on a wet, grey day. You'd see so much more if the sun were out." He leaned back against his seat, and my pulse returned to near-normal. "The Faubourg Saint-germain, where many of the nobility live, is coming up to our left. It doesn't look like much today, but I assure you it houses only *la crème de la crème.*"

I glanced at the Faubourg Saint-germain and shrugged. I'd left one aristocrat behind me and wasn't the least interested in any others. But it reminded me how desperately cruel fate could be. There I was, a runaway from the baron, while poor Genevieve still tormented herself over losing her supper and along with it, the baron's favour.

The fiacre hit a bump as it crossed onto a bridge. I glanced down at my feet and wished for a thousandth time that I'd been less blessed with what Papa called my "good understanding."

The Seine flowed serenely under the bridge. A tugboat pulled a row of barges with a little black and white dog the sole occupant of its deck, barking and snapping at the rain.

"And now where are we?" I asked.

"We're crossing the Seine, from the Left Bank to the Right Bank. This is one of the city's most famous bridges, Pont Neuf. Hardly new, is it? It was built early in the seventeenth century."

I fought back disappointment as I looked down into the river's dark, swirling waters, expecting the Seine would be much wider and faster. It was, after all, the most famous river in the country and it flowed through the City of Lights. All in all, it wasn't much more lively than the sluggish Mayenne that wound through my home town.

"Notre Dame Cathedral is at the far end of the island."

The famed Gothic cathedral's silhouette appeared through my rain-streaked window. How grand! Its twin towers and spire speared the grey skyline far above any other buildings, still too far away to pick out the stone *grotesques* crouched on its roof, but I could imagine them.

Philippe broke into my thoughts. "Soon we'll be able to see the Louvre Museum. Surely you have heard of it?"

"Of course." I leaned toward him to catch a glimpse of the Louvre through his window. A thrill chased through me as the stone fortress-like walls came into view, rising solidly along the Seine. "I've wanted to go to the Louvre museum since I was a little girl. As soon as I'm settled in, I'll need to apply for official permission to copy paintings there."

He looked surprised. "I thought you were simply visiting your grandmother. How long are you staying in Paris?"

I hesitated. "Actually . . . I'm moving here to study at the Académie Julian."

His remarkable blue eyes held mine.

I waited for him to scoff. "I am destined to become an artist."

He surprised me, nodding with no hint of a smile. "I wish you every success."

"Thank you." I failed to keep the bitterness out of my voice as I added, "Not everyone wants me to succeed."

Maman was first in that line. She'd rejected even my early artistic attempts. When the first of my baby brothers had been stillborn and Maman refused to leave her bedroom, Grand-mère moved in with us. At nine years of age, I understood that Maman was grieving over baby Arthur's death.

It was late afternoon, weeks after the baby's funeral, when I dared to enter her bedroom. The drapes were drawn so the room was dim, the air stale. "Maman?"

She sat up with effort and patted the mattress. "Come, Gabbi."

I gasped. Maman, normally carefully groomed, looked as though she'd crawled out of the gutters. Long dark hair hung down her back in limp strands. Her face was pale and puffy around her eyes. I buried my head in her bosom, relieved to cuddle with her after so long.

Then I remembered what was in my pocket and took it out. "I made something for you." I handed her a crayon drawing of our family—Papa, Maman,

Charles, Genevieve and Nacia, Grand-mère and me, each person's name carefully printed underneath their likeness. No baby, for Maman needed reminding that she still had the rest of us. Sure that my drawing would cure her of her melancholy, I had worked on it all morning with Grand-mère's help.

Maman peered at my drawing until, with a grunt, she lit the lamp beside the bed. Her voice sharpened. "Where's Arthur?"

"He's gone, Maman." Didn't she know?

She tossed the drawing on her bedside table, turned out the light and pulled the covers up to her chin. "Leave me, child."

I ran back to the kitchen, sobbing. The pain of that rejection never really left me, but lay dormant like a buried thorn, only to resurface whenever we quarrelled. And yet, just recently when I'd searched her bedroom for Grand-mère's address, I had found my crayon drawing in her écritoire. She'd kept it, all those years.

The fiacre lurched around a hairpin curve. I turned away from the window to discover Philippe's gaze on me.

"Nothing worth having comes easily," he said.

I nodded. I wasn't completely naïve about what lay ahead. I'd forsaken the comfort and financial security of my parents' home for an uncertain future, but at least it would be a future of my own making.

"Gabrielle? Could I, perhaps, escort you to the Exposition Universelle?"

"Oh!" I clasped my gloved hands together, considering his bold proposal. Could I accept? I didn't know Philippe or his family or what he did for a living. Or was I fretting over superficial things, things that Maman would fuss over? Despite his old-fashioned views about women, he had proved himself to be a true gentleman. I really wanted to see the famous Expo and yet wasn't prepared to go alone. Not quite yet. "I'd like that, merci."

"Of course, you must have a chaperone. Would your grandmother join us?"

I bristled. Modern women didn't require chaperones. Yet perhaps this one time, it would be a good idea. "I'm sure she'd love such an outing."

"Bien. I'll send a message when I've concluded my business in the city."

A wide grin spread across my face. My first day in Paris and already I had made a friend.

"Perhaps your brother would care to come as well, provided you finally locate him," he said with a smirk.

"Mmmm," I mumbled, reminded of Charles' phantom presence. I turned away, hoping there'd be no more need for deception. It was getting hard to remember what I'd said.

The fiacre struggled across an intersection jammed with traffic, and the horse began a steep climb. I peered out the window, fixing landmarks in my mind for later exploration. Twin windmills made a strange sight, silhouetted against the grey sky from their perch on the top of the butte.

"Perhaps another time I can show you the shops and cafés along the Avenue des Champs-Élysées and the Bois du Boulogne," Philippe said.

"Perhaps," I murmured vaguely. No doubt he thought I was like any other young woman. How little he understood. It wasn't shopping that had brought me to the city. I longed to visit all of the art galleries and museums, the cafés favoured by the art elite. What a thrill it would be to see famous women artists such as Suzanne Valadon or the American, Mary Cassatt.

"Oh, look at all the statuary and crypts!" I exclaimed as we looked down upon an old cemetery, filled with large vaults, beautiful sculptures and crypts. "I love cemeteries," I said, and then Madame Dijon's voice chirped, "A proper lady would never profess interest in something so grotesque." I glanced at Philippe to see his reaction to my very unladylike comment.

He bit his lip, whether to hide amusement or dismay, I couldn't tell.

A spotted pig trotted across the street, momentarily halting our carriage. "Montmartre still behaves much like the village it was before being annexed by the city," he said, changing the subject. "Look. On that side of the street is an elegant *hôtel particulaire*. On the other side, it's all ramshackle housing, pig pens and chicken coops."

I laughed. Montmartre was certainly less elegant than the arrondissements we'd driven through on the way to the Butte. But somehow it felt right. I could see Grand-mère striding down these streets, equally comfortable with *le gratin* or the rag pickers.

The fiacre continued to climb and eventually turned onto rue Cortot. It appeared somewhat more prosperous. One side was filled with four-storey buildings boasting bay windows and elaborate plaster frontages. Number 16 sat apart on a large lot with its own groomed gardens, the entrance framed by an elegant stone archway.

"Thank you for sharing your cab." I opened my handbag to pay the fare.

He waved away my money. "It was my pleasure to have your company. I look forward to seeing you again soon." He handed me his card, which simply bore his name and addresses in both Paris and Le Mans.

As I slipped it into my handbag, I thought about designing my own calling card. I'd need one, once I started to receive commissions for my work. A bold calligraphy script font in gold perhaps, declaring my profession: "Gabrielle de Villiers, Artist."

Philippe got out and stood hunched against the rain. I handed him my parasol, which he held over the step, waiting with one hand outstretched.

When he grasped my elbow to steady me as I stepped down, an unexpected shock ran from his hand to the base of my spine.

"Au revoir." He handed me the parasol with a slight bow.

"Au . . . au revoir." I picked up my skirts and stumbled inside Grand-mère's building, unsettled by the reaction his touch stirred in me. "Until we meet again," he'd said. I hadn't expected to see him after the train journey, but he showed up when I most needed his help. True, I'd insisted we share the carriage. Now, he knew my address in Paris, and I'd agreed to a *rendez-vous,* albeit chaperoned. Maman wouldn't have tolerated such familiarity with a stranger, but I was certain Grand-mère would approve.

Chapter Eight

AN ELDERLY PORTER SAT HUNCHED behind a metal screen inside the dimly lit vestibule. He squinted through heavy glasses at a newspaper and ignored me completely.

I cleared my throat.

He peered over his paper with cloudy blue eyes that showed an utter lack of interest. "Oui?"

"Excuse me, monsieur. What room is Madame Lucille Cribiere in?"

He turned back to his paper. "Don't know," he muttered.

"Perhaps you could look in your register?"

He made a show of turning the page of his paper, rustling the sheets and smoothing them down again. No response.

"Please, monsieur."

"Humph." The porter sighed loudly, glanced down at a sheet of paper on the counter and shook his head. "Doesn't live here."

"Look again, monsieur, s'il vous plait." I tapped my fingers against the counter. Why was he being so difficult?

He lifted the page and gazed at another one beneath it. "Just as I said. No one by that name lives here."

How could that be? I'd ransacked Maman's bedroom and found the envelope hidden in her écritoire, after the baron had revealed Grand-mère was living in Paris. It had to be the right address. "But I sent a telegram . . . ."

He shrugged.

"Have you even heard of her? Madame Lucille Cribiere?" I repeated my grandmother's name, emphasizing each syllable as if instructing a child. I didn't care if he was insulted. I needed Grand-mère.

"Go away, please." He snapped his paper open once again and stared at it.

My hands shook, and I gripped my purse tightly. "You must be mistaken." I drew out Grand-mère's photograph. "Here's what she looks like—the woman on the left."

He glanced at the photograph, lower lip thrust out. "Never seen her."

"The photograph is four years old. I suppose she's aged since then. Please, look again."

He took a closer look but shook his head once more. "I told you, I've never seen her before. Now, please, go away."

This simply couldn't be happening. I handed him the creased envelope. "See this letter? It's from her. See the return address? Sixteen rue Cortot. That's this building, isn't it?" My voice rose as I tapped the lettering with a trembling hand.

He snatched the envelope, examining it with care as he turned it over. "This was mailed over a year ago."

"Over a year ago . . . ?" I hadn't noticed the postmark. When I'd discovered the envelope, I'd been so certain that my guardian angel had put it in my hands, that God or fate or whatever it was called was conspiring with me to ensure I would get to Paris. "But . . . ." Tears welled up, filling my eyes and spilling down my cheeks. My brave new future was stillborn. Without Mémère . . . .

"Ach, don't cry, mademoiselle. No need for tears." The porter peered at me, his brow furrowed. "Wait here, I will check farther back." A large mantle clock ticked away each heartbeat as he shuffled into a back room.

He returned with a thick register. "Aha! Madame Lucille Cribiere. She was here. She moved."

Of course, that was it. "Where to?"

Another shrug. "Don't know. I wasn't working here then."

"Are you sure there's no forwarding address?"

He made a show of consulting the book. "I am sorry."

"When did she leave?"

"December."

Six months ago. Small wonder she hadn't replied to my hasty telegram of last week. She could be anywhere—anywhere in the world. "Can I at least search her rooms for any clues?"

"Certainly not. The rooms are occupied."

"Then can you suggest how I find out where she is now?"

Once again, that maddening shrug of the shoulders. "I've done what I can. Now, please leave me alone." He turned away.

Leave? Where could I go? Not home. Not after leaving the way I did, as if a thief in the night. Tingling in my fingertips spread up my arms. I felt as if my future had been erased as surely as my gum eraser wiped out strokes of graphite. My legs buckled under me, and I had to grip the counter's edge.

"Mademoiselle? Do you need to sit down?" The porter came out from behind his wicket, took my elbow, and led me to a sofa by the window.

"Merci." I sank onto the cushions. The rain beat against the window, heavier than ever. The porter hovered over me. I waved him away. "I'll be fine. Please, go back to your desk."

Alone in Paris. I knew no one here. No one. A lump rose in my throat, threatening to choke me. I closed my eyes. This couldn't be happening. Not after everything began so well—the train ride, Philippe, Paris. Several minutes passed as I stared at the crumpled envelope clutched in my hands. How did it all go so wrong? Where could Mémère be? How could I manage without her?

But the mere thought of turning back to the train station and home to Laval in defeat caused bile to rise in my throat. I bent over, stifling a sob. No! Maman would be smug or even worse, furious and insufferable. And nothing would have changed.

I straightened my back. I'd given up too much to get here. There had to be a way to stay in Paris! I forced myself to take several deep breaths. Nacia's kid gloves were water-stained and clammy, no longer a symbol of independence. I pulled them off and shoved them into my handbag. My fingers brushed Philippe's calling card. I drew it out, stared at it. No, I could not ask him for help. It was an outrageous idea. Preposterous. Unthinkable. I started to tear up the card, then stopped and slid it back into my handbag. Just in case.

Outside the window, a city of two million people carried on their lives without concern for my desperate circumstances. I hadn't the first idea of how to track down my grandmother. Yet, somehow, I had to.

I had enough money for perhaps a week or two in a respectable hotel. Surely that would gain me enough time to find Grand-mère. But a respectable hotel wouldn't give a room to an unaccompanied young woman. I thought briefly of throwing myself on the mercy of a convent. But no—that was no solution. They would surely contact my family and send me back. I ground my teeth in frustration. Our entire society was structured to thwart a woman who wanted to strike out on her own.

My stomach growled. I hadn't eaten since the previous evening at home, the meal I'd jokingly thought of as the Last Supper. How telling that sounded now. Perhaps I could think more clearly if I ate. I approached the porter. "Could you recommend a good restaurant nearby . . . something inexpensive?" I murmured, blushing.

"Try La Bohème, a café in Place du Tertre, not far from here." He gave me directions.

"Would you keep my bags, monsieur? I won't be long."

He pulled at his lower lip. "Mind you come back, then. I won't keep them forever."

Chapter Nine

I OPENED MY PARASOL, stepped out the door, and turned left as directed. The pounding rain had eased into a fine drizzle. I kept my eyes down, huddled under the slight protection of my parasol, avoiding puddles on the slick pavement and the risk of destroying my once-fine slippers.

I collided with someone.

"*Regardez!*"

I looked up to see a woman staring at the wet sidewalk now scattered with glittery hair combs and a silk dressing gown. I bent to gather them up for her, and we bumped heads. Our eyes met.

"*Je suis très désolée*, madame," I apologized. "It was very clumsy of me."

She stuffed her belongings into a damp paper bag and regarded me with a frown. She didn't appear to be much older than I was. Petite, blonde and blue-eyed, she reminded me of Bernadette and a fresh pang of loss struck me. Tears sprang to my eyes, and I blinked them away.

The woman continued to look me over. Something made me uncomfortable about the spots of rouge on her cheeks and the way her clothes hugged her bosom and hips. If this was Laval, we probably wouldn't have spoken at all. But I was in Paris, determined to leave that kind of snobbishness behind. I studied her closely, looking for common ground. Then I spotted her bare hands. "Are you an artist?"

"How did you know?" she asked suspiciously.

"The paint under your nails," I said. "I'm an artist, too."

"And a detective," she said, finally grinning. "I must be careful."

I shook my head and laughed—an antidote to growing panic. I introduced myself and she told me her name was Babette Chienne.

"Bonjour, Mademoiselle Babette."

"Your accent isn't Parisian," she said.

"I'm from Laval. I came here to live with my grandmother. But . . . ." I bit my lip.

"Ah." She cocked her head, lips pursed. "Where were you going in such a hurry?"

"To a café, La Bohème. Do you know it?"

"Yes, of course," she said. "I live nearby. Let's go."

The rain had stopped, so I folded my parasol and walked beside Babette, listening to her chatter. For a moment, I could pretend she was Bernadette, and we were promenading the boulevard and pursuing our dreams together.

But then Babette gurgled roughly and spit on the side of the walk. An elderly gentleman, leaning heavily on a cane, swerved around us, muttering about the loss of manners.

Embarrassment reddened my face, but Babette didn't seem bothered by the old man's disapproval. She linked her arm through mine. "I moved to the city from a small village, too. Vézelay, in Burgundy. Do you know it?"

"No."

"Of course not," she said, laughing. "It's tiny. Everyone there is stuck in the Middle Ages."

"Laval is a city, but it is just as backward," I confided. "It's why I had to leave. There's no place there for women who want something other than marriage."

"I know exactly what you mean."

"Is Paris really as modern as they say? That artists come here from around the world? That there's opportunity for everyone, even if you're a woman?"

She nodded. "Oh, yes. In Paris, you can do anything! I've met artists from America, Russia, and even from Japan."

"C'est vrai?" That was what I'd been hoping for. What I'd imagined. My shoulders lifted slightly, and I swung my arms as I walked beside Babette. Good fortune had surely put her in my path today.

"Myself, I'm saving to enroll at the Académie Julian."

I stopped and stared at her. "What an extraordinary coincidence! That's where I'm going to study." Although, without my grandmother I was unlikely to study anywhere. "At least, it's what I had planned."

She pursed her lips. "It's a very good school. Everyone wants to study there, if they can't pass the admittance examinations of the École des Beaux-Arts, that is." She spat once again, very nearly splattering my shoes. "What good is state-sponsored tuition if only those who attend the best schools can pass?"

"I thought the École des Beaux-Arts didn't accept women. Not after the riot when two women were admitted a few years ago."

Babette shrugged. "A handful of women study there, but only the ones who will put up with the daily abuse the men dole out."

I touched Madame Magne's reference letter, still tucked safely in my handbag. Its presence gave me heart. "My art teacher advised me to apply at the Julian. The École des Beaux-Arts is too tradition bound and won't allow women to draw models in the nude, which is imperative for an artist."

"The Académie Julian is very prestigious," Babette said with a frown. "They might not accept someone as young as you."

"I'm not too young! Elisabeth Vigée Le Brun was painting commissioned portraits at fifteen years of age."

"Humph." Babette's pretty mouth turned down, and she picked up her pace. Had she not heard of the woman who went on to become Marie Antoinette's official portraitist? Perhaps I'd been especially fortunate with Madame Magne, who taught art technique and history in my final year of school. Perhaps most importantly, Madame had taught us the importance of dreaming. Over her desk hung a quote by Marcel Proust that I read every day that year: "*Si qui rêve est dangereux, le traitement pour lui n'est pas de rêver moins, mais de rêver davantage, pour rêver à toute heure.*" If a little dreaming is dangerous, the cure for it is not to dream less but to dream more, to dream all the time.

We also learned of French women who had devoted their lives to art: Sophie Anderson, Rosa Bonheur, Camille Claudel, and Berthe Morisot. Over the course of that year with Madame Magne, a revolutionary question had taken root within me: if those women could succeed at forging their own lives, why couldn't I?

By the time we arrived at Place du Tertre, the sun streamed down from the clouds and warmed my back. La Bohème, one of many cafés lining the square, struck the right note with its bright red-and-white striped awning. An aproned waiter dried off two chairs for us at an outside table. My sense of *bonheur* increased when the waiter brought steaming cups of strong coffee and a small selection of pastries, bread and cheeses.

I cradled my cup and inhaled the bitter aroma, remembering happier times at home, seated at our kitchen table with Cook. But I gave that up for a reason.

I reached for a slice of bread. My companion had nearly decimated the basket already and much of the cheese as well. "Mademoiselle, I hope this isn't an impertinent question, but how do you afford to live in Paris?"

Babette avoided my gaze and picked at the paper tablecloth with a broken nail. "I used to model in some of the studios for a while. Now, I live on selling my paintings."

"That's wonderful! How much can you sell a painting for?"

"Ah, that depends." She licked her lips. "Sometimes as much as ten francs, perhaps even twenty."

"Ten francs?" I quickly calculated how much I could earn from a week's worth of painting. "Well, that's a start, I suppose."

Babette frowned, her eyebrows knitted together.

"Have you shown your work at the annual Salon yet?"

Her face filled with scorn. "The Salon? You must be joking. In Paris, it's not how good you are but who you know. I'll never be chosen by that pompous club of old men."

Her disparaging comments burrowed under my skin, stealing some of the sun's favour. "I'm sorry. I didn't mean to offend. It's just that I've dreamed of exhibiting in the Salon for so long."

Babette shrugged one shoulder and flicked her hand. "Paris is—Paris." Then she leaned forward. "So, now you will tell me your story?"

"My story?"

She nodded. "Yes. Here you are, all alone in the capital without parents or a chaperone." She made a stern face, and we both laughed.

I hesitated to confide in her, yet she looked interested and sympathetic. "I've . . ." My face crumpled. I drew out my handkerchief and blew my nose. "I've run away from home."

A small smile played on her lips. "*Pour quoi?*"

"My parents refused to allow me to study art. Instead, they promised my hand in marriage to a horrid old man. So I've come here. I planned to live with my grandmother. But she's . . . she's gone."

"Gone? Whatever do you mean?"

I looked down. "She's moved away. I don't know where she is. Or why." My voice cracked with worry.

Babette reached over and put her hand on mine. "How terrible for you. What will you do now? Go home?"

"Non!" A couple at the next table looked over so I lowered my voice. "I can't go home a failure. I will stay and become an artist—like you. It's why I'm here."

She put her finger to her chin and regarded me for several moments before speaking. "I might have a solution."

I leaned forward. "Yes?"

"You could stay with me. It's only a small *chambre de grenier,* but if you can pay a share of the rent, it might work out. For both of us."

I sat up straighter. "I would love to. But . . . . "

"Yes?"

"I can't afford much. I was counting on Grand-mère to pay my expenses."

"Oh, I see." She paused. "It's a shame. I think fate meant us to meet."

"Why is that?"

"Why, because I live on rue Gabrielle. "

"Rue Gabrielle? That would be something, to live on a street with my name. At least I wouldn't forget my address." In spite of my feeble joke, my heart felt leaden. My dream was within my grasp, but somehow I had failed to reach high enough.

Babette eyed me, tapping a finger on the gap between her front teeth. "There's still a way to make it work."

"Really? How?"

"Modeling."

I looked down at my hands as heat rose up my neck into my cheeks. I tried to imagine posing for an artist. "Modeling?"

"The artist may even give you free lessons as well as a sitting fee. A good deal, n'est-ce pas? Or are you too proud?"

Too proud? My chin rose at her challenge. "I can do it."

"Bien. I have a friend, Gaston Lachance. He has his own studio and is always hungry for models. And he would be a great teacher."

"Monsieur Gaston Lachance? I copied one of his paintings from an art journal." Philippe had expressed surprise when I'd told him my sketch was only a copy. He'd replied he preferred my other work to the copy. But perhaps only an artist understood copying as a means of study. It had been a challenge, but I'd learned from the exercise.

I squared my shoulders. To have Lachance as a teacher, even if it meant modelling? It would only be until I began to sell enough of my own paintings or until I found Grand-mère.

"So, what do you think? Do you want to live with me?"

"I . . . I'm not sure. How much rent would you want me to pay?"

She shrugged. "How much do you have?"

I pulled out the roll of bills from my handbag and counted them. "I have nearly one hundred forty *francs* left."

Babette licked her lips. "It's very expensive to live in Paris. And it can be dangerous, nothing like the countryside. If you live with me, I will look out for you."

Still I hesitated.

"You really shouldn't carry so much money in your purse. I'll keep it safe for you." She reached out and whisked the entire roll of bills out of my hands and into her handbag. "That should do for a while."

Anxiety welled up within me. That money was all I had, aside from a few coins in the bottom of my handbag. "But, Mademoiselle—"

"We're friends now," she said, smiling widely. "You must call me Babette."

Chapter Ten

AS BABETTE PAID THE WAITER—with my money—I walked the few short blocks back to rue Cortot to retrieve my bags. What could I do? How foolish of me to show her all my money! Yet I had a place to stay. I swallowed hard. What was done, was done.

The surly porter at number 16 looked up and scowled as I entered the vestibule.

"I have a *petit bleu* for you. Bah, you don't even live here, and I have to deliver your mail."

I took the flimsy blue envelope and ripped it open.

> *Dear Mademoiselle Gabrielle,*
> *I would be honoured to escort you and your grandmother to the Expo on Monday.*
> *I shall come to pick you up at 11 a.m. if you are agreeable.*
> *Sincerely yours,*
> *Philippe Lucien*

I held the handwritten note against my heart. Dare I accept? That gave me only Sunday to find Grand-mère.

"Will there be a reply?" the porter asked.

I hesitated, looking at Philippe's note once more. The speed with which he'd corresponded unsettled me slightly. Propriety surely required at least a day's interval between meeting and an invitation. I shook my purse and fished out the remaining coins. "How much is a reply?"

"Fifty *centimes*," he said.

I tore a sheet out of my sketchpad and wrote a brief note: "We accept your kind invitation and shall be expecting you." I handed the coins and note to the porter. "Will you please have this delivered to Monsieur Lucien? And may

I have my bags now?"

He held my bags out, his rheumy eyes fixed on me, expectant. I scraped up the last of my coins. "Merci." I was now truly broke, truly reliant upon my new friend.

On my walk back to the café, I realized I still clutched Philippe's invitation. I folded it and tucked it into my handbag, a token of my first *rendezvous*. I tried to calm my swirling thoughts. Had I made a mistake, accepting? Madame Dijon's voice came unbidden into my thoughts. "Always, always remember: an acquaintance begun on a railway terminates when one of the parties leaves the carriage."

Out the window with Madame Dijon's etiquette standards! I pitched her to the back of my mind. It was getting crowded there with Maman, the baron, and Madame DuPont.

Babette chatted non-stop on our walk from the café to her attic apartment, the damp silk dressing gown and hairclips firmly parcelled under her arm. It was early evening, and the streets were filled with the creak of carriage harnesses and wheels, the shouts of rag pickers and hawkers. Chickens and stray dogs roamed freely, pecking and scrounging for scraps.

"Babette, can you do me a favor?" I asked, dodging two shrieking children who raced past.

"That depends. What is it you want?"

"A gentleman friend has offered to take me to the Exposition Universelle on Monday. If I haven't found my grandmother by then, will you come as my chaperone?"

She wiggled her eyebrows and smirked. "*Ooh la-la*, you work fast." She swivelled her hips back and forth rudely.

My cheeks flamed. "It's not like that."

Still smirking, she said, "If he pays my way, I'll do it."

I bit my lower lip to keep from reminding her that she had plenty of cash. Mine.

Just ahead, three shabbily dressed young men lounged against a crumbling stone wall, smoking. They stared insolently as we approached. The tallest of the three straightened and leered. "Take a look at what's come our way, boys."

I flinched but Babette smiled and swayed her hips, swishing her skirts. Her tight jacket showed off every curve, leaving little to the imagination. The men whistled.

She laughed and blew kisses over her shoulder.

Walking next to her, I felt as awkward as a schoolgirl, even though my hair was styled up, and I wore my best dress.

"This is it." We stopped outside 17 rue Gabrielle, a tall, narrow half-timbered building attached to its neighbours. Babette led me through a dingy entrance and up a dark, narrow stairway. The heat trapped inside the building increased as we climbed. I tried not to notice the peeling, stained wallpaper or the peculiar cooking smells from apartments we passed. I drew out my handkerchief and covered my nose to filter the most objectionable odors.

So much for fate. Rue Gabrielle wasn't living up to its promise.

When we reached the fifth landing, a heavy-set man opened a flimsy battered door. He stared at us, idly scratching a belly inadequately concealed under a filthy undershirt. "Eh, Babette, who's your new friend?"

She gave him a withering stare and didn't answer. He belched loudly and crossed the landing, entering a smaller room.

"We have to share the toilet with that pig, Victor, his wife and eight brats," Babette said over her shoulder as she led me higher. "Make sure you lock the door when you use it."

I shuddered. There were no locks on any of the doors at home, but we respected one another's privacy.

Finally we reached the top floor. Babette unlocked the door and lit an oil lamp on a low table, depositing her parcel there.

She had called her place "small," but it was more than small; it was claustrophobic. Clothes hung from nails on the walls and lay strewn across an old, worn sofa. An unmade narrow bed huddled against the far wall with a rough wooden chair next to it. A grey sheet hung across the only window. At least it faced north, the most advantageous light for artists. Babette crossed the room and pushed the window open, creating a slight breeze.

A wooden stand held a tiny coal stove, washbasin and jug. A tin-framed mirror was nailed to the wall above. Dirty dishes were piled next to the basin. The room smelled of fried onion, smoke and cheap perfume. At least there were signs an artist lived in the attic. An assortment of glass jars squatted beside the basin, filled with brushes and tubes of paint. Several canvases of varying sizes leaned against the wash stand.

I set my bags down near the door, wondering where I would sleep.

"Home sweet home," Babette said. "*La vie bohème.*"

"May I look at your work?"

She shrugged, so I crossed the room and flipped through her canvases slowly. Some were portraits of children, others portrayed street scenes of sidewalk cafés. Some showed haste, the brushstrokes careless and perspective ignored. A few watercolours lay amongst the oil paintings, cheaply framed but too amateurish to be for sale, in any event. However, a few of Babette's oil paintings showed real promise, especially a series of portraits of an older woman in a café. The troubled expression on her face drew me into the paintings, curious about her story. "You're very good. I'm sure these will sell."

"What do you know?" she replied bitterly. "I've been trying for weeks without a single sous to show for it." She slumped onto the lone chair, her head bowed.

Unease curled within me. "But you told me you had sold paintings."

She looked up slowly, like a naughty child caught in a lie. "I meant I hadn't sold any of that series. But earlier, of course, I sold many."

"Oh."

After an awkward silence, she scooped an armload of clothes off the sofa. "You can sleep here for the night. I'll ask the landlord to find us a bed tomorrow."

"Thank you. It's just until I find my grandmother."

"If you find her."

"I will." But my roiling gut told me otherwise.

Babette pulled out the silk dressing gown from her parcel and draped it across her chest. It was cherry red with birds and dragons embroidered in golden thread. "What do you think?"

What did I think? The bright gown was out of place in the slovenly room. "It's lovely."

"A gentleman friend bought it for me. It's from Japan." She stroked the gown lovingly.

I wondered what kind of gentleman bought silk lingerie as a gift.

"Let's go out tonight, shall we?" she asked.

"I . . . I don't know." The past sixteen or so hours had been more than enough. What I really wanted was a steaming, scented bath and one of Cook's delicious hot suppers. I wanted to curl up in my own downy bed and slip into a heavy sleep—the sleep I did not have the night before, restless with excitement about my impending adventure. I looked around the cramped space. The sagging sofa wasn't likely to offer much rest. And what would I do here alone if I stayed? "All right. After all, I've dreamed of being here for so long."

Babette changed into a yellow-and-white striped gown with a scandalously low neckline trimmed in black lace. She placed a small straw boater on her head, a confection of tulle and ribbons, then painted her lips in front of the mirror. "I'm nearly ready. Come on, clean up quickly. Saturday night is waiting for us!" She grinned.

Her smile seemed so genuine that I had to return it, and my spirits lifted. Paris was indeed waiting—waiting to be explored and enjoyed. Wouldn't Bernadette have loved this adventure? Determined to make the most of it, I smoothed out the wrinkles in my dress and brushed my hair until it shone, arranging it up in the style Bernadette had so admired on Nacia. Using the tiny mirror, I swept back stray strands of hair and re-pinned my soft blue hat into place.

Babette waited, perched on the edge of her bed smoking a cigarette. The acrid smoke blended with her perfume.

I prayed I would find my grandmother the very next day.

Chapter Eleven

IT SEEMED THAT EVERYONE in Montmartre was out strolling the boulevards or lingering in the squares dotted around the neighbourhood. Babette linked her arm through mine, leading me on a winding rue Lepic, ever downhill.

The afternoon's oppressive stillness had given way to a light evening breeze. We passed a young girl selling flowers from a barrow on a street corner. The contrast between the bright yellow and red posies she held aloft and her drab grey attire made an intriguing composition. Two young boys intent on floating a paper boat in the gutter water also piqued my interest. I hoped they'd be back, so I could sketch them, too.

As we descended rue Lepic, the streets grew more crowded with a greater variety of carriages than I'd seen back home: broughams the colour of cigars, fiacres for hire, landaus with the tops down so their occupants could see and be seen. A crimson red carriage approached, its hood folded back. Of its three female passengers, one was grossly fat, the other two gaunt. All three wore large, gaudy hats sporting long feathers.

"Who are they?"

"Showgirls," Babette said. "They're the lucky ones—the Moulin Rouge dancers. The one in yellow is Zafira, the belly dancer. That one in the middle is La Goulue. She was a cancan dancer before she got too fat."

The one called La Goulue, the Glutton, wore a garish amount of red, from her black-lace trimmed dress to her unnaturally bright lips and cheeks and the feather springing from her hat. Her expression shouted disdain. Or boredom.

"What's the cancan?"

"You know—*le chahut!*"

I shook my head.

Babette's eyes sparkled. "It's very naughty. The girls link arms and dance in a line to wild music—like nothing you've heard before. They throw their legs so high it looks like they'll kick the ceiling. Men love it." She lifted her skirts and kicked one leg high to demonstrate, revealing her petticoats and stockings. She lost her balance and nearly fell backward. "Whoops!"

I grabbed hold of her arm to catch her, and she almost dragged me down with her. My cheeks flamed as I looked around. No one paid us any attention. Such a show of undergarments on a public street would have elicited sharp comments in Laval. Thank goodness I wasn't home any more.

"Sarah Bernhardt has a sculpture studio on the butte," Babette said. "She's opening her own theatre this year at Place du Châtelet. People say she knows all the best artists and actors and hosts grand parties."

"Maybe one day we'll be invited."

She snorted. "Not likely." She pointed out studios of other artists as we continued to walk. "Monsieur Vincent van Gogh lived on rue Lepic for several years, you know. And Monsieur Degas has a studio nearby."

Madame Magne had taught us about both those artists. The Impressionists, they were called. My pulse quickened. "Have you ever seen Monsieur Degas?"

"Mais oui. All the time."

Her offhand tone made me wonder if it were true.

"All the modern artists have studios here. It's cheaper than the other arrondissements. Some are poorer than church mice and have no future. Like that naïf, Henri Rousseau."

"I haven't heard of him."

She laughed, a harsh sound. "He's much loved by the Salon des Independents right now. I think his paintings are childish and garish. Too much use of primary colours, not realistic at all." She turned and looked at me. "Ah, but I forgot. He's from Laval. I'm surprised you don't know of him."

"I'll have to look for his work. If he's truly from Laval, he might have painted the same landscapes as me." I smiled. Move over, Henri Rousseau, and make room for Gabrielle de Villiers. "Perhaps there will soon be two famous Lavallois painters."

"That's the spirit." Babette laughed again and squeezed my arm.

We continued to stroll, sharing the warm summer night with families, old and young couples, and groups of men or women not much older than myself. I breathed in the atmosphere of Montmartre too deeply and coughed. La vie bohème didn't smell very good, but all in all, it was thrilling to live in the midst of it. Oh, if only this really could work out.

When rue Lepic intersected with a broad boulevard, Babette steered us east. I tried to take note of landmarks along the way, so I wouldn't get lost when I was on my own, but the buildings and churches all looked the same. "Are we going in circles?"

"No," Babette said, but she avoided my gaze. "Don't worry, you'll find your way eventually."

After that, I paid closer attention to my surroundings. I caught sight of a sign—Boulevard de Clichy—and relaxed slightly. Eventually we began to climb a steep hill via what seemed to be a never-ending series of stairs, elbowed and bumped by a steady stream of people. Babette scanned the faces of men we passed.

"Are you looking for someone?" I asked.

"No," she snapped. She stopped, hands on her hips, breathing hard. "Over three hundred."

"Three hundred what?"

"Stairs. I thought I'd save you from counting them." She laughed. "But don't worry. Soon, we can take the *funicular*." She pointed to a long ramp next to us.

A dozen or more sweaty men toiled over machinery near the base. I'd never seen such a contraption. Steam and black soot puffed into the air with a raucous noise.

"How does it work?" I shouted over the machine.

She shrugged. "All I know is it will save me from walking these goddamned steps every day, once it's open."

I flinched at her swearing.

"I just hope it's cheap enough for the likes of us," she continued.

Cheap enough for us? She could afford the funicular for the rest of her life with the francs lining her purse. My francs! I gritted my teeth and continued to follow her. The money issue could be tackled when we got back to her attic.

As we joined the stream of Saturday evening strollers at the top of the hill, I took a steadying breath. I was in Paris. Soon I'd find Grand-mère and leave Babette behind, with or without my francs. In the meantime, I owed it to myself to enjoy my first day of emancipation. "Let's stop here, shall we?" I asked, looking around. We'd made nearly a full circle and were close, I was sure, to where we'd started at rue Gabrielle.

Babette raised an eyebrow. "Tired already?"

"I'm fine," I lied. I was, in truth, exhausted from the long day and previous sleepless night but wasn't going to admit it to her. "It's simply my first day in Paris. I want to soak it all in."

"Even the pigeons?" She laughed and pointed to a boy feeding pigeons nearby. One sat in his cupped hand, while the others fought over morsels of bread at the boy's feet.

"Especially the pigeons." Another potential picture. The city teemed with characters waiting to be sketched.

The setting sun caught my eye. Pink light bathed the tips of three shining white domes above a stone archway, marking the front of an immense white church covered in scaffolding. Wide stone stairs led up to the entrance.

Babette spat again. "That's the Basilique du Sacré Cœur. They've been building it for years and still aren't finished."

"It's impressive." The church probably housed beautiful art waiting to be explored another day, but just then, another view caught my breath. All of Paris spread out below us.

As dusk settled, thousands of twinkling gas lights surrounded the Seine. Stone houses stretched out to an indistinct horizon under their glow, making the city appear unbounded. Monuments I'd learned about in school rose from the chaos of stone—Emperor Napoleon's Arc de Triomphe, the distinct double spires of Notre Dame Cathedral, the Opera Garnier, the solid mass of the Louvre Museum.

But farther east, a different picture emerged. Decrepit wooden sheds and houses hunched near ugly factories. A yellow haze hung in the air. My first instinct was to look away to avoid spoiling the fairy-tale effect of the rest of the city. Instead, I scrutinized the soot-covered rooftops as only an artist could. I smiled, recalling the reaction of my classmates to my painting of the dead finch. They'd rejected its beauty, but I hadn't. My fingers itched to start sketching, to attempt to capture Paris in all its guises.

"Bonsoir, *Mesdemoiselles.*"

I turned toward the voice. A priest in a long black cassock descended the church stairs. Behind him, the triple domes of Sacré Coeur shone white against the darkening sky.

"Bonsoir, Monsieur l'Abbé," I answered with a smile. "What a beautiful church you—"

"Let's get out of here." Babette grabbed my arm and pulled me away from the priest.

"What's wrong?"

Her eyes darted around. "Don't be fooled by the priests. I can't stand their holier-than-thou attitude." She spat on the sidewalk.

Horrified, I yanked free of her grasp but continued to walk beside her. What else could I do? The city lights below us sparkled with promise, but just out of reach. How torn I was! I physically ached to be a modern, independent woman, an artist like Babette—but not with her sensibilities. I had one foot in her lifestyle, la vie bohème, while another sought familiar comforts and the hope of rescue by Grand-mère.

We walked on in silence for a few blocks until an illuminated tower came into view. Lights flashed from red to blue to white like a patriotic chameleon. "What's that?"

"That, ma chérie, is the Eiffel Tower and the Exposition Universelle. Quite the sight, non? We'll be there Monday, if your gentleman friend comes through." Babette squeezed my arm. "Aren't you happy you left your little country life for this?"

"Oui." I shoved the niggling worry about my grandmother away and focused on my newfound freedom. For that, I truly was happy. I could talk to whomever I chose, explore the city's art museums and galleries. Even stay out all night if I wanted to! I stifled a yawn. Maybe tomorrow night.

"Babette!" Two men in top hats crossed the street toward us, the taller of the two waving. By the familiar way he kissed Babette on both cheeks, he seemed to know her well. I averted my eyes when he hugged her, but not before his hand slid down and quickly squeezed her buttocks. Both men looked almost as old as Papa and at least as wealthy, judging by their tailored suits, silk cravats, starched white shirts, and gold-tipped canes.

What connection could they have with her?

"Henri, Edgar, this is my new roommate, Gabrielle," Babette said. "Today's her first day in Paris."

"Welcome to the city that never sleeps," Henri said with a slight bow, stroking his pointed goatee. "Edgar and I were headed for the Moulin Rouge. Won't you ladies join us?"

Babette linked her arm through Henri's. "I love to dance. But let's go to the Moulin de la Galette. So much more casual, don't you think?"

Henri patted her hand. "Whatever my lady wishes. And Mademoiselle Gabrielle? You will join us, won't you?"

Edgar's green eyes narrowed as all three waited for my answer.

I stifled another yawn. "I've been up since before dawn . . . ."

Something hard flared in Babette's eyes, but she smiled sweetly. "Only children go to bed this early. Children or lovers." She winked at Henri, who grinned.

I straightened my shoulders, not about to be cast as a country naïf, and forced a smile. "Where is this Moulin de la Galette?"

"Not far, just to the top of the butte." He gestured uphill. "Come on, ladies." Henri held out his arm to Babette, leaving me with the silent Edgar.

Babette's head bobbed, and she gestured animatedly while walking arm in arm with Henri. After a block passed in silence between Edgar and me, I asked, "Have you been to the Moulin de la Galette before?"

He nodded. He was supposed to throw the conversational ball back to me. Evidently he missed my etiquette teacher's lessons.

"Are you a native Parisian?"

"Oui."

"How nice."

He snorted but whether it was in disagreement or disgust at my inane comment, I really didn't care any more. I gave up. Hopefully the dance hall would offer livelier entertainment.

We eventually stopped at the base of one of the two windmills I spotted when first arriving in Montmartre. The Moulin de la Galette, an enclosed pavilion, was in better condition than its namesake windmill, its sails broken and idle. A sign, "Bal Dubray," was lit by white globes above a pink and green entrance.

Inside, the *salle de danse* was bursting with patrons. Cigar and cigarette smoke wafted up to the high ceiling. An orchestra played from a balcony festooned with banners and flowers. Palm trees filled each corner of the hall. Around the walls, couples or groups leaned against pillars or shouted at one another across tables laden with glasses and wine bottles.

Henri paid our admission, twenty-five centimes for Babette and me, twice as much for the men, and led us to an empty table. "I'll wager you've not seen anything like this where you come from," he shouted to me over the tinny music and loud conversations swirling around us.

I nodded, mute, for there was nothing like it in Laval. Here was a wild, chaotic garden of dancing flowers. Women wore dresses and hats of all colours: brilliant crimson, forest green, and sunny yellows. Even the men in their dark suits wore stylish bowler, boater, and top hats with colourful bands. I stored the images away for later use in a sketch. My fatigue lifted and my pulse raced.

If only Philippe were across the table from me instead of dour Edgar.

A waiter brought a bottle of red wine and four glasses. Henri paid him, waving away my thanks. "Santé." He filled the glasses, raised his and drained it at once. His cheeks flushed from the wine or the stifling heat of the hall, or both. "A dance, Babette?"

She rose eagerly, and they joined the spinning dancers, leaving Edgar and me alone at the table. He watched the dancers with intense concentration, so I did the same.

A sure-footed, middle-aged man in a top hat and dark suit swung past, skillfully guiding his partner between other couples. Something in his posture or the set of his jaw momentarily reminded me of Papa. "Don't do anything foolish," he'd said. Surely he wouldn't have taken the same train I did to be here, tonight, in Paris. I would have seen him at the station. Or would I? I had been distracted, keen to get away from Philippe.

Nonetheless, I scanned the crowd for familiar faces. Dim lighting and darkened corners thwarted me. I gave up and shook off my suspicions. Paris had over two million souls living here. Naturally someone would remind me of home.

I swallowed my wine. It burned the back of my throat, but I managed not to cough or choke. It wasn't as fine as the wines we had at home, and normally I drank mine watered down. But things were different now. No more being treated like a child. Small, ladylike sips were the wisest choice.

The orchestra ended their song. In the pause before the next piece, Edgar edged his chair closer to mine. His green eyes flickered in the gas lighting. "How do you know Babette, Mademoiselle?" he asked stiffly.

"I've only just met her today. I am staying with her, for now."

He raised his eyebrows. "You are on your own in the city?" He fixed his gaze on me, much like our cats stared at a mouse before pouncing.

Unnerved, I stared out at the dance floor without responding. Still his eyes bore into me.

He cleared his throat. "Would you care to dance?"

"Non, merci. I will spare you, for I have stepped on more than my share of partners' feet."

Clearly offended, he poured himself another glass of wine with stiff, jerky movements. Guilt niggled at me, but I was too tired to go through the motions of social niceties, especially when he so clearly lacked the ability to respond in kind.

We lapsed into silence again, sipping wine. The dancers began la Farandole, a familiar folk dance. They formed an open chain by holding hands and skipped to each beat of the music, knees high. I pushed away a wave of homesickness and blamed it on the lack of sleep. I wanted nothing more than to lay my head down. The stuffy air in the crowded room and the tight bones of my corset wouldn't allow me to breathe deeply, increasing drowsiness. My eyelids drooped and my shoulders sagged. More than once, I began to nod off.

Babette and Henri waltzed past. I stood and waved, hoping to catch Babette's attention. I wanted to leave.

Edgar grasped my arm. "Is something wrong, Mademoiselle Gabrielle?"

"No." I pulled away and darted onto the dance floor, dodging couples who twirled in the dust. I caught a glimpse of Babette's yellow dress at the far end of the hall. Someone knocked into me and I lost my footing, stumbling.

I fell hard on my bottom with a sharp stab to my tail bone. I stayed there, my legs splayed out in front of me like a child, ankles exposed beneath my skirts. The clamour of the orchestra pulsed in my head and raucous laughter crashed around me. Inhaling deeply triggered a sneezing fit from the dusty floorboards. I peered up into the faces of dancers side-stepping around me.

Embarrassed, I painfully dragged myself to my feet and searched in vain for Babette and Henri amongst the weaving couples. Edgar was slumped over our table, pouring another glass of wine. At least he hadn't witnessed my disgrace. I didn't want him insisting that he accompany me back to the apartment. It took some time to push through the dancers and customers queued outside before I emerged on the street, gasping for air.

I leaned against a low stone wall until my breathing slowed to normal. Perhaps Babette had already left with Henri, forgetting about me. When the fresh air cleared my head enough to notice a few guiding landmarks, I headed back toward rue Gabrielle. After wandering down a few streets that circled back upon themselves, the right building appeared. I stared up at the steep flight of stairs. Would I have to sleep on the landing outside the door until Babette returned? With my utter lack of money and no friends to call upon, I had no alternative.

I climbed the six flights breathing through my mouth to avoid the stench. After using the toilet on the lower landing as quickly as I could without touching anything I didn't have to. I tried Babette's door. It was unlocked. Grateful for that one small blessing, I stumbled through the dark to the sofa, undressed and lay down in my chemise, praying for sleep.

Despite complete and utter exhaustion, images of the day's events swirled before me like water colour paint dissolving in a jar of water. Madame DuPont's shocked look of recognition at the Laval station. Pastures and villages passing by the train window. Meeting Philippe. Sketching him, those remarkable blue eyes. The unexplained jagged scar along his jaw. The rain-streaked windows of the carriage fogging up as we shared a ride, unaccompanied. Paris! The Louvre, Notre Dame, the view from Sacré Coeur . . . .

I took a leap of faith toward my dream and left the baron far behind. What a triumph! But where was my grandmother? And what should I make of Babette? Tomorrow, I would demand my money back. And on Monday, I had the Exposition to look forward to with Philippe. Philippe, with his crooked smile and that *je ne sais quoi* . . . .

As sleep finally descended, a small, niggling question returned, one that I had asked myself when he'd offered me the use of his carriage: had he followed me from the train station?

Chapter Twelve

CHURCH BELLS RANG DISTANTLY, dragging me out of a fitful sleep. Light snoring drifted across the room, and the scent of cheap perfume rose from the same direction like an ill miasma rising from stagnant water.

I sat up. Where was I? Clothes hung on nails, not hidden in beautiful armoires. A tiny coal stove squatted on a table, surrounded by a pile of dirty dishes. No maid in sight.

Oh, yes, I was in Paris. In Babette's chambre de grenier.

Nightmares weighed down my head. Vague fragments remained: Mémère sitting stiffly on a chair as I painted her portrait. A dove exploding through an open window . . . a flurry of feathers . . . . a paintbrush skidding across paint and canvas. Claws and beak scratching Mémère's face, tearing out hair. Someone screaming.

Was it me?

I stood quickly, as if I could discard the *cauchemar* and leave it twisted in the blankets. It was a new day. Time to take charge. Without Claudine to help me dress, I left my corset where it lay on the floor and slipped my traveling dress over my chemise. The buttons on my bodice were tight but manageable. I breathed deeply, arched my back, twisted side to side. Much better. And I managed it myself.

"Babette," I called softly as I approached her. "Wake up."

"Hnnh?"

"It's morning. We need to talk."

More muffled noises. I wrenched off her covers. She lay curled in a tight ball with her eyes screwed shut, her chemise ruched around her hips. "Leave me alone," she muttered.

"It's not my fault you didn't get back until a few hours ago."

She glared at me through narrow slits. "Go away." Her breath was sour with alcohol.

"I want my money back." I crossed my arms and stood over her.

She pulled the duvet and blankets back over her head.

"Babette! I'm broke. You took every sous I had. I need money to find my grandmother. Now."

"All right, all right, if you'll leave me be," she grumbled. She reached under her pillow and slipped out a few notes. "Here. The rest is for the landlord." Her head disappeared once again.

I counted the money and made a face—only five francs. "The rest can't be for rent!" I shook her again with no results. With a sigh, I slipped the money into my purse along with a stale heel of bread and a lump of hard cheese I found near the stove. On my way out, I scooped up my sketchpad and pencil.

As I walked down the stairs, I mused about where to start searching for Grand-mère. She'd last lived in Montmartre. That should narrow it down considerably. People probably contacted the local gendarmerie when a family member went missing, but Grand-mère had been arrested and jailed back home. Would the Paris police know that? I hesitated to involve them unless all other avenues failed.

A family of six passed me on the sidewalk. The mother held a babe in her arms, with two small girls in frilly dresses clinging to her skirts. A boy in a dark tunic with freshly slicked back hair clutched his papa with one hand and sucked the thumb of his other. He popped out his thumb to wave at me, and I waved back.

The entire family looked as if they were dressed in their Sunday best. I hadn't planned on attending Mass, but began to follow them. My own family was probably waiting for the baron's arrival, so they could take him to the Basilica for Mass. Or had Maman managed to cancel in time? My stomach twisted as I imagined her humiliation at confessing to the baron that her ungrateful daughter had run away. No, she would have surely avoided that. I refused to consider the alternative.

The gleaming white domes of Sacré Coeur towered over the neighbourhood from blocks away. Instead of climbing the stairs to the basilica, however, the family turned down a narrow winding street that led to a much more modest old church tucked under the basilica's wing. The sign above the door read "Église Saint-Pierre de Montmartre." I followed them inside, and my eyes slowly adjusted to the darkness of the vestibule. Why was I there? Attendance was no longer forced upon me. Yet surprisingly, the sound of an organ playing familiar hymns, the musky aroma of incense and oiled wood, and the hushed voices and rustlings in the pews brought on a sharp nostalgia.

I dipped my hand in the font, crossed myself with holy water, and entered the sanctuary. Mass had already started. A robed, white-haired priest with a bent back presided at the altar. The back pews were filled with elderly parishioners and young families like the one I'd followed. I found an empty seat in a middle pew. Shafts of cadmium green, rose madder, and yellow ochre poured through the stained-glass windows and fell across my folded hands.

During the homily, I closed my eyes and imagined Grand-mère seated beside me. This unpretentious house of worship would have suited her. No doubt she had come here for Mass instead of the new basilica. My eyes flew open. Mémère? I looked around me in the semi-gloom, hoping for a glimpse of her profile, her bright eyes. No one nearby resembled her, but I could hardly search every face without causing a commotion.

Immediately following the final benediction, I slipped down the aisle and waited in the vestibule. There was no shortage of elderly women amongst the worshippers, and I scanned each one as they filed out, but none of them were my grandmother. I waited while parishioners stopped to speak with the priest until finally, I was alone with him.

"Monsieur l'Abbé?" I introduced myself. "May I have a few minutes of your time?"

A smile softened the deep lines in his face, and he nodded. Despite his age, he had a full head of shaggy white hair, and his eyes were bright with intelligence.

"I'm looking for my grandmother, Lucille Cribiere. She lived in this parish until recently. Do you know her?"

The priest's brow furrowed. "I'm not sure, mademoiselle. We have several Lucille's, but Cribiere? That name isn't familiar."

"Here's her photograph. The woman on the left."

"Ah," he said, squinting at the picture I held out for him. "Yes, of course. I never knew her last name; she simply went by Madame Lucille. 'Nothing fancy about me,' she'd say." He chuckled. "She visited the rectory every week and brought me such treats—éclairs, beignets, brioches. And then one week she didn't come. I don't think I've seen her since."

"Was it around Christmas?"

He wagged his shaggy head. "It could have been. I assumed she'd gone to visit family." He sighed. "I miss her company. She was always quick to laugh. And the pastries were delightful, too." He grinned impishly. He probably shared her sense of humour.

"And?"

"I started to worry when she didn't appear again. She hadn't said she was intending to move away."

"Didn't you make any inquires?"

"Oh, yes. Madame Lucille was well-liked. She worked with our St. Vincent de Paul Society, delivering clothing and food to the poor of the parish. I asked the other ladies in the Society, but no one knew anything about her leaving. It was as if—poof!" he snapped his fingers, "She disappeared. She's in the Lord's hands now, my child."

His passivity irked me. "I certainly hope not, Abbé," I said, struggling to be respectful. "I expect to find her soon, very much alive."

He merely patted my shoulder and left through a side door.

I stepped out of the dark vestibule into the late morning sunshine, feeling worse than ever. I shook my fist at the heavens. *Why won't you help me, Lord? You know where she is. I need her.*

Abruptly, I stopped. Was I so shallow? Was I only searching for my sake, so I'd have a comfortable place to live? My cheeks flushed with shame, and I made a vow, then and there. Somehow I'd find a way to support myself. I'd model for Gaston Lachance and work hard at my lessons until I could proclaim myself an artist. And I would search out my grandmother to ensure she was safe. Wherever she was.

Chapter Thirteen

GRAND-MÈRE'S APARTMENT building wasn't far from the church, so I returned to rue Cortot. A scowling, elderly woman took the place of the old porter.

With my best smile-for-strangers, I said, "I'm looking for my grandmother. She used to live here. Madame Lucille Cribiere. Did you know her?"

She made a chopping gesture with her hands. "How many people do I have to tell? She doesn't live here, and I don't know her! Now stop wasting my time."

"Pardon? Someone else asked about her?"

She merely scowled and turned her back.

Unease curdled my belly. "Madame? What do you mean? Who else was asking about her?"

She shrugged. "I told him the same as I'm telling you. I started working here last month."

As she turned her back to me, a middle-aged couple descended the staircase and headed to the door.

I quickly followed them outside. "Excusez-moi. Can I ask you something?"

"Oui?" The woman smiled, but her husband harrumphed and pulled out his pocket watch.

"I'm looking for my grandmother, Lucille Cribiere. She used to live here. Did you know her?" I held out her photograph. "The woman on the left."

"*Bien sûr!*" the woman exclaimed, the feathers on her hat bobbing as she nodded. She put her hand on her husband's arm. "You remember her, Georges. She lived on the floor above us. She was very friendly."

Relief flooded me. "Do you know where she is now?"

She shook her head. "I don't know, but she mentioned a daughter in Laval."

"That's my mother. We haven't seen Grand-mère for four years."

She sucked in a sharp breath. "Four years! Mon Dieu, what a shame. She spoke of her family with such love."

I bit my lip. It wasn't the time or place to explain the estrangement between Maman and Grand-mère. "Can you remember anything else? It's very important."

"I'm sorry. I hope you find her soon. She seemed a bit . . . odd, the last few times we spoke."

Foreboding crept up my spine. "Odd? In what way?"

She lowered her voice. "Lucille was terrified of the gendarmes. More than once, she asked me if any police had been prowling around, inquiring about her. Naturally, I said no, and she seemed greatly reassured. Why in heaven's name should she be worried about gendarmes?"

"Perhaps she was losing her mind." Georges tapped the side of his head. "It happened to your mother, didn't it, Eugénie?"

His wife nodded slowly.

I shook my head. "Not my grandmother."

"Excuse us, mademoiselle. We must go." Georges tugged on his wife's arm.

Eugénie stood firm, her gaze on me. "Wait. I remember when we last saw Lucille. It was nearly Christmas and we were leaving for our daughter Maryse's home. We passed Lucille in the lobby. I asked her if she was spending the holiday with family. She said no, but she had friends in Le Havre she was going to visit."

"Le Havre? Are you certain?"

Her brow wrinkled. "I think it was Le Havre, or was it Le Mans? Oh dear, now I'm not sure. Do you remember, Georges?"

Georges shrugged. "*Viens,* Eugénie." He once again tugged on his wife's arm.

"*Bonne chance!*" Eugénie hurried down the sidewalk with her husband.

A knot formed in my gut. The woman was mistaken. Grand-mère couldn't have gone to Le Havre. It was a seaport; its steamships departed for all corners of the world. But surely she would never leave France. Where would she go?

Canada. My uncle Luc and his wife and children were there. Charles would soon be too, although Grand-mère wouldn't know that. Who would tell her, when we'd all been cut off from her?

The knot in my stomach tightened. Perhaps she had sailed to Canada. But Eugénie said maybe Le Havre or maybe Le Mans.

Le Mans. Philippe's visiting card had two addresses, and one of them was in Le Mans. What an odd coincidence that would be . . . .

Perhaps Grand-mère returned to Paris after Christmas and moved into another apartment. She could be living down the block from me. Or perhaps something terrible happened to prevent her return. Surely the authorities would have contacted Maman if that were the case.

I needed to find someone who was close to her, someone who would know for certain where she went. I squared my shoulders and returned inside to wait for any other residents I could query. The *portière* glared, but I ignored her and sat on the sofa by the window, the same one I'd collapsed on when I'd first learned Grand-mère had moved. Only yesterday, I realized with a start. So much had happened since then. I yawned and settled into the soft cushions. Warm sunlight streamed through the window and spilled over my shoulders like a blanket.

"Eh, mademoiselle!"

I blinked sleep from my eyes. The portière's narrow, pinched face hovered near mine. I bolted upright, my cheeks flushing.

"You must go." She waved her hands as if she were shooing away a stray cat. "This is a respectable establishment, not some *bordel*. I'll call the gendarmes if you come back."

Too embarrassed to protest, I scrambled up from the sofa and left the building. Long shadows indicated it was late afternoon. The only remaining clue about my grandmother was her friend in the photograph: Séverine. I stopped on the sidewalk and took the photo from my handbag, examining it carefully. Arms linked, Grand-mère and Séverine stood in front of a building with large script painted across the glass windows. The name of the shop. La Fronde.

Where had I seen that name before—an art gallery? An art journal? Perhaps it was on one of the newspapers at the rail station kiosk. The name was certainly unusual. History classes taught me that "la fronde" referred to the civil war in the 1600s, but why would a shop be named after a war?

Finally, unable to puzzle it out on my own, I stopped at Place du Tertre. The waiter who served me yesterday was clearing a table at La Bohème.

"Excuse me, monsieur, may I ask you something?"

He frowned, but nodded.

I showed him the photograph, pointing at the lettering in the window. "Do you know where this shop is?"

He grunted as he swiped a damp cloth over the rough wooden tabletop, scattering crumbs onto the pavement. "*La Fronde*," he said with contempt. "That ridiculous rag that pretends to be news."

"So it is a newspaper?"

He glowered at me. "Don't get taken in by those women and their dangerous ideas," he said. "It causes nothing but trouble in the home." He tucked the cloth into his apron and returned inside the café.

I breathed a sigh of relief. Why was he was so angry? At least I had another piece to the puzzle. It didn't take long to find a news vendor's stall squatted on the square below Sacré Coeur. The day's papers lay folded in neat rows as if tucked into bed.

"Excusez-moi, madame, I'm looking for *La Fronde*. Do you carry it?"

The woman quickly glanced around. Then she lifted the stack of *La Croix* and whisked out a copy of *La Fronde*. "Five centimes." She grinned, her two front teeth missing, and put one finger over her lips. "Don't tell my husband."

I nodded and gave her one of my precious francs. She dropped the change into my hand and passed me the paper. I scanned the front page, looking for a clue, any clue. Somehow, there had to be a link between Grand-mère, her friend Séverine, and the newspaper.

The front page of *La Fronde* proclaimed it was written, printed and managed entirely by women, for women. That fit with what I knew of Grand-mère; she certainly would have approved of such an enterprise.

A rich aroma wafted on the air from a nearby coffee cart so I permitted myself the indulgence of a *café au lait*. Coffee in hand, I returned to the fabulous view of the city from the Basilica's steps. The sweet café au lait fragrance helped me stop worrying about the ten *centimes* it cost. At home, everything was provided for me and money didn't matter. Suddenly, it mattered a great deal.

I read *La Fronde* while savoring my coffee. The name of the paper was bold, even confrontational. Feminism could be seen as a type of civil war, pitting men against women, citizens against one another.

The name of my grandmother's friend—Séverine—appeared in a list of contributors. So she was a journalist. Her article demanded the French government change the laws so married women would be free to control their own finances.

Less controversial topics, such as fashion and the stock markets, were also covered in the paper. A headline about the Exposition caught my eye. A major art exhibit was on display in the Grand Palais, built especially for the Expo. *Parfait*. My first date with Philippe tomorrow would go hand-in-hand with my first Paris art exhibition.

When I finally closed the paper, the sun was sinking toward the horizon. Shadows lengthened, casting interesting shapes on the square below. A pleasant breeze cooled the air, and Sunday evening strollers had emerged onto the streets around the church. I opened my sketchpad and concentrated on the faces of people around me.

I sketched a middle-aged man on a nearby bench, smoking a cigarette and pretending to read *Le Figaro* while ogling young women passing by. A group of four elderly men at a table, playing dominoes and drinking cold beer. I made a separate sketch of one of them—a man with a toothless smile and a lifetime of wrinkles scoring his face.

A couple sat on the steps just below me, their hands linked. The woman leaned her head on the man's shoulder. He kissed the top of her head, and she smiled up at him with a look of complete trust. I stopped drawing to watch them, mesmerized by their absorption in one another. What would that feel like? But no man would support a wife who desired a career. I tried to capture their intimacy on the page—the curve of the woman's neck, the man's cheek pressed against her hair. I couldn't get it right. After several attempts, I tore up my pages in frustration.

An outrageously large straw and tulle hat drew my attention away from the lovers. I moved down a few steps to study the woman under the hat more clearly. Seated on a bench at the base of the stairs, she looked up at an elderly male companion whose back was to me. Her gloved hands gestured wildly when she spoke. She wore expensive-looking fashionable clothing, yet her companion was shabbily dressed, creating a curious but intriguing composition.

She had a striking but not beautiful face with eyes too wide apart, a generous mouth with full lips too large. Yet when she threw back her head and laughed, she shone with an honest beauty. I sketched an outline of the ridiculously large hat and her animated face, exaggerating her features slightly.

Working quickly to escape the couple's notice, I outlined her shoulders and waving hands, her companion's gnarled hands clenched behind his back, his baggy trousers and scuffed boots. It was more caricature than portrait. Just as I was about to add finishing touches to the boots, the woman turned her gaze away from her companion and toward me.

My face blushed hot and I looked away. Philippe would think me a hypocrite. I'd happily invaded the couple's privacy for my own artistic needs—just as I had accused him of doing with his camera.

The woman stood quickly and strode over to me.

I braced myself for a scolding.

"Are you sketching me?" she asked in an imperious voice. Clearly, she was someone used to giving orders and being obeyed.

"Oui, madame. I am sor—"

"Let me see," she demanded, holding her hand out.

I passed my sketchbook to her. "It's not finished . . . ."

"I can see that." She frowned but studied the drawing intently. Then she flipped through the other pages of my sketchbook without so much as a "by your leave," nodding at times, pursing her lips at other times. Finally, she handed it back. "Forgive my manners. I'm Madeleine Chaudière."

"Gabrielle de Villiers." I was annoyed by her presumptuous manner yet oddly desperate to hear her opinion of my work at the same time.

"You show talent," she said in a clipped voice. "I've had my portrait done many times but yours . . . ."

I bit my lip to prevent myself from apologizing again.

"I like the caricature. Shows personality." She gazed at me for a few moments. "As for the rest of your sketches, you have talent. I know good art. Been collecting it for years."

"Thank you, Madame." My shoulders sagged with relief. She wasn't offended.

"Do you paint?"

"Yes, Madame. Mostly pastels for portraits and *aquarelle* for landscapes."

"I prefer oil paintings, myself, but I've seen some pastel paintings lately that are equally wonderful." She cocked her head, a smile playing on her lips. "Why don't you come to one of my salons? This Friday evening, after eight. You would be a delightful addition. Bring a companion with you. Someone interesting." She winked as she handed me a card.

"Of course, Madame." A salon! Madame Magne had told us about the sophisticated set that held such parties. Wine and food, entertainment by poets or musicians, all in support of the arts. Some artists claimed they were launched by the "right" salon. "Merci."

"And bring along some of your work." She waved at her companion. "Guillaume!"

I gaped as her companion joined her, and they disappeared within the basilica. She wanted to see my work! Hands trembling with excitement, I checked her card. She lived on Boulevard Saint-germain, where Philippe had said le gratin of Paris society lived. But this Friday? Only five days. I couldn't possibly have something ready . . . could I?

"God bless you, Madame Chaudière!" I laughed aloud and spun in a circle. The lovers on the steps above stared. I didn't care.

The day's sketches might yield paintings Madame would enjoy. The old men playing dominoes? Or the study of the oldest player, cigarette ashes dropping onto his wool jacket, his eyes narrowed in concentration? Not oils, though, they wouldn't dry in time for Friday. Watercolour, then, or pastels. What would she think of a portrait of herself and her companion? Perhaps not at first. Something safer. I hurried back to Babette's.

Chapter Fourteen

I EXCITEDLY SLAMMED the attic door behind me. I'd need oil paints and canvases and stretchers, although not immediately. Pastels would best for portraits, so I needed more paper, frames, and—oh! I could hardly wait to get started.

"Slamming the door wasn't necessary, chérie." Babette, seated on her bed, bent over to slip on her stockings and attach them to her garters. Her dress looked suspiciously new.

"Are you on your way out?"

She straightened and checked her image in the mirror, tucking loose strands of hair into her combs. "Yes, with Henri and Edgar. You could join us."

"I can't. I have to start painting right away. I'll need more of my money to buy supplies."

She continued to gaze at the mirror, applying red paste to her lips. "I gave the rest to the landlord. I told you I would."

"Surely not all of it?" My voice rose in disbelief.

"All of it." She faced me then, hands on her hips.

"But . . . that's nearly a hundred and thirty francs! This place can't cost that much per month." I flung my arms out, surveying the cramped space. "What's the rent here? Ten or twenty francs at most, I'd venture."

"I was behind a few months," she snapped.

I stared at her, incredulous. How could she have spent all my money? My face flushed. "That dress you're wearing; it's new, isn't it? You bought it with my money."

She shrugged. "What if I did?"

"That money was all I had!" My hands curled into fists as the implications of my situation sunk in. "You have to give it back!"

She smirked. "And how will you prove that you gave me anything at all?"

I imagined horns growing from Babette's head. She was right, of course. I'd been such a fool. With no receipt, she could throw me out! Where would I go? Home? Impossible.

I had to create and sell my work—right away. I checked my art box. Only one sheet of decent paper for a pastel, the rest dog-eared or torn. How could I make any money if I didn't have supplies? I slumped onto the sofa and blinked back hot tears, my spirits sagging lower than the make-shift bed's aging springs.

Babette sat down beside me. "Look, I'm sorry but it's done. The money's gone." She lit a cigarette, blowing the smoke through pursed lips. "Don't forget you can model for Lachance. He pays a sitting fee, on top of free lessons."

I straightened my back. I could use the sitting fees to buy proper paper and frames. But would it be soon enough? "When can I start with him?"

"He has to meet you first and decide if he'll take you on." Babette rose and checked herself in the mirror once more. "Besides, I haven't seen him for a while. He often leaves the city to escape the summer heat."

Suspicion sharpened my tongue. "Do you really know him?"

"Are you calling me a liar?" She spun back, her eyes flashing.

I swallowed hard and bit back a reply, hating how dependant I was on her.

Her eyes flickered. "Look, Gabbi, let's not fight. It's so boring!" She thrust out her lower lip. "All the art students go to the Lapin Agile. Come out and have some fun."

Staying in the stuffy little attic wasn't appealing, yet I hardly wanted to be with her. A sharp sofa wire poked into my buttock. "No."

What ill luck to have bumped into her on my first day in the city.

Babette slipped on her shoes. "The Lapin Agile is where I first met Gaston. Perhaps he'll be there tonight."

I shook my head and crossed my arms, even though the chance to meet Lachance and other artists was tempting.

"Don't be such a wet rag." She threw her hands in the air with a sound of disgust. "You're in Paris, for heaven's sake! Are you going to hide out here all night?"

My arms fell. She was right. It wouldn't be fun stuck in the attic, and I wasn't yet ready to strike out on my own. Not in the evening. At least with Henri and Edgar, I had male chaperones, of a sort. More importantly, if there were truly a chance she could introduce me to Lachance, I had to take it. Then I could start painting sooner. And the sooner I had money, the sooner I'd be free of Babette. Perhaps Madame Chaudière would purchase a painting from me on Friday—provided I could have one ready by then.

I pushed all my misgivings aside. "Bien. Give me a few minutes to get freshened up."

"You'll have fun. You'll see." She winked. "Henri and Edgar pay for everything."

And what did those men expect in exchange for footing our bill? Was the pleasure of our company enough? Or did they expect more? I shuddered and pushed those thoughts away too.

As I washed up with cold water and changed dresses, Babette patted powder on her face and rubbed a hefty dose of rouge onto her cheeks. She offered to make me up but I declined. I preferred my clean, plain look to her heavy hand with *maquillage*.

"Let's go!" The giddy Babette was back, unnaturally bright eyes, chattering non-stop. "Henri said they would meet us at the corner, but he is an impatient man. I don't want to keep him waiting." She winked.

We crossed Place du Tertre on our way. The square was filling with patrons as the evening began. Workmen in shirtsleeves gathered around outdoor tables, cool glasses of beer in their fists. Dressed in rags and a dirty felt hat, an older woman with a vaguely familiar face threaded her way through the tables. She stopped at each one, bracing herself against chair backs with her left hand, holding her right one out in supplication. The men simply turned their backs on her as if she was a long-standing nuisance.

Of course. The old woman was the subject in Babette's series of oil paintings, the ones I'd liked. I found coins in my pocket and strode toward her, but Babette caught my arm.

"What are you doing?" she asked.

I shook my arm free and crossed to greet the woman, handing her the coins. Only one franc in all, but it was nearly half of what I had. Enough for a decent meal, certainly, or possibly even a night in a cheap hotel.

"Waste of money," Babette muttered.

"At least it's mine to waste," I shot over my shoulder, but Babette had stayed behind. She gave the old woman a quick hug and dropped something shiny in her palm.

I smiled, even though it was undoubtedly my money she'd parted with. Babette was not as hard as nails after all.

Something—a flash of black silk, a silver-topped cane—caught my eye. Something that didn't fit the plebeian surroundings. I stared at the spot, unsure of what I'd seen. What I thought I'd seen.

"What is it?" Babette came up to me, following my gaze. "Someone you know?" She laughed as if such a thing were impossible.

I didn't argue with her. The vision of a well-cut coat and too-high top hat was gone. A gentleman who looked remarkably like Philippe. I shook that suspicion out of my head, for I'd thought I'd seen Papa at the Moulin de la Galette, and it hadn't been him, at all.

Relax, Gabbi. You are safe.

"You're going to break your neck, you fool," a man with a cigarette shouted. "Get down, Pablo!"

As Babette and I entered the Lapin Agile with Henri—Edgar begged off to my great relief—a cheer erupted from a noisy group occupying two tables. The man, apparently named Pablo, wore a bright yellow scarf around his neck and danced on top of a third table. He tottered dangerously until the man with the cigarette grabbed him and hauled him down. His heels barely missed the flickering candle in the centre of the table.

"No more wine for you, *mon ami,*" The man with the cigarette slapped him on the back of his head. "Sit down, sit down." He turned and spied us and waved his cigarette. "Babette! Henri!"

"*Bon nuit,* Alphonse." Babette took Henri's arm and guided him toward her friend. I edged away and took a seat next to the only other woman in the group.

Babette greeted everyone with kisses on cheeks. "I've brought you a new member, *mes amis.* Gabrielle de Villiers."

As a singer's voice rose from the back of the café, Alphonse introduced himself to me. He stood, a trifle unsteadily, and bowed, gesturing with his burning cigarette. "*Bienvenue,* Gabrielle." He hiccupped loudly. "We have a little tradition when someone new joins us . . . to see whether you are worthy of our august company." Another hiccup. "Tonight, our topic shall be . . . what is art?" He cleared his throat, paused and swept his arm out in a theatrical gesture. "Art is . . . poetry of the eye."

"Not a bad start, Alphonse." The tall, slender man seated across from me saluted his friend. He tipped back his wine and then stood and bowed in my direction. "I'm Paul, from Chicago." He paused and stroked his chin, squinting at the ceiling. "For me, art is a mirror to reflect reality," he said in nearly flawless French.

"*Très bien!*" Light applause followed, for which Paul bowed.

Mon Dieu! Would I also be called upon to expound on what was most dear to me? What is art? That was like asking what was the meaning of life! Creating art is like breathing the air, like opening my eyes each morning to a new day. But I couldn't say that, not to strangers, even if they were artists. I sat on my hands to hide my nervousness.

The woman beside me introduced herself. "Welcome to our band of misfits, Gabrielle. I'm Julie, from Montréal, Canada." She stood gracefully and paused for several moments before delivering her pronouncement. "The act of art is dipping a paintbrush into one's soul and recording its vision."

Everyone clapped and she curtsied before sitting again. She leaned toward me, but her eyes were on Alphonse. "According to Alphonse, I have a Canadian accent," she said, loudly enough for him to hear. "What do you think, Gabrielle?"

I shrugged. "I, too, have an accent. The Parisians sound like they are gargling, their *r*'s are so guttural."

"Enough!" Alphonse laughed in reply. "We'll have you both speaking proper French before the end of the summer."

Julie grinned. Their banter was genuine and light-hearted, the kind that good friends shared. The kind I had with Bernadette. Melancholy threatened to descend on me like a dreary rainy day. I sipped more wine, determined to create new friendships.

Alphonse rapped the table with his glass. "Babette! You're next."

But my roommate's eyes were glassy, and she simply waved him off, her cigarette smouldering. I wondered if she'd get off so easily, but Alphonse looked over her head, apparently distracted. "Konstantin."

A burly man, hair greying at his temples, stood at the far end of the table. Clearly older than the rest of us, he seemed out of place.

"Oui, Konstantin," Paul jeered. "Let's have a real artist enlighten us. What is art, old man?"

Konstantin ignored Paul and bowed in my direction. "I am pleased to meet you Mademoiselle," he said in a thick Russian accent. "Art is art. It speaks for itself." He sat back down, thick arms crossing his broad chest.

Loud boos followed.

"That's cheating!" Paul shouted.

"Not fair!" Henri protested.

Alphonse held up his hands. "Now, now. Let's not let petty jealousies taint these proceedings."

Julie tilted her head to me. "Konstantin's too modest to brag, but he just finished a four-man exhibition at Durand-Ruel's gallery. And two of his paintings were accepted at last year's Salon."

"Time for our new initiates. Pablo, your turn," Alphonse said.

Pablo shot an intense look at me from under his dark eyebrows. I met his gaze, trying not to appear intimidated by his fierce expression. Did this other newcomer feel threatened by me?

He had a flair for the dramatic, whoever he was. "I'm Pablo. You may call me 'the Spaniard.'" He stood, flung his scarf over his shoulder, stuck out his chest and waited until everyone was silent. "Art washes from the soul the dust of everyday life."

"I'll drink to that!" Alphonse cried, tossing back another glass of wine. Heads nodded and a respectful silence followed. How would I follow such a gilded tongue?

Alphonse turned to me. "And finally, Mademoiselle Gabrielle."

I stood, clutching my shaking hands behind my back. "I'm Gabbi, from Laval." I took a deep breath and picked a phrase from somewhere in the back of my brain, something I'd learned in Madame Magne's art classes. "The purpose of art is to form a bridge between painter and viewer." I sat quickly, praying no one noticed that I had paraphrased the great Eugene Delacroix.

Light applause followed. Not an auspicious beginning, but a beginning nonetheless.

Julie leaned in close to me as conversations started up around us. "I like what you said about art being a bridge. Well done, especially being put on the spot like that. Tell me, are you studying at one of the academies?"

"I hope to attend the Académie Julian."

Paul turned sharply. "Forget the Académie Julian," he said with a wave of his hand. "Julian's a terrible artist! If only I'd known before Father paid for my entire year's tuition." He drained another glass of wine.

"Ha!" Pablo said, slapping Paul's back. "The misfortunes of the pampered."

"Trust me, Gabrielle," Paul said, waving Pablo away. "The *ateliers* are dying. You'll learn more by finding a mentor who will take you to paint *en plein air*. Take your easel and paints outdoors and capture your impressions on the spot. Like Renoir and Monet."

"Don't listen to Paul," Alphonse said, frowning. "You must learn academic art by copying the Masters as I do, at the École des Beaux-Arts. Seven or eight years, maybe more. Only then should you even attempt your own compositions."

Julie leaned in, her dark eyes dancing in the dim light. "These clods are full of hot air. And too much cheap wine." She winked at Paul before turning back to me. "We can study together at Julian's women's atelier, Gabbi. Many of the weekly guest tutors come from the Beaux-Arts, so you won't miss out on the classical training they offer."

Her kind, welcoming words stung my eyes. I blinked away tears. Julie painted an image of exactly what I'd hoped to find in Paris. Working side by side with artists of the same spirit. How could I confess I didn't have the money for the academy? At least, not yet.

"The Julian is a better choice for women. Trust me," Julie continued. "Our life drawing classes are all female, and we help one another. Unlike the men, who tear each other apart in hopes of promoting themselves."

"What did you just say?" Alphonse leaned across the table, addressing Julie. "Tell me you're not a *femme nouvelle* who hates men!" He pouted, perhaps an attempt at a wounded expression, but he appeared more like a sad puppy dog.

Heat flared in my cheeks. "Why does the notion of independent women scare men—"

Julie put her hand on my arm and cocked one eyebrow. "If being a modern woman means thinking for myself and speaking my mind instead of pandering to men, then I gladly accept the name!" She reached across me and patted Alphonse's hand. "But I most certainly do not hate men. My beloved father is, after all, a man. One who supports what I'm doing. And you, Alphonse, are my friend, even when you spout nonsense."

He grunted but smiled. "I admit some of us are asses. But if you are cosseted away in an all-female cocoon, how would you know what the real art world is like?"

Alphonse may not have intended his words to be insulting, but Julie jerked her hand away. In a tart voice, she said, "I know enough that I've got a painting accepted in this year's Salon."

"C'est vrai?" His face reddened, and his hand tightened on his wine glass, but he was gentleman enough to struggle to his feet and make an announcement. "Everyone! Join me in a toast to Julie! She has a painting accepted in this year's Salon." He raised his glass to her. "Santé!"

"Bien!"

"Salut!"

"Félicité!"

Everyone joined in except Babette. She slouched next to Henri, arms crossed and her expression sullen. It must be difficult to see another woman succeed when you had given up the race.

I looked away from her and watched the others congratulate Julie. I fled home for a moment like this, immersed in a group of fellow artists. It was exactly what I'd been missing—a place I truly belonged. I breathed deeply and my shoulders relaxed. Eventually, I'd join Julie at the academy. Until then, all I needed was my own mentor, as Paul suggested. A mentor like Gaston Lachance. Such a pity that Babette was my only link to him, for it tied me to her until she introduced us.

I had to press the matter. Soon.

Henri called for more wine, bread, and cheese although an army of empty bottles of *vin ordinaire* already littered the table. Everyone cheered as the waiter appeared with the bounty. I tried not to make a face when I sipped the wine. It was even worse than what they'd served at the Moulin de la Galette, but it had one advantage. It was cheap at only three *sous* per liter and didn't leave me feeling beholden to Henri, who paid for everything as Babette had promised.

"To Henri!" Alphonse made a toast.

"To art!" Paul added.

"To patrons of the arts!" Konstantin added.

"Non, non . . . to anarchy!"

My glass stopped halfway to my lips. Anarchy? I knew little about anarchy, only that when I was ten, the man who had assassinated President Carnot was accused of being an anarchist.

I looked at the half-lit faces around me. Who made the last toast? Konstantin's face was stony. He set his glass on the table. But the others were either too drunk to care or had no qualms about cheering anarchists. Babette leaned against Henri, her cheeks flushed as she downed her wine.

I put my glass down too. Konstantin caught my eye and nodded. His heavy-lidded eyes unnerved me. His gaze was direct and clear.

The singer, who was moving throughout the café, approached our table. Everyone in our group suddenly gave her their undivided attention. She raised her arms encased in elbow-length black gloves, a stark contrast to her sunflower yellow gown. Her gestures became increasingly exaggerated as she sang a folk song about the madly cheering crowds awaiting her execution by *guillotine*. At the end of her song, she made a slashing motion across her own throat and collapsed dramatically into Konstantin's lap.

Scowling, he grabbed her by the shoulders and set her back on her feet firmly, but not roughly. She planted kisses on both his cheeks and left us for another table.

Babette's voice, sharp as glass, cut through the chatter. "I think it's time we truly initiate the newest members of our group." She smirked at me, then Pablo.

"I'll drink to that," Alphonse said, raising his glass.

Babette's smile made me uneasy. "What does this initiation involve?"

Alphonse belched. "Nothing bad, nothing bad."

Julie grabbed my hand and said, "You don't have to, Gabrielle."

Pablo stood up, unsteady. "I'm ready."

"Bravo, Pablo!"

"Well, Gabrielle? Are you with us? Or not?"

Eight pairs of eyes turned on me. Music buzzed in the background, heightening my sense of unease. Isn't this what I came to Paris for? La vie bohème, the camaraderie of fellow artists? "What do I have to do?"

"You'll see," Babette said with another smirk that set off alarms.

I desperately wanted to prove myself as one of this group. How bad could it be? "All right."

Eight shot glasses were quickly lined up on the bar. Henri slopped a murky greenish spirit into each glass and diluted it with a splash of water from a carafe. Absinthe. Papa carried it in his store. Only a foolish few bought the liquor called the Green Fairy for its hallucinogenic properties. Pablo and I were made to stand in front of the bar. Alphonse flipped a coin. "Gabbi first. Four shots for each of you . . . if you can remain standing that long."

As a woman, I could have refused. The men wouldn't likely have minded. But that was exactly why I had to do it, to meet men's standards regardless of how ridiculous they might be. My face already flushed from cheap wine, I shot back the first glass without hesitation. It burned with a raging sweetness that took my breath away.

Pablo didn't wait for me to finish and downed all four of his shots in quick succession. Leaning against the bar, he folded his arms across his chest and regarded me through eyes now narrowed to slits. "Can't keep up?" he taunted, his voice slurred.

"More water," Julie insisted and tipped the carafe into the three remaining glasses.

I picked up another shot. "Santé!" I tipped it back. This time, the burning abated somewhat. Flavours of anise or fennel and other herbs and flowers bloomed inside my mouth quite pleasantly. A misty halo spread out from the oil lamps behind the bar, endowing everyone with a gentle aura. A grin spread across my face. I could hold my own amongst the men, just as I could hold my own at art.

As I reached for the third glass, the chanting around me swelled to a crescendo. "Gabbi, Gabbi, Gabbi!" Faces around me blurred, came into focus again and dissolved into the smoky haze . . . vaguely familiar faces. We met . . . yes, tonight. Artists. I grinned, downed the third glass, and slapped it upside down on the bar. There was Julie. And Alphonse. Who was the American, the one who loved to paint outdoors? And the dark burly Russian?

I looked past the bar to a sullen woman seated at a nearby table, glaring at me. Babette. This had been her idea. And I'd agreed. Why was she angry?

The man with the yellow scarf—Pablo?—was passed out, head on his arms. I won! My grin stretched wider.

The Russian . . . Konstantin . . . spoke into my ear, but laughter and chatter and the drum beat inside my head made it impossible to hear. "Pardon?"

"No more for you, Mademoiselle." He put his hand over the remaining shot glass.

"You're no fun!" I reached around him for the last glass, but I slipped on something slick and fell backward. "Whoops!"

He caught my elbow and righted me.

"I need to sit down." My voice came from somewhere far away, not my own at all.

Konstantin guided me toward our table. The floor turned soft underneath me, and I sat down with a very unladylike thump.

Henri teased me from across the table. "Gabbi, Gabbi, you disappoint me. Only three?" He stroked his goatee, arm around Babette, who nuzzled his neck.

I blinked and tried to focus on him. There were two of him, then one. I leaned toward him before he could split into twins again, and I stroked my own chin. "Perhaps Monsieur would like to demonstrate how a man can hold his liquor?"

"Hah!" Alphonse slapped Henri on the back. "You have to defend our manhood."

A full bottle of absinthe appeared on the table. But Henri didn't just drink it with a splash of water, like Pablo and I. "Now, I show you how to drink absinthe properly!" Henri announced with a grand swing of his arm. "Messieurs and Mesdames—the Green Fairy Ritual!"

One part absinthe, a cube of sugar in a slotted silver spoon, three parts water poured over the sugar, and the emerald liquor turned murky white.

"One . . . Two . . . Three . . . Four!"

"Well done, Henri!" someone shouted from across the table.

"You don't have to prove anything, Gabbi." Julie's voice travelled toward me garbled and indistinct, as if underwater.

I planted my elbows on the table to steady myself, so unladylike. Maman's disapproval crossed my mind. I giggled, for she was not here to scold me. I pointed at Henri. "I can hold my liquor as well as a man. In fact, I bet I can paint better than Henri. Right here, right now."

A round of hoots followed.

Henri chuckled. "I'm a patron, not an artist, chérie."

"A patron?" someone jeered. "Is that what you call yourself?"

"So you don't need lessons from Gaston?" Babette's crimson lips sucked on her cigarette and blew smoke at me.

I leaned away and waved to dispel the smoke, nearly falling backwards.

"Gaston?" Konstantin asked.

"Oui, you know, the famous painter. Gaston La . . . La . . . " I tried to wrap my tongue around the name, but it had thickened, threatening to stick to the roof of my mouth.

"Lachance," Babette said.

"Yes, that's it." I squinted through the cigarette smoke, trying to focus on Konstantin's face. "He's going to give me art lessons for free. I just have to model for him now and then."

No one spoke.

"Lachance?" Konstantin looked incredulous. "Not that *cochon?*"

Pig? Harsh words for a famous artist. Was the Russian jealous?

Babette interrupted, her voice sharp. "Watch what you say, *Ruski*. He's a good friend of mine and a celebrated French artist."

"Babette!" Julie frowned at her. "We are all friends here. You'd do well to remember that."

Babette pouted. "And you'd do well to remember that you are a foreigner."

"Girls, girls." Alphonse hugged them close. "We are all artists. We must stand together against the rest of the world."

"I'll drink to that!" a voice shouted from somewhere close by.

I stood unsteadily. The floor suddenly gave way beneath me and my knees crumpled. I caught the edge of the table and clung to it. "I don't feel so good."

Konstantin jumped to his feet, grasped my elbow and propelled me to the back door.

I rushed into the alleyway and vomited. Long after I'd thrown up the contents of my stomach, my gut still convulsed with dry heaves. "I need to go home."

"Come." Konstantin drew a handkerchief out of his jacket like a magician and wiped my chin. Then he formally offered me his arm as if we were promenading the grand boulevards, not skulking the dank alleyways of Montmartre. "As much as I regret it, I must leave for Moscow tomorrow, Mademoiselle Gabrielle. Promise me you won't be so foolish as to drink so much while I'm gone."

"I won't. I never want to feel like this again." I silently lectured my roiling gut to settle.

He led me down the alley instead of re-entering the café. As we emerged onto a dimly lit street, I stopped and stared at a shadowy figure walking away, disappearing into the dark.

"What is it?" Konstantin asked.

"Nothing." But the cast of the man's shoulders looked familiar, with dark curly hair beneath a silk top hat. Philippe? Could it have been? But he would have no reason to come to Montmartre. I thought I'd seen him earlier, too, but that didn't make any sense. There must be many men with a similar build and profile. It was for the best. It would be embarrassing for Philippe to see me staggering and clutching Konstantin's arm for support.

"I'm staying with Babette," I told Konstantin. "On rue Gabrielle."

He grunted. "Everyone knows where Babette lives."

His strange comment tugged at my brain but was swept aside by an overwhelming need to vomit again. The hammering in my ears intensified, and I shook my head in disgust.

"One more thing," Konstantin said as we reached rue Gabrielle, and he guided me up the stairs to Babette's attic.

I pointed above the lintel where he found the key and unlocked the door.

"Be careful around Babette. She's . . . changed . . . in the past few months." His face darkened into a scowl. "And avoid Gaston Lachance at all costs."

"What? Why?" I focused on placing one foot in front of the other. The floor tilted and I stumbled.

Konstantin grabbed my elbow. "Trust me. He's trouble."

So who was I supposed to trust? I closed the door and staggered toward the sofa.

Chapter Fifteen

DAYLIGHT STREAMED THROUGH the tiny attic window, warming my face. I swallowed to loosen my swollen tongue and opened my eyes only to shut them again, assaulted by the brightness. Images from the previous night flooded back: drinking wine, debating art with my new friends, tossing back absinthe. Konstantin's kindness. The humiliation of vomiting while he held my head. The glimpse—I was sure of it—of Philippe last night as I left the Lapin Agile.

Philippe!

Merde. The Expo! It was Monday. I sat up like a shot. My head pounded, and the room swam before my eyes. What time was it? No clock in sight. Dear God, don't let me be late. No time to first visit the offices of *La Fronde* like I'd hoped. I pushed away a rush of guilt in delaying the search for my grandmother. And when on earth would I have time to complete a project for the salon on Friday?

But I could not miss the Expo.

After downing two glasses of water from the pitcher, I pulled the covers off Babette. "Wake up. I need you to chaperone."

"Chaperone? Me? That's a good one." She turned over and burrowed back under her blankets.

"I can't be late for Philippe. Please, Babette, get up." I left her groaning while I slipped into my light seersucker dress, *sans* corset. I scowled at my reflection in the cheap mirror before splashing cold water on my face and brushing my hair up into a simple knot.

"How is it you are up so early, bright eyes?" She sat up, her night dress slipping off one shoulder. She had the same dark bags under her eyes as I did, but her eyes were swollen to narrow slits. "I thought you drank enough last night to sink a ship."

"I slept like a baby," I said brightly. "How about you?"

She grunted and started to curl up on the bed again. I rushed over to keep her upright. "Come on, I'll brush your hair out for you."

After I styled her hair, she dressed in a scarlet chambray dress and matching heeled shoes. As I brushed the dust off my skirt, it struck me I'd need more clothes than what I brought. Babette's clothes were scattered carelessly around the room on her bed and on hanging on nails. I looked more closely at her. "That's a pretty dress. Did you make it?"

She laughed. "Do you see anywhere to sew?"

"How can you afford so many clothes?"

She smirked. "There are lots of second-hand dress shops. And if you know where to go, you can even rent dresses by the hour. I'll show you."

What possible reason would a woman have to rent a dress for only an hour?

Babette insisted on applying makeup, so I took a few moments to brush my teeth and rinse my mouth. Why did I drink so much last night? What would Philippe think if he knew? I had never consumed more than one glass of watered-down wine in an evening before. But the camaraderie of the other students, even stodgy Konstantin, and the lively atmosphere had made it all seem right somehow. Until now.

"Come on!" I pinned on my straw boater and grabbed my handbag and parasol. "I don't want to be late."

She raised an eyebrow. "He must be quite the looker."

"I want to see the Expo, that's all."

She wagged a finger at me. "Don't try to fool Babette. I can see you're in love."

Love? I pulled on her arm to hurry her. "Don't be ridiculous!" How could I love someone like Philippe, whose ideas about women—and women artists in particular—so irritated me? Regardless, I found myself looking forward to seeing him.

When we reached the street, the sun was already quite high in the sky, the day hot. I turned my face upward, eyes closed, and enjoyed the warmth for a moment before hurrying down the sidewalk, cursing my long skirt as it caught at my ankles and threatened to trip me. Madame Dijon's voice slipped into my mind unbidden: "A proper lady does not rush anywhere. She glides." I laughed aloud, lifted my hem above my ankles and rushed.

By the time we arrived at Grand-mère's building, a four-seat *vis-à-vis* carriage was waiting on the street, its half hood folded back. Perfect for a gentleman escorting two women, as we would be seated across from one another. Very thoughtful. I straightened my bodice and patted my hair, ignoring Babette's wink as I left her by the carriage and entered the building. Philippe's broad back was to me, but I recognized the unruly dark curls under his top hat. He was gesturing at the old portière.

"Philippe!" I stood just inside the door to draw him away from the old woman. "Good morning."

He turned. "Ah, Gabrielle. You are here after all." He muttered something to the portière and then escorted me outside with his hand on the small of my back.

I stiffened at the warmth of his hand. Would he notice I wasn't wearing a corset? What would he think? The sour reek of alcohol surely seeped from my pores. I stepped back to a proper distance. "Philippe, this is Babette." I nodded at my roommate, who lounged against the building. "Grand-mère is unable to come today, so Babette will be my chaperone instead."

He looked from me to Babette. His remarkable blue eyes took in her garish dress. Surprised? If he was, he was too much of a gentleman to show it. He bowed over her hand. "It will be a pleasure, Mademoiselle Babette. Shall we, ladies?"

He helped us into the carriage and sat facing us. We took off with a lurch, the lanterns banging and the horses' iron-clad hooves clattering on the paved street. I opened my parasol with a snap.

Philippe leaned toward me, a puzzled look on his face. "The portière didn't know anything about you or your grandmother."

"Phht!" Babette answered him with a flick of her wrist. "Pay no attention to that old woman."

I twirled my parasol. "It's a beautiful day, isn't it?"

Philippe's eyes narrowed, inspecting me like a bug under a magnifying glass.

"Did you bring along a hidden camera today?" I asked, eager to change topics.

He smiled. "I have, indeed. I acquired it yesterday. If it amuses you, you might try to discover it by the end of our day together."

"A hidden camera? How very *risqué*…even naughty, one might say," Babette murmured, eyelashes fluttering.

"Not at all, Mademoiselle. I'm merely interested in photography, how cameras work, the complicated processing of the plates, that sort of thing." His mouth tightened. "It's nothing more than a hobby."

Undeterred by his flat tone, she leaned forward and gazed directly at him, her bosom bulging above her scarlet *décolleté*. "Gabbi, you didn't say your beau was so handsome when you asked me to chaperone."

I resisted the urge to kick her.

She leaned closer still. "What is it that you do, Monsieur?"

"Business should not be discussed during pleasure," he said, sharply.

"Oh, a true gentleman. This is a real treat." She twirled her parasol, her eyes never leaving Philippe's face.

"Are you an artist, too, Mademoiselle?" Philippe asked politely.

"Yes. It is both my pleasure and my business." She placed her hand on his knee, the sun shining on her pale breasts. "Do you have any activities that you do for pleasure?"

"Of course, Mademoiselle." Philippe shifted his gaze to me and raised one eyebrow. "However, they are probably not to your interest." He lifted Babette's hand from his knee and placed it back on her skirts. I hid a small smile as Philippe turned to address me. "When do your studies begin at the Académie?"

"I . . . I haven't registered yet."

Babette smirked. "They have no room for beginners."

"Babette is waiting to get into the Académie too," I retorted with a smile.

She gave me a dark look, pulled out a cigarette and lit it. She sucked deeply and blew the smoke at Philippe. He sat back and wrinkled his nose.

An awkward silence fell between us. I twirled the parasol while Babette continued to smoke. Her fingers drummed on the seat between us until I wanted to swat her with my parasol. She really wasn't at all the chaperone type, but then I'd had little choice. I took a deep breath and leaned toward Philippe, a determined smile pasted on my face. "What shall we see at the Exposition?"

His eyes lit up. "Whatever you want. There are thousands of exhibits, from the latest inventions with electricity to automobiles and moving pictures."

"Ah, oui," Babette said in a bored voice. She blew another smoke ring. "Le cinéma Lumière. I've seen that."

I remembered an article in *La Fronde*. "There's an art exhibit at something called the Grand Palais. It includes contemporary artists, even the group they call the Impressionists. Paintings by Monet, Pisarro and Manet, among others. My art teacher admires their work greatly. I'm hoping to see Berthe Morisot's paintings there, too."

"Then we shall," Philippe said, his eyes crinkling at the corners as he smiled at me, just as they had when I'd sketched his portrait on the train. "There's more than we'll hope to see in one day, of course. Every important country has a pavilion. There's also the Eiffel Tower, if you haven't had the chance to travel up on its elevator yet. What a sight to behold. And the Grande Roué—"

"I've heard of that—a giant mechanical wheel you can ride!" I pressed my palms together against my mouth. "And the moving pictures sound wonderful."

"Children's entertainments," Babette said, her chin high.

Philippe frowned at her. "Not at all. I can't wait to ride the Grand Roué and see moving pictures at the Galerie des Machines."

I smiled with gratitude at him. He'd come to my defence, much like Bernadette would have done. Why couldn't she have been here with me, rather than Babette? If wishes were horses, beggars would ride.

Babette sank into the seat, smoking and scowling. Her moodiness stole some of my excitement, so we traveled in silence as the carriage left Montmartre and entered the river of traffic on the grand boulevards. I rubbed my temples to relieve a growing headache.

"Are you ill?" Philippe asked.

"Oh no, I'm fine." I grasped my hands in my lap. I wasn't about to admit that I drank too much the previous night. I wanted him to think better of me, as a modern woman firmly in charge of herself and her future.

If only my head would stop pounding!

Then I saw her: the tall, scrawny flower girl I'd noticed on my first day in the city. This time, she was minding a smaller child, likely a young sister. The flower girl waved a bouquet of daisies at passersby but no one seemed interested. Why was I so taken with her? I couldn't say, but the sight of the rags around both girls' feet and the barrow full of unsold blooms tugged at my heart. The flower girl's eyes were enormous, as if she could satisfy her hunger by devouring the luxury around her with her gaze.

"Stop!" I cried.

Philippe's eyebrows rose in alarm. "Driver—stop!" He leaned forward. "What is it, Gabrielle?"

"I . . . I'd like to buy some flowers. From that girl—there." What a capricious, even impolite, request!

Philippe cocked an eyebrow.

"Isn't it terrible that a young girl has to work? What fault of hers is it that she's not in school or playing with other children in the parks? But for fate's hand in whose family we are born into, that could have been me." He didn't need to know that I might soon be reduced to peddling my sketches on a street corner much like the flower girl and would be grateful if someone took pity on me.

"Hah!" Babette scoffed. "Don't waste your time on that gutter girl."

Philippe gave Babette a hard stare before he jumped out of the carriage. He pressed some coins into the girl's hand in return for flowers. She clutched his hands in gratitude, as if it was her biggest sale of the day.

"For you, Mesdemoiselles," Philippe said gallantly as he gave us each a long stemmed rose.

Babette stuck hers down her deep neckline. I buried my nose into mine, inhaling its delicate scent. I stole a glance at Philippe. He regarded me in silence, a slight smile on his lips. I blushed and looked out at the stores along the boulevard.

"We'll soon be passing the Bon Marché and Au Printemps," Philippe said.

Babette perked up at the mention of the fashionable department stores. She leaned out the open carriage as we rolled by gaily coloured window displays.

"And there's the Académie de France." Philippe pointed out a gold-ribbed dome thrusting up over the other buildings. "I'm sure you both know the Académie des Beaux-Arts is housed there."

"Humph," Babette said, her pert nose in the air. "It's nothing more than a bunch of old men who wouldn't know good art if it bit them on the ass."

Philippe stared at her, his lips in a tight white line.

Babette could have benefited from Madame Dijon's etiquette lessons—if she were willing to listen.

For the rest of the ride, Philippe hardly spoke at all, and I feared that he regretted his invitation. Yet I could hardly explain that I was dependent on Babette. Not unless I was willing to recant all my lies.

My unease lightened as we neared the Expo grounds. Up close, the Eiffel Tower was even more impressive than when I first saw it from the bluff in Montmartre only a few nights ago. More pleasing, however, was its clean-lined silhouette, curving like a woman's waist yet also strong, as steel girders are. A thrill chased through me. I was in the city of my dreams, and despite a few setbacks, attending the World Expo in the company of a new friend and a handsome man. Even if they sniped at one another.

Chapter Sixteen

HUNDREDS IF NOT THOUSANDS of people thronged the streets as we neared the Expo gates. A long row of carriages and omnibuses lined the sides of the streets, but pedestrians streamed past them.

"You'll have to walk the rest of the way," the coachman explained when he stopped.

Philippe leapt down and held out his hand. I accepted his help but couldn't resist saying, "If women were allowed to wear trousers, I wouldn't need assistance."

His eyebrows rose and his mouth tightened. "You are jesting, of course, Mademoiselle." He dropped my hand the moment my feet were firmly on the pavement and turned away to help Babette.

"Oh!" She slipped on the carriage step and fell forward into his arms. As he caught her by the waist, she looked over his shoulder at me and winked.

"Take care, Mademoiselle." Philippe's face reddened as he extricated himself from her embrace.

As he paid the driver, a decidedly unwelcome squirm of jealousy hit me. He hadn't responded to Babette's obvious flirting, but she was quite good at playing the role of a helpless woman around men. And isn't that what men like Philippe preferred? Independent women, like me, were entirely undesirable. And that was just as well, for my plans for the future had no room for romance.

"Regardez!" Two dark-suited men in bowler hats pushed past me. As I moved to avoid them, I was jostled from the other side by a nanny pushing a perambulator. A small boy darted past, nearly taking my legs out from under me.

The closer we got to the gates, the more crowds pressed in from all sides. My chest tightened and my pulse raced.

"Let me assist you." Philippe took my hand and tucked it into his arm, his voice quiet and calm. "Just remember to breathe."

"Merci." I took several deep breaths as we approached the gates. "Back home, we never had such crowds," I said, but that wasn't completely true.

Laval's town square once burst with suffragists, on the day that sealed my grandmother's fate. Oh, how I had wanted to join those marching women with Grand-mère! As I watched her go, Papa had tugged gently on my arm. "She'll be fine, petite," he promised. "Tonight, she'll entertain us all with stories from her little adventure."

"It's not the same as being there, Papa!" I had complained as he led me away. But when I looked back, Grand-mère smiled broadly and waved. The jostling, shouting crowd didn't bother her.

I took heart from her example and loosened my grip on Philippe's arm.

In front of us, a large swarthy man and the woman at his side stopped suddenly and looked up, craning their necks, and I nearly ran into them.

"Hah! *La Parisienne?*" the man grunted. "Busty, bustling and arrogant, is more like it."

Frowning, I regarded the object of his displeasure—a larger-than-life statue of a full-figured woman mounted over the elaborate entrance.

"I heard the model was Sarah Bernhardt," the woman said in a nervous, high voice.

"Bah! How can any woman represent my city? Ridiculous notion." He straightened his top hat and strode through the gate, his female companion struggling to keep up, hampered by high heels and tight skirts.

"I knew Paris was modern!" I said. "To choose a woman—an actress!—to represent the city to the world? That would never happen at home."

"It might be one artist's idea but make no mistake," Babette said, her tone bitter. "Women are not the equals of men in Paris or anywhere else."

Her cynicism bothered me. I turned to Philippe. "What do you think?"

He cleared his throat. "The statue certainly is magnificent."

"I wasn't asking for your opinion on the sculpture."

He laughed self-consciously. "Ah, well . . . I suppose I'm glad that men and women are different. After all, women are meant to take care of a home and children, aren't they?"

"Hah!" said Babette. "Spoken like a true male."

I frowned. "If a woman wants to work, why shouldn't she? Why can't the man do his share of running a home?"

Philippe laughed. "You can't be serious!"

I flinched as if I'd been struck, and heat rose up my neck to my cheeks.

Babette smiled. "See? There is your Parisian man."

Flushed, I stayed silent as we waited for the crowds ahead of us to get through the gate. When it was our turn, I dropped Philippe's arm, stepped in front of him, and paid my one-franc admission before he could do so. Babette, naturally, waited for him to pay her admission.

"That was unnecessary," he commented quietly as we walked through the gates together, his voice tight with annoyance or perhaps even anger.

I gazed at him for several moments, willing him to understand. "On the contrary, it was necessary. For me."

He pursed his lips but didn't reply. For what could he say? That he preferred his women to depend upon him for everything? Well, I was certainly not "his woman" and had no desire to be such. With a mental shake, I turned my focus to the sights and sounds around us.

Old and young filled the grounds: women wearing fashionable hats as big as dressing tables; men in top hats and morning suits; children clinging to nursemaids' hands; country folk in homespun cotton frocks with wooden *sabots,* heavy clogs, on their feet. A dark-skinned man with a black turban brushed past me. He turned with a slight bow, as if in apology, and hurried on. And the noise! Megaphones and music competed with one another, together with the conversations of thousands of people, so that we had to shout to be heard.

"Ladies, hold onto me so we don't get separated." Philippe held out both elbows again. Still irritated, I took his arm but kept as much distance between us as possible. Three abreast, the throngs swept us past the pavilions and cafés lining the main streets of the Exposition.

"Ah, *le trottoir roulant!* I've heard about this." Philippe guided us to one side and stopped to stare at three elevated platforms before us. The first was stationary, the second moved at a moderate pace. The third whirred past alarmingly fast. Waist-high poles dotted the moving sidewalks at intervals. People of all ages were being transported, some standing stock still, clutching the poles, and others walking quite without concern.

"Come on!" Philippe urged, grinning as he led us onto the first platform.

"You look like a boy who has spied a new toy," Babette teased, but her wobbly voice betrayed nervousness as she eyed the invention.

Philippe's grin grew broader. "Afraid to try something new, Mesdemoiselles?"

Gripping my parasol in one hand, I lunged with my free hand for one of the poles on the slower of the two moving sidewalks. I missed and stumbled. A stout man on the sidewalk caught my elbow and righted me.

"Merci, monsieur." I clutched the pole and looked over my shoulder. Nearly ten meters back, Philippe leaped onto the sidewalk, Babette still clutching his arm. They wove through the other people on the sidewalk until they were at my side.

"Isn't it grand?" Philippe asked, his eyes shining. "Let's move up to the faster one."

I laughed. "It is fun!" His excitement was contagious. Despite the headache pounding my temples, I let go of the upright pole. Timing my move with the appearance of a pole on the fastest sidewalk, I hopped up. Proud of myself, I glanced back to see Philippe, Babette still attached to his arm like a leech, right behind me.

"We're going eight kilometres an hour now." Philippe's excitement hadn't abated.

"I don't see what all the fuss is about." Babette fanned herself but kept a tight grip on Philippe's arm. Her sour face let on what she thought about the electric sidewalk.

"Don't be such a wet rag," I said, echoing her words from the previous night.

She glowered back at me and gripped the pole tightly. I let go and spread my arms out slightly for balance, my feet wide apart, determined to enjoy the ride past elaborate pavilions and cafés that lined the main boulevard. An imposing and beautifully ornate stone building with bronze statues of rearing horses and riders crowning its curved glass roof, rose above the crowds to our right. The sidewalk glided past without stopping, so I had to admire the building over my shoulder.

"Perhaps we should find some strong coffee and a *beignet*?" Philippe suggested.

"Oh, yes, please," I said. While he scanned the streets for a café, I turned my back to him and tested the smell of my breath against my cupped palm.

"What about there?" Philippe pointed ahead to a simple native hut with a thatched roof. A small stencilled sign read, "Ceylon Tea House". Tables covered in linens were spread under plane trees, providing welcome shade from the hot sun.

Babette smiled for the first time since we'd boarded the moving sidewalk. "Perfect."

Disembarking proved to be easier than boarding once I had the measure of how to change platforms running at different speeds, but it was a relief to be on stationary ground again. Babette, naturally, had the benefit of Philippe's support, yet still looked incredibly relieved to be off the moving sidewalks. The contrast between her sour expression and his delighted one was comical.

"Wasn't that fun?" Philippe asked, his grin unabated.

"It was. I believe I'll make a little sketch of our adventure later," I said.

"A caricature, you mean," he teased with a warm smile. "Should I be worried?"

"Only if I sell it to *Le Petit Journal*." I grinned. As we approached the tea house, a light sense of wellbeing settled over me. Perhaps we could be friends, especially since I was free of Maman's strict rules about whom I could associate with.

At the Tea House, we were seated by a brown-skinned waiter in a crisp white suit, his long black hair knotted at the back of his head. He handed us menus. Philippe slipped his glasses on to read his. Babette and I ordered black coffee and pastries, Philippe an iced tea.

I looked around as I drank my coffee, grateful as its bitter heat spread through my veins and invigorated me. Men and women in fashionable clothing filled the other tables. Two women, not much older than me, sat across from us. One wore her hair in a style I hadn't seen before that I liked. It was pulled back loosely, gathered up on top and knotted around itself. Hair combs held stray locks in place, and a loose curl hung down either side of her cheeks. Bernadette would have loved to copy it, I thought with a stab of melancholy.

Someone at the table behind us gossiped loudly. "Look, Emmeline. It's the Marquise and Marietta. She hasn't worn a new hat all spring. I heard he's is in deep financial trouble."

I turned to see who was talking and smiled. I would have drawn the speaker as a squawking magpie. Dressed entirely in black and white, her hat sported what looked like an entire bird's wing. What would she and her companion think of Babette's crimson dress, painted lips and cheeks? I involuntarily smoothed down my own dress, suddenly self-conscious of wrinkles.

Just then, a large group of women marched into the grassy area around us, carrying signs high above their heads.

Philippe cast an uneasy glance at them. "Ladies, drink up quickly, s'il vous plaît."

Babette teased, "Frightened by a few free-thinking women, Philippe?"

"One woman, one vote!" shouted the leader

"Women are equal to men!" yelled another.

More shouts arose and signs waved in rhythm with marching feet.

"We demand the right to own property!"

"Women can manage money as well as men!"

Most of the women appeared to be upper class, judging from their expensive ankle-length dresses and tailored jackets, yet they were not behaving in a way Maman would have approved.

"There's Hubertine," exclaimed the gossiping woman behind us. "I told her not to get mixed up with those feminists."

Her companion tutted, peering through her *lorgnette*. "They're nothing but a bunch of ridiculous women dressed in mannish suits, making fools of themselves."

One of the marching women circled our table. Her round, smiling face and determined demeanour reminded me of Grand-mère. "Please, madame, tell me what's going on," I said.

She stopped, holding her sign high as she answered. "We're protesting unfair treatment of women." She thrust a newspaper at me, her white-gloved finger tapping the front page. "Join us. There's a Women's Congress on right now as part of the Expo. All around the world, women are speaking out and demanding . . . ah, well, here they are, as expected."

I clutched the newspaper and turned to follow her gaze. A group of uniformed gendarmes arrived.

"Thank goodness," Philippe muttered.

Babette shrank into her seat.

The gendarmes reached for the protest signs. A sharp whistle blew and more policemen arrived. Palpable tension filled the air as the gendarmes' demands to halt competed with shouted slogans. Tension escalated. A beefy, red-faced gendarme shook his fist in a woman's face and grabbed at her arm. She resisted and struck him over the head with her sign. He staggered and fell.

"Let's get out of here." Philippe stood sharply, pulled me to my feet. He guided me behind him, using his body as a shield. "It's getting dangerous."

Babette stood and pressed herself against his back too. "Oh, dear." She winked at me, tossed her head back and laughed.

I glanced at the newspaper in my hands. It was *La Fronde*. A bold headline announced the opening of the Women's Congress at the Expo. "Wait, Philippe, I want to ask that woman about Grand-mère—" I bit off the rest of the words. He thought my grandmother was merely indisposed, not entirely missing.

Luckily, he didn't appear to hear me. He pushed his way through the panicking crowds and led us toward a quieter spot. We stared at the mêlée. I thought again of my grandmother. Was this reminiscent of what happened in Laval that fateful day? My already uneasy stomach swirled as I imagined her struck down in a maelstrom of anger and righteousness. Were her principles—were any principles—worth taking such risks? I looked at the paper in my hands, torn between pride in the women willing to risk ridicule or arrest for what they believed in and resentment at their role in the loss of Grand-mère.

Babette looked over my shoulder. "Ah, *La Fronde*. You know that name refers to the sling anarchists used to smash windows in their riots, don't you?"

"I'll take that!" Philippe snatched the newspaper out of my hands and tossed it in a nearby trash bin.

"Philippe!" I protested. "Why did you do that?"

"You don't need a paper like that."

"But I want to read it!"

His brow furrowed, but his voice softened. "Gabrielle, you don't want to get mixed up in that."

"Perhaps I do," I replied, thinking of Grand-mère's friend, Séverine.

"You could get arrested."

Babette nodded. "It's true."

"Just for reading a newspaper?" I shook my head. "You can't be serious."

"Gabrielle, be reasonable. I'm trying to keep you safe." His lips tightened into a narrow line. "After all, I'm responsible for you."

Heat flared in my cheeks. "I didn't ask you to take responsibility for me." My hands curled into fists. "I am quite capable on my own."

He raised his eyebrows. "C'est vrai?"

"I don't like your tone."

"Now, Gabbi, don't be so touchy," Babette said, practically purring as she hooked her arm through Philippe's. "And Philippe, my dear gentleman, surely you aren't going to spoil this beautiful day with a quarrel."

"Quite right," he replied, his voice strung tight. "Let's continue." Several minutes of strained silence passed while we rejoined throngs of visitors on the main avenue. Then we came upon a mechanical wheel, several stories high. Dozens of windowed cars were affixed to the outside of the wheel, swinging as it rotated.

"That's the Grande Roué," Philippe said. "Why don't we ride it and get a view of the fair grounds? That way, we can decide what we want to see next."

Babette rolled her eyes and sighed loudly.

"An excellent suggestion, Philippe," I agreed. Really, Babette was here as my chaperone and should remember that. But she rarely behaved as expected.

We queued in front of the ticket booth and then took our place in a long line of customers. My neck began to ache from watching the giant wheel and its passengers slowly rotate through the sky.

After only a few minutes of waiting, Babette said, "I'm not wasting my time here. I shall meet you at the Pont Alexandre. In an hour." And off she flounced, parasol twirling.

I stared at her back. How embarrassing! "Not quite the chaperone I was hoping for."

"No," Philippe agreed, shaking his head. "Are you prepared to continue our sightseeing or do you wish to be escorted home?"

Miss this opportunity to see the World Fair? "Oh, non. I truly wish to stay. As I told you, I can take care of myself. Requiring chaperones is just another silly rule that mothers made to control their daughters."

Philippe's expression turned grave. "You're wrong. Those rules are to protect you. If I thought we would be alone, I would have insisted that Babette stay." He looked around, and gestured at the press of people pushing forward to get on the ride. "But you're safe here with so many chaperones."

Maman and Philippe shared many of the same opinions. I smiled slightly. "You worry far too much." Of course I was safe at the Expo and had no need of a chaperone.

He turned to me, his eyes earnest. "There's something else I've been wanting to say all morning." He looked around before locking his gaze on me once again. "I want you to be careful around Babette. There's something about her I don't trust."

I couldn't very well defend her; she'd behaved abominably to both Philippe and to me. Small wonder he warned me about her. And yet . . . "You want me to trust you, but I know nothing about you."

He gazed at me, head cocked to the side. "All right. Let's see, what can I tell you?" He stroked his chin. "I grew up in Le Mans. My family still lives there. My three older sisters are married and have several children each. I adore my nieces and nephews." He laughed. "Most of the time."

"What are your sisters like?"

He smiled. "Not at all like you."

"That sounds suspiciously like an insult."

"Oh, no. It's just that . . . well, they are happily married, raising their children and trying to run orderly households. I admire them and envy their husbands."

My face flushed. "Perhaps your sisters have given up on dreams of their own. You might not know them very well at all."

"Perhaps." He nudged me forward in line, his hand touching the small of my back for the briefest moment.

A treacherous lurch of pleasure bloomed in my chest, catching me unaware. I touched my cheeks, hoping I hadn't blushed as I tried to pick up the thread of our conversation. "So you are the youngest? No other brothers?"

He shook his head. "I'm the only male. Papa is putting a lot of pressure on me to join the family business."

We moved ahead again, nearing the front of the line. Delighted at finally coaxing personal details out of him, I asked, "What's the family business?"

"My father and uncle are lawyers. So far, I have managed to avoid joining the practice, but the pressure is mounting as the months go by since I graduated from studying law."

"But it sounds perfect for you!"

"What do you mean?" He looked at me, one eyebrow raised.

"You would have a ready-made business. Your life would be set for you."

"Exactly." He scowled.

"You want to make your own way in the world. On your own terms."

His gaze intensified. "Yes, that's right. But how did you know?"

"My parents are the same. They think they know what's best for me. However, they don't care what I want."

"And what does Gabrielle Carmen Désirée Jean d'Arc de Villiers want from her life?" He was no longer smiling, but his voice was serious, gentle.

"Freedom."

"Freedom? From what?"

I paused to gather my thoughts. "From Maman. No . . . no, it's more than that . . . I want the freedom to choose. To choose what I do, whom I spend time with. To marry or not to marry at all. Above all, the freedom to pursue my art." Deep inside, those words stoked a fire. They were true.

"Ah, you are one of those modern women." He said it as if being a modern woman was either a joke or a mental affliction.

"Yes, I am." I frowned. He'd better know who I was, right up front.

"Don't give me that sour face," he said. "I was only teasing you. Truly."

He sounded sincere. What did I expect anyway? A man who understood what it was like to have dreams bigger than Society deemed proper? Hardly. "I accept your apology."

When our turn came to board the ride, Philippe took my hand and helped me into the waiting car, and then manoeuvred us to a window. Passengers continued pushing into our car until the attendant shut the door.

The car lurched as it began its climb and threw me against Philippe. A warm feeling rose inside. Startled, I pressed my hand against his chest to regain my balance and detected a bulge under his cravat. "Found it!" I pulled my hand away. "Your camera. It's hidden under your tie, isn't it?"

He nodded, a smile curving his lips. "Clever girl. It's a *photo-cravate*, invented by a Parisian, Edmond Bloch."

I peered closely at his neatly tied cravate. "Is the lens hidden in your cravate pin?"

He laughed. "Very observant of you. The plates, no larger than a postal stamp, are hidden in the mechanism behind. Quite miniature and almost impossible to detect. Here, feel." He caught my hand and pressed it under his cravat. I felt the hard oval outline and discovered a narrow tube running from the camera to somewhere lower down.

I snatched my hand away. "You are a scoundrel! What if someone saw you?"

He grinned, his eyes crinkling with mischief. "You started it."

"Hush," I pleaded, turning from him to look out the window.

"We can see the whole of the Expo from up here," he murmured, but I felt his eyes on me.

We were suspended high above the grounds. The car rocked each time the wheel stopped to board or disgorge passengers below. My stomach turned liquid, but I ignored it and concentrated on the sights below on the boulevards. "Everyone is so small. It's like Lilliput from *Gulliver's Travels*."

"It's a unique sensation, isn't it? Like floating over the city."

I followed his gaze. From the height of the wheel, I saw not just the Exposition pavilions but much of the city. The Seine River sparkled as it ribboned past the grounds, with the Eiffel Tower a gleaming sentinel beside its banks, its peak ascending toward the clouds. The nearest stone bridge shone like a white beam arching over the river. Its rows of gold-gilded horses and cherubs glinted in the sun. My fingers itched to sketch this incredible perspective.

Philippe pointed down at the vista in front of us. "The square to the east is the Place de la Concorde. See that tall obelisk? It was a gift from Egypt to King Louis-Philippe. It stands at the very spot where Louis XV and Marie Antoinette were guillotined."

I shuddered, imagining crowds of crazed spectators during that bloody period. We'd studied it, of course, in school. "Thank God, that's ancient history."

"On the contrary, it's far from over."

"What do you mean?"

"The last Commune was thirty years ago, but there are still anarchists active in the city. Vaillant was beheaded only seven years ago." His voice turned harsh. "They've infiltrated those Soup Kitchen Meetings and the artists who support them. Ordinary citizens are afraid they'll be blown to bits. A bomb went off two days ago in the Bois de Boulogne. Luckily no one was harmed."

Artists supported the anarchists? Uneasiness crept in. Our group toasted anarchy at the Lapin Agile. "I never read about a bomb in the newspaper."

Philippe's eyes crinkled, and the corner of his mouth curled up. "You read the newspaper?"

I looked at him closely. Was he teasing or just being his usual chauvinistic self? "Of course I read the papers. I'm not simple-minded."

He put up both hands as if in surrender. "I never said you were. In fact, I feel quite intimidated in your presence."

"Good." I scowled at him and turned back to the window. Couldn't he accept that I was not unlike him—trying to create a future for myself that wasn't dictated by family?

The car lurched into the descent. In no time at all, the ride ended, and we were herded out for the next rush of passengers.

Philippe checked his pocket watch. "We still have time before we meet Babette. What would you like to do next?"

"I would love to see the art exhibit at the Grand Palais. If we can find it, that is."

He tucked my hand under his arm. "Of course."

How far I'd come in only a handful of days. Here I was, un-chaperoned with a man, very nearly a stranger, seeing the Expo with millions of others from around the world. I was a thoroughly modern woman, indeed.

"Monsieur Lucien?" A young boy slipped out from the crowd and tapped Philippe's arm. He wore a soft cap and clutched a stack of papers or pamphlets.

"Oui?" Philippe said, bending down. "How can I help you?"

"I was told to give you this." He handed a folded note to Philippe.

"What the devil . . . ?" Philippe muttered as he slipped his spectacles on. He opened the note and read it quickly before shoving it in his vest pocket. He looked around, but the boy had already disappeared. Grabbing my elbow, he propelled me in the opposite direction. "We have to leave immediately."

Chapter Seventeen

PHILIPPE'S TONE FRIGHTENED ME. "Leave? Why? What did that note say?"

His mouth tightened. "Gabrielle, trust me and leave now."

I crossed my arms. "I'm not going another step until you explain."

"It's not safe here." He clenched his jaw looked out over the crowds. "That's all I can tell you."

What was in the note? A warning or threat to his life? Or to the life of someone dear to him?

"Well?" I demanded.

"Is it enough if I tell you that a colleague needs my assistance? It's important, or I wouldn't ask you to leave without me."

"A colleague?"

"Yes. Look, Gabrielle, we're wasting precious time." He ran his hand through his thick curls. "Now, can we go?"

"All right." My pulse raced as I tried to keep pace with Philippe's long stride. He clutched my elbow with one hand and held the other out to deflect anyone in our way, guiding me through throngs of visitors toward the entrance gates.

"Wait." I pulled back. "Babette! I can't leave her here."

"I'm quite certain that woman can take care of herself."

As badly as she'd behaved, it didn't feel right to simply abandon her. If there truly were danger on the grounds, and something happened to her, I'd blame myself for not warning her. "I can't leave without her." I stood stock-still in the centre of the avenue, buffeted by the crowd of sightseers.

Philippe frowned, clearly frustrated with me. "All right, we'll go back for her. But if she isn't at the bridge, you must promise to leave at once."

I agreed. We walked hurriedly toward our meeting place, the Pont Alexandre III.

"You'll be able to catch an omnibus from the gates to the base of the Butte, and hire a carriage from there to your grandmother's."

"You aren't coming with us?"

"No, I can't. I'm sorry. I'll wait until you are with Babette, but I can't leave the grounds with you. Please, just follow my directions."

We had reached the bridge. Its golden statues reflected the bright sunshine as if they were beacons to a better life, yet I spotted a trio of rough-looking *clochards* huddled in the shadows underneath. The tramps reminded me all was not glitter and gold, not for everyone in Paris.

In her crimson dress and parasol, Babette was easy enough to spot. She leaned over the rail in the middle of the bridge next to a well-dressed older man. He held one hand on her waist and pointed to something below.

"*Allô!* Babette!" I waved.

Babette turned and waved her red parasol. "Allô!"

I glanced at Philippe. His eyes narrowed as he regarded Babette and her companion.

"Don't look so disappointed we found her," I said, tapping his arm. "She'd be hurt if she knew you disliked her."

Babette embraced her companion before she headed toward us.

Philippe shook his head. "I doubt if she cares much about what others think."

I nodded. That was the one thing I liked about her.

As Babette sauntered toward us, Philippe cleared his throat. "I'm sorry we didn't see more of the Expo. I'd like to make it up to you. We could return to see the Grand Palais and the moving pictures. Or perhaps you'd rather visit the Louvre?"

He wanted to see me again! I wanted the same thing, yet I needed to find Grand-mère.

Philippe's gaze bored into me.

"I do intend to visit the Louvre soon . . . ."

"Shall I send a note to your grandmother's apartment again?"

My mind raced for a way around the portiere. "There's a nearby café in Place du Tertre, La Bohème. What about Wednesday, say at eleven?" That would give me a full day to find my grandmother.

"Two days from now, then." He glanced at his watch again. "You won't need to invite Babette. I'll bring a chaperone—in case your grandmother isn't up to joining us."

I looked at him sharply. His eyes glinted and for a moment, I was afraid he suspected I hadn't been entirely truthful with him.

He placed neatly folded francs into my hand. "This is for the cab fare. Au revoir."

My cheeks flushed. No one had ever thrust money into my hands before. True, he'd asked for the outing, and I naturally assumed he would pay for everything. Still, a strange distaste filled me.

Babette caught up to me. "Where's he going?"

"He was called away suddenly."

"How very strange," she said, frowning.

Strange, indeed. We watched him disappear into the crowds. His words of warning returned to me. "It's not safe here." Assured I would leave the grounds, he was running toward whatever unnamed danger his colleague had warned him about in the mysterious note.

Henri arrived that evening and whisked Babette away to the Moulin de la Galette. I was content to spend the night alone. It was raining again, so I stayed indoors, the attic's tiny window propped open for fresh air.

I flipped through my sketchbook looking for something to render in pastels, something suitable for Madame Chaudière, and stopped at an early family sketch. Papa and Maman, seated together on the settee, posture stiff. Maman's expression was severe, Papa's amused. "I miss you," I whispered and stroked their faces with my thumb.

On the following page, Charles posed beside his gasoline powered bicycle with his arm in a sling, riding goggles in his good hand. I chuckled. He'd been as excited as a boy when the bike newly arrived, but an hour later, he limped home, one arm fractured. It hadn't deterred him in the least. A pang of loss hit me. Soon he would leave for Canada. I swallowed back tears. I might never see him again!

After flipping through more family sketches, I chose one from a vacation four years ago. Our entire family had gone to Dinard in Brittany, just after Grand-mère had left. We rented a house by the sea for an entire month, although Papa often returned to Laval for business. My brother and sisters and I spent much time together on the promenades along the beach during the day or playing cards in the evenings. One hot day, we ventured into the frigid Channel water, all in modest bathing costumes. Maman surprised us by sitting on the sand nearby, watching as she embroidered yet more handkerchiefs for our *trousseaux*.

The sheer delight of shoving and splashing my siblings as if we were young toddlers washed over me again. It was a time of pure fun. Try as I might, I could not bring to mind any other like it.

I readied my pastels and considered how to use the sketch for a proper composition, fighting melancholy. As my hand hovered over the paper, I recalled sketching Philippe's portrait. Philippe—the last I'd seen of him, he was rushing toward some unnamed danger. Was he safe? There was nothing I could do, either to help or to discover how he was. The best way to deal with worry was to throw myself into my work.

With a deep sigh, I began to work, determined to imbue this piece with the sense of frivolity and spontaneity that had inspired it. While we'd never have the chance for such a day again, I longed to re-capture its magic. A tribute of sorts to innocence, to carefree times. Hours later, after making good progress, I yawned and set the drawing aside. Sleep came easily.

"Mon Dieu!"

I jolted awake. Someone—no, at least two people—burst into the room. Giggling, stumbling in the dark.

Drunk.

"Merde!" Henri's voice, slurred and angry. "My toe's been broken on your goddamned wash stand."

I clutched my covers to my chest and dared not breathe. Did he know I was here?

The sound of clothes being removed, tossed aside. Bedsprings squeaked. Dear Lord! He crawled in bed with her!

"*Mon amour*," Babette murmured.

Henri began to sing an off-key rendition of *La Marseillaise*. "*Allons enfants de la Patrie, le jour de gloire est arrivé . . . !*"

Babette giggled.

"*Aux armes citoyens. Formez vos bataillons . . . .*"

I stifled a groan and clapped my hands over my ears. Please make him sleep.

He belted out a few more lines and then, blessedly, began to snore. But it was impossible to get back to sleep. I lay on my back, staring into the dark. In the same room as a man all night! How could Babette put me in such an intolerable situation?

Stiff with tension and exhaustion, I rose pre-dawn and dressed quickly without the benefit of a lamp. Anxious to leave before Henri awoke, I grabbed my art box and paper, slipped downstairs, and bought a coffee from a street vendor, a *baguette* at the nearest *boulangerie*, and a copy of *Le Figaro* from the newsstand. I took stock of my dwindling supply of coins. Fifty more centimes gone.

I spread out the paper on a nearby bench and scanned the headlines. If anything terrible had occurred at the Expo, the newspaper would report it. Nothing. Fear for Philippe's safety became annoyance. Had he deceived me? What reason could he have had to abandon us at the Expo? Doubts and possibilities plagued me as I replayed our conversations the previous day. We'd had fun, but we also sparred. Had he simply tired of my difficult opinions? But the note was real. I'd seen it with my own eyes, even if I hadn't seen its contents.

The front page of the newspaper was devoted to an evolving scandal about a senior military official and his German mistress. It made accusations about the improper disclosure of confidential political information and referenced the Dreyfus Affair, which was still unresolved in the public's opinion.

The article prompted another thought. Perhaps the mysterious note Philippe received was actually from a mistress, and he had to rid himself of me so they could meet. An ugly and unwelcome anxiety settled into me. By the time I finished consulting my city map for directions to the *La Fronde* office, it hit me: I was jealous.

With great effort, I shoved thoughts of Philippe aside and descended Montmartre, heading southwest to the 9th arrondissement. Grand-mère deserved my full attention. I had to find her and ensure her safety. And I had to keep my eyes on my dream, which most certainly did not include any man, not even Philippe.

The premises of *La Fronde* at 14, rue Saint-Georges were easy enough to locate. Inside, there wasn't a man in sight. A rather stout woman in a prim shirtwaist and long skirt rushed past me, clutching a sheaf of paper. The receptionist, a petite elderly woman, regarded me over her spectacles, nose pinched. "What do you want?" she demanded brusquely.

"I . . . ." Had I made a mistake in coming here? Séverine's name was the only real clue to my grandmother's friends in the city. I straightened my shoulders and raised my chin. "I'm looking for a journalist named Séverine. I'm told she works here. Is she in?"

"Who are you?"

"Mademoiselle Gabrielle de Villiers."

She sighed and rose with visible effort. "Stay here."

"She won't know me," I added, "but please tell her I'm a granddaughter of Lucille Cribiere."

Her eyebrows rose at the mention of Grand-mère's name, and I wondered whether or not that was a good thing. I didn't have to wait long to find out. A middle-aged woman walked briskly toward me in a light shirtwaist, a large cream bow tied at the neck. A long, plain skirt fell from her narrow belted waist. Her red hair, carelessly pinned back, was striking, as was her face, full of interest and liveliness. She was definitely the woman in Grand-mère's photograph.

She held out both hands to me. "So, you are Lucille's granddaughter?"

"Oui, Madame." My knees wobbled as I accepted her grasp. Merci Dieu! How good to finally talk to someone who knows Grand-mère. "It is so very kind of you to see me. Thank you."

She waved off my thanks. "Please, come." She led me down a narrow hallway to a small office. An upholstered chair sat behind an untidy desk heaped with papers and files. Beside it, a sideboard overflowed with more piles of paper and a small teapot. She motioned to a hard wooden visitor's chair in front of the desk. "Please, be seated. How can I help you?"

"I'm looking for my grandmother. I was hoping you could tell me where she is."

"You need her address?" Séverine opened a drawer and pulled out a book, flipping it open.

I suddenly felt lighter.

She ran her finger down the page, then stopped. "Here it is: 16 rue Cortot."

My shoulders sagged. Another dead end.

Séverine studied me with concern. "Is Lucille in some kind of trouble?"

"Oh, no. At least, I don't think so. It's just that . . . ." A burden shared is a burden halved. That was one of Mémère's sayings. And I wanted so badly to share my story, but I knew almost nothing about this woman, other than she was a friend of my grandmother. Best to stick to an abbreviated version of the truth. "I came to Paris by train last Saturday from Laval, my home, to stay with her for a visit. But when I got to her apartment, they told me she wasn't living there any longer."

Séverine nodded slowly as she listened.

"She left sometime before the end of December," I continued. "I'm very concerned about her and want to make sure she's all right."

Séverine stood and paced her tiny office. "The last time I saw Lucille was at a little Christmas party we held here. She told me that she was looking forward to spending the holidays with friends in Le Havre. She hired on a younger woman as a companion, so I didn't worry about her."

So. Le Havre, not Le Mans. "Do you know the names of her friends there?"

"No. But she never intimated that she was leaving Paris for good. Perhaps she's back in the city now?"

I threw up my hands. "Perhaps. But I'm at a loss for how to find her." I swallowed the note of hysteria that was creeping into my voice. "I've asked residents of her apartment building and spoke to the priest at the church she attended. No one seems to know where she is."

Séverine cocked her head and studied me. I met her gaze, wondering if my appearance stirred up memories of Grand-mère.

"Try to remain calm, Mademoiselle. I will ask around, in case someone else has seen her recently. But there's something you should know." Her voice lowered. "Lucille used to come here frequently when she first moved to Paris. Through her work with the poor, she often visited the women's prison. She insisted I write an exposé of the deplorable state of conditions there. I took it on. Later, she'd drop by and suggest topics for other articles. But in the past year, I've seen much less of her."

"Why? What changed?"

She looked at me with kindness mixed with pity, the same look that Eugénie, the woman at Grand-mère's apartment, had given me. "I think she was suffering in her mind, perhaps a form of dementia. She started to repeat herself and would forget simple things, like someone's name or a date. Those are natural effects of age, of course, but so unlike the Lucille I knew. Once, she told me a wild story about the Paris police following her, questioning her neighbours and even harassing her. I'm no fan of the gendarmes, believe me, but I couldn't accept that they would treat an elderly woman in that manner."

"One of the residents at her old apartment building told me something similar." I gripped my hands tightly to prevent them shaking. What happened to my dear grandmother since she left home? "When I last saw her four years ago, she was completely sane. I hate to think that she may be losing her mind. And she's all alone."

Séverine bit her lower lip, her brow furrowed. "I am worried, too, Mademoiselle, but I have many friends around the city. I'll do what I can to find her."

"Thank you. Any information would be helpful." My eyes stung with tears. I blinked them back. "What do you think of making inquiries of the police? You may know she was arrested at one time, although it was in Laval. Would involving the police be a mistake?"

"I'm not so sure. As I said, I'm no fan of the gendarmes, although they can be useful at times." She pursed her lips. "Give me a few days to see what I can find out. In fact, why don't you come with me to the Women's Congress at the Expo? It's the best place to find other suffragists. Many would know Lucille."

"Certainly." A weight rose from my shoulders. Finally, another clue to act upon. Perhaps this was the one. "When?"

She checked a calendar on her desk. "How does Thursday morning suit you?"

"Très bien. Where should we meet?"

"Let's make it the west gate to the Expo. Ten a.m.?" She stood.

"Thank you, Madame." I scribbled down Babette's address and gave it to her. "If you do find out anything at all about my grandmother before then, please send a message to me at that address."

She nodded as she looked at the address. "In Montmartre? That's not far from Lucille's apartment."

"I keep hoping I'll turn a corner and there she will be, striding down the street in bloomers." My voice cracked. I had nearly given up on such serendipity.

Séverine reached forward and lightly squeezed my arm. "Lucille will be fine. She's a survivor."

I took a deep breath and stood, praying she was right. As I turned to leave, I remembered Philippe's mysterious note. "Madame, do you know if anything . . . untoward happened yesterday at the Expo?"

She looked startled. "No, I don't believe so. What exactly do you mean?"

"I'm not sure, actually. Never mind. Thank you for your time. I look forward to Thursday."

Back on the street, I reviewed the few facts I had. Grand-mère had been in Le Havre during the Christmas holidays. People who knew her thought she was acting strangely, perhaps suffering delusions. She was afraid of the Parisian police.

What I didn't know made a much longer list. Who were her friends in Le Havre? How could I get in touch with them? Had she returned to Paris after Christmas or boarded a steamship to God knows where? I didn't know whether she had reason to be suspicious of the police, or if she really was suffering dementia. I didn't know if she was even alive.

Oh, Mémère.

What an impossible task. In a city of two million souls, how would I ever find her? And what about me? What would I do if I failed?

Chapter Eighteen

IT WAS LATE MORNING by the time I left *La Fronde*. The sun shone, promising another hot humid day. I shook off fears for Grand-mère. The hunt would resume on Thursday. In the meantime, it was a perfect day to work en plein air.

I needed a cool, shady spot to sketch from. A few blocks shy of the river, I spied the flower girl and her sister again with a full barrow of blooms beside them. I sat on a bench to study the girls without seeming to stare and sketched their figures in black. I coloured the flowers in bright reds and yellows for contrast. The distant spires of Notre Dame Cathedral made an iconic but perhaps foreboding background.

"Gabbi?"

I turned. Julie, the student from Montréal, strode toward me with a sketchpad under her arm.

"Julie! What a nice surprise."

She leaned over my sketch. "What a wonderful idea to use colour so selectively! I've never seen that before."

"Thank you." I blushed with her praise. "Don't you have classes?"

"Every Tuesday we're sent out into the city to be inspired." She laughed and linked her arm through mine. "Let's inspire one another, shall we? Do you need more time here or would you like to find something new to draw?"

"I've got enough that I can finish this later. But give me a moment, will you?" I crossed the street to the flower girl and purchased a bunch of daisies for two sous. I gave her fifty centimes, over twice the stated price, which left me with less than a franc.

"Merci, mademoiselle," the girl curtsied. "Merci." Her little sister, hiding behind her skirts, darted out as I was about to re-cross the street and tugged on my hand. "*Merci*," she said in a soft, fluted voice before racing back to the older girl.

I waved to them before crossing back to Julie. The children's gratitude for such a small sale saddened me.

Julie accepted one of the daisies from me and tucked it into her hair. "Where shall we go?"

"You know the city better than I do."

"We could sketch the Cathedral or the Louvre, but they've been done by hundreds of others. Do you want to try somewhere a bit different?"

"*Certainement*. What do you have in mind?"

"One of my favourite places is the menagerie at the Jardin des Plantes; it's the world's largest zoo, but it's a long walk from here." She paused. "How does Place Pigalle sound? It's near where you live in Montmartre, where the artists' models line up for hire. Although I should warn you, their language is from the gutters."

We began walking in a northerly direction. I'd worn my demi-boots for a change, and was glad of it.

Julie hummed a tune while we walked. "There's something I wanted to ask you the other night in the café, but didn't get a chance."

"*Oui?*"

She gave me a sideways glance. "Please don't be offended, but you don't seem like the type of person who would be friends with someone like Babette."

"She's certainly nothing like my friends at home," I admitted. Nothing like Bernadette at all. "I'm afraid I didn't have much choice."

"What do you mean?"

I tried to keep my voice light. "I left home without my parents' permission after they promised me to an old man. I came here to study art, expecting to live with my grandmother. Only she's gone and . . . ." I bit my lip and quickened my pace.

"She moved? Without telling you?"

"She . . . might not have known I was coming." How ridiculous my impulsive flight from home sounded.

Julie's eyebrows rose into her bangs, but she didn't press me. "So, you are all alone."

I swallowed hard. "I met Babette my first day, and she offered to let me live with her."

Julie pursed her lips. "Are you paying her?"

I nodded, not prepared to confess she had all my money.

"And let me guess, the price is very dear."

Avoiding Julie's eyes, I nodded once again.

"May I speak plainly?"

"Of course."

"Beware of her, Gabrielle. She's been part of our group for some time, but lately, she seems to have given up on art completely. Late nights, excessive drinking and dubious male companions are more her style now. She's out for herself, no one else."

Her words confirmed what I'd suspected, yet I felt compelled to defend Babette, all the same. She'd given money to the old woman at Place du Tertre, so there was a heart inside her somewhere. "She is a bit rough around the edges, but I can take care of myself. At least I have a roof over my head until I find my grandmother." I ignored Julie's searching gaze and stared at my feet. "But in the meantime, my money is a bit thin. Too thin to buy canvases and stretchers. Or tubes of oil paints."

"Some junk stores sell used canvases and frames quite cheaply. They sand and re-finish the canvases and then you simply paint over them."

"Oh. I hadn't realized." At home, supplies were never short, and I'd given no thought to the cost of it all. Babette had a stack of canvases in the attic. If she had given up selling them, why couldn't I re-use those? She certainly owed me.

"You could even try some of the suppliers in the 9th arrondissement, on rue Clauzel. Old Tanguy used to take paintings as credit for supplies but his widow—well, I hear she's of a different sort. Perhaps there are others, though . . . ."

"Rue Clauzel?" I made a mental note to try later if nothing else worked out, but it was hard to imagine screwing up the nerve to ask for such an indulgence.

"I could easily loan you some money," Julie said, her tone light. As if it wasn't a matter of pride or delicacy at all.

Tempted? Yes. But impossible to accept. "Non, merci."

"Gabbi." Julie put her hand on my arm. "I imagine tuition for art school depends on your grandmother also? Please don't be offended by my suggestion, but perhaps the Julian has scholarships for students who . . . who might need some assistance."

I stopped walking and stared at her. She was suggesting that I beg for charity at the academy, that I confess my sordid story to the very people I'd hoped to find a place amongst. I shook my head. "I . . . I couldn't."

"I know it would be hard," she said softly. "But what's the worst that might happen? They could say 'no,' and you're no worse off." She tore a piece of paper from her sketchpad, roughed out a map and wrote down an address on it—La Passage des Panoramas. "You'll find me in the women's studio upstairs, through the arcade. Speak with Amélie. She's Monsieur Julian's wife and administers the women's ateliers. Most classes are suspended during the summer, but there's a few of us who toil away every morning except Tuesdays. I'll come with you to see Amélie, if you like."

"Merci." I slipped the address into my pocket, rubbing it between my fingers. It wasn't a magic lamp I could summon a genie with, but it was worth trying, wasn't it? If I could humble myself. "I could meet you there this Friday morning, if you'll be there?"

"Absolutely."

As we resumed walking, my stride lengthened, and my feet nearly floated over the sidewalk. Possibilities beckoned once again. Shops along the way shone with a golden patina that had nothing to do with the bright morning sunshine and everything to do with my future. Maman would be horrified at the thought of me begging for a scholarship. Truly, I felt slightly nauseous about it too. Yet somehow, it would be worth it. I wouldn't be the first artist to make sacrifices for her art. And if it worked out, I'd soon brush shoulders with other artists, trading critiques, creating the art that was burning inside me.

We arrived at a large square with shops, cafes, and apartments on all sides.

"Here we are. Place Pigalle," Julie said.

In one corner of the square, a gypsy woman danced to music by an accordion player whose upturned hat was filled with coins. Young children perched on the edge of a large fountain in the centre of the square, giggling and pushing one another under its spray.

Julie pointed to a group of woman gathered around the fountain. "See those women? They're hoping to be picked up as models."

I gazed at the ragtag group. Varying ages and appearances, they slumped against the stone, smoking cigarettes and talking. Small children clutched skirts. One woman nursed a baby, breasts bared.

This was not Laval. I shuddered. I'd told Babette I would model for Lachance. Could I do what these women did? "Modeling for an artist would be hard enough, but I simply couldn't display myself here like a fatted calf at market."

Julie made a strange, strangled noise deep in her throat. "Oh, you'd be surprised what some women have to do to make a living."

I stared at her. What an odd thing to say. Her words brought back snatches of whispered conversations, gossip about girls who had lost their reputation by being alone with a man. Girls who ended up pregnant or in houses of ill repute on the fringes of town. But surely modeling for a well-known artist such as Lachance was respectable, an entirely different thing altogether from these women gathered around the fountain.

We found an open bench in the square and sat in companionable silence. I studied the would-be models for a time. A much older woman caught my eye. She had to compete with much younger, more beautiful women, yet her expression held only *hauteur*. I drew her lined, narrow face and framed it with grey-streaked chestnut hair that hung in dank strands down her back. And if that weren't enough to advertise her circumstances, she wore heavy sabots. Compassion welled within me, but something about her demeanour and expression rejected pity. I created several studies of her—alone and with the other models—weighing each one's suitability for Madame Chaudière.

I glanced at Julie. "I've been invited to bring my work to a potential patron's salon."

"Oh, Gabbi! That sounds wonderful! How did that happen?"

I added a few strokes to my drawing. "It was pure luck. I was sketching a woman near the base of Sacre Coeur and she saw me. She marched over and demanded I show her the drawing, and she actually liked the caricature I'd done of her!"

"Luck indeed! She saw you have talent. When is her salon?"

"This Friday." So soon. A lump of anxiety formed in my belly. "I can bring a friend. Would you . . . could you come with me?"

Her shoulders slumped and she frowned. "Oh, I so wish I could. I've never been to one. But I promised my aunt and uncle that I would take care of my cousins that night."

"It's fine." I bit my lip. There was no one else I could invite to the salon—certainly not Babette.

"I'm sorry." Julie sighed and put down her pencil. "I'm going to miss Paris."

"You're not leaving!"

"Not quite yet. I won't go home until I see my painting hanging at the Paris Salon this summer. I've worked too hard to miss that, but I miss my family."

I nodded, understanding. I'd only been gone four days but found myself thinking about home more frequently than I expected. Something as simple as the aroma of freshly baked baguettes from a boulangerie inspired a wave of longing. "Tell me about Canada. My brother is emigrating there soon."

"Where is he going?"

"St. Boniface, where my uncle Luc lives." I frowned. "I'm not sure where that is, actually."

"It's in Manitoba, but I haven't been that far west so I can't tell you about it." She smiled. "Canada's a big country—so much bigger than all of Europe in fact, yet so new. I've barely been out of my home province of Quebec. I can tell you about the city of Montréal, though. It's nothing like Paris, but it's a large city by our standards."

"But not large enough to have a good art school?"

"Oh, no. There's quite a good school, run by the Art Association of Montréal. I studied there under William Brymner and Maurice Cullen for two years. They are well-known and respected artists that have studied abroad, including at the Julian here in Paris, and exhibited widely. They both encouraged me to come to Paris to see the great Masters in person, and to study and exhibit to advance my career. But my parents were afraid to allow me to travel so far from home, so they sent me to New York for a year of study."

"How did you like New York?"

Her face lit up. "There's an energy to the place like nowhere else I've been. As if everything important is happening there on that tiny island—art, dance, drama, business!"

"It sounds marvellous."

"Oh, yes." She nodded enthusiastically. "It has the largest art museum in America, the Metropolitan Museum of Art. And there's a terrific art community and lots of schools, private ones and the universities. In some ways, I liked it better than here. There's a sense of innovation and freedom for women as well as men. But I learned in New York that one has to exhibit in Paris to establish the necessary reputation."

"Why not go back to New York instead of Montréal?"

Julie blushed. "Montréal has something—someone—no other city has."

"Tell me about him!"

Her eyes softened as she described her beau, Daniel. He was well educated and worked in the university's science department. He even sounded romantic; he wrote long letters to her every day she was away.

"Still, is he really worth leaving Paris for?" I couldn't help but think of Philippe and our promised date the next day. Was it a relationship worth continuing? He'd called me a "modern woman" and claimed he was teasing, but I still suspected he was no admirer of *la femme nouvelle*. "I'm not sure any man thinks a woman should be serious about art, or any other career."

Julie laughed. "Well, Daniel wasn't very open-minded about my artistic endeavours at first, but he really doesn't have much choice. Not if he wants a future with me."

"Ah, it sounds as if you are very serious about him." I was still determined to never marry, but I wouldn't have minded being so happy, so obviously in love.

"We're secretly engaged," she said. "When I get back home, we'll tell our families."

"Why keep it a secret?"

She frowned. "Parents are no different in Canada than they are here. Daniel isn't Catholic and I'm not Jewish."

"Mon Dieu! You're very brave."

"No braver than you, Gabbi, leaving home on your own to pursue your art."

I shook my head. No, not brave at all. If the baron hadn't forced my hand, no doubt I'd still be home, dreaming about making my own way instead of actually doing it. I had to thank Maman and the baron for my being in Paris! I smiled.

Julie and I went back to our work, helping one another with perspective and shading, and chatting about the other students at the Lapin Agile. Julie's easy nature was so similar to Bernadette's. How I missed my old friend.

"I wish you weren't leaving Paris," I admitted.

"It won't be for a few months yet. But I know what you mean. We've only just met, and I feel as if we'll become best friends." She reached over and squeezed my hand. "But we have the summer, n'est-ce pas?"

"Oui." I couldn't help wishing I'd met Julie instead of Babette when I first arrived in the city. How different my life in Paris would have been.

"Perhaps," Julie said, "if your brother is moving to Canada, surely you will come to see him. You'll have to travel through Montreal on your way west, so you can visit me!"

"Me? Travel to Montreal? I've never thought beyond Paris."

"But you must!" Julie tore out a sheet of paper and scribbled down an address. "I've written my parents all about you, and I know they will be delighted to welcome a friend of mine."

I folded the slip of paper and tucked it into my pocket with a shiver of anticipation. Perhaps the world was much more accessible than I'd ever thought. Daydreams of transatlantic steamships and foreign art exhibits formed in my mind. Was it even possible? Why not?

"It's getting late. I'm expected for dinner." Julie packed up her materials. "You know, Gabbi, the École des Beaux-Arts doesn't charge tuition. You simply have to write the entrance exams. Although I don't know how often they offer them." She wrinkled her nose. "I hear the men make it nearly im-possible for women to study, though."

I shrugged. "I think I could stand that, but I can't write the entrance examinations without my baccalaureate. I've only my *brevet*." I had only myself to blame for that, but studying another two years for the *bac* had seemed impossibly long and unnecessary. "In any event, they don't allow women in the life drawing classes at the Beaux-Arts. Madame Magne, my art teacher, insisted I need to draw live models. It's why she recommended the Julian, so I'm not ready to give up on it quite yet. And that ultimately depends on finding Grand-mère."

"I hope you locate her very soon."

"Thank you." I quelled a sudden stab of guilt. I'd spent hours sketching and thinking about Friday's salon when I could have been searching for Grand-mère. But that seemed an impossible task. "I'm beginning to doubt I'll ever find her. I've asked around everywhere I can think of. I even located one of her friends, but she didn't know any more than I did." I swallowed the fear rising in my throat.

Julie slapped her forehead. "I'm such an *imbécile*. My uncle is an inspector of the Sûreté. I will ask him to help."

"The Sûreté?" France's national police force. I could feel the blood leave my face. "That is a kind offer, but please, do not bother him about this, Julie. If I need his help, can I contact you, and we can ask him then?"

Her eyebrows arched but she didn't press me. "So I will see you Friday morning at the Julian?"

"Absolutely. Thank you."

She hesitated, then opened her portfolio and handed several sheets of paper to me. "I've extra watercolour and pastel paper. Take these."

My cheeks flushed. "I couldn't."

"Don't be silly. It's no time to be unnecessarily proud. And it would make me happy to know you can use them. Truly." She smiled, her voice gentle.

"Merci." I slid them into my art box, burning with humiliation. So this is what it's like to accept charity. Better get used to it, if I'm to go begging at the Julian.

"Au revoir!" Julie crossed the street and waved before boarding the omnibus. As I began the uphill climb to Montmartre, I thought of what lay ahead. Somehow, I'd find Grand-mère and life would be back on track. Her reappearance would solve so much.

But what if I couldn't find her?

I shoved the question away. I would continue working on paintings for Madame Chaudière. I would demand more of my money back from Babette to buy canvases for oil paintings, for those were what Madame preferred most of all. If Babette refused, I'd be forced to take her canvases and paint over them, as Julie had suggested.

My feet nearly flew up the stone stairway to rue Gabrielle.

When I entered the apartment, Babette stretched like a cat and yawned, still in her nightgown.

"You've slept all day?" I asked. "It's nearly evening."

She laughed. "What's it to you?"

"Nothing, except that you and Henri woke me during the night with your mad singing and clomping around."

She shrugged, unconcerned. "It's none of your business."

I gasped. "You're wrong! It's very much my business. I'm not comfortable with a man sleeping in our attic."

"Our attic?" She snorted. "I'll invite who ever I wish to sleep over."

My cheeks flamed. This was intolerable. I had to get away, but I needed money for that. "I need money—my money—for canvases and paint."

"I told you. It's all spent." She picked at her sleeve, eyes averted.

"Then I have no choice. I have to sell some art." I picked up an amateurish rendering of the Eiffel Tower, clearly intended for the tourist trade, and held it at arm's length. "I'll just paint over this one."

"Give that back!" Babette wrenched the painting from my hands and clutched it to her, chest heaving.

Her vehemence surprised me. "I thought . . . ."

Her face crumpled and her lower lip quivered. Tears formed in the corners of her eyes. Her armour of bravado slipped momentarily, revealing a sensitive, damaged child beneath all the rouge, lipstick, and garish clothing.

For a moment, I stared in alarm. I touched her arm, but she jerked away. "Forgive me, Babette. I . . . I didn't know you still cared about any of this." Shame flooded over me. I couldn't steal another artist's dreams, no matter how tattered. "Never mind about the canvases. I can do pastels or watercolour instead. Please, forgive me."

With visible effort, Babette straightened her shoulders. She wiped her eyes with the back of her hand, streaking her cheeks with her makeup, and strode to the door. She paused, as if gathering her strength, before throwing parting words over her shoulder. "You'll see what it's like. To fail, to realize you'll never be an artist, just a cheap—" She choked back a sob, jerked the door open and fled.

I stood rooted to the spot as her heels pounded down the stairs. Her parting words echoed in the airless, dingy room. It wasn't difficult to guess what words she'd choked on. Just a cheap *putain*. Whore. Prostitute. Tears sprang to my eyes. The rawness in her voice, the glimpse of her shame in that unguarded moment—she deserved compassion, not condemnation or humiliation.

Shaking, I returned her painting to the stack. I donned my smock, unfolded my easel, and pinned up one of Julie's sheets of watercolour paper. The image of Babette's pain haunted me as I spread out my paints and brushes. She had probably been a lot like me when she first came to Paris, full of hope and sure of her path. Despite the heat, a shiver of fear ran down my spine. What happened to her? What separated my fate from hers?

Something fierce rose up from deep within me. I shot up and paced the room. No! I wasn't going to become Babette. I couldn't!

Unlike her, I wasn't alone. I had Julie's offer to help me get into the Académie Julian. I still had hope that I would find Grand-mère and have her support too. I suspected Philippe would be more than willing to help me also, if I could bend my pride enough to ask. And I had a deep faith in my destiny to be an artist. It wasn't as if I had a choice. I had to create art. Somehow, if I tried hard enough, it would all work out in the end.

But if I didn't actually create anything, nothing else would happen. I forced Babette from my mind and returned to my sketches. What was best—the flower girl by the Seine or the old model at Place Pigalle? I sighed deeply. Until I better understood my potential patroness's tastes in art, I should create a safer composition

I chose an earlier sketch of the tenth century castle in Laval. After reproducing the scene outlines, I looked over my limited selection of paint—a split-primary palette, warm and cool tints of each of the three primaries. I'd left most of my paints at home, certain that Grand-mère would buy me a full set of everything I needed. These would have to be enough: Cadmium scarlet, Quinacridone carmine, Cadmium yellow medium, Cadmium lemon, ultramarine blue and phthalo blue-green, plus black and white. I wet my brush and dipped it into the blue-green, welcoming the familiar thrill that pulsed through my veins as I worked.

Babette's bitter words crept back into my thoughts. Would I end up a failure too? Every cell in my body resisted the accusation. Madame Magne had praised my work. Madame Chaudière liked my sketches enough to invite me to her Salon. And Julie saw something fresh in my style. She was only five years older than me, yet she already had a painting accepted at the Salon. Why not me? With those settling thoughts, I focused solely on my task.

Hours later, I stood back, stretched, and tried to view my painting as a critic would. The old castle made a striking composition with its medieval tower and stone walls looming beside the medieval bridge that arched like a cat's back over the Mayenne. Graceful weeping willows skimmed the riverbanks to create a strong contrast against unyielding stone walls. I hoped the bright blues I'd used for the small boat, the shutters on the lockmaster's house, and a fisherman's smock weren't too bold for Madame Chaudière's tastes.

It wasn't finished, though. It was missing the final brushstrokes that would set it apart. I worked until late evening, not stopping until the lamp light sputtered, nearly depleted of oil. As I cleaned my brushes and packed my paints, Victor Hugo's words returned to me, and I wondered if I had courage to be the bird who sang despite alighting on boughs too slight, for she had wings.

Chapter Nineteen

I AWOKE THE NEXT MORNING with a smile on my face, for I'd dreamed all night of my first visit to the Louvre. In my dreams, I had been the only patron in the museum and had run freely from gallery to gallery. The thrill of being amongst the great masterpieces I'd only seen reproduced in art journals lingered long after I had risen. It stirred a desire to paint, Friday's salon never far from my mind.

Babette was, of course, still sleeping so I dressed quietly. I had a few hours to wait before meeting Philippe at the Place du Tertre. What would he have to say about the Expo and the so-called danger there? I passed the next few hours sketching the attic's interior, but tore them all up. Finally, I could wait no longer and set out for the square. Clouds filtered the sun's heat, promising a pleasant day. By the time I arrived at La Bohème, Philippe was already seated at an outdoor table beside a much older woman.

"Bonjour, Gabrielle." He rose and greeted me. "This is Madame Pinot, my aunt and landlady. She's our chaperone for today."

"Bonjour, Madame." The woman's severe appearance reminded me at once of Maman. She wore an armour of black crêpe de Chine. Her hair was parted in the centre and pulled back to a tidy knot at the nape of her neck. A brilliant yellow straw boater hat, festooned with ribbons and flowers, was her one saving grace. "Thank you for coming today, Madame Pinot."

"It's my duty," she said in a clipped tone, glaring at me from under the brim of her hat. "Philippe is like a son to me."

Ah, that explained her fierce expression.

"I thought we could have lunch here before going to the museum." Philippe held a chair out for me.

"That sounds wonderful." I took a seat and read the menu, failing to quell the growling in my stomach as I considered a selection of delicious options for lunch. Cassoulet or quiche; beef sandwich or roast capon? Wouldn't it be glorious to order them all?

The waiter appeared with coffee and took our orders. Against all rules of etiquette, I chose the heartiest chicken meal on the menu. I thought I detected a glint of amusement in Philippe's expression and perhaps, satisfaction. No doubt he was thinking something unflattering about my unseemly appetite, but I was too hungry to care.

"Did you stay long at the Expo on Monday?" I asked, watching his face closely.

"No, I left shortly after you," he said, evenly. But his mouth tightened, and his eyebrows drew together.

"I read yesterday's papers. Nothing unusual was reported at the Exposition." What was he hiding?

Madame Pinot looked at me sharply, then at Philippe. "What's going on, Philippe?"

"Nothing, *Tante*," he said, patting her hand. "I had to leave the Exposition on short notice, for business reasons. Gabrielle and her chaperone had to find their own way home, I'm afraid."

I noted his emphasis on the word chaperone and had to smile. Babette had been an absolute disaster. I also noted his excuse, if that's what it was. Business reasons? What kind of work would bring him into personal danger? "Speaking of business, Philippe, you've still not told me what it is you do."

"As I told your chaperone, business should never be discussed during pleasure." He tipped cream into his coffee. "How have you enjoyed the city so far?"

"I have met one mysterious man," I said, keeping my voice light while thinking of the times I thought I'd spied him lurking in the shadows.

"Ah," he said, meeting my gaze with intensity. "And what were you up to yesterday?"

"I spent the day sketching. And reading the paper."

Philippe gazed at me, his lips pursed. "I assume you also found time to register at the Académie Julian."

"I'm going there on Friday to do just that." I looked away so he wouldn't guess I would be going to beg. Every mention of art school served as an unwelcome reminder of what I wasn't accomplishing. When I dared to glance at him again, he was frowning. Surely he guessed that something was not right.

"The Julian? Is that one of the women's studios?" Madame Pinot asked, her lips pursed.

"No, Madame, they teach both women and men. The women's only studios don't allow the use of live models."

She drew a sharp breath. "Live models, Mademoiselle? Do you mean models without . . . clothing?"

I nodded, slightly amused.

"That's highly indecent."

"Why? The human body is beautiful. It is important to draw it in the flesh."

"Well, I never!" Madame Pinot exclaimed. She fanned herself with vigour. I concealed a smile behind my hand.

"Gabrielle has very strong views about many things," Philippe said.

"Yes, I can see that," she replied with starch in her voice. "Please excuse me. I believe I see someone I know." She pushed her chair out with a metallic screech and walked brusquely away.

"Well, you've made quite an impression on my aunt." He grinned.

"Sorry."

We sat in silence for a moment before he laid his hand near mine on the table. "Are you ashamed of my company, Gabrielle?"

"Not at all. Why would you say such a thing?"

"I haven't yet met your grandmother. Either you don't want her to meet me, or she doesn't exist. Which is it?"

"Oh." I looked away, my mind spinning.

He leaned closer. "You can trust me. What's wrong?"

I wanted to tell him the truth. "What I told you on the train—about my grandmother—"

"Where is that *garçon*?" Madame Pinot returned in a huff, her neck craned as she looked in vain for our waiter.

Philippe frowned, but rose dutifully to hold her chair. "I'm sure he'll be along soon, Tante."

"Please continue, Gabrielle," he said to me.

I bit my lip and shook my head. I couldn't bear his aunt's righteousness. Perhaps it was for the best. He certainly had his own secrets. And telling him my troubles would have been as good as admitting I couldn't make my own way. Life with Babette was becoming intolerable, but with Séverine's help, I'd soon find Grand-mère. Then, and only then, could I confess to him everything I'd been through. He would have to admit that I could manage quite well on my own. I was relieved, of a sudden, that I hadn't told him anything at all.

"Gabrielle?" Philippe repeated. "What were you saying?"

"Nothing of any importance," I said, meeting his gaze.

Madame Pinot sniffed loudly and narrowed her eyes as if the very sight of me was displeasing.

The waiter appeared at that moment and placed our meals before us. My mouth watered. As I cut into the meat, the sweet scent of tarragon rose flooded me with memories of Cook's delicious meals, generously spiced with fresh herbs from our *jardin potager*. No regrets, I reminded myself, for I was soon to experience the greatest art museum in the world.

After lunch, Philippe left briefly to hire a fiacre from the nearest cab stand. The air between myself and Madame Pinot nearly crackled with tension until he returned and escorted us to the waiting cab.

The cab stopped on rue de Rivoli. We approached the Louvre on foot through the Place du Carousel. Barely glancing at the enormous monument to politician Léon Gambetta, I stopped in front of the ornate façade of the Louvre Museum and simply breathed in deeply, for I stood on the threshold of my dream. In a moment, I'd be inside this monument to the allure and power of art.

Its carved stone walls extended for blocks along the Seine. The Louvre had endured for seven centuries and would undoubtedly endure hundreds of years more. Waiting inside were the very best of the world's paintings, sculptures, decorative arts, graphic arts, and antiquities. Tears pricked my eyes, and I clasped my hands to my chest.

Philippe moved closer to me, touching my elbow. "What's wrong?"

"Nothing. Nothing whatsoever." I accepted his arm, nearly skipping beside him.

His dour aunt shot me a dark look.

Philippe strode to reception, paid our admissions, and came back waving a *Guide Populaire du Musée du Louvre.* "What do you want to see, first? The paintings, I imagine?" He handed the guide to me.

The contents included a map with the layout of the galleries and listed the major exhibits on each floor. I hesitated, torn between rushing upstairs to the galleries of famous paintings or delaying such gratification and savouring the entire experience. "Perhaps the ground floor pavilions first? I want to leave the best for last."

His eyebrows rose but he agreed. When we stepped into the first pavilion of Greek and Roman sculptures, I wondered with a smile how our chaperone would react to such stony displays of nudity.

Madame Pinot lasted only a few minutes. "Philippe! Why in heaven's name did you bring me to such a place? I can't tolerate this indecency." Muttering in disgust and crossing herself, she announced that she would wait for us by the entrance to each of the rooms.

"We seem to have trouble finding a suitable chaperone," Philippe said, his voice laced with humour.

I nodded in agreement. We stopped in front of Michelangelo's *Dying*

Slave—a larger-than-life male body. Unclothed. My first encounter with male genitalia and it had to be on a statue over seven feet tall. My cheeks flamed, fully aware of Philippe standing next to me. What kind of artist was I if the human body provoked such a reaction in me? I ordered my cheeks to cool. "Perhaps Madame will find other galleries less unsettling," I muttered.

Philippe laughed softly. "Perhaps."

Each time we exited one gallery to the square before re-entering the next, I was afraid Madame Pinot would demand we leave. Fortunately, the exotic displays in the departments of Roman and Greek Antiquities, and the Egyptian and Assyrian exhibits were more acceptable to her sensibilities. I even caught her eyes alight now and then as she examined cases of gold amulets and elaborate pectoral necklaces from Egypt. Philippe kept a proper distance as we viewed sarcophagi, bronze lions, the famed armless statue of Aphrodite, and exotic sculptures of human-beast idols.

At last we stood at the foot of the grand staircase that led to the premier étage galleries exhibiting the painting collections. Madame Pinot slumped onto a bench in an alcove, arms crossed, her expression sour.

"My old legs are aching," she said, rubbing her knees. "I can't take another step."

Philippe glanced at me and frowned. "Perhaps we should return another day."

My heart sank. "Oh, please, we've only just begun! I want to see everything."

"Aren't you concerned someone might see us without a chaperone?" He appeared concerned, his lips in a disapproving line, but his tone was off. Was he teasing me, or was he going to insist we leave? I could hardly refuse and stay on my own, not when he was my escort.

I hid my hands behind my back to hide my distress. "Please, don't give up now, Philippe." Mon Dieu, not when the best paintings in the world are so close I could smell them! "I don't know anyone in Paris to worry about gossip."

"Aren't you forgetting your grandmother?" he asked, his eyes pinning me in place.

My cheeks flamed as I was caught in my lie. "Ah, well, of course, but she's at home, indisposed."

"Very inconsiderate of her, if you ask me." Madame sighed heavily, no doubt to remind us she was listening to our repartee.

"We appreciate you taking her place, Tante." Philippe patted her hand before turning to me. "And what of my reputation?" His lips curled into a half smile, and my hands unclenched. He was most certainly teasing, after all.

Much lighter, of a sudden, I lifted my skirt hem and started up the stairs. "I'm certain your reputation would only be enhanced," I said over my shoulder, "if you were to be recognized with an unchaperoned woman."

"Touché," he said with a soft laugh, running to catch up to me.

At the top of the stairs, we consulted the guide once more. The Department of Paintings, at last. So many eras and schools of painting to choose from, so many rooms—the Salle La Caze, Salle Henri II, Salon des Sept Cheminées, and of course, Carré and the Grande Galerie, plus many, many more. Where to begin? Acutely aware of the limits of Madame Pinot's patience, I stood frozen at the top of the stairs. How could I leave without seeing all of the Masters, the Flemish painters, the paintings by the Romantics, or pastel portraits by de la Tour, or . . . oh!

I pressed my hand against my chest and took a deep breath. Once I sold a few paintings, I could come here every day. My heart slowed, and I stepped onto the threshold of the Salon Carré, barely aware of Philippe by my side.

My eyes widened. Framed paintings covered every wall, some stacked three high to the lofty ceilings. Two suited men in top hats swung their canes as they strolled past the canvases and murmured to one another. But for them and us, the room was empty.

I took another deep breath before stepping into the Salon and was immediately assaulted. Colours poured off the canvases. Emperors in crimson and gold uniforms on rearing chestnut brown horses, sorrowful scenes of the crucified Christ against blackening skies, straw yellow corpses writhing in agony amongst flames of violent orange; dying soldiers from violent battle scenes—all bombarded my senses. Tears welled as I turned, slowly, trying to absorb the shock of so much beauty, so much passion.

"What's the matter?" Philippe hovered at my elbow, his voice urgent.

I shook my head, unable to speak. Tears slid down my cheeks. It was if my mind, my heart, and my body were overtaken by these long-dead painters who had thrown their wild imaginations onto the canvases. Lives spent serving the fire burning within, their work leapt from the walls and invaded me.

I don't know how long I stood captive to the images, but eventually I dragged my eyes from the paintings to Philippe's face. He handed me his monogrammed handkerchief.

I took a deep breath, dabbed my eyes with the handkerchief, and tried to summon words to explain. I recalled my lame attempt at defining "what is art" at the Lapin Agile, and felt the heat of shame. I'd had no idea what I was talking about, nor did any of the others, likely. There were no words to capture the magnificence of the paintings on the walls before me. Or the sacrifices those artists must have made to realize their vision. But a sense of it pulsed through my veins, from my heart to my trembling hands.

"It's . . . it's so . . . ." I shook my head and gestured wordlessly at all of the canvases.

"I know." Philippe nodded. "I was overwhelmed on my first visit, too." I must have looked surprised for he laughed softly. "Don't be so shocked. You don't have to be an artist to appreciate great art. Now, come, let's take our time and go through each gallery as slowly as you desire."

Grateful for his patience, I stood before each painting for several minutes, allowing the colours, brushstrokes, and images to wash over me. Slowly, I absorbed the names of individual works and artists. *L'Ange Raphael* and *Le Bon Samaritain* by Rembrandt van Ryn. A portrait, *La Joconde*, by Leonardo da Vinci. So many religious-themed paintings: *Jésus-Christ donne a saint Pierre les clés du paradis* by Jean-Auguste-Dominique Ingres, the *Wedding Feast at Cana* by Veronese, and so many more.

A smaller but luminous Ingres canvas, *The Bather*, beckoned me closer. Delicate light on a woman's naked back as she perched on the edge of her bed made her skin appear so real I yearned to reach out and stroke the canvas. How had he accomplished that quality of voluptuousness and yet simultaneously, a sense she was chaste? The realization of how much I had yet to learn—a lifetime!—washed over me like a wave and tears sprang to my eyes once again.

I moved down the long corridors of the Grand Gallérie as if in a trance, yet every nerve, every cell of my body tingled, alert like never before. I was reborn.

If I were condemned to wander those halls of art for the remainder of my life, I would not be unhappy.

I traversed the galleries several times, the Guide clutched in my hands but almost forgotten, as my gaze fixed first upon the vibrant, living canvases lining the walls, then briefly upwards to the ornate ornamentation of the columns and painted ceilings before returning to the masterpieces. I repeated the names of the artists as I read the descriptions, in awe of each of them while acutely aware that none were women: Delacroix, Fragonard, Decamps, Veronese, Raphael, Titian, Corot, Rembrandt Van Ryn, da Vinci, Rubens.

Each canvas elicited a new wave of emotion, pricking my eyes and making my pulse race. Such loss of control frightened me, but I couldn't bear to leave.

We came upon a whiskered man, hunched over a sketchpad, in front of a massive oil painting, *Dante et Virgile* by Delacroix. The copy artist's figures of the tortured souls writhing beneath the barque weren't nearly as dynamic as the original - but who could ever approach the subject of Dante in Hell once Delacroix had created this masterpiece?

I waited until the copyist paused in his work before speaking. "Is it difficult to get permission to copy here?"

"Are you referring to a *carte de copiste*?" A look of annoyance creased his face. "They don't give them to just anyone." He wrinkled his nose as his gaze swept from my shoes to the tip of my hat before shifting his back to me.

I was glad he'd turned away, so he didn't catch the sting of tears in my eyes or my shaking hands.

Philippe put his hand on the small of my back, ever so briefly, and guided me away from the artist. "Don't let him bother you. You will soon be seated here, an easel in front of you as you create your own masterpieces." He gestured at the upholstered circular bench in the centre of the room.

I sat on the bench and shut my eyes. I imagined squeezing shiny dollops of oily colour from tubes and blending them on my palette. Warmth glowed deep inside. I belonged here.

When I opened my eyes, Philippe's gaze was upon me.

"Thank you for . . . for your encouragement. God willing, I will be back here within the week." I took a deep breath. God willing, for I'd meet Julie at the Académie on Friday, gain admittance, and surely get my carte de copiste then.

We took another grand staircase to the second floor. There, a gallery of drawings and pastels held many sketches by great painters like da Vinci and Michelangelo, done as studies for larger paintings.

"Ah, here she is." I pointed to two pastel portraits by Élisabeth Vigée Le Brun, the eighteenth century artist I'd told Babette about. *Portrait de Jeune Fille,* a portrait of a girl about my age hung next to *Le Baron de Breteuil,* a middle-aged baron. A shiver ran through me as if a hand had stroked the back of my neck. The Baron de Breteuil resembled the Baron d'Argente—the same fleshy jowls, grey eyes, a cupid's bow mouth above a weak chin. The *Jeune Fille* averted her gaze from the baron's portrait as if she were seeking escape. Like me.

Oui, jeune fille, run as fast as you can!

"The Baron de Breteuil," Philippe murmured, his voice low and so close to my ear that I felt his breath upon my neck. "I believe these are the first paintings that I've seen here by a woman."

"I'm sure there are others," I said, "but it is true, very few from prior to mid-nineteenth century. Madame Magne told me that more women are pursuing art seriously, but of course their work isn't here in the Louvre." I smiled at the young girl's portrait and silently promised her I'd be back. "At least, not yet."

"Not yet," he agreed, inclining his head. "Tell me, Gabrielle, is it important for you to see art by other women?" His aquamarine eyes were earnest, and his mouth held no trace of mocking.

I nodded. "All of the masterpieces here in the museum are inspiring, yes. But knowing there are other women who feel the same as me, that art is what we're meant to create, is . . . empowering." My cheeks flushed at my grand statement, but it was true.

"Then I suppose you will search out these women. Where will you find them?"

"Madame Magne first saw paintings by Berthe Morisot, a popular follower of the Impressionist movement, at a private art gallery last year. I suppose that is where I will find more female artists. I have some names to look for— Suzanne Valadon, Mary Cassatt, Marie Bashkirtseff."

We continued down the corridor of the *Salles Des Dessins* toward a large pastel portrait of a seated woman. I approached it slowly, taking in the details of the composition and the skilful use of various shadings of blue. *Portrait of the Marquise de Pompadour*, Maurice-Quentin de La Tour, 1755. 178 x 131 cm.

Philippe stood close by with his hands clasped behind his back, gazing at the portrait. "What do you see when you look at this?"

I took my time, sensing he was truly interested in my opinion. "At first, it's the impression the painting makes, that of a wealthy woman surrounded by her favourite objects. The music scores, the books and novels, portray a patroness of the arts." I studied the pastel in more detail. "Then I take note of the composition. Her body and gown form a pyramid, which gives the painting a dynamic feel. The carpet in the foreground, a *trompe l'oeil*, gives the illusion of depth. La Tour has created a harmonious colour scheme—Spanish blue background paper, grey-blue wall panelling, blue-green shadows on the ruffles of her bodice, her azure eyes . . . ." I glanced at Philippe's eyes and lost my train of thought. Their colour seemed to darken from aquamarine to indigo as our gaze lengthened. Shaken, I broke away first and walked a few paces farther into the room to examine another drawing.

Philippe remained in front of the *Marquise de Pompadour* for several minutes, whether to see it anew or to gather his own thoughts, I could not guess. Had he, too, felt his blood heat or experienced a sudden thrum in his chest? I shook my head to dispel my own feelings. It was the grandeur of the museum and its masterpieces that stirred up such emotion, nothing more.

We spent only a short time viewing the various sketches and studies in that section for I wanted to return to the first floor to the Veronese painting, *The Wedding Feast at Cana*. It occupied an entire wall and depicted the first miracle performed by Christ, turning water into wine. This time, I did more than allow the colours and imagery to wash over me. I studied it for technique.

Philippe followed me silently as my eyes roamed over the canvas, first from across the room and then much closer. He cleared his throat. "I'm so glad that we are here together. It's been quite an education, being the first time I've visited with an artist."

I shook my head. "Amidst all this amazing art, I can hardly call myself an artist . . . yet." The musicians in the foreground of the painting were said to reflect the likenesses of Veronese and other Venetian artists of the time, including Titian and Tintoretto. I turned away from the painting to face Philippe. "Creating art is my life's purpose. And I don't mean painting or drawing as something to occupy my idle time."

His cheeks flushed, as he no doubt recalled his comment on the train about his sister "dabbling" in painting. "I am trying to understand."

"I have to be immersed in it, devoted only to my art. Becoming the very best that I can be demands it."

"An admirable goal. But how will you accomplish it?" His voice teased, but his smile took away any offence.

"If you stay around long enough, you'll find out." I matched his teasing tone and turned back to the Veronese.

He moved closer, so close I fancied I heard his heartbeat. "I accept your invitation." Then he cupped my chin with his hand, turning my head to face him.

My skin warmed under his touch, but I didn't pull away. I held my breath.

He gazed at me for several heartbeats—and then withdrew his hand. He stepped back to a slightly more acceptable distance. "For the record, I believe you will accomplish whatever you set out to do, Gabbi."

It was the first time he'd called me Gabbi. I loved the shape of his lips as he said it. My cheeks flushed. "Thank you."

I'd violated all of Madame Dijon's rules of etiquette. "A lady never speaks about herself. She always directs a conversation to the man—his interests, his work, his opinions," she'd say.

Perhaps her advice was worthwhile, at times.

"You must have a passion that you'd risk everything to pursue." I said.

Philippe shrugged. "I've never thought about it. I have my work, which I enjoy, but that's not the same thing, is it?" His eyebrows drew together. "Does art mean so very much to you? Enough to give up everything else—a marriage, children, a home?"

I thought carefully before answering. "I don't want to reject all of that, but how can I do both? I believe that art is what I have to give. It's what I'll leave behind. My footprints, if you will." I gestured at the Veronese canvas. "Even one painting such as this in a lifetime would be worth the sacrifice, don't you think?"

As we both gazed at the painting, I hoped he could appreciate the vision, the skill, and the passion of such an artist.

"Is it fame and fortune you are seeking?"

"No, although the regard of other artists is important. What I really want, no—what I need—is to create what's in here," I pointed to my head, "and here." I touched my chest. "It's hard to explain. I only know it's what I must do."

"I hope what you seek is what you really want," he said softly, placing his hands on my shoulders. "You are the most frustrating yet intriguing woman I have ever met."

The heat of his hands burned through my shirtwaist. I tipped my head back and met his gaze. He leaned toward me. Eyes closed, I held my breath. I'd never been kissed unless my cousin Anton's kiss in infants' school counted.

Philippe's lips brushed mine so softly that I imagined a butterfly alighting on my lips, yet his kiss lingered long enough that the shape of his mouth was impressed upon my own. I waited for more.

Someone, perhaps the guard by the doorway, coughed.

Philippe dropped his hands. "I'm sorry."

"*Moi aussi*," I whispered back, sorry only that we'd been interrupted.

"We'd best leave," he said, abruptly.

I didn't argue, although I longed to stay. As we descended the grand staircase, Philippe offered me his arm. My hand on his sleeve, his scent—a clean smell of soap, pomade and something very male—just like the day we'd met, when we shared the carriage from the train station. It seemed so long ago, yet less than a week had passed since then. Now here we were in the Louvre, fulfilling a long-held dream of mine. I glanced up at him. Was he already regretting our kiss, or had he enjoyed it as much as I had?

We paused at the base of the staircase. "Thank you for everything." I handed him the guide.

"Please keep it as a souvenir." He covered my hand with his. "It's important to mark one's firsts."

I blushed. Which first of mine was he was referring to?

Our chaperone still sat on the bench where we'd left her, snoring soundly with her chin on her chest.

"Tante?" Philippe touched her shoulder gently.

She blinked and looked around as if for a moment, she didn't remember where she was. She held onto Philippe and managed to stand.

"I'll fetch a carriage." He disappeared outside.

"Madame," I said, "please take my arm and we can walk out together."

She nodded, tight-lipped, and took my arm. As we stepped into the court-yard, late afternoon sunlight washed over us. Madame Pinot spoke to me in a brittle tone. "Philippe has a promising career that requires all his focus. He shouldn't be sidetracked by anything or anyone."

"You don't need to worry about me, Madame," I said. "I have my own career to be concerned about." But her comment stung me back to reality. What on earth was I thinking, indulging an attraction to Philippe? He had, at times, shown that he expects women to be like his sisters—marry, bear children, and run a household. As much as he appeared to be trying, I doubted that he understood art as an obsession, as a life.

What man could accept such a quality in a wife?

Chapter Twenty

ON THURSDAY MORNING, my concern for Grand-mère warred with Friday's impending deadline. I pushed thoughts of Madame Chaudière aside and spent my last franc on admission to the Expo. Then I paced under *La Parisienne*, the larger-than-life female statue adorning the top of its gates.

As I waited for Séverine, I wondered whether a fashionably dressed woman was indeed the right portrayal of the "femme nouvelle." I would have preferred she wore bloomers astride a bicycle. Grand-mère could have posed for that sculpture, I thought with a smile.

"Gabrielle?"

I turned and spotted Séverine waving to me, the large crimson bow atop her straw hat helping me identify her amongst the crowds.

I elbowed my way towards her, surprised at the change in her appearance. At the newspaper office, she'd worn the same blouse and plain skirt as the other women, perhaps a sort of uniform. Yet now she wore a very feminine but tailored suit in robin's egg blue. The skirt silhouette was more slender than mine with buttoned and low-heeled demi-boots peeking out below her hem. She wore a light but well-fitted waist jacket over what looked like a man's shirt, although a frothy crimson bow replaced a cravat.

"Good morning, Gabrielle."

"Good morning, Madame Séverine."

"Just Séverine, please," she said. "I'm sorry I'm late. We'll have to hurry. The Palais de la Femme is at the foot of the Eiffel Tower." She consulted the gold watch pinned to her bosom. "I hope we're in time to hear Marguerite's speech."

"Marguerite?"

"Madame Durand. She owns *La Fronde*. She might be able to help us. She knew—sorry, knows—your grandmother."

Knew my grandmother. Despite Séverine's quick correction, her words hit me in the gut like a fist and took my breath away. "Wonderful," I muttered.

Although I was a good deal taller than my companion, I struggled to keep up with her brisk pace. "What's her speech about?"

"She's introducing a resolution in favor of women's right to the vote." Séverine stopped abruptly, and I nearly ran into her. She pointed a white-gloved finger at me. "Young women such as yourself must take up the cause. Don't be content to entertain at your five o'clock teas or swoon at the first glance from a handsome man."

"I—I won't," I said, but she didn't wait to hear my response. She was off and running, or as close to it as she could manage with her slender skirt and the crowds that seemed to deliberately thwart our forward progress. I lifted the hem of my skirt and scurried to catch up to her.

Séverine glanced at me. "You never told me why you came to Paris, Gabrielle."

"To study art."

"Eh bien!" She grinned. "Have you heard of Auguste Renoir?"

"Oh yes, he was one of the Impressionists, I believe."

"He painted a portrait of me." Her eyes had a faraway look. "When I was much younger, of course."

Once again, I considered Babette's suggestion to model for Gaston Lachance. Konstantin had warned me away from Lachance. But surely if a woman like Séverine modeled for Renoir, I could do so for Lachance. I appreciated the Russian's kindly concern for me, but I hadn't left home for a man to dictate who I spent time with. I would form my own opinion. "Do you have the Renoir portrait? I would love to see it."

"Non, I couldn't afford it, back then." She sighed. "Come, we don't want to be late for Marguerite." She picked up her pace, with me on her heels.

As we approached the Eiffel Tower, a loud female voice sliced through the air. "We are not your playthings!" A short stout woman stood atop the elaborate staircase of the Palais de la Femme, shouting through a megaphone and gesturing wildly with her arms. "We demand respect."

"Merde!" Séverine swore under her breath.

I skidded to a stop beside her.

"We demand equality!" the speaker continued. It was more like a protest than a speech.

A large group of men and women were gathered at the base of the stairs. Some were shouting in reply.

"Return to your kitchen!"

"I pity your husband!"

"Down with petticoat politics!"

The speaker responded to the crowd's jeers. "We have proven ourselves in the domain of men. We are doctors! Lawyers! Scientists!"

"We don't want you outside the home!"

She ignored the hecklers. "Give us our own bank accounts! And we demand more opportunity for our young women!" she shouted.

"Close the universities to women." Ripples of loud agreement followed this comment. "Close the Sorbonne to women!"

"It's only going to get worse," muttered Séverine. "You may wish to leave."

The unmistakable antagonism within the crowd unnerved me, and I was sorely tempted to take her advice. "What about you?"

She regarded me with fiery eyes. "I'm a reporter. Naturally, I'll stay."

I thought of Grand-mère the day I last saw her, leaving me with Papa in the square to join her sister suffragists. "I am staying too."

Séverine elbowed her way through the throng and up the broad stone steps. I followed in her wake until we reached the speaker. Up close, the woman appeared much older than I'd first thought, older than someone I'd have thought capable of such passion and vigor. I looked back down at the crowd, growing louder and angrier by the minute.

"Go home, old woman!"

"Police! Arrest that woman for disturbing the peace!"

Séverine snatched the megaphone from the woman. "Isabelle! Can't you see you're not helping our cause?"

Isabelle glared at Séverine. "I have an opinion. And a right to express it." She jerked her thumb toward the entrance to the Palais de la Femme behind her. "Have you seen what those fools in there are doing? Do you want the world to see Frenchwomen as pretty playthings with air for brains? Nothing better to do with our time but shop, shop, shop? Non! Now give me back my shouter." She reached around Séverine to grab the megaphone, but the journalist was quicker, holding it high.

Heckling from the crowd continued.

"Take her down!"

"Harlot!"

"Putain! Whore!"

Shocked by the profanity, I turned and scanned the crowd, looking for the source. It had been a man's voice. But which one? The older man with a face like a bulldog, jowls piled up in folds against his high starched collar? Or the scowling stocky man in the suspenders and homespun blue shirt? Two bearded men wearing silk top hats and immaculate three-piece suits stood shoulder to shoulder, frowning. Was that malice in their expressions? A woman in a boater hat, her wrist in the grip of an older man, caught my eye as her father—or husband—hauled her away.

Something dark flew through the air toward us. Instinctively, I ducked. Isabelle cried out and I turned. Shattered glass lay in the ground around her. A trickle of blood poured from a cut on her brow. Séverine grabbed Isabelle by the elbow and dragged her toward the pavilion entrance.

Heart pumping, I shielded Séverine and Isabelle with my body, spreading my arms out to fend off the crowd, which was quickly becoming a mob. More bottles shattered around me. A quick glance over my shoulder re-assured me that Séverine and Isabelle were safely inside. Picking up my skirts, I turned and sprinted toward the pavilion.

When the entrance was mere steps away, something struck me in the back of my skull and sent me stumbling forward. Fortunately, I managed to catch myself before falling. But as I stood teetering on the steps with the world spinning around me, I stupidly turned to see what had struck me, and my feet skidded on shards of glass. I fell backward, my elbows striking the stone steps. Dizzy and in pain, I couldn't force myself to rise. Frightened faces peered through the glass entry, but no one came to my rescue.

"Mademoiselle?"

A shadow hovered over me. I blinked. Double images blurred and dis-solved into one: a pair of coffee-brown eyes above a blue tunic with shiny gold buttons. Good. A gendarme.

"I . . . I think I've been hit." I felt the back of my head. When I brought my gloved hand away, it was covered in blood.

The gendarme gave me a handkerchief. "Here, press this against the cut." He helped me to my wobbly legs. "Let's get you inside."

I nodded, dazed, and leaned on him. I glanced back at the crowd. Blue-uniformed gendarmes were scattered throughout, but people were still shouting. Another glass shattered on the steps not far below me. A decidedly too high top hat covering dark curls above a broad set of shoulders slipped in and out of view.

The gendarme tugged on my arm. "Viens, it's not safe here. You must come with me."

"Just a moment."

I searched the jostling crowd again. Gendarmes formed a line in front of the staircase and held people from pushing forward. Hecklers grew louder, perhaps emboldened by the sight of us fleeing inside.

"Shame! Go home!"

"Where are your children?"

There, near the front of the crowd—the face I'd been seeking out. I wasn't mistaken, not this time. And Philippe wasn't alone. A woman clutched his arm rather possessively. She stared back at me. Even from the distance, I couldn't fail to notice her beauty. And she was fashionably dressed in a cream chiffon dress, her blonde hair swept up under an enormous tulle hat.

The gendarme tugged on my elbow again. I allowed him to lead me inside the pavilion, unsure what left me more shaken: the blow to my head or the sight of Philippe with his female companion.

The gendarme led me to a chair and left briefly, returning with an ice-cold cloth. He pressed it against my skull, and the hammering inside my head abated slightly. "Thank you, monsieur."

"*De rien,* mademoiselle," he said. "I only wish we'd arrived sooner to prevent your injury."

I nodded, although I wished I hadn't. Movement brought a new sharp stab of pain. I lifted the cloth away. Still bloody. I pressed it back against the rapidly rising bump. How many others were injured?

Oh no, Isabelle and Séverine!

"The two women I was with . . . Madame Isabelle and Séverine . . . do you know . . . how are they? Isabelle's face was cut and bleeding. She's elderly . . . ." I looked around the chaos in the foyer but couldn't spot either of the women. I stood, but nausea hit me immediately, and I swayed before dropping back into the chair.

The gendarme hovered by my elbow. "Please, mademoiselle, stay seated. I will inquire after your friends."

I leaned back in the chair, my eyes closed, and waited. Is this the kind of chaos Mémère had been part of? Had some of her companions been hurt during the arrests in Laval? Had she faced the same anger and spite demonstrated by the crowd today? Oh, if I could only turn back those four years and remain with her, my arm linked with hers in solidarity. A smile lifted my mouth. She would be proud of me today.

The gendarme broke into my thoughts. "I am sorry, mademoiselle, but do you feel well enough to answer the inspector's questions?"

Before I could answer, a large man pulled a chair in front of me and sat down. An enormous black handlebar moustache nearly obscured his mouth. Shrewd eyes shone out from under the bushiest eyebrows I'd ever seen. My fingers itched for my pencil and sketchpad, so I could capture him. He'd make a wonderful caricature—perhaps a walrus in uniform.

His impressive moustache twitched as he spoke. "Did I hear you say Isabelle and Séverine? Are those the names of the women who stirred up this hornet's nest?"

Blood rushed to my cheeks. Was he suggesting it was Isabelle's fault she was hurt? I struggled to speak evenly and not lose my temper. "Séverine is my friend. Isabelle was the woman who was hurt." I shuddered briefly. How could an elderly woman stir up such intense feeling simply with words?

The inspector opened a small notepad, a stubby pencil at the ready. "Tell me what happened."

I tried to collect my thoughts. "When we—Séverine and I—arrived at the pavilion, the crowd was already agitated. We pushed through to the top of the stairs. There were some hecklers but no violence at first." I paused, trying to figure out how things had escalated so quickly. "We spoke with Isabelle for a few moments. Someone yelled obscenities. Then bottles flew through the air. Isabelle was struck and hurt. Séverine took her inside the pavilion, to safety."

He frowned. "This woman—Isabelle—what had she said?"

Again, the implication of blame. "I wasn't there long enough to hear her speech." I sensed I would soon have to choose where to place my loyalties. I shifted in my chair, distinctly uncomfortable. "Have you managed to arrest the hooligans who attacked us?"

His nostrils flared as if my words offended him. "I am asking the questions, mademoiselle. Are you a part of this Women's Congress?"

"I will be happy to answer your questions, Inspector, but I am most concerned about my friends."

He gave a long piercing look before turning to the younger policeman. "Constable, go find out about the other two."

As I watched the constable do his superior's bidding, a ludicrous thought passed through my mind. The inspector reminded me of my mother. It had nothing to do with his appearance, so it had to be his demeanour. He struck me as someone accustomed to others jumping to his every command. And very little missed his sharp eyes.

"My question, mademoiselle, was whether you are one of these trouble-makers?"

I sat up straighter. "No. I mean, I'm not an organizer. But I am friends with Séverine. We came to hear a lecture by Madame Durand."

"Unfortunately, all speeches have been cancelled for today." A half-smile curled his lips, and I knew he wasn't at all sorry. "I hope this little incident teaches you to be careful about whom you associate with in the future."

"On the contrary, Inspector—"

"Inspector?" The young constable reappeared and bowed to me slightly. "Mademoiselle, your friends asked me to assure you that they are fine."

The Inspector scowled at me, his eyes boring into mine. "Good. I will question them immediately. I believe that you aren't responsible for today's mob, mademoiselle. But as soon as you feel well enough, I advise you to leave the pavilion and stick to the shops and cafes on the grounds. Much safer and more suited to your delicate feminine disposition."

I smiled despite his goading, for Séverine and Isabelle would prove to be more than a match for him.

The constable stayed behind, hovering over me. "It looks as if you are free to leave, mademoiselle, once you are able."

I stood too quickly again and the young man took my elbow, steadying me until I straightened. I shook his hand off. "Thank you. I'm fine now."

He cleared his throat. "I could escort you home, mademoiselle, if you would permit me."

I looked more closely at him, surprised by his suggestion.

His close-shaved cheeks reddened under my scrutiny.

"Non, merci. However, you could assist me by telling me where my friends are."

"The inspector may detain them for some time, mademoiselle. He will ensure they get home safely, so you'd be best advised to go home and contact them later."

"Detain them? They've done nothing wrong."

"That is for the inspector to determine."

"Nonetheless, I wish to wait for them." A thought struck me. "I would appreciate your advice on something else. A hypothetical question, I suppose."

"Oui, mademoiselle?"

"If someone asked you to find a friend who was missing, how would you go about locating her?"

His eyes narrowed. "Hypothetically, you said?"

I nodded, slightly uncomfortable under his scrutiny.

"I suppose I'd talk to relatives and friends of the missing person. Find out her normal routine. That sort of thing."

"And if that didn't work?"

He shrugged. "I'd wait until she turned up. They usually do, you know. If not soon after they've gone missing, then in the hospital or the morgue." He coughed. "You shouldn't be afraid to go to the morgue, mademoiselle. There's a glass wall separating the public from the corpses. Many frequent the morgue for free entertainment. I myself have done so. It's quite educational, I daresay."

Bile rose in my throat, but I swallowed, barely. "I see." I pushed aside the vivid picture he'd portrayed. "Are you familiar with the city's hospitals?"

"We have at least seven, maybe more." He cocked his head. "I'd start with the Hospice de la Salpêtrière or the Hôtel-Dieu de Paris. I believe they are both *hôpitaux d'enfermement.* "

I flinched. "Insane asylums? Why?"

"Mental insanity is often a reason someone goes missing."

A shudder spun up my back. "Which is closest to Montmartre?"

He withdrew a notepad from his tunic. "If you give me your friend's name and address, I will do what I can to find her."

"Oh, no, thank you. It was mere curiosity. Please, forget I even mentioned it."

He frowned. "Perhaps you would give me your name and address, then? In case you change your mind and wish to locate your hypothetical friend."

"Oh, I . . . ." Did I have to give him information? What if Maman and Papa were looking for me? They might have already contacted the police. I couldn't bear being dragged home, defeated.

"Gabrielle?" a familiar voice called out. "Is it you?"

I turned to see Philippe stride toward me. His furrowed brow, those intense blue eyes, tightened my chest. Was it relief I felt at the sight of his solid, familiar male presence? Or something deeper, a longing for his hand on my cheek again? He'd been with a woman, I reminded myself, no doubt more than a mere friend. I shook myself and frowned. I hated the stew of emotions he caused in me.

"I thought I saw you outside." His voice betrayed anxiety, which was gratifying. "Are you hurt?"

I touched the back of my head lightly. "Just a small bump."

The gendarme looked at Philippe with great interest. "Are you a witness? Anything you saw would be of great assistance, monsieur."

Philippe put up his hands. "I'm so sorry, but I didn't see much. I heard the shouting and noise from down the street and was curious. I arrived in front of the pavilion to see you escort Mademoiselle Gabrielle inside."

The man gave Philippe a long look. "If you do recall anything helpful, be sure to contact us."

"Of course, officer." Philippe bowed slightly. "Are you well enough to leave, Gabrielle? I would be most happy to escort you safely home."

"Thank you, Philippe, but I am waiting for my friends."

"Friends?"

The constable put his notepad away and gave me a slight bow. "It appears that you are in good hands, mademoiselle. If you don't need me any longer, I have other duties."

"Thank you. You've been most kind." I was relieved to see him leave. My mind turned to Philippe. Who was his companion, and where was she now?

"Are you certain you are recovered?" Philippe asked.

"As well as can be, considering."

"May I see your bump?"

I nodded.

He turned my chin, so he could see the back of my head. I could feel his fingers gently parting my hair, probing. "Ouch!"

He withdrew his hands. "You should go home and rest. You have probably suffered a concussion."

"I'll leave once I know Séverine and Isabelle are all right."

"Séverine?" His concern transformed into a scowl.

I nodded, forgetting that every movement intensified my headache. "We came to hear an official lecture, but a woman, Isabelle, was giving an impromptu speech outside. Séverine tried to dissuade her, as we could see the crowd was getting angry. Then it got ugly and confusing. Someone threw something, possibly a wine bottle, and hurt Isabelle. Then I was hit . . . ." Tears pricked my eyes, but I blinked them away.

He shook his head. "That woman, Séverine, she's not the type of company you should be keeping."

"She's a friend of Grand-mère's," I said, taken aback by his harsh tone.

"She's an anarchist, or at the very least, sympathizes with them."

"Why on earth do you think that?"

"I don't just think that, I know it," he said in a clipped voice.

I crossed my arms. "You can't simply accuse my friend of such a thing, without proof."

"I have proof."

I stared. Who was this man? "Philippe, what are you talking about?"

He leaned in toward me and took my hands in his. "You must understand that anarchy is nothing to play with. It's dangerous. Many otherwise good people agree with the ideology. But make no mistake, anarchists are deadly. Their sole goal is to destroy our entire society. They will kill to accomplish that."

My head jerked back. Kill? Séverine didn't strike me as violent. On the contrary, she seemed more of an intellectual. Thoughtful and kind. But truly, I hardly knew her. I trusted her because she was my grandmother's friend. And I trusted my grandmother. On the other hand, why should I place my trust in Philippe any more than Séverine? "How do you know so much about anarchists?"

"I happen to know a lot about them. It's . . . it's my job." He looked around and leaned closer. "I'm a private investigator," he said quietly.

On the train he'd told me that secrecy and discretion were at the heart of his work. So he wasn't involved in anything illegal, after all. Quite the contrary. Things began to fall into place, like puzzle pieces. The penchant for hidden cameras, his reticence to discuss his profession. Except for one detail.

"Is that how you got your scar?"

He looked away and sighed deeply. When he returned my gaze, there was something guarded there. Something lurking in the dark, wounded and wary. "It was a duel."

I longed for him to tell me more, to convince me he was telling the truth, but I bit my lip and waited.

"My eldest sister's first suitor—not her husband—had insulted her virtue. Papa wasn't going to do anything about it." His bitter tone made me wonder if that had something to do with him rejecting his father's law practice. "I was young and foolish."

"Do you regret it?"

He shook his head, a faint smile curling his lip.

There was much more to the story, I was certain, but equally certain he wasn't about to tell me anything more. We both had our secrets. "Why didn't you tell me earlier? About being a private detective, I mean?"

He looked away, avoiding my gaze, but his voice was nonchalant. "I suppose secrecy is such a part of my work life that it's become second nature."

"Are all those hidden cameras for your work?"

"Partly, although they have become a bit of a hobby of mine. Do you want to see my latest?" He held out his cane, which I assumed somehow contained a miniature camera.

I patted the back of my head gingerly, hoping the bleeding had stopped. "Perhaps later."

"Of course," he said, apologetically, but he fingered the head of his cane nonetheless, and I knew he was disappointed at missing the opportunity to show off his latest toy. I would have been more interested if my headache wasn't so horrid, for even if it was just a hobby, he was most animated when talking about his little cameras. I understood how one's passions could become essential to one's existence. It was the same with my art, a filter through which I saw my world.

"I still can't believe you're right about Séverine," I said.

Philippe pressed his mouth into a thin line. "Even if she's not an anarchist, she has publicly supported them."

"That doesn't mean she's dangerous. No more dangerous than the woman you were with outside the pavilion."

"Claudette? She's a colleague."

"A woman detective?" I couldn't hide my smile as the implications set in. "That can't sit very well with you."

"What do you mean?"

"Oh, come on. You think women aren't intelligent enough or strong enough to work outside the home. You said as much that day at the Expo." I laughed. "I would like to meet your colleague. She and I might have a lot to talk about."

Philippe tried to frown, but the beginnings of a smile played on his lips. "You're changing the subject. I want you to . . . . " He stopped and bit his lip. "I would be happier if you would refrain from associating with women like Séverine."

"You would be happier?" A sharp pang of disappointment lanced through me. Just when I thought he was becoming enlightened, he came out with statements like that. We weren't friends after all. I tried to keep my tone civil, but I shook. "I will go where I choose and associate with whomever I want."

He flinched, and his face flushed crimson. "You don't understand—"

"It's you who doesn't understand!" I jumped to my feet and dashed out the front doors of the pavilion.

"Gabrielle!"

I didn't look back. Shards of glass crunched under my shoes as I ran down the stairs.

"Gabbi!" Footsteps pounded over broken glass behind me. Phillipe was hard on my heels, but I dared not turn or slow down.

The crowd at the base of the pavilion had thinned considerably, and it was easy enough to plunge in and weave amongst them. After several blocks, I finally stopped and looked back. No sign of Philippe. Of course, now that I knew his true profession, I couldn't be sure he wasn't still following me undetected.

It wasn't until I stood outside the gates that I thought again of Séverine and Isabelle. My purse was empty but for a few sous, so I couldn't get back into the Expo and return to the Palais de la Femme. I consoled myself with the constable's reassurances and with Séverine's promise to contact me if she learned anything useful about Grand-mère.

I walked home, once again cursing too many layers of clothing as sweat dripped down my back. On top of that discomfort, my head pounded with every step. Philippe's accusations about Séverine crept into my mind, creating doubts. Worse, I was no closer to finding my grandmother, which would have solved my money problems.

And over it all, disappointment over the loss of what could have been a wonderful friendship with Philippe hung like a suffocating grey cloud.

Chapter Twenty-one

BACK IN THE ATTIC, I lay down to settle my roaring headache, intending only a light nap. I slept for several hours.

When I awoke, it was early evening—too late to search the hospitals or the morgue for Grand-mère. Guiltily relieved that I could put that off for another day, anticipation for Madame Chaudière's salon finally took front and centre stage. Could I use the drawing I made of my family? Non. Too safe. My watercolour of the old castle, although attractive, was safe too. Something unconventional seemed necessary.

Perhaps a portrait in pastel? I flipped through my sketchbook in search of inspiration. There, the studies of the old model at Place Pigalle. Her expression of insouciance, her slovenly posture and clothing. She was once someone's child, excited to attend school perhaps, or to skip rope with her friends. What had happened along the way? That was my challenge. I'd call her Madame X.

A familiar rush surged through me as I began to work on the paper Julie gave me, once again imagining Berthe Morisot advising me: "Perhaps begin with an outline in *fauve clair*." Quick, rounded strokes for the shape of her head, her heart-shaped face. Time fell away, meaningless, as I worked until the lamp sputtered.

When I fell into bed that night, my shoulders and back ached and my headache from the mob at the Expo returned. Yet a blanket of peace fell over me as I thought about the portrait of Madame X.

I rose late the next morning. Babette, predictably, was still sleeping.

As quietly as possible, I slipped into my light seersucker dress and sensible demi-boots for my walk to the Académie. After I gathered my art box and sketchbook, I searched around the tiny stove looking for a heel of cheese or bread—anything to eat. Nothing but crumbs. Grumbling to myself, I wiped the table down and was rewarded by the clink of a coin. Dropping to my hands and knees, I captured it before it could disappear between the floor-boards. Five francs! Merci Dieu for Babette's slovenly cleaning habits! Still crouched on the floor, I gleefully pocketed the coin. How very far my life had shifted from my privileged bourgeoisie life at home.

I had plenty of time before meeting Julie so sought out La Bohème and happily scanned the menu. Ravenous, I splurged on breakfast—eggs, cured ham, a croissant and a steaming café au lait. When I was finally sated, I tipped my face to the warming sun, eyes closed, hands cupped around a second mug of coffee.

Somehow, with Julie's help, I had to convince the Académie Julian to admit me without payment. If no scholarship was available, what options were left? Some kind of concocted story about my grandmother paying my account upon her return to the city? My throat tightened at the very idea. Despite deceiving Philippe about Mémère, lying didn't come easily to me. No, I'd have to throw myself on the academy's mercy.

More worrisome was Mémère's disappearance. And not just because of what that meant to me, but true anxiety over her well-being. Oh, how I longed to lose myself in making art and simply wait for her to turn up. I conjured a vision: sitting at my easel, painting a scene of this very square. The bright striped awning shaded a handful of café tables, couples laughing as their children chased a ball in the centre of the square. A bird swooped in for a scattering of bread crumbs on an empty table. Someone called my name, and I turned to see who it was. Mémère waved, walking briskly toward me with a bright smile of welcome.

My imaginings were so vivid that I opened my eyes and searched the faces around me. Nothing, of course. The sharp pain of disappointment robbed me of breath for a moment. Wishful thinking would not bring her back, yet I hardly knew what else to do. Yesterday, the constable at the Expo had sug-gested simply waiting until she turned up at the morgue or an asylum. I shud-dered. Could I find the courage to search the hospitals and morgues for her? The very thought of it brought on a wave of nausea. Yet I knew that feeling for what it was. Fear. Fear that I would never find her.

Church bells rang throughout the square, reminding me of the hour. Relieved that I could delay any decision on Mémère for one more day, I checked Julie's directions to the Académie Julian. South on rue des Martyrs to L'église Notre-Dame-de-Lorette. "You can't miss it, looks like a Greek temple rather than a Catholic church," she told me. South again, across the Boulevard Montmartre and so on. I made more than a few wrong turns but finally found La Passage des Panoramas.

It was nearly noon by the time I faced the entrance to a glass-roofed arcade of shops and restaurants. It had taken only about thirty minutes from Place du Tertre, a good omen. I ignored displays of jewellery and clothing inside the arcade, seeking out the narrow staircase Julie had mentioned and passing it twice before I succeeded.

The first door at the top of the stairs led to an empty office. I strode down the airless stuffy hallway to the next door. As I opened it, the stench of tobacco and sweat nearly gagged me. The students, all men, worked at their easels with their backs to the door. Through a gap between their backs and easels, I spied a male nude on a round dais at the far end of the room. My mouth fell open.

The model was tall, his arm, leg and abdominal muscles well defined. His male parts were fully exposed. He posed in the classical tradition as a warrior with a sword and shield aloft, reminding me of Michelangelo's statue at the Louvre, *Dying Slave*. It was impossible for him to be the same model of course, but the striking resemblance kept me rooted to the spot.

Eventually, the model turned his face slightly toward me. I returned his gaze as coolly as I could—and then he winked.

I smothered a giggle. Several artists turned and stared at me.

"Mademoiselle! You are in the wrong studio!" An older man, presumably one of the instructors, crossed the room swiftly and shut door in my face.

Never mind. I would soon be drawing from the undraped figure like them. The next several doors were locked or opened into empty ateliers. A final door revealed a crowded room of men and women. Some stood at easels, others sat on low stools as they sketched plaster casts and busts displayed on pedestals and tables scattered around the studio. I scanned the crowd of artists, spying Julie near the back. She waved.

I waited at the door.

"Perfect timing, Gabbi. I'm finished for the day. Let's go find Amélie." Julie led me out of the studio and back to the office at the top of the stairs. "Strange. She is usually working here. Shall we wait a bit and hope she shows up, or do you want to go down and get a coffee in the arcade?"

"If I leave, I may lose my nerve and not return." I clasped my sketchbook tightly as we seated ourselves on two hard wooden chairs in front of a large desk.

"Don't think about the hard part." Julie squeezed my hand briefly. "Think about how wonderful it will be to study here, to be taught by some of the best art teachers in the world! Not to mention the fun we'll have together."

I had no time to consider her advice. An attractive, middle-aged woman, smartly dressed in a pale green seersucker suit, entered the office and slid behind the desk. "Bonjour, Julie. How may I help you?"

We stood. "Bonjour, Madame," Julie said. "This is a friend of mine, Gabrielle de Villiers. She wishes to begin studies here at the academy."

"Ah, you are most welcome, Mademoiselle. I am Amélie Beaury-Saurel and I administer the women's ateliers. Are you another Canadian artist? We've had great successes with our Canadian women." She pointed at a certificate on the wall. "Sophie Pemberton won the Prix Julian last year for her portraiture."

"I hope I don't disappoint you, but I'm no foreigner. I'm from Laval. It's been my dream to study here, Madame." I handed her my sketchbook and Madame Magne's reference letter. "I'm hoping to start right away."

"Please, be seated." She took my letter and skimmed it, a flicker of what I thought was approval in her expression. Then she opened my sketchbook and flipped through it slowly.

I fiddled with the pleats in my skirts until Julie placed a cool hand upon mine. Instead, I concentrated on my breathing until I lost count of how long Madame looked at my work. Surely the longer she examines my sketches, the better?

Finally, she looked up. "You appear to have been taught well to date." She opened a drawer and pulled out a bound book that appeared to be a ledger. "Fees for women are eighty francs per month, payable on the first of the month."

I'm broke. The necessary words wouldn't form on my tongue. Asking for charity was a thousand times harder than I'd imagined. I blushed and looked at my feet as if they could rescue me.

Julie cleared her throat. "There's one small, delicate matter, Madame. Gabrielle finds herself without the necessary funds at the moment, but she's terribly talented, and I thought that perhaps there was some sort of scholarship or . . . ."

The three of us sat in silence, broken only by the ticking of a mantle clock. Madame Amélie re-opened my sketchbook, looking at my work more carefully. When she came to my recent sketch of the flower girl and her barrow, she paused.

I knew I'd managed to create something special with it. Hopefully, it captured not only the girl's persistence and work ethic despite poverty, but her strength of character as she held fast to the younger child's hand while hawking her goods. And the risk I'd taken in colouring only the flowers in the barrow while leaving all else black and white emphasized the bleakness of the young girl's life while offering a glimmer of hope. At least, I thought so.

As I viewed my own work upside down, I felt humbled. If that child could hold her head high despite the rags on her feet, surely I could swallow my pride in order to accomplish my dreams. I straightened my shoulders and met the woman's gaze.

She snapped the ledger shut. "I am sorry but we have no scholarships, and my husband would never allow me to take on a non-paying student."

"What if I were to work for my tuition?" The words slipped out before I'd formed the intent. I dared not look at Julie, for no doubt she'd be horrified.

Amélie looked at me closely. I could guess by her expression she knew I'd never done a spot of work. My gloves disguised soft, blister-free hands. My tailored clothes were of the highest quality, although slightly worse for wear after nearly a week in Paris.

She pursed her lips. "It so happens that the char-maid hasn't shown up for the past three days. Another drinking binge, perhaps." She frowned. "I don't suppose you'd take on her duties?"

Julie gasped. I sat back, shocked. Char-maid?

"It's back-breaking work," Amélie warned. "And you'd likely have to work for at least a month to earn enough for a month's tuition."

A char-maid? Dear Lord, help me find Grand-mère quickly. I swallowed hard. "I'll do it."

Amélie pursed her lips but nodded, then stood to end our interview. "Can you start immediately? I'll show you her cupboard. The men's life study class will end soon. You can clean up after them before you move onto the other studios."

"Gabbi, are you sure?" Julie whispered as I rose to follow Amélie down the hall.

I put on a brave face. "It can't be that hard. And it's only until I find Grand-mère." I squeezed her arm in reassurance and left her staring at my back.

Men are pigs, I decided later. Ashtrays were strewn around the studio yet cigarette butts were ground into the hard wooden floors, tossed onto window sills and stubbed out on porcelain saucers. With the former char-maid's grey smock covering my dress and a rag over my hair, I dragged mop and bucket around the room, unsure about exactly what was expected. Judging from the state of the room, perhaps very little.

After a length of time, Amélie stuck her head in the room. "How are you managing, Mademoiselle?"

I couldn't resist a groan as I straightened from leaning over the bucket. "Are they always this filthy?"

She laughed and disappeared down the hallway, her smart heels clicking on the hard floors.

Finally, by late afternoon I stowed the cleaning supplies back in their cupboard. My walk uphill to Montmartre took considerably longer than my morning's carefree stroll down, but when I began to feel sorry for myself, I thought of the flower girl and scolded myself. Still, I longed for a soak in the lovely deep bathtub at home, or one of Cook's delicious fragrant meals. Instead, I bought a day old croissant on my way home, nibbling it as I climbed the six flights of stairs to Babette's attic. Lord, please ensure my roommate isn't home so I could stretch out on her bed and ease the ache in my lower back.

Chapter Twenty-two

"WHAT'S THIS?" BABETTE GREETED ME, waving Madame Chaudière's card. "Classy address, in the Faubourg Saint-germain."

I gasped and sank onto the sagging sofa. "I forgot. It's tonight." How could I possibly attend a high class salon after the day I'd had? "It's just someone I met the other day. She invited me to her Salon."

"Wonderful! It so happens I'm free, and I'd love to go with you."

"But . . . ."

"Don't you want me?" Her voice was girlish, tentative.

I chewed on my lip. I hated the idea of going to the salon alone. Madame Chaudière had invited me specifically for this Friday. I doubted she'd be pleased if I didn't show and simply assumed I could come another time. Most importantly, she'd asked me to bring some paintings. She was a potential buyer or even a patron. There was no question of inviting Philippe to accompany me, not after everything said between us at the Expo.

Ignoring a queasy feeling in my gut, I reasoned that Babette was better than no one at all.

"Well?" Babette demanded.

Perhaps it would encourage her to give painting another try and ease the guilt I felt for trying to paint over her old paintings. Surely she'd behave better in high society.

"Of course you can join me. It will be fun."

"There's bound to be free food and drink!" Babette bounded out of the attic. Over her shoulder, she added, "Don't worry. I'll be back in time!"

I dragged myself to my feet, washed up with cold water and collapsed again on the sofa. Far too soon, it was time to get ready for the Salon. Only then did I wonder what I could wear.

Foolishly, I'd counted on expanding my wardrobe with Grand-mère's help.

I had packed only two dresses, one of which I'd spoiled, despite the grey over-smock. Wishing I'd brought an evening gown was fruitless, though. The blue silk suit with black piping was all I had. I brushed the bodice and skirt in an effort to freshen them up.

Babette breezed into the attic with little time to spare. She must have read my expression. "You didn't think I would forget, did you?"

"Not at all." I turned my back to her. "You can help me with my laces."

She tightened my corset until I could scarcely breathe. I slipped into my petticoats and skirt, eyeing Babette. "We haven't got much time. You'll have to dress quickly."

She spun around, her long skirts billowing out. "I'm already dressed."

I bit my lip, unsure how to reply. Another red dress, this time persimmon-coloured. The bodice was trimmed in black lace and the neckline scooped deeply into her bosom. The skirt, also red, hugged her hips and fishtailed behind, emphasizing her curves. A wide black sash circled her tiny waist. You had to look closely to see the sweat stains on the bodice or the caked mud on the hem, but propriety would not approve of the colour. Maman's voice invaded my thoughts: "Red says only one thing to a man."

"It's . . . lovely."

Babette flashed a genuine smile. Not a smirk or fake smile, but one that was transformative. For a moment, the worldliness and bitterness in her expression vanished. She looked like any other girl, excited to be going to a party. "All I need to do is freshen my makeup."

Biting back a suggestion to remove rather than apply makeup, I turned to the mirror. "Good. I need a few minutes for my hair. Then I'm ready." At least I had some jewelled hair pins and combs. I piled my hair on my crown and gathered it into a loose bun, pulling a few curls down by my ears, in an attempt to copy the hairstyle I'd admired at the Ceylon Tea House. Perhaps a stylish *coiffure* would deflect attention from my less than elegant clothing. I padded the blisters on my feet with some cotton batting sprouting from Babette's worn duvet and stuffed my feet into my heeled slippers.

How far I'd fallen from only a week ago. As I hid my reddened hands in gloves, a wave of self-pity rose. Straightening my shoulders, I countered it by tallying my successes. I wasn't in the baron's clutches, I was living independently from Maman's strict rules, and I was in the City of Art. I knew other artists and had seen the Louvre. And yes, spent time with Philippe—fun, opinionated, alluring but irritating Philippe. Babette preened in front of the tin-framed mirror. "Do you want me to do your makeup?"

"No, thank you," I said firmly, unwilling to submit to her heavy hand with the rouge and lipstick.

"What's that for?" Babette pointed at the watercolour paintings I'd just picked up.

"Madame Chaudière asked me to bring samples of my work. It's all I have to show her."

"Well, you can't take them unframed." Babette strode to the pile of her paintings and handed me two watercolours of her own. "Use these frames. Just for tonight, mind."

Surprised but grateful, I slipped her paintings out and replaced them with my own. Perhaps I was right to give her another chance. Perhaps tonight would turn out a success, after all.

It would be a long walk to the Faubourg from the apartment carrying my work, so I convinced her to spend the few centimes it took for the omnibus at the base of the Basilica.

My hands clenched with misgiving by the time we stood, at last, in front of Madame Chaudière's mansion. It was six windows across and three stories high. Stone lions, jaws agape, guarded the entrance. We watched two handsome carriages stop and discharge elegantly dressed passengers before leaving again.

"What are we waiting for?" Babette said, tapping her toe. "Let's join the soirée!"

I winced. Why had I let her bully me into bringing her? Because you're afraid of her, answered a small voice in my head as we climbed the imposing steps.

"Oui?" A uniformed butler answered the bell, looking down his narrow, pointy nose at us.

"We're expected," Babette said, taking my paintings from me and thrusting them into the man's arms. She pulled me past him into the foyer. A fullsize nude sculpture of Venus dominated the immense, round foyer. Babette stroked the stone lovingly before poking her nose into the various doorways that led off from the foyer. "Nice place. Very fancy. Lots of valuables."

"Be quiet, for heaven's sake!" I hissed. Luckily, the butler was occupied at the door with new guests. "Someone will mistake us for thieves."

"Don't worry so much, Gabbi." She laughed and continued her inspection of the house.

Clinking glasses and the rise and fall of voices greeted us as we reached the top of a winding staircase. Summoning all I'd learned at Madame Dijon's, I quelled my nerves, pasted on a bright smile, and led Babette inside.

The room was large enough to be a ballroom, with a high coffered ceiling and gilded pillars throughout. Groups of potted palm trees adorned each corner. Electric lights glowed in wall sconces. Guests packed the room so tightly that I couldn't see our hostess immediately. A uniformed servant offered plates of delicate canapés while another served glasses of champagne from a tray. I accepted one. Babette grabbed two. I shook my head at her, but she grinned impishly and downed one, then the other.

We drifted toward a group surrounding a mustachioed man who tunelessly plucked a guitar, his foot resting upon a stool. Conversations buzzed around the musician, nearly drowning out his song.

". . . I insist that Dreyfus is innocent. Why would the army ship him halfway across the world to rot on Devil's Island if not to isolate him . . . ?"

" . . . must be guilty . . . a court convicted him of treason after a second lengthy trial . . . ."

"Then explain the Presidential pardon!"

As the conversation progressed, voices heated up. Most Frenchmen felt passionately about the Dreyfus Affair and were staunchly in one camp or the other. Papa and I had discussed the matter at length the previous year, after the military re-trial was held at Rennes, near Laval. We were in agreement. Dreyfus was likely innocent and the army was protecting someone very high in authority. I stepped forward to join the conversation and glanced over my shoulder. "Babette, what do you think—"

But she was no longer behind me; she'd made her way to the centre of the room. Barefoot, she faced a round fountain with plump stone fish spewing red-tinted water into a low round basin. By the time I caught up to her, she had dipped one foot in the water.

"Stop!" I hissed, pulling on her arm as my eyes darted around. Did anyone witness such behaviour? "This isn't Montmartre!"

"You're not much fun." Babette hiccupped, but she slipped her shoes back on and allowed me to link arms with her.

My heart sank. I would have to supervise her much like a naughty toddler—and on such an important night for me. "Stay close to me," I muttered, dragging her through throngs of guests. Where was our hostess?

Light applause came from the far end of the room. We headed to the sound and discovered a woman reciting poetry. She wore an unusual outfit of a short crimson tunic over billowy white trousers. Her hair hung freely down her back, and her tiny feet were bare, toenails painted crimson. Heavy black kohl lined her eyes, giving her an exotic appearance. I relaxed slightly. Perhaps Babette's red dress wouldn't raise eyebrows after all.

"Ah, Mademoiselle Gabrielle!" Madame Chaudière glided toward us, elegantly dressed in a shimmering sapphire silk gown that trailed behind her in a lengthy train. The sleeves were short puffs of pleated silk, showing off elbow-length white gloves. Her hair was swept under a matching sapphire turban, long jewels dangling from her earlobes. She grasped my hands. "I'm so happy you decided to come to my little party."

She did appear genuinely pleased to see me. The knot in my stomach eased. "Thank you for your gracious invitation, Madame Chaudière."

"You must call me Madeleine, chérie. We're going to get to know each other well, I think. Did you bring any paintings for me?"

"Yes, I left them with your butler—"

Babette stepped fiercely on my toe.

I barely smothered a gasp from the pain. "This is my . . . roommate . . . Babette, a fellow artist."

Babette must have noticed my omission of "friend," for her eyes flashed at my hesitation, much the same as Maman's did when she was displeased.

Babette curtsied to our hostess, her breasts threatening to overflow the deep *décolleté*.

Madeleine's face briefly registered disapproval, but she spoke to Babette with the same courtesy she'd shown me. "Welcome, Mademoiselle Babette. Please mingle. Enjoy the entertainment, food, and wine. My guests tell me my salon has the best kitchen in all Paris."

She slipped my hand under her arm. "Would you mind terribly if we leave you on your own, Mademoiselle Babette? I have someone I want to introduce to Gabbi. You don't mind if I call you Gabbi, do you?"

Madeleine swept me away as Babette snagged another glass of champagne from one of the servers.

I managed to forget my anxiety about Babette soon enough, though. Madeleine quickly put me at ease. She hugged my arm tightly, in a way that reminded me of happier times with Bernadette, and introduced me as the "young artist she was collecting" to poets, politicians, musicians, and authors. Her generous praise caused me to feel lightheaded—or was it the champagne?

After we'd met what seemed like everyone, Madeleine approached a middle-aged couple just entering the large salon. Tipping her head close to mine, she whispered, "I've been inviting this man for months, and finally he is here! Mind what you say, he's the head of the Sûreté."

Julie's uncle. My armpits dampened as I worried whether to mention my grandmother to him. Perhaps fate was determined we meet. My anxiety rose when I stood face to face with the senior policeman.

"Inspecteur Générale and Madame Charest, I want to introduce my newest discovery, Gabrielle de Villiers. She's a fresh new artist I'm collecting. And if you're smart, you'll start buying up her work, too."

"*Enchanté*." Monsieur Charest took my hand and bowed slightly.

"*Enchantée*, Mademoiselle," Madame Charest said, inclining her head. "How charming to meet a young artist. Our niece from Canada is staying with us and also studying art."

I nodded. "Julie Laliberté, I believe. We've met a few times."

"Ah, what a marvelous coincidence!" Madeleine beamed at us as if she'd been responsible for our connection herself. "Please excuse me, I see more guests have just arrived." She winked at me as she turned to leave me with the older couple.

The inspector frowned as he regarded me. My hand tightened around my glass of champagne. "Are you the young woman who has lost her grand-mother?"

Mon Dieu, Julie, what else did you tell him about me? I forced my voice to remain steady. "Yes, I suppose I am."

"Oh dear, that sounds quite tragic." Madame's eyes softened with concern. "I'm sure Claude can help you. Can't you, dear?" She placed a hand on his arm and squeezed.

Her husband cleared his throat and patted her hand. "I'm not sure this is the time or place, Marie."

Quite right. "Thank you for your concern, Madame," I said. "But I couldn't bother your husband with my little problem."

"Nonsense. You're a friend of Julie's and therefore a friend of ours. I'm going to leave you two to discuss this alone, however. I see Alphonsine by the piano and wish to speak with her." She pressed my hands in hers and gave her husband a dazzling smile, which he returned. "Claude will find your grandmother. Never fear."

The Inspector General and I stood together in an awkward silence. He cleared his throat twice and shifted his weight from left to right foot. He was, no doubt, embarrassed by his wife's insistence that he help with something that was most certainly undeserving of his high ranking attention.

He sighed. "Well, perhaps you'd best tell me your story. Marie will pester me until your grandmother is safe and sound." He gestured at a nearby settee.

"It's nothing, really," I started, after we'd sat down. When I met the police-man's steady gaze, I ordered my queasy gut to settle. I could not concoct lies, although careful fact-pruning was clearly called for. I drew a deep breath. "I arrived at my grandmother's apartment on rue Cortot in the 18th arrondisse-ment only to discover she'd moved away months before." The pain of aban-donment from that rainy, grey afternoon descended over me, and I blinked rapidly. "She didn't leave a forwarding address."

Julie's uncle eyed me much the way the senior gendarme at the Expo had done. I pressed my lips together to avoid blurting out any more details.

"And your parents don't know where she moved to?"

"Ah, non, monsieur. There was a . . . a falling out." A flash of shame swept through me. To admit family problems to a stranger! I clutched my hands in my lap. The full truth was much, much worse.

"Have you looked for her in the hospitals or the morgue?" His expression softened a bit. "I'm sorry but in my line of work, well, it's only natural to consider even the more dire of circumstances."

"Thank you, Monsieur," I managed.

"I could make inquiries at our women's prisons as well, if you wish." His offer sounded half-hearted to my ears.

"I am sure that will not be necessary," I said firmly.

He nodded. "Of course, it was a poor idea. Most likely, your grandmother is simply visiting outside the city and will return, hale and hearty." He slapped his hands on his knees and stood abruptly. "I'd better join Marie."

"Léon?" Babette's sharp voice cut through the chatter nearby.

Along with everyone else in the room, I rose and looked to see where her voice was coming from.

"It is you, León!" Babette waved at a middle-aged man in evening dress. He was entirely bald, although he sported enormous black sideburns. A matronly woman in a cream evening gown, a heavy pearl choker at her throat and feathers in her hair, held onto his arm. As Babette approached them, teetering slightly, expressions of horror consumed their faces. The man turned his back and resumed a conversation with another couple.

An awkward silence ensued. Babette stood alone. Her face registered hurt, then anger. A stab of pity hit me. Slowly, people began to circulate once again, talking and drinking as if the scene hadn't happened.

Madeleine caught my gaze, held it, and then tipped her head toward Babette. Her message was clear. With a sinking feeling, I slipped through the crowded room and headed toward Babette who still faced Léon's back.

"Babette?" I joined her and put my arm on her shoulder. "Come with me."

Her painted mouth set in a deep line, she shrugged me off and strode toward the bald man and tapped on his shoulder. "Léon? Surely you remember?" she asked shrilly. "At the Moulin Rouge. It's me, Babette."

The man turned and looked down his nose at her for several seconds, his eyes as cold as caviar canapés. "You must be mistaken. I've never been to the Moulin Rouge. And we have most certainly never met."

His wife continued to clutch his arm, the only hint of her emotion in the frenzied flicker of a painted Japanese fan.

Babette's face reddened. She stepped backward into me.

"It's time to leave." I grabbed her elbow and pulled her toward the door and down the staircase to the foyer.

The butler escorted us outside rather hastily, shoving my paintings at me.

I hugged the paintings to my chest. I hadn't expected to cart them home, at least not quite so soon. But there was no point on insisting Madeleine keep them. Even though her praises rang in my head, I could never apologize enough for Babette's outburst. Once we were back on the street, trudging home, I asked, "What was all that about, with the man you called Léon?"

"That old goat," Babette spit out. "He remembers me all too well."

I bit my tongue, afraid of the angry words that would fly from my mouth. She was oblivious to how her behaviour affected anyone else, including me. True, she'd been humiliated, but I most certainly lost a potential patron. Maman's voice came to me again. "We are judged by the company we keep. So choose your friends wisely." This time, she was right.

As I brooded over all the damage Babette had caused in a single night, an unwelcome thought hit me. My own situation was precarious, but it was, in large part, my own fault.

The fact that I had told half-truths to the head of our country's police force couldn't be laid at my roommate's feet. I had to accept responsibility for leaving home so impulsively. I should have waited until I knew Grand-mère was expecting me. I should have been better prepared for the possibility that I might be on my own.

I glanced at Babette, trying to see through the heavy makeup and hard expression. Where was the girl I'd first laughed with when we'd met? The one I'd glimpsed when we'd set out for the Salon? Both of us had been in high spirits and full of hope. I put my arm through hers as we ascended the final stairway to rue Gabrielle. "One day, when we are successful artists, we'll look back on this and laugh."

She pulled her arm away. "It doesn't matter." Her voice caught and contradicted her words. "Becoming an artist—that was just a childish notion—a stupid castle in the air. Phht!"

Chapter Twenty-three

WHEN I ROSE EARLY THE NEXT morning, Babette wasn't buried under her covers. I hoped she hadn't left during the night to seek solace from Henri or another man of his persuasion, but her choices were hers.

She may have given up on her own dreams, but I would not. If Madeleine liked my art, perhaps another patroness would as well. First, my chores at the Julian, then I'd meet Julie at the Jardin des Plantes. I dressed into my light seersucker dress and sensible boots, grabbed my art box and sketchpad. I still had four francs so breakfast at La Bohème was once again possible. With eggs, *pain au chocolat* and a steaming café au lait in front of me, I could think. I still needed to find Mémère, more urgently than ever, for I couldn't fool myself any more. I could no longer tolerate living with Babette.

As I fished through my purse to pay the waiter, my fingertips brushed Philippe's calling card. I withdrew it and stared at it for some time. Who better to locate a missing person than a private investigator? If only we hadn't quarrelled. But it was inevitable. We were so different.

But wasn't Mémère's welfare more important than my pride? I squashed that thought and hid Philippe's card back in the bottom of my handbag. When I was truly desperate, perhaps I would reconsider.

Amélie wasn't in her office when I arrived at the Julian, so I found the cleaning cupboard, donned the apron and headscarf, and did my best with mop and bucket. It was late morning before I was satisfied enough with my efforts.

I crossed the Ile de la Cité, stopping briefly to admire the Gothic architecture of Notre Dame with its twin pillars, menacing gargoyles, and elegant flying buttresses. I promised myself I would spend time inside the cathedral. Soon. Once I crossed the River and followed the Quai Saint-Bernard, I arrived at the Botanical Gardens. I easily spotted Julie amongst the crowds of visitors, made up largely of nursemaids with perambulators and young children.

"Gabbi!" she called, waving gaily.

We exchanged cheek kisses like old friends and entered the gardens. They were free, much to my relief. I had three francs remaining after my splurge on breakfast and appreciated the jingling sound the coins made in my pocket. One never knew when expenses would arise.

"The gardens are quite beautiful," Julie said as we walked down circuitous gravel paths. "However, what I want to show you is farther along."

My nose wrinkled with disgust as a breeze brought a stench of what I could only assume was a combination of animal dung and the odour of so many animals caged in great proximity.

"I've been here several times already," Julie said as she led me through the gardens, striding briskly. "My nieces and nephews adore the animals, and their nursemaids appreciated my help with supervision."

I gaped at the animals I'd only previously seen in school book illustrations or artwork. Elephants, with skin so wrinkled and textured I longed to stroke them. Crocodiles, sheathed in impregnable scaly armour, sunning themselves. We passed the monkey house, their raucous cries filling the air. Just beyond the aviary, where vultures crouched in trees, following us with unblinking eyes, Julie stopped and pointed.

Large wild cats paced in a long row of double-barred cages. Lions were caged in pairs. Next to the lions was a solitary tiger. I stood in front of its cage and stared, transfixed.

As it paced, shoulder muscles rippled under its impossibly soft-looking fur. What would it be like to curl up against it and run my hands through its luscious coat? Perhaps the tiger sensed my intent for it stopped abruptly, right in front of me. Its golden eyes, unblinking in their intensity, bored into me. The bars of the cage threw striped shadows against its already camouflaged coat.

Just like my self-portrait, the one I slashed through with golden bars.

Sympathy for the magnificent creature stabbed me sharply. To be caged and put on display for the public's entertainment seemed unbearably cruel.

"Gabbi? What's wrong?" Julie's voice interrupted my thoughts. "Are you afraid?"

"What? Oh, no," I said. "It saddens me to see these animals like this."

She pursed her lips. "I hadn't thought of that, but I see what you mean." She paused. "I was going to suggest we sketch the big cats. But if it upsets you, perhaps we should try somewhere else. The rose gardens will be in bloom."

"No, I'd like to draw the tiger, actually."

We set to work on our own compositions in companionable silence. After I'd watched the tiger for several minutes, I resolved to sketch it in what I guessed would be its natural environment. The sign said it was an Indian tiger so I imagined a dense, tropical jungle as its home. I studied the cat's form, its musculature and the stripe patterns of its perfectly camouflaged coat. Its long sinuous black-and-white tail tip flicked relentlessly. Wickedly sharp claws flashed from soft, broad paws as it paced in front of me. I shuddered, imagining meeting this tiger in the wild. As if sensing my fear and fascination, the tiger stopped in front of me once again and stared. It yawned, exposing deadly fangs and a wide, pink tongue. Crisp white whiskers sprouted from its snout.

After I made several studies, I chose a fresh page and started a full page drawing. Then I tried to capture the right reddish-orange for his coat with my pastels. I looked over at Julie. She was sketching the male lion in the adjoining cage.

"I went to that Salon last night and met your uncle and aunt," I said.

She looked surprised. "Isn't it a small world?"

"Your aunt was quite kind, and your uncle made suggestions of how to find my grandmother. Please tell them I appreciate it."

"How was the salon?"

I scrunched my face. "Babette came with me. It was a complete disaster."

Her eyes widened. "You took Babette to a Salon in the Fauberg?"

"We were very nearly thrown out, after she caused a scene with an older gentleman she seemed to know rather intimately." I reddened, aware I was becoming too well-versed in my roommate's dubious lifestyle. "You probably think I got what I deserve, taking her along."

Julie shook her head. "I wasn't judging you, although I can't wait to see you leave her company. I could ask my aunt and uncle if you could live with us. But with nine children and all the servants . . . ."

A vision of a happy, hectic but comfortable home rose up, threatening to choke me with a sweet sharp yearning. I tried to make a joke of it. "Nine children? That makes Babette sound positively lovely."

"Nonsense. Wouldn't we have a grand time together, at least until end of August? And by then, surely you'll have reconnected with your grandmother. I'll ask Uncle tonight." She waved away my thanks. "Now that's settled, let's get back to work. I need a finished piece for Monday morning."

We sketched for the remainder of the day. I replaced the bars of the tiger's cage with waving golden grasses, allowing the beautiful cat its escape onto the pages of my sketchpad.

"I only wish I could actually transport you from here to your home, dear

Tiger." I fancied it understood me, for it stopped its pacing long enough to gaze at me once again. Its black and golden eyes were lacklustre, and I wondered how long it had been captive. My own freedom was suddenly sweeter, and I pitied the tiger its fate.

As Julie and I worked, she told me funny stories about her nephews and nieces. I was looking forward to meeting them all. It seemed like no time at all before we were packing up and promising to meet up for another sketching session. My feet nearly flew up the hill to Montmartre as I thought of how my fortunes were changing. Somehow, I'd find a way to approach Madame Chaudière and apologize for Babette's behavior. Somehow, I'd find my grandmother. All things were once again possible.

"I'm taking you to Gaston's tonight." Babette dropped her silk dressing gown and stepped into her *pantalettes*.

I stood still, my mouth agape. "You heard from him?"

"Oui. He's anxious to meet you." She winked before she pulled on her stockings and fastened them to her garters. She wiggled into the same tight persimmon-coloured dress she'd worn to the Salon.

So, she had been truthful about Lachance after all. And yet uneasiness curled inside me. It was more than Konstantin's warning to stay clear of the man, or the look that passed between the other students when his name was mentioned. I shrank from any further dependency on my unreliable roommate.

"What's wrong?" Babette stopped dabbing perfume between her breasts and frowned.

"I . . . I'm surprised, that's all." I stared at my hands, red and dry, fingernails cracked and broken from cleaning up the studios at Julian's. Modeling would surely be easier than being a char woman. And Amélie had said it might be several weeks before I actually got to join a class. Madeleine's praise aside, I had much to learn if I wanted to do more than society portraits.

I thought of the Veronese in the Louvre. Of my art teacher's passion when she spoke of famous French artists, women who defied convention and devoted a lifetime to art. Art remained the reason I was in Paris. Gaston could be a valuable ally in the art world. It didn't pay to alienate such people.

"Well?" Babette's sharp voice jolted me into a decision.

"Of course I'll go." I took off my seersucker dress, deciding I needed to look my best. As I wriggled into my corset, I promised myself I would abandon it once I'd been accepted as his student. "Babette, would you help me with the laces?"

She tightened my corset, and I put on my only good dress, topping it with a light bolero jacket.

"You'll need *maquillage* tonight. Gaston likes a woman who is made up."

"Why would he care?"

Babette pursed her lips. "If you're prepared to model for him, he needs to know what you'll look like once you are made up. It's only a bit of paint, silly."

"All right, but only if you promise to use a light hand." I held still as she brushed powder over my face and rubbed rouge into my cheeks.

"Now, your mouth." She took a slim brush and painted red paste onto my lips. "Look. You aren't a country mouse anymore. You're a city woman."

The face staring back at me from the mirror certainly looked older, but I wasn't sure it was an improvement. I stuck out my tongue at my reflection and laughed at myself. Well, if this was what it takes to get ahead as an artist, I could put up with it, even if it made my skin itchy. I turned from the mirror to resist the urge to wipe off the rouge and paste.

Babette stood at the door, tapping her foot with nervous energy. "The night awaits."

"I'm coming." I grabbed my hat, purse, and sketchpad. I fished Nacia's gloves out of the bottom of my purse and pulled them on over my rough hands.

The prospect of quitting my charwoman's work spurred me into meeting Lachance. He was my second chance. I pinned my felt hat into place with Grand-mère's beautiful silver pin. She would have encouraged me, telling me I belonged in the company of successful artists. "I need your confidence tonight, Mémère," I whispered.

Babette pointed at my sketchpad. "Why are you bringing that?"

"Monsieur Lachance will want to see some of my work, won't he? How else can he decide whether he'll take me on as a student?"

She laughed and wiggled her eyebrows. "Oh, he has his ways."

Her innuendo stirred vague unease into a witch's cauldron in my gut.

Once we were out on the streets, I only half-listened as she chattered about the previous night's fun with Henri. What would Bernadette say about my roommate? She'd say Babette was a flighty songbird, pretty but unsteady. She'd warn me not to trust someone I barely knew. But that advice could apply to Philippe and Julie, also. I had only myself to rely upon and would have to be on guard. I shivered despite the warm night air.

We left Montmartre, crossed Boulevard de Clichy and entered a more upscale neighbourhood. The entire block was made up of five-storey apartments, their street fronts elaborately decorated with plaster cornices and gargoyles. Bright flowers cascaded from iron balconies.

"Monsieur Lachance has done very well as an artist," I noted.

Babette laughed. "Oh, Gaston comes from money."

The building's uniformed doorman merely nodded at her as we walked through the lobby. We took a lift to the third floor.

A uniformed butler answered the door and silently led us across the marble-tiled entry to an elegant but darkened parlour. The walls were covered in red-and-black flocked wallpaper. The furniture was heavy and dark. Definitely furnished by a man. Did that mean he was not married? I knew nothing of his private life: where he was from or how old he was. I shook my head. Those were the criteria Maman used to judge people. I was more modern than that.

I edged closer to the only painting in the room, a vaguely familiar life-sized portrait of a young woman standing on a beach. The cerulean blue of her dress was repeated in the clear sky, a child's sand toys and the lacy parasol that partially obscured her face. I imagined posing for such a composition, tilting my head. Peering down at the lower right corner, I drew in my breath when I read the signature. Lachance. Yes. It was the painting I'd seen in Madame Magne's art journal. For a brief, guilty moment I was glad Grand-mère had disappeared. If she were in Paris, I wouldn't have met Babette and wouldn't be in Gaston's flat, waiting to be introduced.

Babette was clearly familiar with the parlour. She crossed to a mahogany cabinet and poured herself a glass of absinthe, undiluted. She raised the glass and smirked. "*A ta santé!* Care for *la* fée verte?"

"No, thank you." I winced, recalling how I'd felt after drinking the Green Fairy that night at the Lapin Agile. "It's too strong for me."

"Phht!" She waved her hand dismissively and tossed back the liqueur. She refilled her glass and poured another, bringing it to me. "Here, this will loosen you up a bit. You might find you need it."

I sniffed the liqueur. Its scent of herbs and anise stirred embarrassing memories. My hand shook, and I set it on a side table. But what if Gaston found my sketches childish and rejected me? Perhaps one small glass would help me relax and provide confidence. I dashed it back, and its warmth curled inside me.

A tall, handsome dark-haired man strode into the parlour. Likely in his thirties, he wore a well-cut evening suit, although his cravat was untied.

"Ah, good evening, ma chérie." He went straight to Babette, kissed her cheeks and hugged her briefly. Then his green eyes fixed on me.

Breathe in, breathe out, Gabbi, I told myself, and smiled at Lachance.

He walked swiftly to me. "And who is this charming creature?"

"This is Gabrielle," Babette said in a rough, saucy tone, making me wince. "She just moved from the country and is living with me. She wants to study under an artist."

He smiled. "And you suggested me, chérie? How kind." He took my gloved hand and bowed. When he straightened, he appeared genuinely pleased to see me, his eyes curious and alight. "Welcome, Mademoiselle Gabrielle. I always enjoy meeting new artists. It's an exciting time, n'est ce pas?"

It was easy to return his smile. "I am honoured to meet you, Monsieur Lachance."

He waved his hand as if waving off my praise. "Why don't we go into my studio? It will be more comfortable there, and I can show you where I work."

He led us down a narrow carpeted hallway that ended at a dark, heavy-paneled door. Slipping a key into the lock, he opened it and ushered us into a large impressive studio. Directly across from us, blood-red drapes framed a sparkling view of the city. A black lacquered screen stood out in one corner of the room, and heavy drapes hid another corner from view.

This was clearly a working artist's studio. A tall easel dominated the room. A paint-smeared palette, assorted brushes, bottles, and half-used tubes of paint were scattered across a nearby tabletop. Pleasantly lightheaded, I crossed the room to a large blank canvas that waited on the easel for the next model.

For me, I thought, with a sharp intake of breath. If I impressed this man, my image could be hung in the next Salon or even in the Louvre. My name could become famous from one well-received painting. Like Berthe Morisot. Madame Magne had told me that Morisot's friendship with Camille Corot and Edouard Manet had given her the introductions she needed in Parisian art circles. I wondered whether I might follow in her brushstrokes.

"Mademoiselle Gabrielle?" Gaston interrupted my daydreaming. He pointed at my bosom. "Is that for me?"

I flinched but then realized I was clutching my sketchbook against my chest as if it were a shield. "Oh, this?" I said with a nervous laugh. "Yes. I brought some of my work so you could see if you want to take me—take me on as a student, I mean. I've never formally studied art other than at school of course. But I've been drawing since I was a young girl . . . ." Suddenly pain-fully aware I was babbling and still clutching my book, I stopped speaking.

"May I?"

Stupefied, I nodded and held my sketchbook out to him, holding my breath as he scanned the pages. His powerful hands caught my attention: those tapered fingers held the secret of success. I felt exposed and fragile, as if criticism from him would snap me in half like a stick of charcoal.

However, I relaxed when he chuckled at my cartoons of the baron and paused at one of my sketches of our carriage horse, Birgitta. "You enjoy painting animals? Perhaps like Rosa Bonheur?"

"Oh yes!" I was thrilled that my name could be linked to such a famous artist, if only in conversation. "I have lots of paintings of horses and cows. But I love to do portraits most of all, perhaps."

"Why portraits, Mademoiselle?"

I'd never asked myself that question and took a moment to answer. "I . . . I suppose I'm looking for myself in the people I draw." What I'd just said surprised me, but I knew its truth by its warmth settling into my heart. I looked at Gaston with awe. He must be a great teacher.

He nodded. "And do you feel the heat of it as you work? To be a great artist, you must be consumed by a fire within before you can release it onto the canvas." He gestured dramatically with one hand, flinging it from his chest to the easel across the room.

His words stirred me. "That is exactly how I feel!"

He smiled and handed back my sketchpad. "I believe you. I see raw passion in your sketches. I will work with you to stoke that fire. We will set Paris alight with your paintings."

I was mesmerized. "Merci, Monsieur Lachance."

"Please, you must call me Gaston. And I will call you Gabrielle." He reached out and took my gloved hands in his own, turning them over and stroking my palms. "We'll make these hands famous, you and I."

It suddenly seemed hot in the studio. I drew my hands back, cursing my propensity to blush at the slightest touch by a man.

"You do want to be my student, don't you, Gabrielle? I think we could work well together, you and I." His eyes locked onto mine. He stood so close I could barely breathe.

My voice and my wits deserted me, but I managed to nod. Awe for his talent was making me an idiot. I wracked my brain for something intelligent to say. "I know becoming an artist takes time and a lot of practice, but I'll work hard. You won't be disappointed."

He nodded, spreading his hands out. "With your raw talent and my experience, we'll create masterpieces, n'est-ce pas?" He touched my cheek.

I took a step back, retreating to a respectable distance.

He leaned closer, his voice breathy. "You're not having second thoughts, are you?"

I hesitated and looked across the room where Babette stared out the windows. She turned to meet my gaze and crossed the room to me, her heels clipping the tile floor. "She's not having second thoughts at all. Gabrielle is grateful for your offer. She's just a little shy, aren't you, chérie?"

I shook my head.

Gaston's eyes narrowed. He stood watching me, rubbing his chin as if considering a sausage in a boucherie. I felt him assess my shape, suddenly not hidden enough under layers of silk and petticoats. I was compelled to fill the silence, to drag his eyes away from my body. "Wha—what days do you teach, Monsieur . . . Gaston?"

He raised an eyebrow. "You want to discuss that now? Very well. You'll model every evening. Not before seven, mind you. Then on Friday nights, I will teach."

"You want me to model every day for one free lesson?" My charwoman's job at the Julian suddenly seemed more desirable.

Babette frowned, placing her hands on her hips like Maman. "Gabrielle, don't you know how fortunate you are to study with Gaston?"

Something much darker than Fortune inhabited the studio, its weight pressing in on me from the corners. Pressing against my temples. Was it the absinthe or the sense of foreboding? "I-I'll have to think about this." I held her gaze and pleaded with my eyes. *Please understand. Let's leave. Immediately.*

She put her arm around me. "Come with me. Let's get you ready to model." She tugged me toward the corner screen.

I pulled back. "I don't want to. Not tonight. I'm too tired. I can come back tomorrow."

"Don't be silly, chérie. We're here now. Get undressed."

I startled. "Undressed?"

She looked at me as if I was an imbécile. "Surely you know modeling is always in the nude."

Liar. Many society women posed for their portraits, fully clothed. I backed away from Babette and found myself next to the easel, my back to the city lights.

The whole sordid scene finally sank in as clues I hadn't seen before leaped out. A regiment of half-empty wine bottles piled up under the table next to the easel. A divan bed with rumpled bedcovers only partially hidden behind the drapes. The heavy scent of a woman's cheap perfume mingled with bitter tobacco and the sour odour of spilled wine. Konstantin had tried to warn me, but I shrugged his comments off as jealousy.

And Philippe had been right about Babette, after all.

Snippets of gossip about fallen women and corrupt men flitted through the growing alcohol-induced fog. My hand flew to my throat, touching the tidy row of buttons on my bodice. "I can't do this."

Babette's voice changed from its teasing lilt to a sharp tone. She rushed over to me and dug her nails into my bare wrist. "Yes, you can. You can and you must." Her eyes flashed an unspoken threat.

I pulled away from her grasp and started for the door. Gaston swiftly crossed the room and leaned against it. His smile reminded me of the sly fox in nursery stories. "You've got nothing I haven't seen already." His voice changed. Rougher, deeper. And the smouldering look in his eyes brought a chill to my gut.

I needed time to think. Still clutching my sketch book, I stretched my lips over my clenched teeth into a facsimile of a smile. "Very well, if you insist." I squared my shoulders, walked over to the lacquered screen and slipped behind it, gulping air to feed my brain. I prayed for a divine rescue: a second parting of the Red Sea or another burning of Sodom and Gomorrah. And if not that, at least an inspired idea.

To steady my thoughts and sort them, I slowly removed my gloves and slipped them into my jacket pockets. I hung my jacket over the screen hiding me from Gaston and Babette. Comprised of six hinged panels, the screen was quite beautiful with gold and red motifs decorating each panel in the style *Japonaise*. I focused on the feel of the glossy lacquer finish, cool to my shaking fingers.

Gaston and Babette spoke in urgent whispered tones. I couldn't make out their words from behind the screen. The sound of clinking coins followed and then Babette's saucy voice. "Au revoir."

Next came the sound of metal sliding against metal—the deadbolt to the studio door opened. Then it closed again like a hammer nailing down the lid of a coffin.

Chapter Twenty-four

"ARE YOU GOING TO TAKE all night to undress?" Gaston's voice, from the other side of the screen, sounded impatient.

"Almost ready." My voice wavered. The harsh reality of Babette's betrayal and Gaston's true nature struck like a fist in my stomach. I wrapped my arms around my waist as tears welled in my eyes and slid down my cheeks. Stupid! Stupid Gabbi!

My sketchpad lay at my feet. Was I going to give up everything I'd fought so hard for already? No! Adrenalin surged through my veins. There must be a way to escape. Either by my wits or, if necessary, by my fists. I'd never struck anyone, even play fighting, but my hands curled into fists naturally. I began to pray once again, while simultaneously casting about for ideas. Inspiration. Or a weapon.

A rack of satin dressing gowns stood against the back wall. Several canvases leaned against the high screen. I turned one over and gasped. It was a painting of a voluptuous nude lounging on a bed. She stared out of the canvas with a vacant expression, fondling one of her own breasts. The next painting depicted three nude women—girls, really—tangled together in bed sheets. Those models had the same empty, hopeless expression as the first. I turned the paintings back with a trembling hand, not wanting to see any more.

As I turned from the stack of paintings, my elbow struck the rack of silk dressing gowns, nearly toppling it. I grabbed it before it could clatter to the floor. Perhaps if I threw a dressing gown over my clothes, Gaston might think I'd undressed. It might give me enough time to run to the door, unlock it and flee. To where, though? I'd still be inside his apartment. Would his butler stop me? I'd have to face that possibility if and when I managed to escape this dead-bolted room.

When I pulled a gown off the rack, I glimpsed a door behind it. The fire exit! Merci, Dieu! I twisted the handle but it wouldn't open. I gave it another firm wrench but it didn't budge.

"What's taking so long?" Gaston's hoarse voice sounded close.

I swallowed my fear, squeaking out, "Just another minute."

I stared at the door. My salvation. With a deep breath to steady me, I wrenched on the handle while shoving my whole weight against the door. It groaned but didn't yield.

Gaston appeared behind the screen. "You're not going anywhere!" He grabbed my arms, pinned them behind me and yanked.

"Merde!" He slipped on my sketchpad and in that split-second of lost balance, I tried to wrench free. He righted himself and half-dragged, half-carried me around the screen. My sketchpad lay spine open on the floor beside my handbag. Grand-mere's photograph, Philippe's handwritten note inviting me to the Expo and the Louvre museum guide, Nacia's blue kid gloves—all spilled out.

"Ouch!" I cried as he twisted my wrists. "That hurts."

His reply was a coarse, harsh laugh. He yanked my arms and thrust me to my knees on the floor in the centre of the studio. He shoved me onto my face, and I bit my lip. The metallic taste of blood filled my mouth, and I gagged.

Gaston released his grip on my wrists. I forced myself to roll onto my back and face him. He sat on my hips, pinning me to the floor. I tried to sit up, but he pushed me back down with hairy, sweaty hands.

He grinned strangely, as if he were insane. Maybe he was.

"Let me go," I begged. "It's not too late."

"Too late? For what?"

"If you let me go now, I won't tell the police."

"Hah!" He threw back his head, laughing like a wild hyena. The eerie, wild sound struck at my core.

I screamed.

Gaston's laughter ended abruptly. He slapped me. He thrust one knee between my legs to force them apart. He groped my breast with one hand and pulled at my skirts with the other. His lips crushed down on mine, his thrusting tongue forcing my mouth open. I couldn't breathe. Panic rose up within me as I fought back. It was useless. His weight kept me pinned even as he fumbled with his trouser buttons.

The nude models' blank faces hovered before me, devoid of hope or decency. I fought the hysteria rising within. I had to outwit him, for he easily overpowered me. I forced myself to stop fighting his kiss, slowly and deliberately until his body relaxed. The sour taste of him twisted my stomach, but

I could think of no other choice. I imagined what Babette might say. "You're hurting my back. The bed would be much better."

He narrowed his eyes, but he didn't shift his weight.

With trembling fingers, I undid one button on my bodice, then another, my cheek still burning from his slap.

He nodded then and got off me. He grabbed my arm and yanked me to my feet.

I gritted my teeth while keeping a smile. He had to think I was willing to submit.

"I knew you'd see it my way," he said hoarsely, licking his lips. "You girls act so innocent, but you want it as badly as I do."

I shuddered.

He pushed me toward the bed. My heart pounded against my ribs and blood thumped painfully through my temples, threatening to overwhelm me. The room spun.

I had to act before he pinned me on the bed. I turned around and forced myself to drape my arms around his neck. "At least let me discard my hat," I murmured. I reached up with one arm, keeping the other around his neck, and withdrew Grand-mère's six-inch pin from my hat. With a deep breath, I plunged it into his neck, twisting it deeper as he writhed.

He screamed and shoved my hand away, pulling the pin from his neck. It skittered across the floor. He swore, cupping his hand to his neck to stem the flow of blood. "Putain!" His eyes widened and he began to sway.

I ran for the door, slid the bolt free and flung it open, my hat toppling behind me, hair sailing free.

"*Salope!*"

I stumbled but righted myself. Heavy footsteps followed close behind.

"Putain!" Gaston lunged and caught my elbow as I ran down the hallway. I pulled away and my sleeve ripped. He grabbed my hair and twisted it so hard that my eyes teared.

I turned and spat at him. He slapped me with his free hand. I punched his face and scratched his eyes and his face, drawing stripes of blood until he let me go with a howl.

I fled past his startled butler. I hesitated in the corridor, panting. Waiting for the lift would waste precious seconds, so I headed for the stairs, tripping on the first. I slid off my high-heeled slippers, tossing them aside. I stumbled down the three flights, my skirts held high with the other hand. I staggered into the lobby.

The doorman turned toward me, startled. "Mademoiselle?"

I hesitated. He could be part of Gaston's game. I flung the door open and flew into the street, running into a man standing directly outside. The wind sailed out of me, and I nearly bowled him over.

"Gabrielle!"

Strong hands gripped my shoulders, righting me. Heart still pounding, I focused on the voice and then the face. "Philippe!" I sagged against him with relief.

'Salope!" Gaston had followed me out into the street. Undeterred by Philippe's presence, he staggered toward me. His nose and upper lip were smeared with blood, as was his white shirt. His demonic leer didn't waver.

Then he looked at Philippe. "Bonsoir, monsieur. I'm sure you don't want to get involved in a domestic squabble. Please, chérie, come home." He held his hand out to me.

I slid behind Philippe—and Philippe slammed his fist into Gaston's face. Bones cracked. I turned my face away as Philippe struck him again. When I looked up, Gaston was doubled over in pain, cradling his face.

"*Bâtard!*" Philippe growled before he turned to me. "Let's get out of here."

Chapter Twenty-five

Philippe hailed a fiacre on the next street and helped me inside. As we passed under a street light, he brushed the hair back from my face and gasped. "Mon Dieu, Gabbi." He touched my cheek so tenderly that tears welled up again. He slid a silk handkerchief from his inner pocket and gently dabbed my tears away.

His knuckles were raw and bloody. My fingernails were torn and bloody. Gaston's stink of sour breath and sweat washed over me; the memory of his hands on my breasts, the tenderness of my inner thigh where he'd . . . I began to tremble violently.

"I'm so sorry," Philippe murmured.

I shook my head, sniffling. He passed me his handkerchief, and I blew my nose. "It's not your fault. I was stupid. So stupid." I looked over at him. "If you hadn't been there . . . ." I shuddered and my stomach flipped. "Stop the carriage!"

"What's wrong?"

"I'm going to be sick."

Philippe pounded on the roof with his cane. "Driver! Stop!"

The driver was slow in releasing the door latch. I bolted out onto the dark street toward a fence with my hands over my mouth. I bent over, and my stomach heaved up disgust, fear, and anger; heaved again and again. I gripped the fence, shaking.

Philippe waited beside me while I wiped my mouth with his handkerchief. "Are you going to be all right? Do you need a doctor?"

I shook my head, too weak to be embarrassed.

He helped me back into the carriage and instructed the driver to continue. "I'm sorry," I said, settling back onto the seat, my head down.

He took my hands in his. "You have nothing to apologize for. That monster, he's the one to blame. Not you."

"Babette's part of it, too. She took me there. I think he paid her! Oh, you were so right about her. I'm sure she knew exactly what would happen." Gaston's nude paintings . . . . Nausea rose again, but this time, I managed to quell it. "We have to tell the police. I'm not the first. They have to be stopped."

"I'll see the police first thing in the morning. Don't worry about it now. You've had an awful shock. Try to put it out of your mind."

I bit my lip. He was trying to comfort me, but he had no idea how dirty I felt, how Gaston's touch burned my skin like a brand. I would never forget.

"Remember, it wasn't your fault."

I shook my head. I was responsible for putting myself in such a vulnerable position. Naïveté and pride were my downfall. Why hadn't I seen the warning signs? I knew Babette was rough and street-wise. Why hadn't I listened to others' warnings? Or to the soft voice inside me telling me to beware? Instead, I gave her the benefit of the doubt. I tried to empathize with her, maybe even thought I could help her.

I rested my head against the high plush seat of the carriage, trying to push away images of Babette and Gaston. Babette coaxing me to drink the absinthe, her eyes hard when I wanted to leave. Gaston's fetid breath, his hand on my breast. My knees forced apart.

Philippe standing there on the sidewalk.

I bolted upright and stared at him. "What were you doing outside Gaston's?"

He looked away. Creaking carriage wheels, the clomp of shod hooves on the cobblestones filled the silence between us. Finally he spoke. "You know I didn't trust Babette. I followed you to Gaston's. I was trying to decide whether to force my way into his apartment when you came flying out."

"You followed me?"

He stiffened, his voice pinched. "Damn good thing I did. I knew Babette was trouble. But you wouldn't listen to me." He sounded like an angry parent.

"I know. You were right about her. But you didn't have to follow me. You're not my guardian, are you?"

He sighed and looked away. "I am your guardian, in a manner of speaking."

"What do you mean?"

He chewed the inside of his cheek. "I have something to confess. Promise you will hear me out?"

Confession was something between sinners and priests. I braced myself against the padded seat, not at all sure I could withstand another shock.

His eyes flickered. Indecision or guilt?

"I can see you're in no condition to hear what I have to say. I promise to explain my presence at Gaston's in the morning, after you've had a night's sleep."

"I'm fine," I lied. "Tell me now."

"You've suffered enough tonight." He looked away into the blackness outside the window.

It was true. I'd endured the worst night of my life. I closed my eyes and tried to fit what I knew into a coherent picture. Philippe was a private investigator, hired to prevent the anarchists from bombing the Expo. He hated any connection to anarchy. Séverine publicly supported the anarchists. She and Grand-mère were friends. I told Philippe I had met Séverine, and she'd offered to help find my grandmother. Philippe followed me from Babette's to Gaston's. My eyes flew open. "You think I'm an anarchist! You followed me as part of your job! Isn't that right?"

"Anarchist?" He looked startled. "No. No. You've got it all wrong."

"Then why?"

He closed his eyes and drew a long deep breath. My heart leaped into my throat. Something significant between us was about to change. I could feel it in my pulse, in my tightened chest.

"I was hired to watch over you when you ran away from home."

The wind was sucked out of me. Someone had hired Philippe. Most surely my father. Somehow he'd known I would run away. Only Nacia knew my plans. She must have told Papa.

"Gabbi?" Philippe leaned toward me, concern in his eyes.

I shook my head and turned away from him, staring out into the night. What was real and what wasn't? Every encounter with Philippe must have been orchestrated by him. We didn't meet by chance on the train. The times I thought I saw him in Montmartre, at the Lapin Agile, in Place Pigalle . . . it was him. He must have seen me drunk, clutching Konstantin for support.

But that kiss in the Louvre. What was that?

I faced him again, the blood pounding against my temples. "You've been lying to me ever since we met!" Tears welled in my eyes once again, and I turned away so he wouldn't see them. Was there no one I could rely upon?

"Not everything was a lie." He sounded at least slightly ashamed. "Look at me, Gabbi. Please?"

I turned to see his face creased with anxiety. "I am so sorry I didn't protect you from Gaston. I beg your forgiveness."

"It wasn't your fault." Not only was I the most naïve, stupid girl in the city, but I'd fooled myself into thinking this man cared for me. My cheeks burned with humiliation. Philippe had been very good at his job, very charming and very good. Stupid, stupid, stupid Gabbi. "And what about the anarchists and the Expo? Were they all lies, too?"

"Not completely," he said. "Our firm has been hired to stop anarchists from disrupting the Expo, but it wasn't my assignment. You were." His voice changed, caressing the word you, as if he considered himself fortunate. "My colleague knew I was there with you that day. He sent that note, warning me of potential unrest."

"And Grand-mère? Is she part of this ruse?"

He had the nerve to look offended. "Of course not. When I discovered she was missing, I began looking for her. I still am."

I shook my head, thinking of the times I'd longed to ask for his help but was too proud. "I hope you're better at finding missing persons than protecting stupid country girls for their fathers."

"You don't know how sorry I am."

I turned away and stared unseeing out of the carriage window. Anarchists. Bombs. *Poseurs*. A rapist posing as an artist. A *lorette* posing as my friend. A bodyguard posing as—well, what did I think Philippe was? A suitor? Hardly. And yet, foolishly, I thought he was romantically interested in me.

Philippe reached for my hand, but I snatched it back. I couldn't stand his pity. I was sorely in need of comfort, but I wouldn't seek it from him.

The shock of the night must have been receding for the pain of my injuries intensified. My face was the worst—my lips were swollen and sore, my cheeks burned from being slapped, and my scalp was tender where that beast had twisted my hair in his fist. My nails were ruined and bleeding. My elbows were raw although I didn't even know why, and one ankle throbbed. Above all, a throbbing pain grew from my spine and exploded through my skull until the slightest movement of air inside the carriage caused me to wince.

Driving anger and fear drained away, leaving me overwhelmed with fatigue. I leaned against the seat cushion, and my eyelids grew heavy. "Where are we going?"

"To my aunt's. You can stay there tonight. Tomorrow, I'll escort you safely home."

"Home." The word left a bitter taste in my mouth. But where else could I go?

Chapter Twenty-Six

PHILIPPE KNOCKED SOFTLY on the door to Madame Pinot's chambers.

A nightcap-encased head poked out. "What's going on? Oh, it's you, Philippe."

"I'm sorry it's so late, Tante. You remember Mademoiselle Gabrielle? She needs a place to stay tonight. Could she have the empty room on the first floor?"

Madame Pinot gave me a barbed look, shut the door, and re-emerged in a heavy flannel wrapper, key in hand. She took me upstairs without a word, showed me a small but clean bedroom, and left.

Philippe turned his top hat in his hands, avoiding my eyes. "I'll say good-night now and see you in the morning. If you need anything, anything at all, my room is two doors down."

"Good night." It was all I could manage. With feet as heavy as marble plinths, I trudged to the communal toilet down the hallway. I avoided looking at myself in the mirror above the washbasin. In the bedroom, I undressed quickly and kicked my corset and torn dress against the door.

Sinking under the blankets, I shut my eyes tightly and prayed for sleep to carry me away from the nightmare my life had become. Despite the warm night, I shivered uncontrollably. My skin burned with shame where Gaston's hands touched me. Shame and filth, as if I had slept in the city gutters for weeks. The headache that began in the carriage only intensified once I was prone. It pounded an unrelenting rhythm inside my skull—thump, thump, thump.

Worst of all, even though Gaston was the real monster, I hadn't protected myself. In my blind ambition, I ignored the warning signs and trusted the wrong people. Now there was no one left to turn to. Everyone I relied on had broken my trust: Babette and Gaston, Philippe, Papa. Even Nacia. I was truly alone. Self-pity released a torrent of tears. I cried until no tears remained, until there was nothing left but a shallow version of who I thought I was.

Yet sleep eluded me. I rose and pushed the window open to lean out into the soft evening air. Faint popping and sizzling accompanied streaks of red, pink, and green fireworks that lit up the inky darkness over the nearby Expo grounds. It reminded me of the gaiety, glamour and false sense of security I'd felt at the fair. Paris had lost its allure for me. The city's beauty was a mere veneer; scratch her surface and underneath was betrayal and corruption.

The street below my window revealed a ceaseless stream of carriages, hoods open to the night sky. Coachmen's whips cracked and tired horses neighed. Occasionally the loud sputtering of a motorcar pierced the air, leaving a harsh gasoline stink in its wake.

Directly below me, a couple strolled along the sidewalk arm in arm, laughing and murmuring. I wanted to lean out and warn the woman to be careful, to trust no one.

I shut the window and crawled back under the blankets to toss and turn, resigned to a sleepless night.

Something soft brushed against my cheek. A paintbrush. Babette sat on the bed, stroking my face with its soft bristles.

I bolted upright and pulled back from her. How had she gotten in the room? Gaston loomed over her shoulder. I shuddered as I stared into his cat-green eyes.

"Why did you run away?" Babette asked. "You can't escape us."

Gaston laughed as he leaned closer, his breath reeking. "You belong to me now, *ma petite lorette*."

Babette smirked and pulled Gaston's face toward her, kissing him on the lips. She turned her round eyes back to me. "You're no artist. You're just like me." She threw the paintbrush over her shoulder. Her lips twisted into a grimace as she stood. Gaston slid into her place and pinned my shoulders with his hands, saying, "You asked for this."

I screamed and bolted upright. Moonlight streamed across the bed and cast flickering silhouettes across the walls. No Gaston. No Babette.

"Gabrielle?" Philippe's voice called from just outside my door.

"It's nothing."

Minutes passed before his footsteps passed my door and faded away.

I sank back on the pillows. It was only *un cauchemar*, a nightmare. But the small voice inside my head asked whether they were right. Had I asked for it? Was I ruined now, no better than Babette? Did I belong to their world of betrayal and abuse? Perhaps Maman would take one look at me and throw me out . . . .

Someone knocked on the door.

I sat up, rubbing my eyes. An unfamiliar water pitcher and bowl sat on the dresser in front of striped wallpaper I didn't recognize. Sunshine streamed through lace curtains, casting delicate shadows on the floor.

"Gabrielle?"

Philippe's voice spilled through the door and triggered a nauseating wave of memories. I hunched over, my face in my hands. "What do you want?"

"I have your dress. My aunt retrieved it and mended it for you."

Wrapping the sheets around me, I opened the door a crack and took my dress from him. "I don't have any shoes."

He glanced at my feet. "Oh, I forgot . . . I'll ask my aunt." He coughed nervously. "The train to Laval leaves in two hours. We should be on it . . . ."

"I'll be down shortly." I closed the door.

I glanced in the mirror and gasped. A purplish bruise had bloomed over-night on the side of my face. I touched my cheek. It was swollen and tender. My fingernails were caked with filth. Gaston's flesh and blood. I poured water from the pitcher and scrubbed my nails with a nailbrush on the washstand. Blood swirled in the bowl as I scoured, purging any trace of him from my hands.

I scrubbed until fresh blood swirled into the basin—my own blood—and pressed a neatly folded facecloth on my fingertips to staunch the bleeding. I poured a glass of water from the washstand and rinsed my mouth, trying to flush away ugly memories of the past twenty-four hours. I thought longingly of my ivory handled hairbrush, now in Babette's care, as I tried to smooth down my hair with my fingers before braiding it into one long plait. At least Madame Pinot had performed a small miracle with my dress. Too bad, bodies don't mend as easily. Or hearts.

The sitting room was empty when I descended the stairs, barefooted, and poked my head into the kitchen.

Madame Pinot was slicing turnips. She pointed with her chopping knife to a large black pot on the stove. "You look as if you could use some food. Bowls over there, plates on the table."

"Thank you for mending my dress, Madame." I scooped the leek and potato soup into a bowl, cut off a slice of bread, and sat at the table.

More chopping sounds, vicious and staccato. "I am sorry for your trou-bles." She paused her work and glanced at me from her chopping block.

I nodded my thanks and bent over my bowl, inhaling its rich, garlicky aroma.

"There's a pair of clogs at the door," she said and resumed her chopping with more vigour.

I glanced at the back door where a clean but decidedly rough pair of sabots sat. Shame flooded through me, and I blinked back tears.

Philippe stuck his head in the kitchen. "It's good to see you up and eating." His cheer sounded forced.

I ducked my head and took a mouthful of soup, avoiding his eyes. Surely he judged me and found me wanting. Just as I had.

"I sent a telegram to your father, so he'll expect us. I also made a complaint to the police. They promised to look into Gaston and Babette." He paused until I looked up. "You'll have to be interviewed about last night," he continued, his voice gentler. "I convinced them to have a local magistrate do that in Laval. However, if Babette and Gaston are charged and brought to trial, you'll need to return here and give testimony. Are you up to that?"

Madame Pinot drew in a sharp breath. "Let the poor girl be, Philippe. She's had enough without worrying about judges and courts."

Her unexpected sympathy surprised me.

"I'll do whatever I have to," I said, but my hand shook. The soup spoon clattered to the table. Would I have to tell the judge every detail? Could I return and face Gaston in court? I squared my shoulders. I must.

"Thank you for the soup, Madame." I rose and left the kitchen with Philippe on my heels.

"Are you ready to leave?"

I had nothing to pack: no gloves or handbag, no art box, no sketchpad, no luggage at all. I hugged myself, trying to warm the bone-deep chill within me.

Philippe touched my elbow, and I startled.

"Gabbi," he said. "Is something wrong? Something I said?"

I took a deep breath before answering, the vein at my temple throbbing a warning of a new headache. "I'm fine. Thank you for your concern."

His gaze sharpened, but he didn't press me. We boarded the carriage waiting outside and rode in silence to Gare Montparnasse. When we arrived, he helped me out of the carriage and clung to my hand. "I'm sorry."

"Sorry for what?"

He closed his eyes briefly before meeting my gaze. "I'm sorry for lying to you about who I was. I'm sorry I didn't stop you from getting mixed up with Babette or Gaston. But I'm not sorry for taking this job."

I pulled my hand away. "We mustn't be late for our train."

Chapter Twenty-seven

I SLEPT DURING THE ENTIRE train journey, partially to avoid talking to Philippe, but mostly because my mind simply shut down. The only way I could deal with what had happened with Gaston was to box it up and shove it into the recesses of my brain. The effort of doing so drained me.

"We're here." Philippe shook me gently awake as the train screeched into Laval station.

I could barely keep my eyes open during the carriage ride from the train station to my home. Philippe hovered over me, treating me like an elderly aunt. At least he had the good sense to refrain from talking.

I stood before the front door of my home, hands clenched, Philippe beside me. The drapes of an upstairs window parted, and Nacia's face appeared. She looked frightened and the weight of my actions bore down once more. Her tiny wave didn't relieve my fears.

My mother opened the door.

"Maman."

She gasped.

I was alarmed at the change in her, too. Dark circles bulged under her eyes, and they glimmered with tears—or perhaps a trick of the evening light. Her eyebrows knotted together, and strands of her dark hair escaped from her normally pristine bun. I did this. "I'm sorry," I whispered.

She hesitated on the threshold before she grabbed me in a fierce hug. I inhaled her faint lavender scent and hugged her back, not wanting to release her.

She pulled away finally and gripped my shoulders, her eyes boring into mine.

"Where's Papa?" I asked.

Her lips tightened. "He's in the parlour." She turned back inside, leaving

Philippe and I to follow.

The parlour drapes were drawn shut. A single lamp illuminated a slumped silhouette in the corner of the room. My father.

"Gabbi?" He leapt up and opened his arms.

"Papa!" I threw myself into his embrace.

"Gabbi," he repeated, his voice shaky.

I clung to him tightly and tried to suppress the rising heat of anger. Anger at his part in Philippe's deception. Anger because he was right, that I couldn't take care of myself.

"It's so good to see you home where you belong." He extended a hand to Philippe. "Welcome, Monsieur Lucien."

Philippe whispered something to Papa, then turned to greet Maman, who stood with her back to the lamp. Her face was shadowed and expressionless, with no trace of the shock apparent when she'd first seen me.

Charles passed the room and halted. "Gabbi." He took me by my shoulders and gently kissed my cheeks. "Petite," he murmured, his eyes moist as he gently stroked the bruise on my face.

"Monsieur Lucien." Charles reached for Philippe's hand, leaned in, and whispered something to him.

All the whispered secrets, shadows, and betrayals. I felt a stranger in my own home. My throat tightened over the words I longed to say to my family. Take me back to my childhood, to my innocence.

Charles nodded and left the room, leaving me hollow, my kinship with him greater now that I was also *persona non grata* in the family.

"Désirée." Papa turned to Maman. "Gabbi has been through a terrible ordeal—"

She put up her hand. "Gabrielle, please leave us." Her voice cracked, and she bit her lower lip.

Surprised at being dismissed, I left reluctantly and stood trembling in the foyer.

"Gabbi, Gabbi, Gabbi!" Nacia ran down the stairs toward me, nearly tripping in haste. She embraced me tightly, her tears wetting my cheeks.

"I'm all right, Nash," I murmured into her hair.

She drew back, linked her arm with mine, and led me upstairs to my room. We sat side by side on the bed.

"Where's Genevieve?" I asked.

"She's at the church, but she should be home shortly. We all knew when the train was arriving."

I nodded and glanced around the room. My self-portrait still sat on its easel. The pearl choker lay where I'd discarded it on my dressing table, as if waiting for me to return and clasp it around my neck once again. My throat constricted. Everything appeared to be as I'd left it the day I ran away. Less than two weeks ago, yet it felt as though months had passed.

"I'm so sorry, Gabbi." Nacia wiped her eyes. "Please forgive me."

"For telling Papa I'd run away?" Resentment sharpened my tone.

"I know I broke my promise, chérie. But the thought of you in Paris by yourself . . . ."

"How did you know I'd be alone?"

"You left without waiting for Grand-mère to reply to your telegram, and when we didn't hear from her after you left, I panicked. I didn't know if you found her, or if you were alone—"

"She's missing," I said, tears welling.

"I know that now. I'm so sorry. Do you forgive me?"

Nacia's skin, always pale, was translucent and blue under her eyes, around her lips. She was so fragile. If she'd been lured to Gaston's instead of me, she wouldn't have survived. Something softened inside me. "I forgive you."

"Thank you, chérie." She squeezed my hand. "What happened?"

"What happened? Do you mean, why am I back?"

She nodded. "All I know is Papa got a telegram this morning that you were coming home with that man."

I sighed deeply. How much could I share without dragging myself down into that abyss?

"A burden shared is a burden halved," she said, reminding me of Mémère's homegrown wisdom.

I closed my eyes. Perhaps telling her would relieve some of the shame. I curled my legs up under me and told her everything. About the time with Philippe on the train, his interest in my sketches, doing his portrait. Arriving at Grand-mère's and discovering she'd left. I couldn't meet her gaze as I told her I'd allowed Babette to take all my money and the state of the attic we'd shared. I left out the night that Henri spent there, less than ten metres away from where I lay.

Some of the retelling made me laugh—the night at the Lapin Agile with Julie and the other students, my inept work as a charwoman, the cast of characters I met at Madeleine's salon, my first outing with Philippe at the Expo.

Nacia listened without interrupting.

As I told her about Gaston's attack, I stood at the window, gazing into the garden, hands clenched to prevent the trembling that threatened to overwhelm me. She gasped and rose to join me at the window, her arm around my shoulders. I was not at all certain the telling had helped.

"Poor Gabbi," she said, stroking my arm. "I should never have helped you leave. It's my fault."

"I'm not sorry I left home."

"How can you say that?" She stared, open-mouthed.

I took a deep breath. Why didn't I regret leaving home? "I proved to myself I could travel alone and that I was resourceful. Yes, I made some bad choices, but isn't that part of life? Making mistakes but getting back up again, a little wiser than before?"

"You're strong," she said. "Stronger than me."

"Not everything in Paris was terrible, Nash. In fact, much of it was marvellous. I wish you could see the Louvre Museum."

Of course, meeting Philippe was also part of it. Bitter and sweet. I let myself remember his piercing blue eyes, the surprise of his kiss in the Louvre. "I can't accept that all this happened for nothing. It has to mean something."

She shuddered. "I'm never leaving home."

"Don't be afraid, Nash. There's so much that is wonderful out there. I met people like me, art students from all over the world." If we'd had enough time, I was sure Julie would have become a close friend.

Oh no! Julie. My hand flew to my mouth. She'd wonder why I didn't show up at the studio. I hoped she wouldn't suffer any consequences for my absence.

"What's wrong?" Nacia asked.

"I've disappointed a good friend. I must write to her." I owed Julie an apology and an explanation.

"Oh! That reminds me. A letter came yesterday from Bernadette. It was addressed to me, so I opened it, but it's for you. I'll get it." She left briefly and returned, handing me the envelope. "I wish—"

A knock on my door interrupted her. A new maid opened the door. "Excuse me, but Madame wishes to see you now, Mademoiselle Gabrielle," she said with a slight curtsy.

I left the letter on my desk and followed her to the parlour.

Whatever had been discussed with Papa while I was absent had restored Maman's composure. She sat by the window, her back ramrod straight. Her dark eyes met mine across the room, and I flinched.

Papa left without meeting my eyes. Coward.

"Who is the new maid?" I asked my mother, deciding to try neutral territory first.

"Demi. She replaced Claudine."

Something in Maman's tone, the way she said Claudine, should have warned me what was coming. "Where's Claudine?"

"I fired her." Maman looked at me calmly. "She was supposed to keep an eye on you. She failed."

I shook my head, silently apologizing to Claudine. Another casualty in the war between my mother and me.

Maman motioned for me to sit beside her. "Do you have any idea how hurt I was when I discovered your letter?"

"I'm sorry, Maman. I didn't intend to hurt you or Papa."

"But you did. Terribly." She shook her head violently. "And I had to lie to the baron about your—disappearance."

"What did you tell him?"

"That you had fallen quite ill and that we had to postpone the announcement of your engagement until you were recovered."

"It's nearly true, Maman. It made me ill, just thinking of marrying him." I was trying to lighten her mood, but it backfired.

She seized my wrists. "How can you joke? You could do much worse than the baron. If what I've heard is true, you very nearly did."

I wrenched my hands from her grip. I didn't refute her. I couldn't. I shut my eyes to block out Gaston's face, but his horrid features were etched into my mind.

Maman stood and paced across the parlour floor. "I told you Paris was nothing but a cesspool of corruption. But as usual, you didn't listen to me. You're fortunate that your father was suspicious and hired that investigator to protect you."

Her assumption that Philippe alone rescued me rankled worse than my corset stays. "I'm not completely helpless, Maman."

"Don't you realize what you've done? You are ruined."

"I am not ruined." The sour taste of Gaston's tongue in my mouth, the shame of his sweaty hand on my breast, the rough crush of his knee between my thighs. Stop! Don't think about it.

Maman's face loomed in front of me. "You're just like your grandmother. You don't care how your behaviour affects me."

"How my behaviour affects you? Don't you care what happened to me?"

She shook her fists in the air. "Don't you realize that what happened doesn't matter? What matters are appearances."

"What happened matters to me! Besides, no one has to know."

"Hah! Celeste DuPont saw you on the train the day you left. She told Madeleine Pierre, who told the rest of my friends. And no doubt someone saw you arrive today in the company of that young man. Soon the baron will hear the gossip, and your prospects will be ruined."

Anger flared. "Do you not realize that the reason I left was because I have no intention of ever marrying that despicable man?"

Maman resumed pacing. "There's only one solution to this mess you've made. You have to marry the baron immediately. I'm sure an exceptionally large dowry will offset any whiff of scandal."

"Non! You aren't listening. I won't be sold off like one of Papa's casks of wine."

Maman stopped pacing in front of me. Her eyes glinted like steel. "You selfish girl. You think only of yourself, your precious dream of being an artist. Our family's honour is stake, Gabrielle."

"Honour?" I stared at her. "Perhaps you should have thought about our honour before agreeing to the baron's proposal, without inquiring of my feelings toward him."

A glimmer of regret flickered across Maman's face before her eyes narrowed. "Regardless, we are bound to the baron now. If you don't go through with this wedding, your father's reputation and business will be destroyed. Who will do trade with a man who doesn't honour his word? No one."

"I hadn't thought—"

"No, you hadn't thought of anyone but yourself. And what about Genevieve and Nacia? Do you think any man will offer marriage to them now, once they learn you refused to marry your betrothed? Your sisters will be spinsters for life. And it will be your doing."

My beloved sisters. My father. I sank into a chair and stared at my feet. I had been blind. Selfish. I risked our family's future and an honour that I had not understood or chose to blindly ignore, in pursuit of my own dream. My anger, worry, and desperate need to save myself from the baron dissolved at the moment. There was no other moral alternative than to marry the baron.

"I'm sorry, Maman. I will do as you wish." An enormous weight bore down on me as I dragged myself to my feet and crossed the room. I couldn't bear another minute with Maman.

The front door opened as I crossed the foyer, and Genevieve stepped inside. She drew in her breath as she gazed at me, her eyes red.

My throat tightened. "I'm sorry, Genevieve. It should be you, not me, marrying the baron."

Her eyes narrowed. "So the wedding is going ahead after all."

"I don't want to marry him! I . . . I'm doing this for the family, not for me." How could she not understand? I took her hand. "I'm doing this for you."

She yanked her hand away and slapped my face, her eyes brimming with tears. "I will never forgive you for this!"

Her words sliced through me. "I pity you," I said, fleeing.

Chapter Twenty-eight

Tears blinded me as I ran for the stairs and the safety of my room.

I ran straight into Philippe at the base of the stairs.

"Whoa!" Philippe grabbed my arm to stop me from falling.

I pulled away, intensely aware of the heat of his skin on mine. "Why are you still here?"

"I was waiting for you. Can we talk somewhere alone?"

I wiped my face with the back of my hand, fumbled in my pocket for a handkerchief, and blew my nose. "We can sit in the garden." I led him toward the back door.

"Gabbi!" Cook gasped and caught my hand as we passed the kitchen. "What happened, chérie?"

I smiled, or at least I tried to, but her gentle, concerned expression brought more tears. I reached out for a warm, pastry-scented hug. She stiffened and pulled away, glancing over my shoulder at Philippe. She dropped my hand and curtsied. "Welcome home, Mademoiselle."

"This is Monsieur Lucien. Madame Favre, our cook," I said.

Philippe bowed slightly. "Madame."

I led Philippe outside to the garden. A delicate scent of jasmine and lavender rose up beside the path as I sought out my favourite stone bench under the beech-nut tree. I took one end, giving him plenty of room to be seated at a proper distance.

"Well?" I regretted my sharp tone as soon as I spoke. A concoction of attraction, anger, shame, humiliation, and something quite sinful—an overwhelming desire for another kiss—stewed within me.

He sat on the opposite end of the bench. "You're angry with me. I understand that. But you must know that I intended to tell you I was hired by your father. There just never seemed the right moment. I never wanted to hurt you." He leaned forward and placed his elbows on his knees, hands clasped in front of him. "In fact, I'm quite fond of you," he said, his voice barely a whisper.

Fond of me. His words jolted down my spine and outward in flash of heat. I shook myself to dispel the *frisson* of pleasure. "It doesn't matter anymore. I am to be married soon. To the Baron d'Argente. Any . . . misunderstandings . . . about our relationship are in the past now."

His mouth fell open and he blinked. "But after what you've been through . . . surely your parents won't force you to marry?"

I laughed bitterly. "That's exactly why I'm marrying him. Once society learns what happened in Paris with Gaston . . . it will taint our entire family unless I am safely married off."

Philippe leaped to his feet and paced in front of me. "That's ridiculous! It wasn't your fault. You shouldn't be punished for it."

Oh, he was so right. But his anger worried me. "Philippe, please understand. You know how unforgiving society is, especially provincial society. We're not in Paris now." I forced the words out, defending my family's decision. "I can't bring any more dishonour to my family."

He stopped pacing and took my hands, pulling me to my feet. "Is it what you want, Gabbi?"

My bare hands thrilled at his touch. I should have pulled away, but I didn't. We were close, close enough to kiss. I stared at his lips. What harm would it do? Maman already thinks I'm ruined. Why shouldn't I have one last pleasure?

"Gabbi?"

"I . . . I'm sorry. What did you say?" My cheeks burned. Would I never learn not to let my emotions swamp my senses?

"Is marrying the baron what you want?"

"It is what I must do."

Philippe cupped his hands around my face and leaned forward. His lips crushed mine. I wrapped my arms around his neck and returned his kiss with abandon, pressing my body to his. How natural, how right it felt to be in his arms.

Philippe was the first to pull away. "Gabbi—"

I put my fingers on his lips to stop him from speaking. Any words of endearment would crumble my defences. This madness had to end. "I think it's best that you don't call on me again." I stepped back and held out my hand. "Goodbye."

He took my hand, kissing it fiercely. When he straightened, his eyes glistened and for a sweet moment, I believed he truly cared for me.

I watched him walk away, knowing that was the last I'd see of him. Choked by sobs, I fled to my room where I paced back and forth like a caged animal. There was no way out. How could I avoid marriage without bringing ruin upon my family? If only Grand-mère could be found! She'd know what to do. And Philippe did promise he'd keep looking.

A light knock rattled my door.

"Who is it?"

Demi spoke through the door. "I've been sent to ask if you are joining the family for dinner."

"I'm not hungry."

"Cook guessed as much." The doorknob turned and Demi entered, carrying a food tray, her eyes cast down.

"Thank you, Demi. Leave it here on my desk."

She placed the tray and left.

An envelope peeked out from under the tray of soup, bread, and berry pie. Bernadette's letter, the one she sent to Nacia for me. I slid it out and scanned the letter, devouring its contents as if it were my dinner. And in a way, it was: food for my spirit.

Ma chère Gabbi,

Your shocking letter is in my hands. I can't believe you left home and are living in Paris with your grandmother. You are incredibly brave, my dear friend. You must write immediately and tell me everything that has happened since that day!

Dinard and St. Malo are lovely and the beaches keep my little brothers entertained, but oh, how I miss you. I picture you in Paris, at the front of the classroom, sketching live models (are they truly naked?) and going to cafés with famous artists. Have you been to the House of Paquin or Worth's to gaze at the beautiful gowns for me?

I'm addressing this to Nacia in Laval as you failed to give me your grand-mother's Paris address. I expect she'll forward this on to you. You told me Nacia knows your plans, and I pray this doesn't fall into the wrong hands (!!) Write me immediately!!

Your loving friend,

Bernadette

I re-read the letter. Bernie was filled with pride and great expectations for my future. Truly my best friend. I wanted to beg her to come home. She couldn't stop the wedding, but she could keep me sane until then.

I slipped a piece of stationary from the drawer along with a pen and inkpot.

Dear Bernadette,

I stared at the page, chewing on the wooden tip of my pen. Could I write the words that would spoil her holiday? It would be terribly selfish. She'd find out soon enough that I was to be married. I imagined her shocked reaction to the news that I was marrying a man nearly thirty years older than me. A man I disliked and could never love, honour, or obey.

I couldn't write about that, yet I couldn't create a fantasy life in Paris to amuse her. I crumpled up the page and threw it into the waste basket, hoping she'd forgive me for failing to reply.

The setting sun shone through my window and lit up the crucifix over my bed. Perhaps there was someone who understood broken dreams and betrayal. And if I believed the Bible, He was someone who could intervene. I retrieved my rosary from the bedside table and knelt, rolling the carved beads between my fingers as I prayed through the Sorrowful Mysteries.

"Au nom du Père et du Fils et du Saint-Esprit. Amen."

I expected an immediate answer—a divine sign of some sort. At least a crash of thunder and lightning and a deep voice telling me what to do. But there was nothing, only the birds trilling outside my open window and muted voices drifting up from the street below.

Did that mean somewhere deep within me lay an irredeemable flaw? Pride or ambition, whatever it was named, was a deadly sin I couldn't release; it fed me and fuelled my art. Could I have chosen a more destructive path?

Yet without pride, how could I achieve any of my dreams? I couldn't willingly live another life than the one I'd sought when I left home. An intense need, an insatiable hunger burned within me to create paintings that existed only because I exist. Surely a loving God wouldn't allow me to feel so compelled to create art, if I wasn't supposed to be an artist. Why, then, would God condemn me to life with a man such as the baron? And yet, that was my fate. I must accept it or go mad.

My family deserved my loyalty and sacrifice. Any path other than marriage would cause suffering for those I loved most. If it was a question of my life alone, I would fight for my art to the very end. But it was no longer just about me. It never was. I'd been too self-absorbed to see that.

My heart grew as heavy as the grave-cold gargoyles atop our Basilica's steep roof. A deep melancholy replaced all hope for a life of my own choosing.

Chapter Twenty-nine

"STAND STILL!" MADAME CHARLOTTE complained through the row of pins clamped between her lips.

"I've been standing for hours," I replied. "When will you be finished?"

The couturière ignored me and stuck another pin in the hem of my new visiting dress. I sighed deeply. Maman had lured Laval's top dressmaker to the house the morning after I returned home. Did the seamstress notice the bruise on my face, or the way I winced when she turned me this way and that for the fittings? If so, she was either too polite or too appreciative of the lucrative work to comment.

Laid out on Maman's bed were several gowns-in-progress—a mud brown morning dress, a delicate blue silk reception dress, a wool travelling suit, and two elegant evening gowns. Maman wasn't doing this for me, for the extent of one's *trousseau* reflected upon the mother's worth, not the bride's.

Maman entered the room and circled me, her eyes narrowed, clearly assessing every detail of the chartreuse *peau de soie*, from the Alençon lace edging on the sleeves and modestly cut neckline to the circular flounces on my hips. "Parfaite, Madame."

"Merci." The seamstress stood with difficulty, her knees cracking as she stepped back and eyed her handiwork with a smile. "*Vous êtes très jolie*, Mademoiselle." She swung a cheval mirror in front of the dress stand, so I could admire my reflection. The now purplish-green bruise on my face clashed with the chartreuse gown. Hardly "jolie."

I stepped down, and Madame slid the dress over my head. Sharp pins maliciously scratched me. "Are we finished, now?"

"Mais non!" She turned to Maman. "My shop is extremely busy. I must do all the fittings today."

A light breeze slipped into the room through the open window and lifted the oppressive heat only slightly. I stood by the window trying to cool off, my chemise sticking to my skin.

"Gabrielle?" Maman's voice pierced my thoughts. "Stop daydreaming and cooperate."

"Oui, Maman." I meekly climbed back onto the dressmaker's stand. Madame approached, hidden under an armful of white silk, lace, and ruched *lisse*. She wrapped a corset around me, pushing my breasts up, tucking and tightening. "This plain one will do for today's fitting, but I'll create a more beautiful corset for the actual day, of course."

"I certainly hope so, Madame." Maman's stern voice carried a warning the seamstress surely understood.

Her nimble fingers flew as she next pinned the silk bodice to me. I took a breath,ever so shallowly. She stabbed my waist.

"Ouch!"

"Stand still," Madame growled.

"That hurt."

Madame fluffed up the leg-of-mutton sleeves until they were as high as my ears.

"No one in Paris wears this type of sleeve," I complained, recalling the gorgeous gowns I'd seen at Madame Chaudiere's salon and at the Expo.

"You are no longer in Paris," Maman replied tartly. "I'd have thought you'd be grateful to leave that all behind."

I winced. Touché, Maman.

Madame continued to weigh me down with acres of fabric, lace, and trimmings. When I glanced in the cheval mirror, a ridiculous goblet of frothed milk stared back at me.

The high lace collar, stiffened by bones, ensured I would keep my head high while mincing down the aisle, for it jabbed my chin if I looked down. The sleeves narrowed below my elbows, fastened by sixteen tiny buttons. The stays of the corset ensured painful reminders to keep one's posture erect. A long line of pins down my back would be replaced with hooks-and-eyes. Multiple petticoats and a crinoline would at least keep anyone, including the baron, at arm's length. Undressing would take a very long time on my wedding night. Thank goodness for that tiny blessing.

"Ah, Gabbi." Maman's eyes moistened. "You look beautiful. You will see that I'm right about this wedding."

I swallowed hard. "Oui, Maman." The words croaked out, and I wiped a hand across my damp forehead.

"The train, Madame?" Maman asked.

The seamstress lifted several meters of matching silk trimmed with tiny pearls and edged in elaborate lace. She pinned it on the back of my waist. Its weight pulled me down: another sign of wealth and status. I shuddered, picturing a lifetime of being assessed by the cut of my clothes.

"I suppose you'll have to wear white slippers," Maman said with a sigh. "It's only for one day, so perhaps you can force those feet of yours into a smaller size."

"Yes, Maman."

"Now the veil," she ordered.

The seamstress fixed the veil's crown onto my hair. Then she lowered its layers of lace, obscuring my view of the room and bringing on a brief moment of dizziness. How many times would I trip walking down the aisle?

"Nacia, Genevieve!" Maman clapped her hands. "Come and see."

My sisters crowded into the room with Demi close at their heels. They stared wordlessly until I felt like the prize cow at a fair.

Nacia stepped closer. "Lift the veil up, Gabbi. I can't even tell it's you." She stroked the shiny silk skirt and sighed deeply. "I can't wait to be a bride."

"You can take my place."

"I'll have none of that talk!" Maman glared at me.

"You will be a beautiful bride," Demi said, clutching her hands together.

"A doll is more like it," I muttered. Or *marionette*, the puppeteer pulling strings to move my arms and legs, speaking for me.

Genevieve stood near the door, her arms crossed and her face twisted with resentment. "This must be costing a small fortune."

Maman nodded, gazing at me. "Oui, but it will be worth it."

And then it all descended upon me—the weight of the gown, the pull of the stays, the heat of the room. "I feel sick." I swayed.

Maman and Madame sprang forward, steadying me as I climbed down from the dressmaker's stand. Their fingers flew over hooks and pins, removing the layers of silk and satin, helping me step out of the skirts.

Nacia drew a dressing gown over my shoulders. "You need some fresh air," she said, leading me out of the room. "Let's get you into something more comfortable, and we'll go for a walk."

She waited for me to change into a simple skirt and shirtwaist. She picked up two parasols, and I followed her outside to the courtyard. A large thud from the carriage house drew us there. We looked in on a growing pile of trunks, carpet bags, and crates.

Charles whistled as he heaved another bag onto the pile.

"Someone's been busy," I said.

He turned. "Ah, bonjour, *mes sœurs*."

Charles's shirtsleeves were rolled above his elbows, his jacket carelessly thrown over the seat of his gas-powered bicycle. He looked more like one of the servants than my smartly-turned out brother. Change was all around me.

"So you are truly leaving France for Canada?"

"Don't look so sad, Gabbi." He hugged me.

I tried to smile for his benefit. "When does your ship sail?"

"July 14, Bastille Day. I'm booked on a steamer from Le Havre to New York City, and then a train north to some God-forsaken French settlement called St. Boniface. It's where Uncle Luc lives." Despite his words, he looked happy.

"Bastille Day. So soon."

He shrugged. "I'm ready for a fresh start. And Canada's just the place for that. I've been reading up on it. Lots of Frenchmen are making their fortunes there. Why not me?"

Why not him, indeed? He was the only male heir with the family fortune backing him. Whereas I was the youngest daughter whose impetuousness caused her family embarrassment and ruined my only asset—my reputation. "Yes, why not you? You get sent off on an adventure in great style, while I am forced to marry a hideous old toad."

Charles and Nacia exchanged worried looks.

"Ignore me. I'm simply irritated from being turned into a human pin cushion."

Nacia smiled and squeezed my hand. "It's all right. Brides-to-be are allowed to be moody, aren't they, Charles?"

He laughed. "I wouldn't know. And I hope not to find out for some time to come."

"You might find Canadian women irresistible, *mon frère*," Nacia teased.

Charles laughed. "From what I know, there are very few women and an abundance of single men. If you're looking for a husband, you'd best come visit me."

Nacia blushed. "Maman would throw a fit if I married a cowboy."

"I'll keep an eye out for one with a title," Charles said with another laugh. "But I think Canada has few of those and a great deal more commoners. It's the country of second chances."

"You make it sound like the Promised Land," I said. "I should be going with you."

Charles took my hands in his. "I wish you could."

I stifled a sob and turned away, pretending to study his pile of trunks, crates, and bags. "It looks like you're taking an entire household with you."

"That's only half of what I need," he said. "I have almost another week to finish packing. I suppose that I'll miss your wedding. Have you set the date?"

"If I'm lucky, never," I muttered. Our carriage horse, Birgitta, neighed and I walked to the back of the shed. She leaned into me as I stroked her muzzle, inhaling the sweet hay-scent of her braided mane.

"Maman has invited the baron here tomorrow to finalize everything." Nacia took my arm and, tucking it into hers, gently pulled me away from Birgitta. "Everything will be fine, won't it, Gabbi?"

As we left Charles to his packing, I realized that "fine" must be the numbness I felt. I had thought that the opposite of passion and joy was anger or fear. But it wasn't. It was accepting other people's vision of who I was, of who I was meant to be. So perhaps I was fine, after all.

Arm in arm, parasols up, we walked toward the castle and chateau. The sun shone on the circular keep's roof and cast irregular shadows along the stone walls. An ache coursed through me. How could I witness such beauty and not despise fate for destroying my destiny as an artist?

Nacia drew me into the sunny meadow beside the castle. "I'm worried about you."

I shrugged.

"I'm serious, Gabbi. You used to be so full of life. Or filled with anger or righteousness! But now, you're as passive as a cow."

I snorted. "Thank you for that compliment, chérie."

"You know what I mean. Why can't you accept marrying the baron? Is it the worst thing that could happen? You can surely still draw and paint."

I shook my head. "I don't want to paint any more." I recalled Babette's words with a deeper understanding. "It was just a dream—a childish castle in the air."

"No!" Nacia groaned and grasped my hands in hers. "How can I help you?"

"There's nothing you can do. Maman watches me like a hawk about to snatch a field mouse, but she doesn't realize she's already won." A tiny spark of rebellion rose within me as memories of sketching Philippe's portrait, drawing with Julie at Place Pigalle flickered in my mind. But it sputtered and died quickly for lack of air.

"Don't worry, Nacia. I'll marry the baron, say the right things to the right people, and smile until my cheeks hurt."

Nacia peered into my face. "You haven't smiled since you came home."

"What is there to be happy about? Everything I cared about is gone or was an illusion."

"Oh, Gabbi." Nacia hugged me fiercely. "I don't care if you marry the baron or anyone else. I'd do anything to get my fun-loving, outspoken, determined, and pig-headed sister back."

She wanted me to smile so I tried. If I gave people what they wanted, they left me alone. And all I wanted was to be left alone.

Chapter Thirty

ANOTHER STIFLING SUMMER DAY indoors, another tedious round of small talk. My eyes drifted toward the parlour room door. Correspondence on a silver tray on the foyer table, invoices from the couturière and florist, a growing pile of visiting cards. The detritus of a business transaction.

"Gabrielle?" Maman's sharp voice pierced my thoughts. "Monsieur le Baron was speaking to you, chérie."

I shifted my attention to him. Seated across the tea table, he was more bird-like than ever in his canary yellow waistcoat, black cravat, and starched white shirt. "I'm sorry, Monsieur le Baron."

He cleared his throat as if a heavy gob of phlegm quivered there. "I was saying how pleased I was that we have a date set for our nuptials."

"What?"

Maman preened as if she'd just become a baroness herself. "July 14th."

"But that's one week from now—the day Charles leaves." I squeezed my hands, trying to stem the tide of panic washing over me.

"That's exactly why we've had to rush the date. You wouldn't want your only brother to miss the most important day of your life, would you?" Maman's voice was calm but carried a steel edge. "Unfortunately, he'll have to depart as soon as the civil ceremony is over, or the ship will sail without him."

The baron took a sip of cognac and picked up his ever-present cigar from the crystal ash tray. "I'm afraid I'm also part of the rush. Travel plans take me to Italy. If we are wed soon enough, we can make the trip together." His gaze fell not on my face, but on my bosom.

I felt the colour drain from me as I faced the smug expressions of my mother and future husband. My puppet master was changing from Maman to the baron. They continued to discuss details as if I were absent. Perhaps I was, in all but physical presence.

"Of course, the guest list will be restricted, as we can't possibly inform everyone so quickly," Maman said. "But I doubt that bothers you, Gabrielle."

My throat tightened. How could I prevent it from happening so quickly? "Maman, have you forgotten about the publications of banns? That takes three weeks at a minimum."

"The Bishop and Mayor made concessions. The banns need only be published once at the town hall and tomorrow at the Basilica and the Cathédrale de la Sainte Trinité."

I sagged against my chair. Maman must have wielded all her influence, backed by Papa's wealth, to ensure all would be accomplished in one week. Extraordinary! And was I the only one who recognized the irony of choosing a holiday symbolic of the ideals of *liberté, égalité,* and *fraternité* as my wedding day? "Surely one can't be married on Bastille Day. It wouldn't be proper."

"It's perfectly acceptable," Maman said, her words clipped. "The civil ceremony takes place at 9:30 a.m. at the town hall. We'll be at the *dejeuner* before the official parade and celebrations start, and the church service will be at 2 p.m. It's not unusual, nowadays, to have both on the same day."

What was more shocking—Maman adopting modern customs, or the sudden rush to the altar? "Will you at least send a telegram to Bernadette, inviting her to the wedding? I must have her here."

Maman nodded and made a note on a pad of paper in front of her. "So much to do." She sighed loudly. "It's a pity we don't have sufficient time to display Gabrielle's trousseau."

One small blessing: saved from Maman's friends pawing through my lingerie and gifts, assessing how much money our family was spending to impress.

"And the *corbeille* . . . ." Maman continued.

"Ah yes, my gift to the bride." The baron shifted in his seat, slightly uncomfortable under Maman's gaze. "It is a pity we are so rushed."

Silence.

So, there would be no gift of the baron's family heirlooms, furs, or jewellery. It didn't matter to me but Maman had clearly expected the baron to follow the tradition, despite his lowly financial circumstances.

He cleared his throat. "With your permission, Madame de Villiers, I would like Gabrielle to give me a tour of your gardens you have told me so much about."

"Bien sur, Your Excellency." Maman purred. "I shall ask Demi to accompany you." She rang her silver bell and flashed me a warning with her eyes.

Demi appeared and curtsied. "Yes, Madame?"

"Please accompany Mademoiselle Gabrielle and Monsieur le Baron as they take a turn around the gardens."

I stood. "Monsieur?"

"Please, Gabrielle, call me Victor," he said as he offered me his arm.

I looked down to hide the contempt in my eyes. "If you insist, Monsieur, but not before the wedding. It wouldn't be seemly."

I'd hoped to annoy him, but he only smiled and pressed his arm against me, squashing my breast. As we entered the garden, I tried to pull away, but he was surprisingly strong. Demi remained several paces behind us.

We walked in silence down the crushed gravel path. The baron stopped by the small latticed gazebo at one end. Bright orange honeysuckle flowers trumpeted their fertility to hummingbirds and bees alike. I shuddered.

The baron leaned close. "There appears to be seating for only two in the gazebo, yet I dearly wish to try the view from that delightful vantage point. Do you think your maid would wait here?"

I asked Demi to wait and stepped into the fairy-tale gazebo Papa had created for Maman. It had been built nearly thirty years ago, before nine pregnancies. It was impossible to imagine my parents desperately in love. Had Maman approached her own wedding as a business proposal?

"There is one small favour I would ask of you," I said, spreading my skirt out on the small bench so he had to stay a suitable distance from me.

"Anything, my dear Gabrielle."

I kept my eyes on my hands, folded in my lap. "Would you object if I lived in the capital for part of the year?"

He let out a bemused laugh. "I would think you have had enough of Paris."

So he had heard. "Nonetheless, I would love to study art there, perhaps only for a few months each winter."

He slid closer and manoeuvred so his back was blocking Demi's view. His voice was low as he held my gaze. "Listen to me. Your family is fortunate that I am a man of my word. Your reputation is tainted, but I agreed to marry you, so I will keep my promise." He took my hand in his clammy one. "But surely you understand I have expectations of my wife."

I swallowed hard.

He tightened his grip on my hand. "My expectations are no more than those of any other husband."

It took all my resolve not to snatch my hand away. Wife. Husband. The words made me cringe inwardly, yet what did I expect? I had chosen this path.

He cleared his throat. "As my wife, you will honour me in all ways, run my household, bend to my needs, and bear me heirs. You will find those duties will occupy all of your time. I will not tolerate a wife who does not obey me. Do you understand?"

The cloying sweetness of the honeysuckle stuck to the roof of my mouth, threatening to gag me. It should be Genevieve sitting here. She would accept such demands willingly, even eagerly. I nodded.

He stood and offered me his arm. "I'm glad there is no misunderstanding between us."

I stood, trembling, and waited until my legs were solid enough to carry me back to the house.

Chapter Thirty-one

AS SOON AS THE BARON LEFT, I ordered Demi to run a hot bath in the new bathing room Papa had installed only weeks before. I stripped down to my chemise and waited impatiently for the large enamelled bathtub to fill. Squatting on bronzed claw feet, it dominated the room. Demi sat nearby on an upholstered stool that hid a silver bed pan.

"You're shivering, Mademoiselle, and yet it's hot as Hades." Demi wiped sweat from her brow. She narrowed her eyes. "Are you ailing?"

"It's nothing." Nothing that could be cured. When I lowered myself into the steaming water, I inhaled its lemon scent and scrubbed with the washcloth until my skin turned red. Perhaps I could wipe away thoughts of the baron's demands.

"Does Mademoiselle have a rash?" Demi asked, peering at my reddened arms.

"No, I do not," I snapped. I dropped the washcloth into the water. Nothing could erase my revulsion for my future with the baron.

I closed my eyes and sank into the fragrant, seductive warmth of the water. I sank like the poor girl in *Ophelia Drowning,* an engraving in an art journal. I fancied seaweed and fishes luring me into their silent, timeless world beneath the surface as my skirt rose gently upward, away from my skin.

Shakespeare wasn't the only man to romanticize drowned women; they were admired and loved because of their tragic deaths. But Ophelia had been a redheaded beauty who drowned innocently in a river; not deliberately in a bath tub. Still, I held my face below the surface. Drowning seemed an attractive option.

A firm hand grabbed my wrist and pulled me to the surface. I rose, gasping for air.

Demi stared at me with a look of blank horror on her face, still holding my wrist. "Mademoiselle frightened me!"

"Shush, nothing happened."

The maid shook her head but bent to her task and soaped my back, gently pouring rinse water afterward.

I ignored her and closed my eyes again. Oh, how intolerable my life had become. I simply couldn't refuse to wed the baron. The wedding plans had gone too far. Important people were coming, gifts purchased, the trousseau nearly finished. And underpinning it all was the reputation of our family.

Could I really drown myself? I'd need an opportune moment. "Demi, you must have other chores. I'm perfectly capable of bathing myself."

Her eyes narrowed. "Mademoiselle, you know I can't do that. You want me to lose my job?"

"I won't tell Maman. Please. I need time alone."

She shook her head.

"You were a jailer before you came here, weren't you?"

She compressed her lips and crossed her arms. She was headed for a long career at chez de Villiers.

Nacia knocked and poked her head into the room. "Gabbi, you have a visitor."

"I don't want to see anyone." I slid back into the steamy water. I couldn't imagine anyone visiting me. Unless . . . . "Is it Bernadette?"

"No," she said. "That rather handsome young man who brought you home from Paris. Monsieur Lucien. He says it is urgent that he speak with you."

"Oh," I said, sliding farther down. Drowning would solve more than one problem.

Nacia's heels clicked across the tiled floor. I looked up. She hovered over me, arms crossed. "I never order you around, do I?"

"No."

"Well, I'm telling you now to get out of that tub, get dressed, and greet your visitor properly."

I sat up straighter and stared in awe. "Demi, hand me that towel."

"But I haven't washed your hair, Mademoiselle."

"I'll do it," Nacia said. "Please leave us, Demi."

What had gotten into my meek sister?

The maid marched out and closed the door behind her.

"Now we can talk," Nacia said. "Or rather, I shall talk while you listen." She rubbed soap into my hair and lathered it. "I've had enough of your moping and gloom. I knew you cared about this Philippe as soon as you told me about meeting him on the train and your outings in Paris. And just now, he confided in me that he cares very much for you. So you will receive him with the respect that he deserves."

She poured fresh water over my soapy hair.

"How can you forget that I'm to be married to the baron? It wouldn't be seemly to receive Philippe."

"You've never worried about propriety before. Why start now?" Nacia ran her fingers through my hair as she rinsed it a second time.

She was so right. I bowed my head for a third rinse. Then I stood and she passed me the towel. Once I was dry with a towel turbaned around my head, I followed her to my bedroom where she helped me dress. She brushed out my hair, braiding the dark wet strands and pinning them up so they wouldn't dampen my clothing.

"There," she pronounced. "You're ready. Now, listen with an open heart. Please?"

Philippe must have charmed her. He certainly could be convincing when it suited his purposes. I knew that only too well, remembering how his eyes crinkled with mischief when we jumped onto the moving sidewalk at the Expo, and how his deep voice thrilled me before he kissed me in the Louvre. I went down to the drawing room to meet him, as nervous as if he were courting me and this was our first encounter.

Nacia sat on a chair outside the door, keeping a discreet distance. I wondered if Maman knew I was receiving this gentleman caller. Or had Nacia managed somehow to keep him a secret? She opened a book on her lap and cast her eyes down.

Philippe stood at the window, gazing out at the garden. I caught my breath when I saw his profile, remembering our last kiss in the garden. He hadn't yet noticed me, so I took this last opportunity to simply gaze upon him. His beautifully shaped lips, his strong dark brow, the jagged scar along his jaw that was not a flaw at all but rather a badge of his loyalty and courage. My heart ached. How difficult it was to be in the same room with him, to be close enough to smell his scent of soap and pomade. Close enough to look into the blue eyes that changed hue every time I saw him.

I wondered if he still had the portrait I'd sketched on the train. So much had happened since that hopeful day. "Bonjour, Philippe."

"Gabbi!" He turned and took a few steps toward me, a wary smile lighting his eyes.

"Please, sit down," I said, trying to sound as if he was just another visitor, not the one person I most wanted to see and most feared seeing.

He waited for me to take a seat near the window before he chose a chair across from me. The late afternoon light filtered through the sheer drapes and cast his features in a soft glow. His expression was apprehensive, and I was afraid of what he'd come to say. I clutched my hands together and waited.

"Thank you for receiving me without notice." He shifted in his chair and gazed at me intently. "It's a pleasure to see you again. You look well."

"Aside from rather hideous bruising, yes, I am well." The stilted, formal conversation made me fidget and shift in my chair. We were acting as if we were strangers, as if I didn't owe him a great debt.

He coughed, a nervous sort of sound. "Have you been painting?"

"No, I'm not . . . interested in it anymore." I shrugged.

"But you love your art!"

"Things change." In the silence that followed, I sought something safe to discuss. "I don't think I properly thanked you for coming to my aid. In Paris."

He inclined his head. "You are most welcome. I only wish I'd acted sooner and thus saved you from . . . well, from unpleasantness."

Another awkward silence. Was there nothing we could discuss without embarrassing one another?

"You will be glad to know I'm a reformed man, because of you."

"Pardon?"

His beautiful carved lips curved into a lop-sided smile. "After our discussions of women and careers, I kept thinking of what you had said. I talked to my sisters, in fact."

"*C'est vrai?*" It seemed that even Philippe was changing. "And?"

"And you were right about one of them. Sylvie. She told me she wished she'd gone on to university to study science." He shook his head. "Science! She's been reading about a woman, Madame Curie, and her discoveries of new chemical substances. When she talked about Madame Curie, Sylvie's eyes lit up, just like yours when you talk about art."

"But isn't your sister married, with children? It's too late for her."

He laughed. "That's what I told her, but she said she was going to tell Giles, her husband. They will have to find a way for her to study and be a mother." He shook his head. "Remarkable."

"I hope it works out for her," I said, trying to feel truly happy for his sister. "Is that . . . is that the only reason for your visit?"

"Ah, not entirely." He cleared his throat and fidgeted. "I've come with news of your grandmother."

My heart lifted. I'd given up hope too soon. She could be on her way to stop this charade of a wedding! I closed my eyes and remembered the soft cloud of white hair around her face, the broad smile that lit up her eyes. Mémère. I opened my eyes and met Philippe's gaze. "You've found her?"

His mouth tightened.

It couldn't be good news.

"She booked passage on a steamer to Halifax."

"Halifax?" I grasped the arm of the chair, seeking an anchor. "Is that in England?"

"No, Canada. The ship sailed last month."

"Are you sure?"

He gazed at me, his eyes reflecting concern. "Yes. There's more news. Are you all right?"

I nodded, not entirely sure.

"I hate to be the one to tell you . . . ." He looked out the window for several heartbeats. "She became quite ill while onboard and died before the steamship docked in Halifax. A death at sea is quite complicated, I'm told. The authorities in Halifax weren't certain how to handle it. Eventually they contacted your uncle in Manitoba as her closest kin. Your grandmother was buried there last week. I'm so sorry."

Mémère. The room tilted.

Philippe knelt before me, his hand reaching for mine. "Are you all right?"

I stood but my legs buckled, and the last thing I recalled was Philippe crying my name as the room went dark.

Chapter Thirty-two

"SHE'S BEEN IN BED FOR HOURS, Charles," Nacia whispered.

"Should we summon the priest? Or a doctor?" Charles replied, concern in his voice.

"Maman doesn't want to cause any alarm. She says Gabbi will come out of it on her own."

I lay curled up under a thin blanket with my back to them, eyes shut and only half listening. My mind was as numb as my heart.

"Gabbi?" Nacia touched my shoulder gently. "Wake up. It's dinner time, and Cook has made your favourite meal—roast beef with fresh asparagus and peas from the garden."

The thought of food caused my belly to cramp. I groaned.

Nacia spoke again. "We have to do something, Charles. She must be ill. It can't just be the news of Mémère's death, as bad as that was."

"Maman took it harder than I thought," Charles said. "They'd been estranged for so long, you'd think she hardly cared."

"She was still her mother." Nacia rubbed my back, her hand scribing circles. "Gabbi's wedding is only a week away, and the prospect of it is killing her. How can we convince Maman she has to cancel the whole thing?"

Dear Nacia, she truly understands.

"I'm hardly the one to do it. Have you forgotten I'm persona non grata?" Charles asked.

"She could delay it."

"Delay won't help Gabbi, will it? It just postpones the inevitable."

Bless my brother for his practical mind. I would have welcomed any delay.

"And Maman wouldn't cancel if the Virgin Mary herself insisted. The baron's family are coming, as are all of her friends. She would never survive such humiliation."

A sharp pain stabbed deep in my abdomen, and I groaned again, pulling my knees to my chest.

"What's wrong, Gabbi?" Nacia pulled on my shoulders, turning me toward her.

I clutched my abdomen. "It hurts. It really hurts!" The pain grew worse by the moment, as if I'd been skewered on a spit.

"Go get Maman," Nacia told Charles. "I'll stay with Gabbi." She felt my forehead. "You're burning up, chérie." She left my side and returned with a cold wet cloth.

For the next three days, I lay suspended in a foggy purgatory of fever and chills, wet cloths, and heavy blankets. Snatches of whispered conversations filtered in with fragments of images that could have been moments of lucidity or dreams. Papa stroking my hair, murmuring. Maman and Genevieve at my side, praying the Rosary. Cook urging me to drink thin soup or sip cool water. Nacia laying cold cloths on my forehead, moving me gently to sponge my body, changing my chemise when it was drenched from fever.

And our family doctor, muttering and grinding medicines, tipping my head to force foul concoctions down my throat.

Once, I was sure of it, Mémère came to see me. She lay on the bed beside me and sang, just as she'd done when I was young. Philippe must be wrong. Someone else died on that ship, not my grandmother.

One visitor kept constant vigil: a recurring nightmare. Dressed in the monstrosity of my wedding finery, I walked down the aisle of our church clutching a bouquet of white lilies. Guests on either side whispered and pointed. I approached the altar and the baron. As the priest began to intone a prayer, a white dove crashed through the stained glass windows above. She fell at my feet, her wings broken. A seeping pool of blood stained my shoes and the hem of my dress crimson. The lilies spouted blood, soaking my dress. Someone screamed; perhaps it was me.

The nightmare tormented me again and again. Details would change—the guests or the flowers I carried—but it always ended the same way.

One day, my eyes opened to a clear view of my bedroom. It was early morning, judging by the thin light in the room. I sat up slowly. I tried to stand, but my legs wobbled, and I had to sit down. How long had I been in bed? I spied a glass of water on the nightstand and drank it slowly, savouring the cool wetness sliding down my throat.

Nacia stirred from her spot in a nearby chair, opened her eyes, and smiled. "You're awake!" She sat up and pulled on her dressing gown. "How do you feel?" She sat beside me and placed her cool hand on my forehead. "Your fever has gone; thanks be to God."

"I think I'm all right." My stomach grumbled. We both laughed.

"I'll bring you something to eat."

"No, I'll come down with you. It would feel good to walk."

Nacia helped me into a dressing gown and supported me as we descended the stairs.

I emerged from my dream world of filmy, fleeting images of weddings gone awry to one of tangible objects: crisp linen against my skin, sturdy walls, and wooden floors. I still wasn't sure what was and wasn't real.

I stopped Nacia before we entered the kitchen. "Philippe. He was here, wasn't he?"

She nodded. "What do you remember?"

"He told me that Mémère had sailed to Canada. That she'd been quite ill and she . . . died onboard. Is that true?"

Her face crumpled. "It's true. And then we thought we were going to lose you too."

We wrapped our arms around each other, tears running. Oh, Mémère. To be so ill, so far away from family, from home. All the times she'd nursed me when I was sick as a child. If only I'd been able to do the same for her. And we couldn't even give her a funeral. It all happened without us.

Finally I drew away. "How is Maman?"

"I've never seen her so upset." Nacia wiped her eyes, blew her nose. "When she wasn't at your bedside, she barricaded herself in her room. She blames herself, you know, for cutting off all contact with Mémère."

"Well, she is responsible for Mémère being alone!"

Nacia shook her head. "If you could see how she's suffered, Gabbi, you wouldn't be so harsh. Imagine how you'd feel if Maman had died while you were away in Paris."

Remorse stabbed me. My behaviour was no better than Maman's. I had run away from home, cutting myself off from the family just as she'd done to her mother. Oh, the past has a way of repeating itself. But it wasn't too late for Maman and me. "Let's find Maman."

"She's in the kitchen," Nacia said.

"Ah, *mon chou*, you are well again," Cook exclaimed as we entered the kitchen. "Like Lazarus, risen from the dead!"

"Don't be sacrilegious," Maman snapped. She rose from the table where Genevieve sat, the household accounts ledger open. Maman placed her hand on my forehead. "Much better, merci Dieu."

She hugged me briefly, and as I inhaled her lavender fragrance, the part of me that had hardened against her softened. She'd suffered these past days too, grieving Mémère. She stroked my hair, her hand lingering on my cheek. "You had me worried, chérie. But with a little rest and some food, and with God's grace, you'll soon be fully recovered."

As I looked into her eyes, circled with fatigue and worry and possibly regret, I knew I couldn't add to her burdens. I was truly trapped. "I hope so, too, Maman."

"And the wedding will go on as planned," Genevieve added with a false smile and a bitter tone.

"Oui, only four days until the blessed event." Maman passed me a copy of the published banns.

My hands shook as I read our names, linked together in bold print: "M. V. Legris, Baron d'Argente and Mlle. G. C. de Villiers." Such a shame it wasn't Genevieve's wedding announcement, for our initials were identical. She was christened Genevieve Clare. She'd wanted this her entire life while I'd never dreamed of marriage. Oh, the irony.

"I know how you feel. It's too exciting!" Maman's cheeks flushed with pleasure, completely misunderstanding. How wide the gap between us.

"You should eat something, Gabrielle, and then rest, while your sisters and I manage everything. We can't have a sick bride, now can we?"

I nearly laughed at her attempt to motivate me to a speedy recovery.

Chapter Thirty-three

AFTER A LIGHT BREAKFAST and a short sleep, I slipped downstairs looking for something to distract me from the pending wedding. I passed through the foyer just as our butler, Gerard, shut the front door. He held an elaborate bouquet of showy white gardenias.

"Those are beautiful," I said. "Who are they for?"

"For you, Mademoiselle."

"Me?" I took the bouquet from the butler and buried my face in them, inhaling their musky sweetness. A tiny envelope was tucked into the stems.

My heart pounding, I tore it open. I recognized Philippe's handwriting on the note at once.

Dear Gabrielle,

"What's this?" Maman's voice preceded her into the foyer.

I slipped the note into my pocket, praying she didn't notice. "Flowers, Maman."

"Who sent them?" She took the bouquet from me, barely gave them a glance, and frowned. "Is there no card?"

I shook my head. I couldn't bring myself to surrender Philippe's message.

Gerard glanced at me and then cleared his throat. "Monsieur Lucien was here, Madame. As you've ordered, I told him Mademoiselle Gabrielle was unavailable. He left the bouquet."

Philippe had been here, just moments ago? Not a delivery boy? My eyes flickered to the door, betraying me.

Maman glared. "Gabrielle, this is your fault. Don't encourage the poor man when you will be married before the week is out."

I flushed and bit back a reply.

She thrust the bouquet at Gerard. "We cannot accept these. Get rid of them."

"Non!" I bit my lip, and lowered my voice. "I mean . . . it would be such a waste to throw them out."

A week earlier, she would have insisted the flowers be discarded. But either Grand-mère's death had softened her, or she was confident in her success. She nodded her assent, turned on her heel, and sailed out of the foyer.

I carried the bouquet to the kitchen in search of a suitable vase. They would make a beautiful still life painting. That unbidden thought tugged at my resolve to give up art. I imagined the brush balanced in my hand, the pressure of each dab and stroke reminding me of Philippe. The urge to create swelled, threatening to choke me.

Cook looked up from kneading dough at the table. "Oh, those are lovely! The vases are in the cabinet, there." She pointed a flour-dusted finger before resuming her work.

After cutting the stems and arranging the bouquet in the vase, I stepped back to admire them. The contrast of pure white petals against a background of glossy, dark leaves would make a perfect composition. Perhaps Flanders yellow with Prussian blue for the upper side of the leaves; viridian or cobalt green for the darker underside. The petals weren't a pure white. Upon close scrutiny, the lower petals reflected the shiny green foliage. Titanium white would need to be nuanced with hints of green. They would make a challenging study . . . if I were painting.

Cook grunted as she pounded the dough with her fists a final time. She straightened and wiped her hands on her apron. "I thought I saw a young man walk past the window a few minutes ago. The same one who visited the day you fell ill."

What did she know, and what did she suspect? "Yes. He . . . works for Papa. He brought these for me."

She pursed her lips, but I couldn't tell if she disapproved.

"He's just a friend."

"Be careful, chérie," she said. "He certainly means to be more than that. White gardenias mean secret love."

My cheeks warmed. I grabbed the vase and rushed out of the kitchen. Only once I closed my bedroom door and set the vase down did I read Philippe's note.

Dear Gabrielle,
I hope you have recovered from your illness. I tried to visit but was refused. I must see you. I am waiting for you at the Basilica Notre Dame. Please come at once.
Philippe

I shuddered at the thought of Maman reading such a note. How could he have been so careless? He had no idea who he was dealing with, that was clear.

I stared at the fragrant bouquet of flowers. It would be nearly impossible to leave the house. Maman might agree to my meeting with the priest about final wedding details, but she'd insist on coming along. Perhaps if I convinced her I was becoming more devout and wished to attend confession before my wedding? I could see Philippe, then, one last time. It would be worth it, even though every encounter with him made marrying the baron that much harder. It would be easier to pretend I didn't care, to ignore his request.

When I sought out Nacia, she had no doubts. "But of course you must go! If you don't, you will always regret it."

"You've changed, Nash," I said, amazed at my sister's certainty.

She took my hand and squeezed it. "I want you to be happy. I need my vibrant, loving sister back."

Nacia told Maman we were going to the Basilica for confession and obtained her permission for the outing. I dressed with extra care, changing three times before settling on an azure blue suit suggested by Nacia. Demi fussed with my hair, taking her time to create a nightmarish Pompadour. Four o'clock, four thirty. Would he still be there?

Nacia watched all of my preparations with a satisfied smile. Finally, I tore out the hideous coiffure and allowed my hair to fall down my back. By the time we left the house and began to walk the short distance toward the Basilica, late afternoon clouds darkened the sky and light rain began to fall. We opened our parasols when the first drops fell, but the wind picked up, and we were soaked through by the time we reached the church. So much for all my primping.

The basilica's tall, carved stone spire still reached for the heavens after seven centuries. Was there a lesson in it for me—to be constant in my attempts to reach for my dreams, regardless of how impossible they may seem?

Inside the dark vestibule, I shook out my parasol and waited for my eyes to adjust to the gloom. Nacia draped a long dark scarf over her hair and handed one to me. I was grateful for the anonymity it provided. I dipped my hand in the holy water and stood at the entrance to the sanctuary, breathing in the faint smoky scent of incense and oiled oak that took me back to the day I stood in the small church in Montmartre. I couldn't see Philippe. Had he given up on me?

"Don't worry, he's here," Nacia whispered.

A shiver ran down my spine as I stared down the long aisle to the altar and wondered at Philippe's choice of meeting place. While close to my parents' house, it was also the site of my pending wedding. Was he aware of that? Did he realize the irony? Or did he have some other reason for wanting to meet me here, of all places?

A queue of people near the elaborately carved wooden stall suggested that the priest was already in the confessional, much to my relief. Surely he would have recognized me, raising questions if he saw me with Philippe.

Nacia took my arm and led me to a pew near the middle of the sanctuary. I genuflected and crossed myself, but couldn't focus on prayer. Memories flitted about like a hummingbird in a field of wild flowers. Philippe posing for his portrait the day we met, the feel of his strong hands in mine, the warmth of his lips. That day in the garden . . . he started the kiss, didn't he?

"Gabrielle!" Philippe whispered.

I jumped.

He slid beside me on the smooth oak pew.

"Bonjour," I whispered shakily and then cleared my throat. "I believe you have met my sister, Nacia."

He nodded. "Bonjour, Mademoiselle."

"Bonjour, Monsieur Lucien."

He bent his head toward mine. "We can talk in the chapel, there," he said, motioning to the side where an elaborate plaster statue of the Virgin Mary invited worshippers.

His breath warmed my neck, and I shivered, nodding, not trusting my voice. I quietly slid past Nacia and tiptoed to the dim side chapel, Philippe at my heels. I felt his gaze on me as we knelt on padded kneelers before the Blessed Mother. I turned to him. The intensity with which he studied me made me uneasy. Did he find me wanting?

"Thank you for coming," he said softly.

Like a magnet, he drew me toward him. I clasped my hands tightly in prayer to ground me. "The flowers . . . they were lovely."

He looked around. We were the only ones in the chapel, yet still he whispered. "Are you recovered?"

"Yes, thank you."

"Merci Dieu."

I was surprised; that was the first time I'd heard Philippe mention God, and realized I had no idea what his religious views were. Our time together in Paris seemed like an illusion; I really didn't know him at all. "I didn't properly thank you, the last time we spoke."

"The last time we spoke." He paused. "Well, there was little time for that."

"I'm not normally the fainting kind."

Someone coughed. We turned but saw no one approaching.

"I am so very sorry about your grandmother."

"Thank you. It's hard to think of her, so ill and without family, somewhere in the middle of the sea." I blinked back unshed tears.

He reached across and took my hand, kissed it. "I hated bringing that news to you. I know how much she meant to you."

That nearly undid me. I bit my lip hard to stop myself from crying, and took several deep breaths. "I failed her."

He shook his head. "She left on that ship before you even came to Paris. How could you have helped her?"

I shook my head. It wasn't logical, but I couldn't shake the conviction I'd failed my grandmother when she'd needed me most. I had to atone for my selfishness. "I'm sure you have heard that my wedding is this Saturday."

"Yes," he said, his voice strained. "Forgive me for insisting upon seeing you. I realize how improper it is, but, well—I'm so very glad you came."

I didn't answer, for an elderly woman shuffled into the small chapel. A coin jangled in the tin donation box. She lit a candle and murmured a prayer. The shadows gave her a dark and unforgiving appearance.

We continued to kneel until she left the chapel. I stared at Philippe's hands as he clasped them over the armrest of the kneeler. Those hands had swept a loose strand of hair from my face, stroked my cheek as a prelude to a kiss. An ugly dark scab graced his right knuckle. Had Gaston's loathsome chin produced that injury?

But that was behind us. I gazed openly at his face to memorize his features, for I would never see him again. He shifted closer to me. The incense-laden air blended with a hint of his scent that I would never forget.

I stood. He stood also. I glanced across the church. Nacia was still kneeling in silent prayer. Worshippers continued to enter and exit the screened confessionals at the back. The priest should be occupied for some time yet. "Why did you ask me here, Philippe?"

"I'm not sure where to start." He took a deep breath. "I'm staying in Laval, at the Hotel de Paris until my future gets sorted. You see, I lost my job because I failed to protect you in Paris—"

"Oh! I'm so sorry." I reached out to touch his arm but stopped, remembering I could have no part in his life.

He shook his head. "It was for the best. Losing my position has forced me to evaluate my life and make some changes. Changes that might affect you."

I clutched my hands tightly. "Oh?"

"I am leaving for Canada." His eyes were alight. "I'm going with your brother, Charles."

No! The room tilted. I clutched the kneeler rail for stability. Canada—that wretched country was taking everyone I loved from me. First Mémère, then Charles, my new friend Julie, and now Philippe! But then, I'd already lost him, the moment Maman formalized my betrothal to the baron. My breath caught in my throat, and I had to look away from him.

Outside, rain pelted the chapel's stained-glass window, running down in streaks. Inside, Christ hung on the cross, blood oozing from the wound in his side. His mother was prostrate with grief at the foot of the cross, consoled by the apostle James. Christ regarded his mother with such tender devotion. I tried to swallow the lump in my throat.

He cleared his throat. "Gabrielle?"

I turned. "Yes."

"I'm going to emigrate to Canada."

"I know. I heard you," I said dully.

"I'm helping Charles get established, to begin with. After that, I plan to open my own photography studio, perhaps in Montreal."

"Photography? I'm not surprised." He was moving across the ocean, moving on with his life. Away from me. I nodded, yet couldn't force my voice past its woodenness. "That sounds wonderful."

"No. You're not listening."

"I am. I'm truly happy for you." And I was happy, despite the growing chasm in my chest. He deserved to follow his own heart. "But why Canada?"

"It's . . . it's because of you. At least, in part."

I turned to face him directly. "Me? What do you mean?"

He grinned, his teeth a flash of white in the gloom. "Ever since you challenged me in the Louvre to discover what I really wanted, I've given it a great deal of thought." He paused. His voice changed cadence, became more confident, more certain. "I want to be a professional photographer. I love the whole process—taking the shots, developing them in my laboratory. It's new and innovative, and I'll be on the cutting edge, especially in Canada. With any luck, I'll soon be able to afford to marry and raise a family."

I struggled between rejoicing over his plans and facing my own bleak future. It took several seconds before the word 'marry' registered on my brain. "Marry? You're getting married?"

And now all his confidence of a moment earlier seemed to vanish. He looked frightened. No, it wasn't fear. It was longing.

"That depends on you." His eyes, now a deeper indigo, locked onto mine. He reached out and stroked my cheek with his hand, gently, as if afraid I'd shatter.

I had to remind myself how charming he could be when he wished. "Me?" I barely whispered.

Chapter Thirty-four

HE REPEATED, "YES, GABRIELLE. I want you to marry me."

My chest tightened and paralysis rendered me unable to speak or move, unable to breathe.

He rushed on. "I intended to propose when we last spoke, but you collapsed before I could."

Propose. He had meant to propose. To me.

"Your mother chased me away, accusing me of upsetting you."

More likely, she realized he would interfere with her wedding plans.

He turned to face me squarely and clutched my hands in his.

"Philippe, I—"

"Marry me, Gabrielle."

His eyes held mine. I saw only sincerity and hope, yet didn't trust my own senses, couldn't find my voice.

"It's the perfect solution," he said urgently. "You don't have to marry the baron. Not if you leave France."

I gazed at his face, so open and vulnerable. But trust no longer came easily for me. Marry him? And condemn my family to dishonour and even possibly ruin? What about my art? I'd given up on it with the baron, yet would life with Philippe give me the freedom to resurrect that dream?

Marrying him wasn't an unbearable idea; quite the contrary. But it would be unbearable to be foisted upon him. "Does Papa have anything to do with this?"

He dropped my hand. "You think your father bribed me to . . . to propose?" Strain showed in his voice and his face turned stony. "Will you never forgive me for deceiving you in Paris?"

"I'm sorry," I said. "That was unfair."

His lips tightened but he nodded. "It's not your apology I'm after."

I blushed. I knew what he wanted. What I wanted, too.

"I know this seems a bit sudden and more than a bit mad. But with your wedding to the baron so near . . . . " He cleared his throat. "My family has tried to talk me out of it. In light of everything that has happened, it's the right thing to do."

Heat flared inside me, a fiery ball that raced to my cheeks. "Are you saying you are proposing against your better judgment?"

His cheeks reddened, and he looked away briefly. "Don't take my words and twist them. You know what I mean."

"I well know what you mean. I'm ruined, tainted, spoiled by another man. But your—chivalry—insists you rescue me."

He had the nerve to look affronted. "That's not it, not at all."

Indignation, with a hefty dose of despair, swirled in my belly. He had to accept my refusal, even if he didn't understand all of my reasons. "My answer is the same. No." I spun away and rushed down the side aisle toward the door. After several strides in the cool damp air, I slowed down and Nacia caught up to me.

"Are you all right?" She hooked her arm through mine, pulling back to slow me down further. She handed me my parasol, but I didn't open it. Though the sky remained heavy and grey, the rain had slowed to a drizzle—a perfect backdrop to my mood.

"You look pale. Perhaps we shouldn't have come."

"I . . . I'm fine, Nash." How could I tell her that nothing mattered anymore? That my future was set and love couldn't rescue me, for love kept me bound to my family, and that love forced me to accept a commitment I did not want to make. I paused for a moment, and clutched my nauseated stomach.

She peered at me closely. "Let's get you home. I couldn't bear it if you became ill again." We walked arm in arm for several blocks, accompanied by chirping birds and the click of our heels on the walk.

"What did he want?" Nacia blurted.

"He . . . he's worried about me. That's all."

"Hmmm." But she respected my reticence, and we reached the house without further discussion of Philippe.

When I entered my bedroom, the sweet scent of gardenias threatened to undo me. I fell onto the bed, staring at the ceiling. How had my life spun out of control so quickly? When I had so hopefully plotted my escape to Paris only a few weeks before, the whole world seemed to be waiting for me to reach out and take the prize. Was I so worthless now that nothing could save me?

Philippe was offering an escape. Yet, running away to Canada with him wouldn't salvage my family's reputation or my sisters' future happiness.

Not to mention the sting of his words: "in light of everything." If Gaston hadn't attacked me, if Philippe hadn't been forced to take me home in disgrace, would he propose marriage? I would never know.

My brain circled around and around the problem like a ravenous wolf. Surely there was a solution, if I just studied it hard enough. A chink in the armour, a crack in the bulwark.

What did I know of Canada? Julie had studied at a prestigious art school in Montreal. Why couldn't I do the same? But she'd had the support of her parents and her future husband. Philippe did not say whether or not he would support me at art school, but I knew he was struggling with modern opinions about a woman's role. And Julie had even admitted that society life was just as constrained in Canada as it was in France.

The sweet scent of Philippe's gardenias wafted over me. Secret love, Cook had said. Perhaps he did love me. But it was equally possible he had no idea about the language of flowers. I re-arranged the blooms, admiring the soft highlights cast on their petals by the afternoon sun.

I turned my back to the flowers and stared out the window. Could I create one last painting, a reminder of what Philippe had meant to me, and still marry the baron? And could I walk away from my art again, after experiencing the pleasure of its creation?

It was no use. I had to paint.

I had only just picked up my brush when someone knocked at the door. I groaned. Could I not be left alone? "Go away!"

The door creaked open, and I spun around to face the intruder.

"Bernadette! You're here!" I dropped my paint brush and flew across the room, pulling her into a tight embrace.

"Surprised?" She grinned as we parted. She looked as beautiful as always, her blonde curls tamed by pins and combs. Her face was lightly freckled, and she wore a sea blue-and-white striped seersucker dress, as if dressed for a stroll along the seashore.

"Yes, surprised. But delighted," I said. "I didn't expect you until Friday."

"I couldn't wait! Your mother's telegram frightened me. What's this urgent wedding all about? What happened in Paris? And why didn't you write me yourself?"

A sudden wave of longing for the innocence of our childhood struck me. I wished we were still schoolgirls, chasing one another around the castle walls, braiding daisy chains. Bernadette reminded me of all I was losing, no matter what choice I made for my future. I swallowed the lump of regret in my throat.

"What's wrong, chérie?" She drew me onto the bed where we sat facing one another.

I shook my head, unable to speak without choking on loss. "I . . . I have made a horrible mess of things." I finally gave into to my anger, shame, and confusion. I wrapped my arms around her neck and between great racking sobs, I told her everything, including the news of Mémère's death. Finally the wave of emotion subsided, and I sat back and dried my eyes.

She tucked a strand of my hair behind my ear. "Poor, dear Gabbi. You don't know how very fortunate you are."

I drew away from her. "Fortunate! How can you say that?"

"Don't you realize? I would give anything to have your ambition. To know exactly what I want to do with my life, as you do." She stood and walked over to my picture, with its bare outline of the bouquet. "The passion you've been born with to create art is a gift, Gabbi. A gift."

I was stunned. She envied me? "But look at you, Bernie. You are loved by everyone. Your parents dote on you. You have absolute freedom to do what you want, with whom you choose."

She laughed. "Ah, Gabbi, we are quite the pair, are we not? Envying the other and not appreciating what we have?"

I sniffled. "Perhaps we could switch places?"

"Too late, chérie, much too late. I don't envy you your baron."

"Ah, yes. The baron."

"But there is Philippe, n'est-ce pas?"

I sighed. "But he wants to marry me . . . ."

"And what's so terrible about that?"

"So many things! He proposed in some misguided attempt at chivalry. I think he's fond of me, and I might even love him, but love doesn't matter. I know marriage won't work out for us. We're too different. He'll come to hate me when I don't live up to his expectations."

"Whatever do you mean?"

"He wants a wife who will make him the centre of her universe. I can't do that."

"Are you so certain of that? If you love each other, isn't that enough?"

I shook my head. "It's only enough in romance novels, Bernie. Real life isn't like that."

She frowned. "I'm not so sure. I can hardly wait for the right man to come along and sweep me off my feet." She swept her arms in a grand gesture and flopped onto my bed, as if she'd been lifted up and dropped there.

I laughed. "I hope that's exactly what happens for you. But I couldn't bear it if I disappointed Philippe. And yet . . . ."

"Yet?"

"I would rather die than marry the baron." There, I said it aloud.

"Gabbi!" She looked at me with a look of horror. "You can't mean that!"

"I do." I groaned. "Oh, Bernie, how did this all turn out so horribly? I tried to follow my dream, just like Madame Magne taught us, but instead everything went wrong."

"Do you regret going to Paris now?"

Was my answer any different than I'd given Nacia? Did I regret the thrill of living in the city of artists or Julie's friendship? Did I regret the time spent at the Louvre, or in Montmartre, sketching the streets, the people? Meeting Philippe?

"I wish I hadn't been so blindly foolish about Babette and Gaston, yes. But the rest? Non." I hugged myself to dispel the queasiness rising inside me whenever I thought of Gaston. "At least I had a glimpse of what my life could have been." That was better than not knowing at all. And it could have turned out differently.

If only.

"Don't despair, chérie. We'll find a way out of this wedding for you." She squeezed my hand.

I shook my head. "There's nothing anyone can do."

"Can't you simply tell your parents you refuse to marry the baron?"

"I've tried that. Things have gone too far. My parents can't refuse him, not after the banns are published and invitations sent out. It would be a terrible public humiliation for my family. And the consequences to Papa's reputation—my sisters' futures. No, impossible."

"What if you told the baron, face to face, that you don't want him? Surely he won't insist on marrying you against your will?"

Bernadette's naïveté surprised me. But she hadn't been through the past weeks that I had. "He doesn't care one whit about what I want. He's a man used to getting his own way." Desperation slid like ice into my belly.

"Then we must pray, Gabbi. Pray for divine intervention. I can't believe God intended for talent like yours, talent He so lovingly gave you, to go to waste."

"Prayers haven't helped me so far, Bernie." Saying it aloud made me realize that wasn't quite true. I'd prayed for divine rescue from Gaston, and with the assistance of Grand-mère's hat pin, I had escaped him. Had God intervened? "And besides, how can I do anything but marry the baron? To do otherwise would bring disaster to my family. I can't—and won't—do that to them."

"What about Philippe? Isn't there a way to make that work?"

I hesitated. What about Philippe? He'd offered me an escape route, but I was afraid. Afraid it would prove to be a dead end. The end of my art. I imagined spending the rest of my life trying to please him, to put my art aside while raising a family, running a household. Most importantly, it wouldn't avoid the disastrous consequences for my parents.

"Mam'selle?" Demi knocked and entered without waiting for my reply. I wondered if she'd been eavesdropping, for her expression was definitely smug. "Your father wishes to speak with you."

I squeezed Bernadette's hands. "I'll be right back. Please wait for me."

Papa met me at the bottom of the stairs. "Gabrielle. I had heard you were recovering. It's good to see you up and about."

"I'm feeling much better today. Thank you, Papa."

"Merci Dieu." He embraced me. "Come in and sit down, petite."

I followed him into his study. I sank into the same chair I'd collapsed into when he refused to let me study art in Paris, the same chair I sat in to plead with him to stop the wedding.

He sat behind his desk, hands folded in front of him. "I thought we should have a little chat, you and I, before the wedding."

I stiffened.

"You know your mother and I have settled on a dowry for you."

"Yes."

"The funds will be under your husband's control, of course." He sounded terribly formal, as I imagined he did when conducting business.

"I realize that," I said, curious as to why we were even discussing money, a subject normally reserved solely for men.

His voice changed to an almost teasing tone. "However, I am not unaware of your . . . shall I say, independent nature?"

"What are you getting at, Papa?" Surely he wasn't having second thoughts.

He cleared his throat. "I've decided, in the interests of marital harmony and longevity, that you'd be happier if you had a little nest egg of your own."

"I don't understand."

He smiled, his dimples deep as he pulled open a drawer and drew out an envelope. A fat, stuffed envelope. He held it out to me. "Fifty thousand francs."

I drew in my breath. "A fraction of that would have made all the difference in Paris." I could have lived on that for years while studying and exhibiting, building a career in Paris.

He looked distressed. "Please don't . . . that's over and done."

The thick envelope sat on his desk between us.

"You'll never know, Papa, what I've lost."

"Life doesn't always give us what we want, petite," he said, his voice weary.

I noted the lines in his face, the grey overtaking his dark beard. I never considered whether he, too, had made compromises and abandoned dreams of his own. Despite everything, compassion and, yes, forgiveness, surged inside me. No, Papa, life isn't always what we hoped it would be. For either of us.

He leaned forward, his face earnest. "I'm not blind to your feelings, petite. If I had any power in this, it would be Genevieve marrying the baron, not you. She's more suited to him, to that kind of life. But we must learn how to make a silk purse out of a sow's ear, n'est-ce pas?"

He was giving me the money to assuage his guilt. Yet I took the envelope, hefting its weight. "It's mine alone?" It wouldn't replace my art, yet perhaps I could salvage some kind of independence. I clutched it as if it were a life raft. I was drowning. "For my sole use?"

"Yes. And you needn't tell your husband about this. Or your mother." He winked. "I think your grandmother would have approved, don't you?"

"Ah, oui." Mémère believed women deserved control of their finances. It wasn't the money itself, she had said, but the ability to make decisions for one's self. I looked down at the envelope bulging with francs. Enough francs for a beginning. An idea, half-formed, began to grow. Was it possible? "It's too much," I protested, yet couldn't release my grip on the envelope.

He waved away my objection. "Not at all. It is but a fraction of your dowry."

I stood. "Merci bien, Papa. I am very grateful." Grateful for his thoughtfulness, but also that he had no idea how much he was helping me, or he would have taken it back at once.

I paused at the door. "I'm so glad Charles will be here for the wedding."

"Yes. It might be the last time the entire family is together." Papa's smile was tinged with regret.

"I do so hope Charles will stop gambling, once he's in Canada." I kept my voice light.

"Don't worry, petite. I've engaged that young man Philippe to accompany Charles and ensure he stays out of trouble."

I tried to sound surprised. "Oh, Papa, you are a wonderful father. You think of everything."

"Actually, it was Philippe's suggestion. I thought it an excellent one."

I nodded, my heart pounding as I left clutching the precious envelope. A glimmer of hope for a way through this debacle arose, a way to a life of my own.

I ran to my room. "Bernadette, will you deliver a note for me?"

Her eyes lit up. "For Philippe?"

A grin spread across my face. "Yes. And a telegram to my friend Julie." I sat at my desk and wrote, my hand shaking with desire. "Now, I have to find Genevieve." She was crucial to my plans.

Chapter Thirty-five

TWO DAYS BEFORE THE WEDDING, Bernadette and I walked arm in arm to the ruins of the castle.

Philippe waited in the shade of the cool stone walls but came forward as we approached. "Bonjour, Mesdemoiselles."

"Bernadette, this is Philippe. Philippe, my best friend, Bernadette."

"Enchanté, Mademoiselle." He bowed low over her hand. "I recognize you from Gabbi's portraits of you."

"Enchantée, Monsieur." She kissed my cheek and stepped back down the path to give us privacy.

"You came," I said, my heart pounding against my chest.

He pressed his lips to my hand. "Of course."

"Thank you. I was afraid you were too angry with me after we last parted."

His mouth tightened briefly. "I was upset, but not angry. I know you are in a very delicate position." He paused. "I was afraid you might be angry at me for my impertinence."

"I was angry. At first." I smiled at him, losing myself in his eyes for a moment. "But I've had time to think."

He nodded. "Marriage isn't something you should rush into." He squeezed my hand. "You do realize that it is possible . . . I mean, you might never return to France."

I looked searchingly into his eyes. "Have you changed your mind? You sound as if you're trying to talk me out of this." I laughed nervously.

"Mon Dieu, non!" He shook his head. "But I don't want you to be plagued by second thoughts, halfway across the Atlantic."

"I need to ask you something important." I paused, wanting to be certain he understood how important. There could be no flinching now. I must know the truth. "When we last spoke, you said you were fond, very fond of me." I had intended to go on, but his smile stopped me.

"Are you asking me if I love you?"

I held my breath, his answer hovering in the air between us. If I breathed, it might blow away and the moment would pass.

"I do love you, Gabbi."

"But then why—"

"Why could I not say it?"

I nodded.

"I wanted to . . . but I had to . . .guard my heart. Were you not to share my feelings . . . ."

"I thought my feelings were obvious." I looked away from his piercing blue eyes, suddenly nervous. "My heart races when I think of you. I can't wait to see your face again after we've parted." The stone weight of the past two weeks lifted off my chest, and I could finally breathe freely. "I love you too."

He grabbed both my hands in his. "Gabrielle Carmen Désirée Jean d'Arc de Villiers, will you marry me?"

Slowly, I shook my head.

He looked confused. "But—"

"I do love you, yes. But I cannot marry you."

He dropped my hands and stumbled as he backed away. His face darkened with shock or perhaps anger. "What do you mean? What are you playing at?"

"I'm not playing with you, Philippe. Surely you know I could never treat you with such heartlessness. Please hear me out." I drew him into the sunshine and over to my favourite sketching spot. "Let's sit here."

He swept an area free of twigs and leaves with his hand and spread his jacket out. I sank onto it, and he sat beside me.

I forced myself to keep my gaze on him, despite the pain and confusion in his expression. "I want you to understand why I'm proposing something other than marriage."

"Other than marriage?" he repeated, eyebrows raised. His face reddened.

A hot flush crept up my neck also, blooming on my cheeks. "Oh, no. I don't mean . . . I couldn't . . . not that." To avoid his gaze, I looked at the sky. Clouds drifted in front of the sun, creating patches of shadow in the meadow. Birds trilled in the nearby trees, perhaps a finch such as the one I'd sketched with such hope of the future. My eyes swept over our surroundings. The stony bulk of the castle, its battlements, and stone keep loomed above us. I would miss its presence, its reminder of what endures and what does not. I breathed deeply, hoping to draw the castle's strength into myself.

"I need time to be myself. Up until a few weeks ago, I had only ever lived at home. In Laval. Now that I've had a glimpse of living on my own—yes, despite Babette and Gaston—well, I want more of that."

I hugged myself briefly before I continued. "It's also going to take time to trust anyone again. People change, I understand that, and we disappoint the ones we love the most. Even if it's unintended. You see, I lost Maman's love when she had all of those stillborn babies; she's never been the same since. I trusted Papa to love and protect me, and he tried to do that by hiring you when I ran away."

He grabbed my hand.

"But Papa won't protect me from marriage to a man I loathe. Ironically, it was through his intervention that I met you: handsome, thoughtful, interested in my art. I thought you were attracted to me—"

"But you know—"

"Please. This is hard enough."

He slowly let go of my hand and nodded for me to continue.

"I thought you were attracted to me, and I began to love you, your strength and your gentleness. Your loyalty to your sister." I reached out and gently traced the scar along his face. "When I saw you outside Gaston's, when you struck him, I knew I could rely upon you. And then . . . and then, I learned you were paid to look after me."

He looked so sad, but he did not try to refute my words. Could not.

"I questioned everything that was said between us, not knowing what was true and what was simply part of your job."

His lips parted as if he was about to speak, but he closed them again. He clasped his hands over his knees while I spoke, his knuckles white.

Was he angry? "It's going to take time for me to trust anyone again," I said softly. "Do you understand?"

He met my eyes. "I'm sorry," he said quietly. "And I think I understand, at least somewhat."

"It's more than simply trusting again." I took a deep breath. "I have to pursue my art. I've found a way to do that and avoid marrying the baron, but it involves deceiving my parents. If they knew my plans, they would either be publicly humiliated or honour bound to force me into the marriage. But if it works, it will save the family's honour." Dear Lord, it must work.

He frowned. "C'est vrai? But how?"

I put up my hand. "I'll tell you the details after—when I meet you at Le Havre."

He drew in a sharp breath. "Le Havre? Does than mean—"

"I will come to Canada with you and Charles. But only as far as Montréal." I forced myself to maintain eye contact. The confusion I saw in his eyes almost made me falter. "Montreal has a reputable art school. It's what I need." My voice shook with fear of hurting him. "The only way to save face for my parents is to go through with the wedding. But I will also be on the train to Le Havre with Charles. We'll meet you at the dock and board the ship together." I paused. "You know, the kind of investigative work you do gave me the idea of how to outsmart the baron."

"I don't understand," he said, but I thought I saw a flicker of interest in his gaze.

"You will." I smiled, thinking about my carefully crafted deception. "When we arrive in Montréal, I hope to stay with the family of a fellow artist I met in Paris, Julie."

"But how will you live?"

"I now have enough money, thanks to Papa. I'll be all right."

He stood abruptly and began to pace. "And what about us?"

"We'll have time together on the ship. Time to truly get to know each other . . . ."

"And?"

"And I hope you will return to me in Montréal, once Charles is settled in Manitoba."

He took my chin and tilted my head. I closed my eyes. He trailed his fingers across the nape of my neck, and I gasped but kept my eyes closed. His lips touched mine, lightly at first. Then he wrapped his arms around me and pressed his firm, warm mouth against my lips. I wanted it to last an eternity, my heart pounding, my lips responding, our breath merged into one.

He stroked my face and my hair as we parted. "I will earn your trust."

"I know my refusal must be hard, but I want you to understand who I really am."

"I love who you are," he said huskily.

My resolve was crumbling under his gaze and his pain-soaked voice. "I'm not sure I can be the woman you want for a wife."

He shook his head. "You're the only woman I want." He touched my cheek with a tenderness I hadn't expected. "And you'll see that I can be the husband you need. I will return to you. And we will marry. You can fill our home with your drawings and paintings . . . ."

Now it was my turn to nod. "And?"

"And, perhaps, children?"

I hesitated. "Perhaps."

"We can make it work."

Oh, how I prayed he was right. Yet my chest tightened at the attempt to envision our life together. "You say that now. But you'll have expectations of me—to run a household, to have babies and change diapers. I'm afraid I'll never have time to create the paintings I know I have inside me. What I'm saying is that I can't be a traditional wife, Philippe."

He shook his head, frowning. "You don't know everything. Your heroine, Berthe Morisot, married and had a child. Yet she continued to paint and show her work."

"How do you know that?"

"Have you forgotten what I do for a living?" A small smile played on his lips but then disappeared. "Do you think I cannot change? Do you think so little of me?"

"No, it's not that at all," I said slowly. "Your happiness means too much to me to make promises I cannot keep."

I paused, waiting for him to realize the meaning of my words. "Is it not enough that I will wait for you? When you return, we'll have time together, and I'll learn to trust again. But I must trust myself first. And I must find a way to pursue my art, above all else."

"Above all else?" he repeated in a faint voice.

Was it only just registering on him what I meant? I held his gaze, nodded. He must understand. Nothing could be as he hoped unless he truly understood this.

Everything I wanted was still possible, and needed only his agreement. I closed my eyes and prayed, *Dear Jesus, show him we have a future together as equals, if he can accept me as I am.*

"It means that much to you, your art."

I opened my eyes and nodded. "You spoke passionately about how important it was to follow your own path, not one of your father's choosing. Well, creating art is my own dream, my life's work. Do you see that?"

He could. It was there in his eyes. I had convinced him. And now?

"I had hoped for so much more."

"Are you . . . refusing me?"

He looked away. After an excruciating wait, he turned back to me. "I don't know."

Chapter Thirty-six

"I'M SO HAPPY!" MAMAN LIFTED three scratchy crinolines off her bed and over my head, settling them around my waist and tying the ribbons. "This morning reminds me of my own wedding."

I was about to disappoint her terribly. I really had tried, but failed, to assume the shape of the dutiful daughter she expected. "Thank you, Maman, for everything," I said. "I'm sure it will be a perfect day, a perfect wedding."

Her eyes narrowed, but my smile was genuine. Luckily she didn't know why I was so agreeable.

I rested my hand on my abdomen to still the fluttering inside. Nervousness about pulling off the deception, yes, but also anxiety over Philippe's final words to me . . . *I had hoped for so much more.* Yet, with or without him, I knew with certainty that I was doing what I had to. Like the bird in Victor Hugo's quote, I would not be deterred. I would spread my wings. And I would sing.

"I knew you would realize this is for the best, chérie," said Maman.

I inhaled sharply, cherishing how good it felt for her to call me *chérie*. It was a pity it would be the last time.

She helped me into the bodice and skirt, then stood back and circled me, assessing every detail of the dress. "You lost too much weight when you were sick. The dress hangs on you as if you were a skeleton. I'll have to pin it." She reached for the cushion of dressmaker pins.

"No!" I shouted, before I remembered my vow to be demure and obedient. It was my parting gift to her. "No," I said again, more softly. "It's fine, really. There's no time. You have to leave for the *mairie* and ensure everything is in place."

She checked the tiny gold watch pinned to her bodice. "Mon Dieu, how did the time fly?" She called in my sisters and Bernadette. "Come and help Gabbi finish dressing. I must get to the town hall before anyone else." She took my face in her hands and pulled me toward her, kissing my forehead.

"*Je t'aime,* Gabbi."

Tears sprang to my eyes. "*Je t'aime,* Maman," I said with honest forgiveness in my heart. She would never understand me, but she loved me and that was enough.

Bernadette, Nacia, and Genevieve stepped into Maman's bedroom as she left and circled me as if to create a protective ring. We stood silently, listening to the voices drifting up through the open window.

Gerard called "*Allez!*" to Birgitta, her harness jangled, and they clattered out of the courtyard.

Bernadette squeezed my hand. "Are you absolutely certain this is what you want, Gabbi?"

"*Certainement,*" I said. "That is, so long as Genevieve hasn't changed her mind." I looked at my older sister, a catch in my throat. Without her assent, I was truly doomed.

She frowned and my heart sank. I closed my eyes and started to pray under my breath.

"Don't be a silly nit. Of course I want this," Genevieve said impatiently.

Doubts still gnawed at me. "You spoke to Papa's notary. Are we sure we have the legalities covered?"

"The banns were published with initials, not first names." Genevieve sounded confident. "The notary assures me that will be enough. Until the vows are exchanged."

"And what if the baron refuses?"

She smirked. "Trust me. He'll agree. Nothing matters more to him than appearances. And of course, the dowry. Besides, I have my ways."

"What?" I asked, shocked.

Nacia clapped her hand over her mouth and giggled, her eyes bright with mischief. "You know Genevieve's right. Look at Maman; she wears the pants in our family."

"Nash!" I could hardly believe she'd said that aloud, even if it were true. My shy sister grew bolder each day. I looked back at Genevieve and tried to keep a straight face. "I'll grant you that. And, you've also been honing your powers of persuasion on Nash and me for years." I giggled too, and soon all of us joined in, even Genevieve. It was a relief to laugh aloud and dispel the tension in the room.

"In all seriousness, Genevieve, I hope that the baron realizes how fortunate he is to be marrying you, instead of me." Dizzy with relief, I demanded, "Get me out of this, quickly. Papa will be knocking on the door any minute."

They went to work, unhooking, untying ribbons, lifting away crinolines and petticoats until my virginal wedding dress was draped across Maman's bed. I stepped off the dressmaker's stand, and Genevieve took my place.

The mechanism on the busk of my corset stuck and for a moment, panic spread through my fingertips.

"Let me do it." Bernadette batted my hands away, easily unlatching it. She passed the corset to Nacia, who wrapped it around Genevieve. It had been especially made for the wedding dress, decorated with tiny seed pearls and silk ribbons that only the groom would see. While Nacia tightened the laces on Genevieve's back, I rubbed my waist and ribs where the sewn-in bones had pinched me, vowing that would be the last corset I ever wore.

Bernadette put her arm around my waist, and we watched Nacia lift the crinolines over Genevieve's head, and finally the ruffled, flouncy, frothy skirt. She attached the metres of train. I wrapped the bodice around Genevieve and buttoned the sleeves while Bernadette laboured at the multitude of hooks-and-eyes. Nacia picked up the veil.

Knock! Knock!

"Ready, petite? Your groom awaits!"

"A few more minutes, Papa." I regretted not saying goodbye to my father. I loved him and would miss him, but I simply couldn't trust him with this secret. He might have acquiesced, but he might also have felt compelled to stop me. "Quickly, the veil!" I whispered.

Genevieve beamed as I pinned the crown of the wedding veil to her pile of curls and then lowered the layers of lace over her face. I nodded with satisfaction. I couldn't discern her features. Merci Dieu for the tradition of the veil!

Nacia slid lace gloves onto the bride's hands.

"Good luck, Genevieve," I whispered as I slid her feet into heeled slippers. They were exceptionally high, and she would appear to be nearly as tall as me. "I hope you are happy."

She squeezed my hand, which I took as a reply, wishing me the same.

I grabbed Nacia into a fierce hug one final time and gave her a pair of fine kid gloves as my bridal present. For Genevieve, with the exception of two of the newly made traveling dresses, I left everything in my trousseau. And what she most coveted, the right to be called "baroness."

"Bernadette, I have something for you, too." I handed her a framed pastel I'd done the previous day of the two of us. In it, we were young girls again, holding hands as we danced at the base of the old castle.

"It's the perfect gift," Bernadette said, her eyes moist. "And it's signed and dated. It's going to be very valuable one day. I'll have an original de Villiers."

We both laughed. "Well, even if I'm never famous, it's a rather good likeness of the two of us, n'est-ce pas?" I gazed at the pastel a final time, content with the finished result. I'd depicted my hair in a mess and my dress torn.

Bernadette was immaculate, of course. And our expressions glowed with the carefree joy of childhood.

"I'm not sure I should give you your gift." She tried to keep a straight face. "Since you're not getting married, it wouldn't be proper, would it?"

"I'm not leaving without it," I demanded, my hand out.

She laughed and waved a slim parcel, wrapped in shiny paper, above her head.

Much taller than her, I grabbed it at once and held it against my heart. "Merci *beaucoup*, chérie."

"Open it now."

Another knock on the door. "Gabbi?"

I tore the paper off the slender package. Nestled inside its satin box was a gold locket. I sprung the catch. A tiny photo of each of us graced the inside. I fastened the locket around my neck. "Merci, Bernie." A deep ache rose in my chest. "I'll miss you so much. You must visit me in Canada."

"I promise." Her tears wet my face as we embraced.

"Gabbi!" Another impatient knock at the door.

"Oui, Papa!" I turned to my sisters and Bernadette. "Don't forget your parts. And remember, after the civil ceremony, the scandalous gossip about the baron's last-minute declaration of love for Genevieve."

"It will spread like wildfire." Nacia bit her lip. "Are you so very sure you want your name sullied in this way?"

"It's the only way. Besides, I shall be out of the country before it can harm me." Despite my brave words, my chest tightened. Heartsick already, I'd never suspected I would leave France to pursue my dreams. But it couldn't be helped.

"Au revoir, mes chéries." I slipped behind Maman's wardrobe to hide while Nacia opened the door.

"Where's Genevieve?" I heard Papa ask.

"She'll come with Charles," Nacia explained. She and Bernadette were my bridesmaids. Charles would stand up as a witness for the baron, arriving at the last possible moment so no one could question him about Genevieve. I was counting on Maman being too engrossed with the proceedings to notice her absence until it was too late.

I was finally alone in the house. I wandered around my mother's room a final time, touching familiar objects, opening her lavender water and inhaling deeply. That scent would always remind me of her. On top of her bureau, she'd propped a faded photograph of herself with Mémère. It must have been taken shortly before she left us, but I'd never seen it before. Perhaps Maman had brought it out after the news of her mother's death. I was tempted to take it, for I no longer had anything of my grandmother's, but no, Maman needed it more. I would, instead, hire Philippe to take my photograph and send it to her. I could only hope she'd place it on her bureau next to Mémère's.

I sat at her écritoire and wrote a long note, explaining myself in words I couldn't find when I was with her. I told her I hoped she would eventually understand and forgive me. I asked her to forgive my sisters for their part in the *charade*; wrote that one day, I hoped she would be proud of me.

Impulsively, I selected one of her hat pins to replace the one I had embedded in Gaston's neck.

In Papa's room across the hall, I left a letter I'd written earlier. I'd included much of what I'd written in my note to Maman, and thanked him for being the wonderful father I'd known for the past sixteen years. I suggested he and Maman might even wish to travel to Canada, to visit Charles and perhaps, even me.

I slipped into my own room and dressed in a pale green traveling suit sans corset. As I fixed my hat with Maman's pin, I recalled how my prayers had been answered after all. Mémère had come to my aid when I most needed her. And I was leaving the baron and his gilded cage behind without dishonouring my family. I left my corset on my bed, aware that the metaphor would likely be lost on my mother. When I passed my image in the mirror on my wardrobe door, I saluted the young woman standing there. "Happy Bastille Day, Gabrielle. To the barricades!"

Chapter Thirty-seven

MY BAGGAGE WAS ALREADY PACKED and hidden amongst my brother's luggage in the carriage house. As arranged earlier by Charles, a hired carriage pulled up to the house. I met the driver, showed him where to get our bags and stepped into the carriage.

As I settled into the seat, I blinked away tears, wishing I could have left openly and with my parents' blessing. The carriage jolted forward, the wheels creaking as they turned over the cobbled courtyard. I told the driver to stop outside the *mairie*. Charles would come out and join me as soon as the ceremony ended. I adjusted the tilt of my hat, removed my gloves before slipping them back on, longing to watch the drama unfolding inside.

Several minutes passed. I could take a peek, couldn't I? It would only be for a few moments. No one would see me. I alighted from the carriage and slipped around the side of the building to the delivery entrance. Inside, stairs led up to a dark hallway which ended at the ceremonial room where weddings and other official ceremonies were performed.

A heavy wooden door stood between me and my great deceit. I took a deep breath and pulled the door open, just a sliver.

Clearly Maman had succumbed to her love of pageantry. The room was crowded, not only with family but guests as well, and a violinist played a sweet melody. The baron stood at the front of the room near the raised dais, his figure in profile from my vantage point. He wore a new black frock coat of the finest cut. With his black silk top hat in hand, his dark waistcoat and white cravat, and dove-grey striped trousers, he completed the picture of a respectable, titled gentleman. Surely any young woman—any but me—would be proud to stand beside him. Charles, seated behind the baron and beside the Comte, the baron's other witness. Charles glanced over his shoulder. I gasped, pulling the door shut. He'd be furious if he saw me peeking.

I waited, ears straining to hear what was happening. The door stubbornly refused to yield any secrets. I cracked it open once more.

Genevieve now stood on the baron's left, a bouquet of lilies in one hand. Bernadette, Nacia, Maman, and Papa sat behind her. I breathed a sigh of relief, for the veil still covered Genevieve's face. Her head was bowed, so she wouldn't be detected too soon. And perhaps it was also lowered out of real modesty. For Genevieve, this was not just a ruse. It was the beginning of her dream life.

Maman's friends craned their necks to and fro, no doubt inspecting the baron's entourage and the cut of the men's suits, taking close note of what the women wore, how they'd styled their hair. Surely they approved of Nacia's elaborate lavender gown with its modest neckline, trimmed with pearls to match those on the bride's dress. Bernadette's pink silk gown with a sweetheart neckline, matching gloves, and tiny lace slippers probably enchanted all the men, married and unmarried.

Papa leaned over and whispered something to Maman.

Were either of my parents regretful about the forced wedding? I preferred to think so.

The Mayor entered from a side door and took his place behind a raised wooden pulpit of sorts. His sonorous voice rang out with words of welcome, and then he began to recite the obligations of husband and wife under the Napoleonic Code. "The husband owes protection to his wife, the wife obedience to her husband . . . ."

Words that had meant nothing before of a sudden were loaded with meaning. I shuddered at my narrow escape. But Genevieve would embrace them whole-heartedly. Dear God, please grant her happiness.

". . . The wife is obliged to live with her husband and to follow him to every place which he may judge it convenient to reside . . . ," the Mayor continued.

The baron stared at his bride's veiled face. Did he suspect anything?

My breath caught. I should not be watching, yet I could not look away.

The baron took Genevieve's gloved hand in his and turned to the Mayor.

The Mayor asked whether the bride and groom consented to take each other as husband and wife.

Genevieve spoke first. "I do." Her strong, clear voice rang through the room—perhaps too eagerly.

The baron's back stiffened. Did he detect a subtle difference in his bride's voice?

He leaned toward Genevieve in a whispered exchange. The whispers grew louder and more urgent. The baron's face reddened.

He knew.

I should flee, yet my feet would not obey. I stared at the scene through the narrow slit in the door, my heart thundering in my chest.

"What's the delay?" The Mayor demanded. He motioned the baron and Genevieve forward. Another heated, whispered exchange, this time amongst the three of them.

My pulse pounded in my temples. Was our deception about to crumble?

The Mayor's face was grave. "Witnesses, come forward, please."

Charles, the Comte, Bernadette, and Nacia joined the knot of people crowded around the Mayor's dais. Maman stood, but Papa pulled her back down into her seat. She waved her fan madly as the discussion continued.

Murmurs rose amongst the guests, spreading like a plague of gnats until the entire chamber was abuzz.

I couldn't hear above the rumble. What were they saying at the front? I pulled the door slightly wider. A loud creak split through the air.

My heart exploded with fear. I released the door and fled down the hall, not daring to look back.

But by the time I reached the exit, thunderous applause erupted.

Fait-accompli!

Somehow, Genevieve convinced the baron to accept her rather than lose his dowry and gain potential disgrace. Dear God, pray let him forgive her the deception and direct all blame to me.

I slipped outside and leaned against the stone building to catch my breath. "Thank God. Thank you, God, for—"

Someone grabbed my wrist. I gasped.

"What are you doing outside the carriage?"

It was Charles. I nearly fainted with relief.

"Are you trying to ruin everything?" he growled.

I shook my head. "No one saw me."

"Let's hope not."

We leaped into the waiting carriage, grateful for a ship departure that ensured Charles had to leave the ceremony as soon as the nuptials were signed and sealed.

"Congratulations," Charles said, grinning, his eyes alight with mischief. "You pulled it off!"

"I thought so, from the applause. But what happened? When Genevieve spoke and the baron looked so shocked . . . I was so afraid!"

"When the baron's face turned brilliant red, I knew he'd caught on," Charles said. "The Mayor called us together and demanded an explanation. Genevieve looked so panicked! But after heated whispering between her and the baron, the baron glared at the Mayor and demanded the ceremony continue. A shrewd and intelligent man. He didn't want to lose face in front of all the guests, but even more, I expect he couldn't bear to lose the dowry."

I grinned, my pulse still hammering through my veins. "And now, everyone has what they want."

"Perhaps not quite as they imagined, but I think you are right."

I offered another quick prayer that it was true. The baron received the de Villiers dowry and a wife who valued marriage and society life, one who would obey him, no doubt beautifully upholding his status. Genevieve would be baroness, which should be a double win for Maman, as her eldest daughter was safely married. Papa also got what he wanted and his word of honour remained intact. He'd given me a portion of my dowry to ensure me some independence, which it would indeed. And Nacia, well, she'd gotten her first taste of rebellion. I hoped the experience would encourage her to stand up for herself even more.

As for our extended families and neighbours, they were not only guests at one of the city's more notable weddings, but they were privy to a scandal. How delicious for many! By the time everyone arrived at the Basilica for the church ceremony, the gossip should have performed its magic. At the wedding déjeuner, Nacia and Bernadette would have ample time to spread the story that the baron had, that very morning, declared his undying love for Genevieve and refused to marry me. My departure would secure the "truth" that our family graciously complied with His Excellency's request and last-minute changes were made.

As for me? I was on my way to study art, free of my mother's influence. True, I was headed to Canada, not Paris. But perhaps, after some success in Montreal, I would return to Paris with an entry in the Salon. It wasn't unheard of.

Finally, I allowed myself the luxury of imagining Philippe's face when I related the entire adventure to him. And an entire week onboard together, with Charles, while we sailed into our futures.

Charles tapped the side of the carriage and shouted, "To the train!"

Chapter Thirty-eight

WE CAUGHT THE EXPRESS train to Paris, changed trains, and arrived at the port of Le Havre at dusk. Thousands of people were dockside. Excitement was palpable, an electric current buzzing through the crowds. The din was deafening. Between frequent blasts of the ship's whistle and horn and the shouting passengers and well-wishers, I could hardly hear Charles' directions to the porters. We slowly wove our way between women wearing brightly coloured hats and matching travel outfits, men in their best suits, starched white collars and black top hats. The sharp tang of salty air exhilarated me.

"I don't see Philippe, do you?" I asked, craning my neck.

"No, but he'll find us." Charles stared at our ship, *L'Aquitaine*. The massive steamship loomed over the pier. Her black stacks were freshly painted and the setting sun bathed her white flanks and sails in soft pastel hues.

"*L'Aquitaine*," Charles said. "That's a fitting name for the ship bearing us away from the Old World and sailing toward the New."

I nodded. "Eleanor of Aquitaine broke all the rules as she became Queen of France and England, didn't she?"

Charles grinned. "She was known to be a headstrong, powerful woman. During the Crusades, she and her ladies wore Amazon costumes to symbolize the power of warrior women. Should I warn Philippe?"

I elbowed him in the ribs. "No!"

Charles laughed. "In any event, she looks like a fine ship. We'll get to New York in less than seven days if we're lucky enough to have smooth sailing."

"I wonder what it was like for Mémère."

"I know. I think of her often, too." He put his arm around me. "Second thoughts?"

"No. But I can't help thinking that I'm standing right where she stood, only a month ago. Did she regret leaving France? Leaving us?"

He shrugged. "I don't know. But I think she'd be excited for us, don't you?

Think of what's ahead—a grand new adventure!"

"Yes, an adventure!" But where was Philippe? What if he had second thoughts? "I had hoped for so much more," he'd said. Mon Dieu, what if . . . there was nothing to do about it now. There was certainly no going back.

We made our way toward a broad gangway draped with banners of the Compagnie Générale Transatlantique Line. A brass band played on deck below flags of France fluttering with blue-white-and-red glory in the onshore breeze.

Farther along the dock, large families lined up before a drab gangway that fed into the belly of the ship. They wore dark, ragged clothing, and many of the men carried large bundles on their shoulders. One woman caught my eye. She held a crying baby in her arms, while older children clung to her skirts. The contrast between her family's drab clothes and the brightly dressed crowd around us was striking, yet her smile was as broad as those of us on the upper decks. The longing to capture it all in a sketch returned to me like a sharp pang. It was another sign that I'd made the right decision. Philippe or not.

Black smoke billowed from the ship's funnels. The ship teemed with sailors preparing her for departure. Over the din of the crowd we heard her engines throbbing to life. *L'Aquitaine's* horn sounded. It was time to board. And yet I held back.

"Gabbi!"

Philippe! His voice reached something deep within me. I turned to see him pushing his way through the throngs toward me. Abandoning all propriety, I rushed toward him.

There was only him—his penetrating blue eyes, his dark unruly curls, his brilliant smile. Suddenly we were within touching distance. I stopped, longing for him to cross the final space between us.

He reached out with one hand and took mine in his, weaving our fingers together. I stepped closer, his warmth radiating toward me. His shoulders rose and fell with the effort of running. I placed my hand on his chest and felt his heart beating.

"Gabbi," he repeated.

I tipped my head back and looked into his eyes. No doubt loomed there, no hesitation, only a longing that matched my own. My heart pounded in my temples. Six days together on the ship! Thank God for Charles' presence, or I'd surely succumb to temptation.

He kissed me, lightly at first, then with more urgency. I wrapped my arms around his neck, and he encircled me with his, pulling me closer. He lifted me off my feet and held me tightly.

When he set me back down, I pulled away and straightened my hat, suddenly self-conscious.

Charles cleared his throat. I turned to see him wink and quickly look at the ship. "Isn't she a beauty?"

Philippe stared at me. "She most certainly is."

I blushed.

He motioned his porter to come forward. From a cart filled with bags and trunks, he fished out a large wrapped parcel and handed it to me with a slight bow and a broad smile. "For new beginnings."

My hands shook as I held the parcel, a large envelope taped on top.

"Open it," he said.

"Now?"

"Yes. You will need it right away, I am sure."

I tore my gaze from his wide smile and slit open the envelope first. Inside was a sheet of paper, folded in half. I hesitated.

"Go ahead."

It was the portrait I'd sketched of him on the train the day we'd first met. A day of such promise. Who knew it would lead me here? I stroked the paper with my thumb, happy that at least one sketch from my adventure had survived. "You kept it." I looked up at him, surprised to see his eyes tearing up.

"Now your present."

Ripping the shiny gold paper, I uncovered a hinged mahogany box, the size of a small suitcase. "Gabrielle Carmen Désirée Jean d'Arc de Villiers" was engraved in a brass plate on the top. My hands shook as I opened it.

I gasped.

A paint box. A most beautiful paint box. A palette was nestled inside the lid. Fine sable-haired brushes lay next to rows of colour tubes in every colour imaginable, even Prussian blue. I touched the array of colours lightly, as if they were the rarest of flowers.

He understood.

"Thank you." Words were inadequate. I touched his cheek for the briefest of moments.

He caught my hand in his and kissed it. "I still want to marry you, Gabrielle. But I'm prepared to wait. At least a short time."

"Merci." I clasped the paint box to my chest as the three of us walked up the gangway.

Charles showed our tickets to the purser at the top, and we joined the press of passengers on the promenade deck. Those onshore waved up at us. A woman in the crowd rushed to the outermost end of the pier, waving a white handkerchief, and the image burned into my imagination. It would make a good composition. When I glanced at Philippe, he too was gazing at those on shore. I wondered, for the first time, whether his family had come to see him off on his new adventure.

Before I could ask, he announced, "Time for a photograph. The first of many, I hope. Charles, Gabbi, stand there by the railing. Quickly now, so we get the pier in the background."

Charles put his arm around my shoulders, and we posed for Philippe, who adjusted his top hat. "Now, stay still, just for a moment."

"Where's your camera, man?" Charles questioned.

Philippe's lips curled into that crooked smile I hoped to see much, much more of. A deep throaty laugh bubbled up within me. When it erupted, I found I couldn't stop. A snort, a giggle, a guffaw, a cackle, my cheeks tight and eyes pricked with tears. It all burst out of me, a glorious light-headed release that seemed limitless.

"Are you all right?" Philippe came close, a look of concern in his expression.

I held onto his arm, gasping for air. "I'm . . . I'm . . . . " I convulsed with laughter again. Philippe laughed along with me, heedless of nearby passengers who halted as they passed and stared, some with alarmed expressions.

Charles frowned, hands on his hips. "I don't see what's so funny."

"Patience, mon frère," I said, wiping my eyes and taking a deep breath. "All will be revealed."

Philippe, still chuckling, showed my brother his top hat camera, and they were soon avidly discussing gelatine dry-plates, exposure times, and apertures. It appeared that Philippe had found a kindred spirit for his love of the technical aspects of photography.

Recovered from my bout of near hysteria, I leaned over the railing to watch as our ship eased away from the dock. Two hemp-nosed tugs came alongside and ushered *L'Aquitaine* toward the open sea.

We stayed on the promenade deck, each occupied with our own thoughts. I breathed in one last look at my homeland. My heart gained weight as the shoreline disappeared and the ribbon of the ship's wake became my only connection to France. To my family, to Bernadette, to the academies and salons of Paris.

With effort, I turned to face the westward wind and inhaled the crisp invigorating air. "Montréal," I whispered. "Montreal." It had the same potential for magic as my first dreams of Paris.

Acknowledgements

This book would never have seen the light of day without a gallery of supporters. Particular thanks to my awesome editor, Deborah Froese, and the rest of the team at Rebelight Publishing—Melinda, Melanie, and Suzanne. Much appreciation goes to my critique partners over the years and to my writing mentors at Banff Centre, Humber School for Writers, and Highlights Foundation.

The historical research wouldn't have been as complete without the SINDBAD librarians at the Bibliothèque nationale de France and the archivists at the Musée du Louvre. Many thanks also to those closer to home who patiently answered my persistent questions about French, art, and design: Julie, Dulcie, Deanna, and Sandra. All errors are mine alone.

Heartfelt thanks to Lanice, Rona, Joyce, Jane, Sandy, and Maureen—you never fail to lift me up—and to many more friends too numerous to name. Thank you to my enthusiastic early readers, Angela, Harriet, and Peter. I am so grateful for my family, most especially my children, Lucas and Maryse. You are the wind beneath my wings. Finally, thank you to God, through whom all things are possible.

Author's Notes

The Art of Rebellion began as a search for the story of my own grandmother, Carmen Gabrielle Sala Morton, who died before I was born. Although Gabbi's journey is fictional, her strength of character, sense of purpose, and independent nature were inspired by Carmen. She, like Gabbi, grew up in Laval, France and had to fend off suitors chosen by her mother from the impoverished nobility. Carmen immigrated to Canada willingly, unlike Gabbi who was forced to escape scandal and pursue her art, but Carmen was also a rebel. She defied her family and societal expectations when she clambered down a ladder outside her bedroom window and eloped to marry a cowboy, Jack (Sundown) Morton. But that's another story.

  The Art of Rebellion takes place in France during *La Belle Époque*, or the beautiful era, a period from the late nineteenth century to early twentieth century. It was a time of relative political stability, but also of cultural revolution and innovations in science, technology, and the arts. Paris truly was the centre of the world for art and was the ideal setting for Gabbi's personal rebellion and coming of age.

  In creating *The Art of Rebellion*, I became indebted to many dedicated authors of scholarly articles, historical reference books, and websites on a multitude of arcane topics, from the interiors of nineteenth century artists' studios in Paris to corsets, detective cameras hidden in revolvers, and the price of pencils in 1900. There are too many resources to list here, so you can find my bibliography as well as maps, photographs and fun facts about Belle Époque Paris, on my website: www.brendajoyceleahy.com. Please check it out and send me your feedback.